Praise for the novels of Sherryl Woods

"Sherryl Woods writes emotionally satisfying novels about family, friendship and home. Truly feel-great reads!"

—#1 *New York Times* bestselling author
Debbie Macomber

"During the course of this gripping, emotionally wrenching but satisfying tale, Woods deftly and realistically handles such issues as survival guilt, drug abuse as adolescent rebellion, and family dynamics when a vital member is suddenly gone."

—*Booklist* on *Flamingo Diner*

"Woods is a master heartstring puller."

—*Publishers Weekly* on *Seaview Inn*

"Once again, Woods, with such authenticity, weaves a tale of true love and the challenges that can knock up against that love."

—*RT Book Reviews* on *Beach Lane*

"Woods…is noted for appealing character-driven stories that are often infused with the flavor and fragrance of the South."

—*Library Journal*

"A reunion story punctuated by family drama, Woods's first novel in her new Ocean Breeze series is touching, tense and tantalizing."

—*RT Book Reviews* on *Sand Castle Bay*

"A whimsical, sweet scenario…the digressions have their own charm, and Woods never fails to come back to the romantic point."

—*Publishers Weekly* on *Sweet Tea at Sunrise*

SHERRYL WOODS

Swan Point

mira

mira

ISBN-13: 978-0-7783-0906-2

Swan Point

Recycling programs
for this product may
not exist in your area.

Printed in U.S.A.

Swan
Point

CHAPTER ONE

Adelia watched with her heart in her throat as the moving van pulled away from the crumbling curb in Swan Point, one of the oldest and, at one time, finest neighborhoods in Serenity, South Carolina. With moss-draped oaks in perfectly maintained yards backing up to a small, man-made lake, which was home to several swans, the houses had been large and stately by early standards.

Now, though, most of the homes, like this one, were showing signs of age. She found something fitting about the prospect of filling this historic old house with laughter and giving it a new lease on life. It would be as if the house and her family were moving into the future together.

Letting go of the old life, however, was proving more difficult than she'd anticipated. Drawing in a deep breath, she turned to deal with the accusing looks of her four children, who weren't nearly as convinced as she was that they were about to have an exciting fresh start.

Her youngest, Tomas, named for his grandfather on

her ex-husband's side of the family, turned to her with tears streaming down his cheeks. "Mommy, I don't like it here. I want to go home. This house is old. It smells funny. And there's no pool."

She knelt down in front of the eight-year-old and gathered him close, gathered all of them close, even her oldest, Selena.

It was Selena who understood better than any of them why this move had been necessary. While they all knew that Adelia and their father had divorced, Selena had seen Ernesto more than once with one of his mistresses. In a move that defied logic or compassion, he'd even had the audacity to introduce the most recent woman to Selena while he and Adelia were still making a pretense at least of trying to keep their marriage intact. His action had devastated Selena and it had been the final straw for Adelia. She'd seen at last that tolerating such disrespect was the wrong example to set for her three girls and even for her son.

"I know you'd rather be in our old house," she comforted them with a hitch in her voice. "But it's just not possible. This is home now. I really think you're going to love it once we get settled in."

She ruffled Tomas's hair. "And don't worry about the funny smell. It's just been shut up for a few months. It'll smell fine once we air it out and put fresh paint on the walls." She injected a deliberately cheerful note into her voice. "We can all sit down and decide how we want to fix it up. Then you can go with me to the hardware store to pick out the paint colors for your rooms."

The girls expressed enthusiasm for the idea, but Tomas remained visibly skeptical.

"What about the pool?" he asked sullenly.

"We can use the town pool," Selena said staunchly, even though there were tears in her eyes, too. "It's even bigger than the one at home, and our friends will be there. And since we're living so close to downtown now, we can walk to the bakery after school for cupcakes, then stop in and see Mom at work. Or go across the green to Wharton's for ice cream."

Natalia sniffed, but Adelia saw a spark of interest in her eyes.

"I like ice cream," eleven-year-old Natalia whispered, then nudged Tomas. "You do, too."

"Me, too," Juanita chimed in. Until the divorce Adelia's nine-year-old had been boundlessly enthusiastic about everything, but this was the first sign in weeks that her high spirits were returning.

Tomas continued to look unconvinced. "Will *Abuela* be able to find us here?" he asked doubtfully.

"Of course," Adelia assured him. Tomas adored her mother, who'd been babysitting him practically from infancy because of all the school committees on which Adelia had found herself and, more recently, because she was working at a boutique on Main Street. "She helped me to find this house."

Amazingly, for once, her mother had kept her lectures on divorce to herself and professed to see all the positives in the new life Adelia was fashioning for her children. She'd told stories about the days when the elite in town had lived in Swan Point. There had been lavish parties in this very house, she'd reported to Adelia. She'd stuck to focusing on the possibilities in the house and the quiet, tree-shaded neighborhood, not the negatives.

Her mother's support had actually given Adelia the

courage to move forward. To her surprise, Adelia had recognized that even in her thirties, she still craved her mother's approval. It was one of the many reasons she'd waited so long to end her travesty of a marriage.

"Can we still go to *Abuela*'s house for cookies?" her son pressed.

"Absolutely," Adelia said. "You can go every day after school if you like, the same as always."

Though he was starting to look relieved, a sudden frown crossed his face. "What about Papa? Is he going to live here, too? He won't like it, I'll bet. He likes our real house, same as me."

Selena whirled on him. "You know perfectly well he doesn't live with us anymore. He's not coming here. Not ever! He's going to live in our old house with somebody else."

Adelia winced at the disdain and hurt in her oldest's voice. Ever since she'd realized that her father had been openly cheating on Adelia, Selena had claimed she wanted no part of him. Her attitude had hardened even more when she'd overheard Ernesto describing her as her mother's child in a tone that made clear he wasn't complimenting either one of them.

Adelia had even spoken to a psychologist about this rift between father and daughter, but the woman had assured her that it wasn't unusual for an impressionable teenager—Selena had just turned thirteen—to react so strongly to a divorce, especially when Ernesto's cheating had been so public and when he'd shown no remorse at all once he'd been caught. In fact, he'd remained defiant to the bitter end, so much so that even the judge had lost patience with him.

At Selena's angry words, Tomas's eyes once again filled with tears.

"Enough," Adelia warned her daughter. To Tomas and the younger girls, she said, "You'll still be able to see your father whenever you want to." Like Tomas, Natalia and Juanita looked relieved, though they carefully avoided looking at their big sister, clearly fearing her disapproval. That was yet another rift she'd have to work on healing, Adelia concluded with a sigh. Ernesto certainly wouldn't make any effort to do it.

As hurt as she'd been and as much as she'd wanted to banish Ernesto from her life forever, she'd accepted that her kids deserved to have a relationship with their dad. It would be selfish of her to deny them that.

Besides, she'd had enough explaining to do to the rest of her rigidly Catholic family when she'd opted for divorce. Then, to top it off, she'd insisted on moving out of the huge house on the outskirts of town that Ernesto had apparently thought was reasonable compensation for his infidelity. Her sisters had been appalled by all of it—the scandal of Ernesto's cheating, the divorce and the move. Keeping her children away from their father—however distasteful his behavior—would have caused even more of an uproar.

Not that Adelia cared what any of them thought at this point. She'd made the only decision she could make. Her only goal now was to make this transition as easy for the children as possible. She'd do it with as much cheerfulness as she could possibly muster. She might not even have to fake it, since on some level she was actually eager for this fresh start.

For now, though, she forced a smile and looked each

of them in the eye. "I have an idea," she announced, hoping to turn this difficult day around.

"What?" Tomas asked suspiciously.

"I think we all deserve a treat after such a long day."

"Pizza?" Natalia asked hopefully.

Adelia laughed. Natalia would eat pizza three times a day if she were allowed to.

"Yes, pizza," she confirmed.

"Not here, though," Tomas pleaded, wrinkling his nose in distaste.

"No, not here. The dishes aren't unpacked," she said. "We'll go to Rosalina's. I'll call your uncle Elliott and see if he and Aunt Karen would like to join us with Daisy, Mack and the baby."

This last was offered especially for Selena, who adored her uncle and who'd become especially close to his adopted daughter, Daisy. Adelia might not intend to keep Ernesto away from his children, but Elliott was the male role model she really wanted in their lives. Her younger brother was loving, rock solid and dependable. She'd be proud to see Tomas grow up to be just like him. And she desperately hoped her girls would eventually find men like him, too.

Once the decision to divorce had been made, Elliott had overcome all his own strong objections to offer her the support she'd desperately needed. She owed Karen for bringing him—and even her mother—around. Her own sisters continued to treat her as if she'd committed a mortal sin.

The prospect of pizza at Rosalina's with Uncle Elliott and his family wiped away the last of the tears, and Adelia took a truly relieved breath for what seemed like the first time all day. Her family was going to be all right. There might be a few bumps along the way, thanks to her determination to shed any of her own ties to Ernesto, but they would settle into this new house.

And, she concluded with new resolve, they would turn it into a real home, one filled with love and respect, something that had been in short supply with her ex-husband.

Gabe Franklin had claimed a booth in the back corner of Rosalina's for the fourth night in a row. Back in Serenity for less than a week and living at the Serenity Inn, he'd figured this was better than the bar across town for a man who'd determined to sober up and live life on the straight and narrow. That was the whole point of coming home, after all, to prove he'd changed and deserved a second chance. Once he'd accomplished that and made peace with his past, well, he'd decide whether to move on yet again. He wasn't sure he was the kind of man who'd ever put down roots.

Thank heaven for his cousin, Mitch Franklin, who'd offered him a job starting on Monday without a moment's hesitation. Recently remarried, Mitch claimed he needed a partner who knew construction so he could focus on his new family. He'd taken on a second family just as he'd started developing a series of dilapidated properties on Main Street in an attempt to revitalize downtown Serenity.

Gabe had listened in astonishment to Mitch's ambitious plans as he'd laid them out. Despite his cousin's enthusiasm, Gabe wasn't convinced revitalization was possible in an economy still struggling to rebound, but he was more than willing to jump in and give it a shot. Maybe there would be something cathartic about giving those old storefronts the same kind of second chance he was hoping to grab for himself.

"You're turning into a real regular in here," his waitress, a middle-aged woman who'd introduced herself a few nights ago as Debbie, said. "Are you new in town?"

"Not exactly," he said, returning her smile but adding no details. "I'll have—"

"A large diet soda and a large pepperoni pizza," she filled in before he could complete his order.

Gabe winced. "I'm obviously in a rut."

"That's okay. Most of our regulars order the same thing every time," she said. "And I pay attention. Friendly service and a good memory get me bigger tips."

"I'll remember that," he said, then sat back and looked around the restaurant while waiting for his food.

Suddenly he sat up a little straighter as a dark-haired woman came in with four children. Even though she looked a little harried and a whole lot weary, she was stunning with her olive complexion and high cheekbones. She was also vaguely familiar, though he couldn't put a name to the face.

There hadn't been a lot of Mexican-American families in Serenity back when he'd lived here as a kid, though there had been plenty of transient farmworkers during the summer months. For a minute he cursed the way he'd blown off school way more often than he should have. Surely if he'd gone regularly, this woman would have been on his radar. If there had been declared majors in high school, his would have been girls.

He'd studied them the way the academic overachievers had absorbed the information in textbooks.

Instead, he'd been kicked out midway through his junior year for one too many fights, every one of them justified to his juvenile way of thinking. He'd eventually wised up and gotten his GED. He'd even attended college for a couple of years, but that had been later, when he'd stopped hating the world for the way it had treated his troubled single mom and started putting the pieces of his life back together.

He watched now as the intriguing woman asked for several tables to be pushed together. He noted with disappointment when a man with two children came in to join them. So, he thought, she was married with six kids. An unfamiliar twinge of envy left him feeling vaguely unsettled. Since when had he been interested in having a family of any size? Still, he couldn't seem to tear his gaze away from the picture of domestic bliss they presented. The teasing and laughter seemed to settle in his heart and make it just a little lighter.

When his waitress returned with his drink, he nodded in the woman's direction. "Quite a family," he commented. "I can't imagine having six kids. They look like quite a handful."

Debbie laughed. "Oh, they're a handful, all right, but they're not all Adelia's. That's her brother, Elliott Cruz, who just came in with two of his. He has a baby, too, but I guess she was getting a cold, so his wife stayed home with her."

Gabe hid a grin. Thank heaven for chatty waitresses and a town known for gossiping. It hadn't been so great when he was a boy and his promiscuous mother had been the talk of the town, but now he could appreciate it.

"Where's her husband?"

The waitress leaned down and confided, "Sadly, not in hell where he belongs. The man cheated on her repeatedly and the whole town knew about it. She finally kicked his sorry butt to the curb. Too bad the whole town couldn't follow suit and divorce him." She flushed, and her expression immediately filled with guilt. "Sorry. I shouldn't have said that, but Adelia's a great woman and she didn't deserve the way Ernesto Hernandez treated her."

Gabe nodded. "Sounds like a real gem," he said.

In fact, he sounded like a lot of the men who'd passed through his mom's life over the years. Gabe felt a sudden surge of empathy for Adelia. And he liked the fact that his waitress was firmly in her corner. He suspected the rest of the town was, too, just the way they'd always stood up for the wronged wives when his mom had been the other woman in way too many relationships.

Funny what a few years could do to give a man a new perspective. Back then all he'd cared about was the gossip, the taunts he'd suffered at school and his mom's tears each time the relationships inevitably ended. He'd witnessed her hope whenever a new man came into her life and then the slow realization that this time would be no different. His heart had broken almost as many times as hers.

Still, he couldn't help thinking about all the complications that came with a woman in Adelia's situation. He had enough on his own plate without getting mixed up in her drama. Much as he might enjoy sitting right here and staring, it would be far better to slip away right now and avoid the powerful temptation to reach out to her. Heaven knew, he had nothing to offer a woman, not yet, anyway.

"Darlin', could you make that pizza of mine to go?" he asked his waitress.

"Sure thing," Debbie said readily.

She brought it out within minutes. As Gabe paid the check, she grinned. "I imagine I'll see you again tomorrow. Maybe you'll try something different."

"Maybe so," he agreed, then winked. "But don't count on it. I'm comfortable in this rut I'm in."

She shook her head, then glanced pointedly in Adelia's direction. "Seems to me that's just when you need to shake things up."

Gabe followed the direction of her gaze and found the very woman in question glancing his way. His heart, which hadn't been engaged in much more than keeping him alive these past few years, did a fascinating little stutter step.

No way, he told himself determinedly as he headed for the door and the safety of his comfortable, if uninviting, room at the Serenity Inn. He'd never been much good at multitasking. Right now his only goal was to prove himself to Mitch and to himself. Complications were out of the question. And the beautiful Adelia Hernandez and her four kids had complication written all over them.

"Looks as if somebody has an admirer," Elliott commented to Adelia. Though his tone was light, there was a frown on his face as he watched the stranger leaving Rosalina's.

"Hush!" Adelia said, though she was blushing. She leaned closer to her brother. "That is not the sort of thing you should be saying in front of the kids. The ink's barely dry on my divorce papers."

Elliott laughed. "The kids are clear across the restaurant playing video games. You're only flustered because you know I'm right. That guy was attracted to you, Adelia. I recognize that thunderstruck expression on a man's face. I wore it a lot when I first met Karen. I saw it in the mirror when I shaved. It happened every time she crossed my mind."

Adelia smiled at the memory of her little brother falling hard for a woman no one in the family had approved of at first simply because she'd divorced a deadbeat husband. Elliott had fought hard to ensure that they all came to accept Karen and her kids and love them as much as he did. After her own marital troubles, Adelia had come to admire her sister-in-law's strength.

"You were a goner from the moment you laid eyes on her, weren't you?" she said.

"No question about it," he said. "I still am, and I don't see that ever changing. I want that happily-ever-after kind of love for you."

"Maybe someday," she said, not really able to imagine a time when she'd be willing to risk her heart again.

Elliott nodded in the direction of the door. "So, any idea who your admirer is?"

"Stop calling him that," she ordered, blushing again.

"Just calling it like I see it," he teased. "And it's nice to see some color in your cheeks."

She gave him a mock frown. "Don't make me sorry I called you tonight," she scolded. "There are some aggravations I can't avoid, but you're not one of them."

He grinned. "You needed me here to help you corral those kids. And don't even try to pretend that you didn't enjoy the way that man was looking at you. You're not just a mom. You're a woman. You've seen far too little of that sort of appreciation in recent years."

"That may be so, but I'm not even remotely interested in dating anytime soon," she repeated emphatically, though she knew she was wasting her breath. Her brother loved getting under her skin and he'd just found a new way to do exactly that.

"You didn't recognize him?" he persisted, proving her point that he didn't intend to let this drop. "You work right downtown. You're involved in every activity in the school system. You see people all day long."

She shook her head. "I've never seen him before. He must be new in town."

"And Grace Wharton hasn't sent out a news bulletin?" he asked, only partially in jest. Grace, who ran the soda fountain at the local drugstore, prided herself on knowing all the comings and goings in town and being the first to spread the word. "Or are you just pretending that you missed the latest edition?"

Adelia tried a stern look that on rare occasions worked with her kids. "Drop this, please. There's been enough turmoil in my life these past months to last a lifetime. These days I'm a mom first and foremost. I need to get the kids settled in our new house and on an emotional even keel. That's my only focus for now."

"You're still a vibrant, attractive woman," Elliott reminded her, clearly undeterred by her expression or her words. "You deserve to find a man, the right man, who'll appreciate and respect you in a way that Ernesto never did." His expression darkened. "I still wish you'd let me teach him a lesson about mistreating my big sister."

She almost smiled at his zealous desire to stand up for her but didn't because she didn't want to encourage him. "I dealt with Ernesto. Thanks to Helen Decatur-Whitney, he'll be paying for his misdeeds with those generous support payments for the kids for years to come. Every penny is going in the bank. They'll have enough money tucked away to attend any college they choose when the time comes."

"I still don't get why you refused any alimony," Elliott told her, his frustration plain. "The man owed you, Adelia. You have a business degree, but you never used it so you could concentrate on being the perfect wife and mother. Who knows what you might have achieved by now if you'd started a career after college?"

"Being a wife and mother was the career I chose," she told him. "I don't regret that for a second. Now that I'm a single mom, I'll put just as much energy into working and being a good parent. Being independent is important to me, Elliott. I need to know I'm in control of my life."

"I'm just saying that Ernesto's money might have made it easier," he argued.

"Don't forget that Helen got enough money in a lump sum to pay for the new house and to keep our heads above water for a year, longer if I'm careful. I'm making decent money at the boutique, especially since Raylene made me the manager. I want to show my girls they can grow up to take care of themselves."

"I guess that's an admirable goal," he said, though his tone was doubtful.

She smiled at him. "Isn't that what your wife did after

her husband left her with a mountain of debt? Karen made a life for herself and her kids. It was a struggle, but she persevered. That's one of the reasons you fell for her, because she was strong in the face of adversity."

"I suppose." He grinned. "But then she found me and now it's my mission to take care of her and our family."

"Funny," she said. "Karen seems to think you have a partnership."

Her brother winced at the reminder. "Sorry. Apparently the Cruz macho tendencies die hard."

"As long as they die," she told him. "But I'll leave it to Karen to teach you that lesson."

Elliott frowned. "How did we get off track and start talking about my marriage? We were talking about you and that man who just walked out of here after giving you a thorough once-over."

"While the idea of any man staring at me appreciatively is a welcome change," she conceded, "I'm not looking for a relationship now. Maybe never. How many times do I need to say that before you believe me?"

Elliott looked dismayed rather than convinced by her response. "Don't let what Ernesto did shape the rest of your life, Adelia," he said fiercely. "Not all men are like that."

"You're certainly not," she agreed. "And for that I am eternally grateful." She touched his cheek. "I imagine Karen feels the same way. She must count her blessings every night."

"*Most* nights," her brother corrected with a grin. "At least when she's not exasperated with me for one thing or another, like forgetting about that whole partnership thing, for instance."

"Yes, I can see how you might test a woman's patience," she told him. "As a boy you were certainly a pest."

"Gee, thanks."

She patted his cheek again. "Don't fret, *mi hermano*. We all wind up loving you just the same. Even though this conversation is making me a little crazy, I know you mean well and I love you for caring."

Elliott's expression suddenly sobered. "Adelia, promise me something, okay?"

"Anything."

"If a man comes along, you'll leave yourself open to the possibilities. I'm not talking about the man who just left here, but any man."

"Any man?" she echoed, amused.

"After I've checked him out thoroughly," he amended.

"Now *that* sounds much more like the overly protective brother I know and love," Adelia said.

"Promise," he repeated.

Though she couldn't imagine it would be a promise she'd have to keep, at least not anytime soon, Adelia nodded. "Promise."

Just then the pizza and the kids arrived at the table simultaneously and, thankfully, further conversation was impossible.

Time and time again, though, she found herself glancing toward the door and thinking about the man who'd cast a lingering look in her direction. Whether it was the openly appreciative way he'd studied her or her brother's teasing, she felt the oddest sensation stirring deep inside. It was a sensation she hadn't anticipated and didn't especially want, but it felt a whole lot as if she might be coming alive again.

CHAPTER TWO

If Rosalina's had become his restaurant of choice in the evening, the bakery was the place where Gabe satisfied his sweet tooth every single morning. Not only was Sweet Things owned by his cousin's new wife, Lynn, but he'd quickly discovered that the woman made the best cookies, pies, pastries and cupcakes he'd ever put in his mouth. If Mitch hadn't beaten him to it, he'd have courted Lynn himself, not that he'd mentioned that to his cousin. He needed Mitch as an ally, not an enemy.

Thank goodness, though, ever since Gabe had arrived in town, Mitch had insisted on starting their mornings here over coffee and pastry warm from the oven as they planned how Gabe was going to fit into the company. His cousin filled him in on the work needed on the neighboring properties. Lynn joined them from time to time, but she was usually far too busy baking to take a break just past the crack of dawn.

At full daylight and after getting his fill of coffee and pastries, Gabe walked the length of Main Street with Mitch, trying to get a feel not only for downtown

Serenity as it currently existed, but for his cousin's vision.

The historic brick town hall at one end of the large, tree-lined green housed the city's offices. Wharton's, which had been in business as far back as Gabe could remember as a combination pharmacy and soda fountain, anchored one side of Main Street. A hardware store revitalized by Ronnie Sullivan anchored the other side.

Sweet Things was in that block, along with Chic, the stylish women's boutique next door. The remaining storefronts were empty and mostly boarded up, victims of the economic downturn and of the tendency in too many small communities for business to flee to the outskirts of town and more modern strip malls. The one exception in the next block was the relatively new and apparently wildly successful country radio station with its studio window facing the green so the on-air hosts could report on Serenity's many holiday festivals and everyday happenings.

Gabe had been able to view the recent progress with appreciation, but he was still mindful that a lot more was needed before downtown Serenity could be described as thriving.

This morning—his first official day on the job— he studied Mitch over his mug of coffee. "You really think turning this town around is possible?"

"I'm counting on it," Mitch said. "Our town manager, Tom McDonald, believes it's possible and is doing everything he can to lure new business to town. I want to be sure there are up-to-date properties available to rent when the prospective business owners come to look things over. I want downtown to be irresistible. I want them to see it immediately as a better bet than one of those strip malls that have started popping up along the highway outside of town."

Gabe smiled. "Were you always this idealistic and ambitious?"

"I don't see it as ambition. I see it as a chance to do something for a town I love, the town where I've built my life. I don't want to see downtown die the way it has in so many towns." Mitch shrugged. "Maybe that is idealistic."

"I hate to tell you, pal, but that ship has sailed. Right now, this downtown is on life support at best."

"I know a few people, my wife among them, who'd tell you otherwise," Mitch retorted. "And Dana Sue Sullivan, whose restaurant lures people from all over the state, would pick a major fight with you if she heard you say that. Sullivan's may not be right on Main Street, but her success speaks for itself."

Gabe laughed. "Well, I'm not about to take on Dana Sue. I've heard too many stories about her temper. But Lynn is what they call a pie-eyed optimist. She married you, didn't she? What does that say about her judgment?"

Mitch didn't take offense at his teasing. He laughed with him.

"She took a chance on me, all right," Mitch said. "I thank my lucky stars for it. After Amy died and the boys were away at college, I was a lost soul for a while." His expression sobered. "I wish you'd come over for dinner one night, instead of existing on pizza. You know you're welcome anytime."

"I know that," Gabe said. "But you're still a newly-wed. I don't want to intrude."

"We're past the honeymoon stage," Mitch said, though the appreciative glance he cast in his wife's direction as she came out of the back to wait on a customer said otherwise. So did the touches he couldn't resist making every time she was in close proximity. "We've been together almost a year now. And with Lynn's two kids underfoot, it's not as if we have a lot of privacy, anyway."

"In my book a year still makes you a newlywed."

Mitch gave him a knowing look. "And in my book, you're just making excuses. You're family, Gabe. You're not an outsider. I know you didn't feel that way as a kid and I'm as sorry as I can be about the way the rest of the family treated your mother."

Gabe waved off the apology. "You were just a kid yourself. You had no control over what the adults did and thought. Besides, I get where they were coming from. My mom had her share of problems. Drinking was the least of it."

Mitch winced. "I came way too close to relying on alcohol myself after I lost Amy," he revealed quietly, startling Gabe. "I'd like to think I wouldn't have judged your mother for that weakness."

Gabe wondered if there was some hereditary inclination that seemed to steer Franklins toward booze. "I took a brush with it myself after Mom died," he said. "Even though I knew firsthand where that path could lead. Now that I've got my feet back under me and can see what dangerous decisions I was making, I feel a lot more sympathy for her myself than I did when I was living with it. I can also see a lot more clearly that she sure as heck had an addiction to the wrong sort of men. It was a bad combination."

"But those shouldn't have become your problems, too," Mitch said. "You took them on when the family should have been there to support both of you, instead of passing judgment. It wasn't right that you got labeled a troublemaker for trying to protect your mom."

"Water under the bridge," Gabe insisted. "Can we stop talking about this, please? You've more than made up for the past by giving me this job."

Mitch dismissed the sentiment. "I have to admit that I'm still a little surprised that you wanted to come back to Serenity. You were awfully eager to put the town and your family behind you when you took off after your mom died."

Gabe shrugged. "Seemed to me like the best place to get a second chance would be in the same place where you blew the first one. I guess I was finally ready to face the past, instead of running from it. Maybe I can shake those ghosts that seem to go with me wherever I am."

"A very mature outlook."

Gabe laughed. "Yeah, well, I imagine that's a surprise for you, too. It sure is to me. Maybe hitting forty somehow turned me into a grown-up." He set out determinedly to change the subject once and for all. "Now, what's on the agenda for today? You've given me enough time to get settled in. I'm anxious to get started and prove you didn't make the wrong decision by taking me on. I filled you in on my experience, but you haven't seen my work firsthand. I meant what I told you—if it doesn't measure up, you can tell me that straight-out, okay?"

"That's not likely," Mitch said. "Your job history

speaks for itself. I know some of those men you worked for around the state."

"Did you speak to them? That's why I gave you their names."

"No need. I trust you," Mitch claimed, giving Gabe's sometimes shaky self-esteem a needed boost.

Just then, the door opened and Adelia Hernandez stepped into the bakery. If anything, Gabe thought she was even prettier with her long hair tousled by the wind and wearing a dress that showed off her shapely legs. That crazy pulse of his skipped a couple of beats.

Apparently the reaction wasn't entirely one-sided. When she spotted him, her cheeks flushed and her step faltered.

Naturally Mitch noticed Adelia's discomfort and Gabe's fascination. His eyes narrowed.

"You two know each other?" he asked Gabe. Adelia hesitated as if she was torn between whatever she'd come in to get and getting away from Gabe as quickly as possible.

"She was at Rosalina's when I was there last night," Gabe replied carefully.

"And?"

"That's it. She was there with her family. I was there by myself. Nothing more to it."

Mitch regarded him doubtfully. "Looked like a little more than nothing just now," he said as Adelia hurried to the counter and placed her order with Lynn.

"I've never even spoken to the woman," Gabe assured him. "And if that gleam in your eyes has anything to do with matchmaking, you can forget about it. I'm here to work. Period."

Despite his very firm disclaimer, he couldn't seem

to keep his gaze from straying to Adelia, whose hand appeared to be shaking as she accepted a container of coffee from Lynn. As soon as she'd paid, she whirled around and practically ran out the door.

"Adelia!" Lynn called after her, then glanced toward Mitch. "I don't know what in the world is wrong with her this morning. She's jumpy as a june bug and she ran off without her pastry."

Gabe was instantly on his feet. He held out his hand. "I'll take it to her."

He saw the startled expression on Lynn's face and heard his cousin's chuckle as he took off. So much for any pretense that he wasn't interested, he thought ruefully. Oh, well. He figured that had pretty much been doomed from the instant he'd laid eyes on her, anyway. It was a darn good thing he'd had a ton of practice at controlling most of his craziest impulses.

This is ridiculous, Adelia thought as she struggled to get her key to work in the lock at Chic, the boutique next door to the bakery. How could a man to whom she'd never even spoken rattle her so badly? She'd been squeezing the Styrofoam cup so tightly since leaving Lynn's, it was a wonder there was a drop of coffee left in there. It was all her brother's fault for planting that crazy idea in her head, for suggesting that the stranger was a potential admirer.

She'd barely set the coffee down by the cash register when the bell over the front door tinkled merrily and she realized she hadn't locked the door behind her. More startling was the sight of the man entering.

"You!" she exclaimed.

She must have sounded alarmed, because he

stopped in his tracks and held out a small pastry bag. "I come in peace," he teased, seemingly fighting a smile. "You left this behind at the bakery. Lynn was worried, so I said I'd deliver it."

She sucked in a deep breath and closed her eyes for an instant. "Sorry. You just caught me off guard. I usually lock the door behind me since we don't open for another half hour. I come in early. Well, I guess that's obvious, isn't it? I like to get started before any customers walk in. I want to make sure the displays are neat and the cash register is set to go, that sort of thing. I'm a little obsessive about it."

She realized she was rambling. She clamped her mouth shut. He held out the pastry bag, and when she didn't immediately reach for it, he set it on the counter, amusement written all over his face.

"I'm Gabe Franklin," he told her. "Mitch's cousin."

Adelia felt herself relaxing ever so slightly at that. Mitch was a good guy. One of the best, in fact. Any cousin of his would surely be okay, even if this man seemed to have the power to rattle her in ways no man had for years. Any rattling Ernesto had done had been to her temper.

"Mitch is great," she said.

"That seems to be the consensus," he responded.

She frowned at the edge she thought she heard in his voice. "You don't agree?"

He winced. "Sorry. It's an old habit. In the interest of full disclosure, I was the black sheep Franklin growing up. Old resentments die hard. He *is* a good man. I can appreciate that now."

"I imagine it can be hard growing up in someone else's shadow," she said. "I know Mitch is a local. We knew each other in school, but what about you? Are you from Serenity?"

He nodded. "Born and bred here."

"Then I'm surprised we haven't crossed paths before. We must be about the same age. I imagine we were in school around the same time. I'm Adelia Hernandez, by the way. I was Adelia Cruz before I married."

"And I spent more time suspended from school than I did in classes," he admitted. "I left town for a lot of years after that. I just got back a week ago. Fortunately I got my act together during that time and picked up a diploma, then went on to college. I suppose I should say I took classes, since I never graduated. I was in too much of a hurry to get on with life."

"Did you regret that later?"

He shook his head. "No point in regrets. It was the decision I made. I try not to look back, just focus on the here and now."

"I'm trying to work on that," she told him. "And I've recently had to face the fact that human beings are an imperfect lot. What matters is how we deal with our mistakes. Sounds as if you've made up for yours."

"Not entirely, but I'm working on it."

She watched as he glanced around the very feminine shop, which was currently displaying summer dresses and a new line of lacy lingerie. His gaze landed on the lingerie. Color bloomed in his cheeks. His nerves definitely showing, he shoved his hands in his pockets and backed toward the door.

"I'd better get back to the bakery. Mitch has a long list of projects he wants to go over with me. It's officially my first day on the job."

Adelia nodded and held up the pastry bag. "Thanks for bringing this."

"Not a problem."

She watched him leave, admired the way his jeans fit snugly over a very excellent backside and felt heat climb up her neck. She thought of Elliott's advice just the night before to keep her heart open and her own very adamant declaration that she was a long, long way from being interested in another relationship. She suddenly couldn't help wondering if Gabe Franklin with the wicked gleam in his eyes and his flirtatious ways was about to make a liar out of her.

It was midmorning before Adelia was able to push all thoughts of Gabe Franklin aside and concentrate on work. Just as she was about to reorganize a display to show off a new shipment of colorful scarves, her cell phone rang. To her dismay it was the principal of Selena's middle school.

"Adelia, I'm so sorry to bother you at work, but we have a problem. Selena's not in her physical education class. The teacher didn't notice it until they were choosing sides for soccer. She'd taken attendance earlier and Selena was there, but she disappeared sometime between that and when they went outside."

"Are you sure she didn't just stay in the locker room?" Adelia asked, trying to tamp down the panic that was already rising. "She hates soccer. Skipping it to sit in the locker room and read a book is something she might do."

"She's not on the school grounds," Margaret Towson told her. "I've had several people checking for the past twenty minutes or so. Do you want me to call Carter Rollins?"

"The police chief? Do you really think that's necessary?"

"It's standard procedure if a child disappears during the school day and the parents don't know where they are, either. Do you have any idea where we might find Selena?"

Adelia felt tears gathering in her eyes. "No."

"Perhaps I should check with her father then," Margaret ventured, her tone tentative.

"No," Adelia said quickly. "I'll handle this. I'll call Carter and start looking myself," she said. "Thank you for letting me know so quickly, Margaret."

"Adelia, I know Selena has been going through a difficult time. Her teachers are aware of it, as well. If there's anything we can do to help, just ask."

"Thanks."

She disconnected the call and immediately called her boss. Raylene Rollins, rather than Raylene's husband, Carter. The minute she explained the situation, Raylene said, "Lock up the store and go. I'll be there in a few minutes to take over, but don't wait for me. I'll call Carter and tell him what's going on. Try not to worry. Selena can't have gone far. She might even be at home. Have you tried her cell phone or the phone at the house?"

"No. I wasn't thinking," Adelia admitted, completely shaken by the oversight. "I'll do that now. Thanks for understanding, Raylene."

"Don't thank me. Just go. And call me the minute you find her."

Adelia grabbed her purse from the office, put a

closed sign on the door, then locked up the boutique. She opened the door to Sweet Things, drawing a startled look from Lynn.

"Is everything okay?" Lynn asked. "You're white as a ghost."

"The school just called. Selena's missing."

Lynn had her own cell phone out before Adelia could finish the sentence. "Mitch will start looking, too," she reported. "What can I do?"

"Just call me if she shows up here or if your daughter has any idea where she might have gone. I know Lexie's older, but kids hear things. I'm hoping this was just an impulsive decision, but with everything that's happened lately, I can't help worrying that she might have been planning to run away."

"I'll check with Lexie right now," Lynn promised just as Mitch and Gabe came rushing into the bakery.

Mitch put steadying hands on her shoulders. "Stay calm," he said quietly. "We're going to find her. Gabe, why don't you go with Adelia. I'll start driving around town. Any place you think I ought to check first?" he asked.

"I don't know," she said, fresh tears gathering in her eyes.

She'd been so sure that Selena was handling the divorce okay. She was angry at her father, of course, but beyond that she seemed to be taking the move and all the rest in stride. The rebellion of a few months ago had seemingly vanished, replaced by resignation. Adelia should have seen through that. Apparently her mom-radar wasn't as sharp as she'd thought.

"I've got this," Gabe told Mitch. "You start looking."

Mitch nodded. "I'll start by the school and fan out

from there. I'll check with Carter, too, so we're not duplicating our efforts."

Gabe turned to Lynn. "How about a cup of tea? Something herbal, maybe?"

Adelia regarded him as if he were nuts. "I don't have time to sit here and sip tea," she said, starting toward the door.

Gabe blocked her path. "We'll get it to go. It'll help to calm your nerves so you can tell me where you want to start looking."

"He's right," Lynn said, already handing her the to-go container. "I've put plenty of sugar in there for you. That'll help, too."

Adelia told herself she only accepted the cup so she could get out of the bakery, but in some part of her brain, she knew they were both right. The tea might help to settle her nerves so she could think straight.

With Gabe watching her closely, she took several sips, then met his gaze. "Satisfied?"

"It's a start," he said lightly. "Now let's go find your daughter."

Something in the way he said it, with full confidence that they'd be successful, reassured her, even though nothing had really changed in the past few minutes.

"I want to go by the house first. I've called and there was no answer, but that doesn't mean she's not there."

"Where's the house?"

"Swan Point."

He nodded and turned in that direction. "Just tell me where to turn once we're there," he said.

The drive through the neighborhood of fewer than a dozen homes took only minutes, as did the search of the house. There was no sign of Selena, no book-bag tossed on the sofa or remnants of a snack in the kitchen.

"What about her father? Would she go to him?" Gabe asked.

"Not likely," Adelia said, unable to keep a note of bitterness from her voice. "She's very angry at him these days."

"Anybody she's especially close to?"

Adelia immediately brightened. "Her uncle. Elliott runs that new men's gym just off Palmetto. You know the place?"

Gabe nodded. "I just joined."

As they made the drive to Fit for Anything, Adelia's mind started racing. "What if—?"

The words were no sooner out of her mouth than Gabe cut her off. "No what-ifs," he declared firmly. "She hasn't been missing long. If she's upset, she'll go someplace where she feels safe."

"But she might not be thinking clearly," Adelia protested, her panic returning. "She's only thirteen, Gabe. I'm afraid I've been forgetting that myself. I should have been paying more attention. Instead, I was so worried about my younger kids, I missed all the signs that Selena was in real trouble. I was just grateful that she was no longer rebelling against the world."

In front of the gym, she bolted from the car practically before it could come to a stop. Inside, she scanned the room until her gaze landed on her brother. He regarded her with alarm, which grew visibly when Gabe came in right on her heels.

Misreading the situation, Elliott stepped between them. "Is this guy bothering you, Adelia?"

She held up a hand. "No, it's nothing like that. Selena's missing. Gabe is helping me look for her. I thought maybe she'd come here to see you."

Elliott shook his head. "I haven't seen her. Let me check with Karen. She's not working today. She's at the house with the baby."

Adelia felt herself starting to shake as her brother made the call to his wife. Then she felt Gabe's steadying hand on her shoulder. He didn't say a word, just kept his hand there until the moment passed.

Elliott listened intently to whatever Karen was saying, his expression brightening. "Thanks, *querida.* Adelia will be there in a few minutes." Smiling, he turned to her. "Selena's at my house playing with the baby. Karen didn't think to call anyone because Selena told her she only had a half day at school and swore you knew where she was."

Adelia finally let out the breath she felt like she'd been holding for hours. "Of course Karen believed her," she said wryly. "Selena's very convincing when she wants to be."

"Want me to drive you over there?" Elliott offered. "I can get one of the other trainers to take my next client."

"I can take her," Gabe said. He looked at her. "Unless you'd prefer to have your brother go with you."

Adelia hesitated, then shook her head. "If you don't mind making the drive, that would be great," she told him. "Elliott, there's no reason for you to miss an appointment. I can handle this."

Elliott looked worried but eventually nodded. "You'll be there when I get home? I want to have a talk with my niece about skipping school and worrying you."

She smiled. "Believe me, she'll get more than enough talking from me tonight. You can save your lecture for another day."

Elliott nodded with unmistakable reluctance. "Whatever you think, but I will have a word with her. You can be sure of that."

"Not a doubt in my mind," she said, then turned to Gabe. "Let's go. That is, if you're really sure you have the time."

"I have the time," he said without hesitation.

On the way to her brother's, Gabe called Mitch and told him they'd located Selena and were on the way to get her. After the call ended, he told her, "Mitch will speak to Carter and let him know to call off the search."

Adelia sighed. "I should have thought to do that."

"You have plenty of other things on your mind," he said, excusing her. "I imagine you're pondering a dozen different things you can say to drive home the point that what your daughter did was wrong."

Surprised by his understanding, she nodded. "How'd you know?"

"Not because I got my share of lectures, that's for sure," he said. "My mom was pretty oblivious to the trouble I was getting into." He glanced her way. "Word of advice?"

"Sure."

"Whatever punishment you decide to dole out, and there should be one, be sure you hug the daylights out of her first."

Adelia felt her heart tumble just a little. "You didn't get the hugs, either?"

"Nope, which is why I know exactly how important they are," he said as he pulled to a stop in front of Elliott's house in a new subdivision outside town.

Adelia turned to him then. "Thank you."

"For chauffeuring you around town for an hour? Don't mention it. I'm just glad there's a happy ending."

"Not just for that," she corrected him. "For reminding me that discipline always needs to come with a hug."

He winked at her. "I saw you with your kids at Rosalina's, remember? Something tells me you already knew that."

Adelia stood in the driveway and watched him leave. She'd seen a different side of Gabe Franklin just now, one that was even more appealing than the flirtatious man she'd encountered before. Something told her this thoughtful, more vulnerable side made him even more dangerous.

CHAPTER THREE

"Thanks for helping out just now," Lynn said when Gabe stopped by the bakery for a large cup of coffee before heading back to the construction site. "Adelia would never admit it, but she had to be scared out of her wits. I know I would have been if it had been one of my kids missing. I'm sure having you around kept her calm."

"I don't know how much help I was," Gabe said. "All I did was drive the car in whatever direction she asked me to."

Lynn smiled at the self-deprecating comment. "And you didn't say one single word in all that time? Didn't offer any support? Maybe insist she drink some tea?"

"The tea made sense," he grumbled.

Lynn's smile spread. He was obviously self-conscious about accepting praise for what he apparently considered to be nothing more than a neighborly gesture. She considered that very telling. Mitch had told her about Gabe's past and how determined he was to fight his old reputation as a troublemaker. This humility was definite evidence that he was well on his way.

"Don't make a big deal about that, or about anything I did, for that matter," he said. "It was nothing anyone else wouldn't have done."

"Whatever you say," she said, laughing. "Something tells me things are about to get real interesting here on Main Street."

Gabe frowned at her. "Just because you and my cousin still have stars in your eyes doesn't mean the whole world is just waiting for romance."

"Adelia would probably say the same thing," Lynn said agreeably. "She just got a divorce. She's not interested in meeting anyone right now. Yada yada yada. I've heard it all before. Said it myself, in fact, when Mitch came along. Doesn't mean I believe a word she says." She regarded him pointedly, then added, "You, either. My theory is that neither of you has a clue what you really need in your lives."

"Well, whether you buy it or not, could you stay out of it?" Gabe pleaded. "I've got problems enough up and down this block without adding your meddling into the mix."

"What problems?" she asked at once, her mood sobering. "Does Mitch know?"

"Of course he knows. I haven't been on the job long enough to make decisions without running them by him. Now, if you'll get that cup of coffee I asked for when I first walked through the door, and maybe a few of those chocolate chip cookies, I'll get back to work, so he doesn't fire me for hanging out too long with his wife."

She quickly poured the coffee and bagged his

cookies, choosing a few from a tray still warm from the oven, but she waved off payment. "Just a reward for helping Adelia," she said. "Where will you be if Mitch stops by here looking for you?"

"In the old supermarket space on the corner trying to figure out how we're going to replace those old beams without the roof tumbling down on our heads. The termites have been living it up in there for ten years at least."

Lynn looked alarmed. "That can't be good. What about Chic? It's right next door to that space. Is their ceiling okay?"

"I'll check with Mitch, but I imagine he did a thorough job fixing up that place and this one. If there was damage, I doubt he missed it."

Relieved, she nodded. "You're right, of course. Mitch pays attention to details. It's one of his best traits."

Gabe grinned at her. "I imagine that comes in handy in more ways than one," he said with a wink, then took off, brushing past Maddie Maddox, Helen Decatur-Whitney and Dana Sue Sullivan in his hurry.

Their arrival wasn't particularly unexpected. Once word of a crisis spread through town, the original Sweet Magnolias were always among the first to respond. The loosely formed group of friends had grown to include many other women now, including Lynn, but these three were still its heart and soul.

"What's his hurry?" Helen asked, her eyes narrowed. The town's—maybe even the state's—most prominent divorce attorney was by nature cynical and suspicious, even after several years now of being deliriously happy in her own marriage.

Lynn chuckled. "I made him nervous."

Maddie regarded her with surprise. "How?"

"By suggesting that his willingness to jump in to help Adelia was something more than a neighborly gesture," Lynn said.

"I knew it!" Dana Sue said, her expression smug. "All day long I was hearing gossip that Adelia and Gabe had crossed paths at Rosalina's the other night and fireworks went off. It was Grace spreading the story, and you know how she is. She can spin a romance out of a passing glance."

Helen held up her hands. "Hold on a minute! The latest Serenity romance alert is fascinating, but shouldn't we be focusing on what we can do to help in the search for Adelia's daughter? That's why we rushed over here."

Maddie and Dana Sue immediately looked guilt-stricken.

"Of course we should," Maddie said.

"It's okay," Lynn soothed. "Selena's safe and sound. Adelia and Gabe found her at Elliott and Karen's house. He stopped in just now to fill me in." She glanced at the three women, who'd been best friends since childhood. "Now who needs coffee and maybe a slice of pie while you fill me in on what you've heard about Gabe and Adelia?"

"I wouldn't turn down a slice of lemon meringue," Maddie said at once.

"Coconut cream for me," Helen said as Lynn poured the coffee.

Dana Sue stared at the display case longingly. As she did, Lynn remembered hearing that she was at high risk for diabetes. That would be a tough diagnosis for anyone, but Dana Sue owned a restaurant and was around food constantly. She sighed now.

"I'll pass on the pie," Dana Sue said with unmistakable disappointment, "but I will take the coffee."

"How about a couple of sugar-free oatmeal cookies?" Lynn suggested. "They have cranberries and walnuts. I promise they don't taste like sawdust."

Helen's eyes lit up. "Ooh, those sound fabulous. Maybe I'll have those, too."

"Instead of pie?" Lynn asked.

"Absolutely not," Helen replied, then hesitated. "But maybe you'd better put them in a bag. I'll pretend I'm taking them home for my daughter."

Maddie and Dana Sue exchanged a look.

"Want to bet they're gone before she gets to the corner?" Maddie asked.

Dana Sue shook her head. "Why would I want to bet against a sure thing?" She grinned at Lynn. "Bring on the cookies and don't waste a bag, okay?"

Helen patted the chair next to her. "And sit right here next to me. I want to know everything you can tell me about Gabe and Adelia."

Lynn chuckled as she imagined how Gabe would react to being linked with Adelia all over town. He'd been grumpy enough when she'd merely hinted at a potential romantic pairing. Now that the Sweet Magnolias and Grace Wharton were alert and watching for every sighting, it was going to make him crazy. In Lynn's opinion, a little craziness was just what he needed.

Gabe found Mitch standing on scaffolding in the middle of the construction site on the corner. Mitch was regarding the damage-riddled support beam with disgust. When he caught sight of Gabe, he climbed down.

"What's your plan?" he asked at once, surprising Gabe.

"You don't have one?" Gabe asked.

Mitch chuckled. "Of course I do, but I put you in charge. I want to hear yours."

Startled by the confidence his cousin was placing in him, Gabe pulled a rough sketch from his back pocket and spread it out on a rickety old table that comprised his office space for now.

"Here's what I was thinking," he said, going over the drawing. "I had Ronnie Sullivan in here earlier for some cost estimates on the lumber. He says if we want a couple of steel beams, he can get prices for those, too, but we're talking big money."

Mitch's expression was thoughtful as Gabe talked. He glanced up at the existing beams, then at the figures Gabe had jotted down, then nodded. "Let's do it right," he said eventually. "If we're going to fix this building up, we need it to be built to last."

"I'll have the prices for you tomorrow," Gabe said, relieved. He'd been cautious, but he, too, believed in getting it right, not cheap. "By the way, your wife's expecting you. I stopped in to grab a cup of coffee just now. She might need a little reassuring about the state of the ceiling over the bakery."

Mitch frowned. "Why?"

"It's possible I planted a few seeds of doubt talking about all the termites," Gabe admitted, then shrugged at Mitch's incredulous expression. "Hey, I had to say something to get her off the topic of me and Adelia Hernandez."

"And all you could come up with was termite damage?" Mitch said with mock exasperation. "She's going to want to go up there and check out those beams herself."

Gabe laughed. "I suspected as much. Where's the trust? That's what I want to know. You did renovate that space for her."

Mitch shook his head. "Which just means we probably should add contractors to the list of people who need to avoid doing business with family." He sighed heavily. "Thanks for that, by the way."

"Anytime," Gabe said.

Let his cousin deal with Lynn's inquisitive nature. That was a whole lot easier on Gabe than having her pecking away at his personal life.

Adelia stood outside the nursery at Elliott and Karen's house trying to calm her temper before she confronted her daughter about scaring her and everyone else. She needed to remember what Gabe had said about doling out hugs before discipline. She thought she'd always been pretty good at that, but today had been a real test. What she wanted more than anything was to give her daughter a good shake and ground her for at least the remainder of her school years. Fortunately, she was wise enough to know none of that was the answer to what had happened today.

When she opened the door, she found Selena sitting in a rocker with the baby in her arms and sunlight spilling over them. Even at only thirteen, she had the serenity of the Madonna about her. It was a terrifying reminder of how quickly she was growing up.

When Selena glanced up and caught sight of Adelia, though, wariness filled her eyes and she was a nervous teenager who knew she was in trouble. "What are you doing here?" she asked, her voice unsteady.

"I think the better question is what are *you* doing here in the middle of a school day?" Adelia responded, careful to keep the fear and temper out of her voice. "You've had half the town running around trying to find you, including the police chief."

Selena had the grace to look shocked by that. "I'm sorry. I didn't think anyone would miss me. I just skipped out on soccer. I'm no good at that, anyway."

"And what about the classes you have after physical education? Were you planning to go back for those? If so, you're already late."

Selena winced. "I lost track of time," she whispered, clearly aware that Adelia wasn't likely to buy it.

"Seriously? You expect me to believe that?"

"I was hoping," Selena said, her expression guilty.

"Afraid not. Put the baby down and come outside so we can talk," Adelia said, pausing to brush gentle fingers over the baby's soft-as-silk curls. With black hair and big brown eyes, she was all Cruz, that's for sure.

Maybe because she knew it was inevitable, Selena did as she'd been told to do, then followed Adelia from the room. As they passed Karen in the living room, Adelia asked, "Mind if we sit on your deck for a little while? We need to talk."

"It's fine," Karen said. "Would you like something cool to drink? I've just made fresh lemonade."

"I'd like some, please," Selena said at once, clearly relieved by any delay she could seize. "I can get it."

She scampered off to the kitchen before Adelia could protest. Karen smiled. "She's awfully eager to make amends, isn't she?"

"Seems so," Adelia said, then released a sigh. "I've never been so terrified in my life."

Karen, who'd been reserved with her for a long time, stepped forward and pulled her into an awkward embrace. "But she's okay. That's what counts, Adelia. She came here, to a safe place. She didn't run away."

"I know and I'm more grateful than I can express for that. Did she talk at all?"

"No. I think she just wanted some space on neutral turf. She asked if she could hold the baby. She's been in the nursery ever since." She gave Adelia an apologetic look. "If I'd had any idea you didn't know where she was, I would have called you immediately."

"I know that," Adelia assured her. "Thanks for being so kind to her."

"She's my niece," Karen said simply.

Selena returned from the kitchen with three glasses of lemonade and looked at Karen hopefully. "Are you coming outside to talk, too?"

"No, sweetheart. This is between you and your mom." She looked at Adelia. "If you need anything, let me know. I can give you all a lift home whenever you're ready, unless you'd like to stay for dinner."

"We'll see," Adelia said. It depended on how this conversation went and whether she thought she needed some backup from her brother to drive her points home with Selena. Her mom would keep the younger kids for the night, if need be.

Adelia led the way outside. She sat on a cushioned bench on the shady side of the deck, then patted the seat next to her. With unmistakable reluctance, Selena sat beside her. Adelia reached for her hand.

"Do you have any idea how precious you are to me?" she asked softly. "You're my firstborn, Selena."

Rather than looked reassured, Selena looked sad. "But if it weren't for me, you might never have married Dad."

Adelia frowned at what seemed to be an entirely out-of-the-blue comment. "What do you mean?"

"Come on, Mom. I can count. You and Dad got married because you were already pregnant with me. If that hadn't happened, then you wouldn't have been trapped with a man who cheated on you every chance he got."

Adelia closed her eyes, trying to gather her composure. She'd hoped this conversation would never be necessary, but Selena had clearly overheard way too many arguments with Ernesto and the accusations that had been flung about.

"It's true that I was pregnant when your Dad and I got married," she confessed, then forced Selena to meet her gaze. "But you need to believe me, sweetheart. I don't regret that decision, not for a single minute."

"How can you not regret it?" Selena asked angrily. "Dad did."

"No, he didn't. Not really."

"I heard him, Mom."

"People say things in the heat of the moment that they don't really mean, even your dad. But let's focus on how *I* feel for now. How can I regret marrying your dad when I have you and your sisters and your brother because of that decision? The four of you mean everything to me. I may hate what's been happening, I may be really angry at him right now, but

I can't regret being married to him, sweetheart. One of these days you'll discover that things are never as black-and-white as we might like them to be. There's a lot of gray in the middle. Good just happens to come with bad sometimes."

Tears streamed down Selena's cheeks. "I'm never getting married," she declared.

Her determined words were as painful for Adelia to hear as her own had probably been for Elliott on Sunday night. She didn't want her daughter's future to be shaped by the divorce. She pulled Selena close and Selena actually allowed it, resting her head on Adelia's shoulder as she had when she was younger.

"That's not a decision you need to be making now," she told her daughter. "And it certainly isn't one you should base on what happened between your father and me. Look at your uncle Elliott and Karen and how happy they are."

"But Karen's first husband was a real jerk," Selena reminded her. "So was Raylene's. I heard all about how he abused her and then came here and tried to kill her."

"But Raylene has Carter now and they're expecting a baby," Adelia reminded her. "She found real happiness this time, the kind that will last."

"But there's no way to know for sure," Selena protested. "I'll bet you thought Dad was great at first or you wouldn't have fallen in love with him. The same with Karen and Raylene. They're smart, too, and look what happened to them."

"Okay, here's what I know," Adelia said, brushing a lock of hair back from Selena's damp cheek. "People make mistakes. And sometimes people change. Human beings are flawed, but that doesn't mean you should never take a risk. The important thing is that it be an informed risk, one you only take after very careful thought. And even then, if you get it wrong, you pick up the pieces and move on."

Even as she said the words meant to reassure her daughter, Adelia realized they were very similar to the sentiment that Elliott had expressed to her. She wondered if she was any more capable of hearing them right now than Selena was.

"How do you do that, though?" Selena asked. "Move on, I mean? You make it sound easy, but it's not."

"No, it's not," Adelia said. "But you do it because you must and you do it one day at a time. Some days will be easier than others."

"I made today harder, didn't I?" Selena asked, real regret in her voice.

"You did," Adelia said, unwilling to gloss over the effect her behavior had. "But I understand why you came here. Sometimes I forget that you're not a grown-up and that all these decisions your dad and I have made affect you in ways I might not even realize. But, baby, you need to talk to me about it, not take off." She tucked a finger under Selena's chin and forced her to look into her eyes. "Deal?"

Selena nodded slowly. "Deal." Her expression turned worried. "How much trouble am I in? Grounded is a given, huh?"

"Grounded is a given," Adelia agreed. "But I imagine we can smooth things over at school, even though they have a very low tolerance for skipping classes. You'll need to apologize to your teacher and to the principal for worrying them."

Selena didn't look happy, but she nodded. "Anybody else?"

"Raylene and Carter for inconveniencing them," Adelia said. "Mitch Franklin, who dropped everything to help look for you, and his cousin Gabe, who drove me around to all the places I thought you might be, then brought me here."

"I don't even know him," Selena protested. "Why did he help?"

"Because that's what people do in Serenity," Adelia told her. "I know you think this town is way too small and old-fashioned and that you can't wait to get away, but the positive side of living here is that we look out for each other. We pitch in when anyone's in trouble."

It was something she was just coming to realize for herself, and in the past few months, when her world had been turned upside down, she'd been grateful for all the support, sometimes from the most unexpected people. Gabe Franklin, she was forced to concede, fell into that category.

Gabe stayed on the job until after eight, running the numbers Ronnie Sullivan had given him for new steel support beams until he had a proposal ready to pass along to Mitch first thing in the morning. While he'd told himself it was the responsible thing to do, he knew the real reason he was still at the construction site was to keep himself from heading over to Swan Point to check on Adelia and her daughter.

"She's not your responsibility," he muttered to himself on more than one occasion when he found his thoughts straying to her panicked expression when she'd first found out her daughter was missing.

For the entire hour he'd been with her, though, she'd lost control only once when *what-if* calamities had crept into her head. He thought he'd done an okay job of diverting her attention before she could sink into real despair. Other than that moment, she'd shown admirable strength. After his own childhood, it had been eye-opening to see how a good mother handled things.

He was about to turn out the lights, lock up and head for Rosalina's, when the door opened and Elliott Cruz walked in. Gabe stilled at the sight of him. He'd seen the protectiveness in the other man's eyes earlier and couldn't help wondering what had brought him here now. A warning to stay away, perhaps? Gabe was ready to reassure him on that point. He intended to steer clear of Adelia as much as possible for his own peace of mind.

"Elliott, right?" he asked, seizing the initiative and holding out his hand. "We didn't really meet earlier."

Adelia's brother looked startled, but he shook his hand.

"What brings you by?" Gabe asked.

"I came to apologize," Elliott told him.

The statement took Gabe by surprise. "Why?"

"Because you pitched in to help this afternoon and I came on too strong and all but attacked you when you came into the gym with my sister."

Gabe shrugged. "You didn't have all the facts."

"No, I certainly didn't," Elliott said. "Adelia would be the first to tell you, jumping to conclusions is a bad habit of mine. In my family I was the only son with three sisters. They were all older, but I took on the role of protecting them when our father died. Sometimes I've been known to get carried away."

"Seems to me they're lucky to have someone looking out for them," Gabe said.

"Tell *them* that," Elliott replied, his expression rueful. "I don't get half the gratitude you might expect, especially from Adelia. She's the oldest and always thought *she* should be protecting *me*."

"That whole dynamic is a mystery to me," Gabe admitted. "I was an only child."

"But you had cousins, right? I thought I heard you and Mitch are related. And there are other Franklins around town."

"Mitch and I are cousins, but we weren't that close growing up. I might as well tell you straight-out that I was the black sheep of the family and my mom was a pariah in the family and around town. You won't hear a lot of good said about either of us."

Elliott frowned at that. "Black sheep?" he repeated, worry back in his expression.

"Reformed," Gabe assured him. "I haven't gotten into a brawl in years. Haven't really needed to since my mom died and I stopped needing to stand up for her."

Unhappy with himself for revealing far more about his past than he was in the habit of doing, he held Elliott's gaze. "You've apologized. I've accepted. Anything else?"

Though Elliott looked faintly taken aback by his direct words, he didn't look away. "Just one more thing," he said. "I saw you at Rosalina's the other night. I saw the way you were looking at Adelia. Saw it again earlier today, in fact."

"Look, I don't know what you think you saw—"

Elliott smiled. "I *know* what I saw," he corrected. "I saw a man who's hungry for a woman. It's a look I recognize, so a word of warning. Don't start something with my sister that you have no intention of finishing. She's feeling overwhelmed and vulnerable these days. I don't want her hurt again."

"Not my intention, believe me," Gabe said, respecting the directness, even if it made him uncomfortable to be having this conversation with a man he'd barely met. "I have plenty on my plate these days. I'm not looking for a fling and I'm certainly not in the market for anything more serious."

"If that's the case, then steer clear of Adelia," Elliott said. "That's the best way I know to avoid any misunderstandings."

Even though it was advice he'd already been telling himself to heed, Gabe took exception to being warned off. "Look, I respect the fact that you're only looking out for your sister, but she strikes me as a woman who's smart enough to know her own mind. I doubt she'd appreciate you running interference for her."

To his surprise, Elliott laughed at that. "No question about it," he conceded. "She'd be furious, so maybe it would be best if we kept this conversation just between us."

Gabe relaxed. Despite Elliott's tendency to come on too strong, he had to respect his intentions. "I can do that. No reason at all for us to be crossing paths except casually. I can't imagine the topic coming up."

Elliott looked relieved. He hesitated, then said, "I missed dinner at home to come by here. Since you've obviously been working late, I'm guessing you haven't eaten, either. Feel like grabbing a pizza at Rosalina's?"

Since he'd been planning to head over there anyway, Gabe saw no reason to refuse the overture. He figured the cross-examination and warnings were out of the way. It might be nice to have some guy talk instead of eating all alone. Eating with Elliott would sure as heck keep his thoughts from straying to Adelia, and that had to be a good thing.

"Sure," he said.

He finished locking up, then followed Elliott to the Italian restaurant. To ensure that the conversation stayed on less disquieting topics, he asked about Fit for Anything and Elliott's role there.

"I'm just one of the partners," Adelia's brother explained, describing the agreement he'd made with several of the men in town to run the place in exchange for a share. "I'm a personal trainer there and at The Corner Spa, too."

"Sounds like a demanding schedule," Gabe said.

Elliott nodded. "You have no idea, especially with two stepchildren and a new baby at home. Fortunately, I'm blessed with an understanding wife who has her own career. Karen's just been promoted to sous-chef at Sullivan's. Between her cooking and my mother's, believe me, I need to work out even harder than most of my clients do."

Gabe laughed. "If I keep existing on pizza, I'll need to add a few extra workouts into my routine, too. I tell myself I'd eat healthier if I were in my own place, but the Serenity Inn will have to do for now."

"That's where you're living?" Elliott asked, sounding shocked.

"I know its reputation as a place the locals go for trysts," Gabe said. He'd known all about that when he'd been a kid, thanks to his mom, who'd been a frequent visitor. "But it's clean and not too expensive."

"Are you planning to look for your own place?"

"Sooner or later," Gabe hedged. It all depended on how long it took for him to get antsy. The instant he sensed he might be starting to put down roots, it would be time to go. That was the pattern he'd established in a half-dozen other towns across the state. His motives for coming back to Serenity might be different, but there was no reason for that particular pattern to change.

"Well, if you decide you want to look at some houses or apartments, I know a couple of good Realtors. Mary Vaughn Lewis or her daughter can probably hook you up."

"Mary Vaughn's still around?" Gabe asked, not sure why he was so surprised. She'd been just a little ahead of him in school. It had always seemed to him that she was ambitious enough to take off at the first opportunity. She'd had her own family demons to battle back then, though she'd handled them better than he had.

"Wait a second," he said. "Did you say Lewis? As in Sonny Lewis, the mayor's son? That's who she married?"

Elliott nodded. "They divorced, but they're back together now and have a new baby, a boy."

Gabe shook his head. The longer he stuck around, it seemed the more surprises awaited him. It was a little worrisome that he found that intriguing.

CHAPTER FOUR

Even though she desperately wanted a morning caffeine fix, Adelia found herself avoiding Sweet Things for the next few mornings, determined to steer clear of Gabe. Involving him in her drama with Selena was one thing. She'd had little choice about that. But the attraction that was starting to simmer, for her, anyway, was a little too disconcerting for a woman who'd declared herself to be single-mindedly independent for now. She wasn't ready to cede that stance. She might never be.

Her determination lasted quite nicely through the weekend. After a busy Saturday at the boutique, she devoted herself to spending time with the children on Sunday, finally caving in to Tomas's pleas to go to the usual family dinner at her mother's.

Just as she'd anticipated, it was awkward and tense from the moment they arrived. Her sisters scowled at her and looked relieved when she finally abandoned the kitchen in favor of going outside to watch the kids. Her brothers-in-law regarded her as if she were deliberately trying to shake up their orderly worlds. Only the determined cheerfulness of her mother, Elliott and Karen made the afternoon tolerable. None of the others would have dared to voice their opinions aloud in front of her mother especially. The risk of alienating the family matriarch was too great.

The children, thankfully, were unaware of most of the undercurrents as they ran boisterously through the house and played in the yard with their cousins. Watching them, she was almost able to believe life would eventually return to normal, or whatever the new normal might be.

By three, though, Adelia had had more than enough. She excused herself to go home and work on the list of repairs needed at her new house. Surrounded by welcome silence, she'd made good progress on her list by the time Elliott and Karen dropped the children off on their way home.

"I'm sorry about today. It won't always be like that," her brother reassured her, regarding her with worry. "Everyone will eventually get past this."

"And stop judging me?" she asked wryly. Her annoyance kicked up a notch. "What right do they have? They know what Ernesto was doing. In fact, I suspect our sisters knew all along and never said a word."

Elliott frowned at that. "You can't really believe that. Why would they do such a thing? What about family loyalty?"

Adelia voiced her theory. "I'm very much afraid because they've been brainwashed to believe that sort of behavior is expected, just the price a woman has to pay for a certain lifestyle."

When her brother's expression immediately darkened, Adelia realized she'd revealed too much about her possibly unfounded suspicions. "Wipe that look right off your face," she ordered. "And don't go roaring over to their houses tossing around accusations. I don't know anything. I just have a feeling in my gut."

"Your gut feelings are usually right on the money," he said.

"Really? I never had a single one about Ernesto, not until the end when he grew careless."

"Only because you didn't want to believe he'd ever treat you that way," Elliott said. "Love sometimes makes people blind. Do you think that's the case with—"

Adelia cut him off and tried to stare him down. "Promise me you're not going to get in the middle of this, not between me and them nor in their marriages," she commanded. "I mean it, Elliott. Our sisters are living their lives as they see fit. I just wish they'd show me the same courtesy."

He sighed deeply. "I hope you're wrong," he said.

"I hope so, too."

But she didn't think she was. Of all people, she knew only too well what it was like to live with delusions just to keep the peace and hold on to a familiar lifestyle.

Adelia was well aware of Mitch's habit of starting his day in his wife's bakery. She also knew she couldn't avoid the place forever, even if steering clear was the best way to give Gabe a wide berth. From the moment the bakery had opened, she'd gotten into the habit of pausing to share a cup of coffee with Mitch and Lynn before heading next door to the boutique. They'd probably make way too much of it if she stayed away too long, especially after Gabe and Mitch had pitched in to help with the search for Selena. The last thing she wanted was for any of them to think she was ungrateful.

But even as she'd reminded herself of that, she let another week pass before she mustered up the courage to return to her old routine. She had work to discuss with Mitch, she reminded herself. That alone was the perfect excuse, if she needed one, to stop by the bakery.

She'd stayed up late the night before fine-tuning the list of projects needed to fix up the house. She needed to get cost estimates and then prioritize those that were essential and those that could wait. The list was a whole lot longer than she'd anticipated. It seemed that history and architectural character came with a host of problems.

Thankfully, when Raylene had promoted her to manager of the boutique she'd given her a nice raise to go along with it. That extra money would allow her to do at least some of these improvements without dipping into her nest egg from the divorce. Adelia was still a little shocked by her promotion. Sure, she'd gotten a business degree in college, but for years the only "jobs" she'd held outside her home had been on the numerous school committees she'd chaired. Raylene had taken a chance on her, and she claimed she'd more than proved herself. Adelia seemed to have an innate sense of fashion and an ability to help customers make choices that flattered them. Sales had skyrocketed in the months after she was first hired.

"To be honest, I'm a little nervous about how I'll handle the whole parenthood thing," Raylene had claimed after the first trimester of her pregnancy when she'd offered Adelia the promotion.

"But you've been raising Carter's sisters with him,

practically since their parents died in the car crash," Adelia had protested. "You've been great with them and they adore you."

"They're teenagers," Raylene had replied, as if that had made her role easier. "I have no idea what to expect with a baby. You're practically running this place for me already, so you deserve the title and the raise that goes with it. You'll still get your commission, too, since you're the best saleswoman I've ever seen. All those lookers who used to leave without buying now can't get out the door without being loaded down with bags."

Adelia had hardly been in a position to turn her down, even though the responsibility had been a little terrifying. Now she was more than grateful for yet another chance to prove to Raylene, but even more importantly to herself, just how capable she was.

It was ironic, really, she thought on her walk into downtown bright and early on Saturday morning. She was a mature woman with an increasingly responsible job. She had a head full of ideas to prove that Raylene's faith in her hadn't been misplaced. She was a good mother, at least according to most assessments. If those things were true, how ridiculous was it that she was scared of a man she'd just met simply because she found him attractive?

Mitch was attractive, for heaven's sake, and he didn't scare her. Neither did any of the other men she knew in Serenity.

Because they were all safely married, she concluded with a sigh. Gabe, it appeared, was not.

Outside Sweet Things, she sucked in a deep breath and wiped her sweaty palms on a tissue. Today was as good a day as any to get back into her preferred rou-

tine. That it was a Saturday, a day she was less likely
to encounter Gabe, was *not* the reason for her sudden
bravery, she assured herself.

As she entered the bakery, she reminded herself
that she was here to have a business discussion with a
man she'd known for years. Mitch wasn't the terrifying
Franklin, after all. That was Gabe, and he frightened
her only because of how easily he disconcerted her.

After the pep talk she'd been giving herself, she was
actually stunned and a little disappointed to find Mitch
all alone at his usual table, sipping a cup of coffee and
studying a blueprint. He glanced up and smiled.

"There you are. Lynn and I have been wondering
where you've been. You've been MIA for a while now."

"Just getting settled in the new house," she claimed.
"I'm glad you're here, though." She reached in her
purse and withdrew several yellow sheets torn from a
legal pad. "I have a list of renovation projects I wanted
to discuss with you, that is, if you're not too swamped
with your Main Street redevelopment these days."

"I'm never too swamped to tackle a job for a friend,"
he said. "Have a seat. I'll get you some coffee. Lynn's
in the back cussing away at some pie dough or something. The woman may make the best pastry in two
states on a bad day, but she's a perfectionist."

"Ah, but that's why she has such an incredible reputation," Adelia said, joining him at the table, which had
been covered with a blue-checked cloth. He'd pushed
aside a Mason jar filled with fresh daisies that added a
cheerful, homey touch. "This place has been a success
since the day she opened. Thank goodness, Raylene and
all those Sweet Magnolias ganged up on her and convinced her this was something she could do."

Mitch laughed as he poured her a cup of coffee. "They're a sneaky bunch, all right."

Adelia regarded him with amusement. "You did your own share of fast-talking, the way I understand it. Isn't that how you wound up buying up all these vacant storefronts with Raylene? Wasn't this downtown revitalization actually part of your plot to lure Lynn into opening a bakery and becoming a tenant?" She laughed at his guilty expression. "Just as I thought."

"It was a sound business decision," Mitch declared, setting the coffee in front of her. "That's my story and I'm sticking to it."

Just then the door opened and Gabe walked in. He was halfway through apologizing to Mitch for his tardiness when he noticed Adelia. A smile broke across his face, one that revealed dimples. They only added to his allure as a bit of a scoundrel.

"Hey, darlin'. Where have you been hiding?" he asked her.

Adelia blushed, flustered not only by his teasing, but because he'd taken note of her absence. "I've been right next door," she told him. "Every day, same as usual."

Mitch apparently noticed her reaction because he stepped in. "Adelia just bought one of those old houses in Swan Point," he told Gabe.

"I saw it," Gabe reminded him. "When we were looking for her daughter."

"Of course," Mitch said. "I doubt you had much of a chance to take a look around that day. She's brought me a list of a few things she wants to have done."

Gabe caught sight of the pages of notes and sketches and chuckled. "From the looks of that list, you sure you wouldn't be better off tearing it down and starting over? It might be cheaper."

"But then it wouldn't have any character," she protested defensively. "I love the house. It just has a few age-related flaws, the same as most people." She studied him with narrowed eyes. "Or are you one of those who thinks anything past a certain age should be tossed away?"

Gabe held up both hands. "Hey, that was a comment based on financial considerations, not age."

His glance skimmed over her, deliberately lingering until she flushed. "Some things improve with age," he commented appreciatively.

Adelia wished she could grab her coffee and run, but she knew that would be far too revealing. She concluded the really courageous thing to do would be to stay put. She took a sip of coffee, instead, to steady her nerves.

"Let me see," Gabe said, taking her list from his cousin. He got to page two and frowned. "Didn't you have the roof inspected?"

"Of course I did," she said impatiently.

"And you knew it was leaking?"

"Yes, and I got a very nice credit for that, thank you very much. Now, though, I need to get it repaired. I've run out of pots and pans to put under the leaks." She turned to Mitch. "That probably should be at the top of the list."

"No doubt about it," Mitch agreed, then unexpectedly stood up. "Gabe, you can handle this, right? I want to check on those reinforcing beams going in down the block."

Adelia stared at him. "But I thought you'd be doing this," she said, then winced. "Sorry, Gabe. No offense."

He grinned, clearly aware of exactly why she looked so rattled. "None taken."

Mitch gave her shoulder a squeeze. "You're in good hands. Gabe has plenty of experience, some of it in historic renovations, as a matter of fact. He knows what he's doing, probably even better than I do. If you have any questions after he gives you an estimate, we'll talk about them. How's that?"

"Fine," she said, though she couldn't seem to hide her reluctance.

After Mitch had gone, she glanced warily toward Gabe. He was leaning back in his seat, the chair on two legs. His own denim-clad legs were stretched out in front of him. While the posture was relaxed, she sensed a coiled tension just beneath the surface.

"If you're not okay with this, just say the word," he said quietly.

"Of course I'm okay with it," she said irritably. "Mitch says you're more than qualified and I trust his judgment."

A wicked gleam sparked in his eyes. "Then it's me personally you're not so sure about. I promise you I'm harmless."

Adelia didn't believe that for a single second, not with her heart pounding like a jackhammer. But maybe that was her problem, not his. It wasn't as if he'd made a blatant pass at her. And despite her impression that he was single, maybe she'd been wrong about that. Maybe he was happily married. Married would be good.

"Are you married, Gabe?"

As if he'd followed her train of thought, he laughed. "Nope. Free as a bird. You?"

"Divorced," she admitted. "*Recently* divorced."

"As in not interested in taking another chance on love anytime soon," he concluded. "Duly warned."

Though his tone was solemn, the wicked spark in his eyes was anything but reassuring. He was going to be trouble, she concluded with a sigh. No question about it.

"How'd things go with Adelia this morning?" Mitch asked Gabe at the end of the day.

"I make her nervous," Gabe admitted.

Mitch frowned at that. "How so?"

"She's a beautiful woman. I can't seem to stop myself from a little harmless flirting. I get the impression she's not used to that."

"She's just getting out of a bad marriage," Mitch told him.

"So I've heard. The guy was a cheater. I imagine that left her with some issues."

"The cheating was certainly bad enough," Mitch confirmed. "But he paraded his mistresses openly around town. The last one lived right in his neighborhood. Even his daughter knew about her. I think that's what nobody in town will ever be able to excuse, the way he disrespected Adelia so openly in front of one of his kids."

Gabe frowned at that. "You've got to be kidding me. What kind of lowlife does something like that?"

"Ernesto apparently thought his marriage vows only extended to providing well for his family, not to fidelity. The way I hear it, he thought he was entitled to play around, that it was part of the deal in exchange for the nice house and lots of spending money."

"That explains why she's now living in a house with a leaking roof," Gabe guessed.

"More than likely. She's a smart woman. She's just discovering that she can make it on her own. Independence is real important to her right now." His expression turned thoughtful. "She reminds me of Lynn in that way. I wanted to rush in about a million times to make things easier for her while she was divorcing Ed Morrow, but she needed to figure things out for herself, to prove that she was strong enough to do right by her kids. Much as it killed me to sit idly by while she struggled, letting her get back on her feet on her own was the right thing to do. She didn't need a knight in shining armor. She needed a partner, someone who'd treat her like a woman with a lot to offer."

"I suppose you think that's the strategy for winning Adelia, too," Gabe said.

Mitch leveled a long look at him. "Do you need a strategy?"

Gabe thought about the question. It was fraught with all sorts of implications. "No way," he said candidly. "I only came here with the intention of getting back on my feet, maybe making amends."

Mitch frowned. "You did nothing wrong, Gabe. You don't owe anybody in this town a thing."

"But my mother was a piece of work. In my zeal to defend her, I made my share of mistakes."

"Okay, let's say you make amends. Then what?"

Gabe hesitated, pondering the question, then shrugged. "I'll probably move on. I can't see myself putting down roots, here or any place else."

"Then a word of advice. Be careful with Adelia, my friend. We all recognize how strong she is, but she doesn't see it just yet. Give her time to get there and don't do anything that might lead her to believe you're staying. And if you think that word of warning is coming just from me, think again. You ever heard of the Sweet Magnolias?"

Gabe shook his head. "Who are they?"

"It's not an official organization or anything, but a lot of the women in town have formed this deep bond. They look out for each other, and heaven help anyone who messes with them. You probably remember Maddie Maddox?"

"Doesn't sound familiar."

"She would have been Maddie Vreeland in school. Then she married and became a Townsend. When that ended in divorce, she married the high school baseball coach. Anyway, she, Dana Sue Sullivan and Helen Decatur-Whitney started calling themselves Sweet Magnolias way back in high school."

Gabe held up a hand. "Slow down." He described the three women who'd been entering the bakery as he'd fled to get away from Lynn's teasing on the afternoon Selena had gone missing.

"They're the women who started it," Mitch confirmed. "Over the years, they've included a bunch of other women, Lynn among them. I'm not sure what they do beyond the occasional margarita night get-together, but they sure do stick up for one another. I wouldn't want to tangle with them or get their backs up, that's for sure. I'm not sure I'd be married to Lynn right now if they'd objected to it."

Mitch grinned. "Fortunately, Maddie, Helen and Dana Sue and I go way back. They jumped on my side. In addition to any wooing I did, Lynn got the full-court press from the Sweet Magnolias, too." His expression sobered. "I'm just saying, if you do anything to hurt

Adelia, they'll be all over you. I have a hunch her recovery's going to be their next project."

The advice was perfectly reasonable, but Gabe took offense just the same. "Whatever my flaws might be, Mitch, they don't include a trail of brokenhearted women. Listening to my mom cry her eyes out at night taught me to be honest and never offer something I don't intend to deliver."

His cousin nodded. "Good to know." A grin spread across his face. "Something tells me, though, that battling wits with you could be just what Adelia needs to get her confidence back."

Gabe waved those yellow pages in his cousin's face. "So, I was right. Despite all those warnings you just uttered, you do have some crazy idea about pushing the two of us together for more than fixing up that house of hers."

Mitch shrugged, his expression innocent. "The work needs to be done. You're good at what you do. If a few sparks fly in the process, all the better." He gave Gabe an amused look. "For both of you. Just keep in mind those boundaries I warned you about."

Gabe scowled at his cousin, suddenly wondering if coming back to Serenity had been as smart a move as he'd once thought it was. "I'm not likely to forget."

Chic closed promptly at six on Saturday, though it was usually closer to seven by the time Adelia wrapped up all the chores she felt were necessary before locking up for the night. When she stepped outside, she was stunned to find Gabe leaning casually against the building. He straightened at the sight of her.

Adelia regarded him with confusion. "Were you waiting for me?"

He grinned. "What was your first clue? You know any other pretty women in the neighborhood?"

"Gabe!" she protested. "You have to stop doing that."

"Doing what?"

What was he doing exactly, other than rattling her, that is? Was he flirting? It had been so long since any man had teased and flattered her, she couldn't be entirely sure.

"Saying things like that," she told him finally, then started striding down the block with the crazy idea that she might be able to shake him if she walked away quickly enough.

He easily fell into step beside her. "Hasn't anybody ever told you how beautiful you are?" he inquired curiously.

"Not in a long time," she admitted wistfully before she could stop herself.

He stared at her incredulously. "Then the men of Serenity are idiots," he declared.

She smiled at his vehemence. "Or maybe they just had good instincts for self-preservation," she suggested. "Until recently I was married, remember?"

"So compliments were reserved for your husband?"

"Something like that."

"And did he lavish you with a lot of them?"

She frowned. She had a hunch he already knew the answer to that. "We're divorced. What do you think?"

"Then I get to lump him in with all the other idiots," he said.

Adelia stopped in her tracks and turned to face him. "Gabe, why were you waiting for me? And why are you walking home with me? If we were sixteen, I'd say you were angling to carry my schoolbooks."

He laughed at that. "If I'd known you back then, I probably would have been." He pulled the now-rumpled yellow pages from his back pocket. "I thought I could look over these projects of yours and try to get a handle on what needs doing first."

For a few minutes, Adelia had forgotten all about the renovations and his assignment to take them on.

Gabe was studying her with unmistakable amusement. "Did you forget about these?"

"Temporary lapse," she assured him.

"Is this a bad time? If you have a date or something…" His voice trailed off as he studied her speculatively.

"No date," she responded tersely. "And this is as good a time as any. I should warn you, though, that my mother's at the house with the kids. That might ensure that you'll get an invitation to a good meal, but it will also come with a lengthy interrogation."

"I made it through your brother's. I imagine I can handle whatever your mother asks."

Adelia regarded him with alarm. "Elliott interrogated you? When?"

"On the day we were looking for Selena. He came by the construction site that evening. He told me he was there to apologize for the way he'd reacted when we stopped by the gym, but it was evident he wanted to clarify a few things for me."

"Such as?"

"My intentions. His concerns. That sort of protective guy stuff."

Adelia groaned. "He didn't! I may have to kill him. He had no business getting in your face like that."

"Oh, he thought he was being subtle about it, but men are rarely as subtle as they'd like to think when they're warning people off. I got the message." He shrugged. "Then we went out for pizza."

"Men!" she said, shaking her head.

"He just wanted me to know you have someone looking out for you. I don't imagine he realizes he's not the only one."

"Who else?" she asked before she could stop herself.

"Mitch chimed in just a couple of hours ago. He also said there's some group of women in town, the Sweet Magnolias I think he called them. He said they'd have my hide if I hurt you."

Adelia actually laughed at that. Though she wasn't an actual member of that unofficial group of women, she certainly knew them all. She also knew their reputation for protecting their own with a ferocity that was a little terrifying to any rational man in town.

"And yet here you are," she said. "Risking life and limb by walking through town with me."

"Darlin', there are some things worth taking an occasional risk for," he said.

Then he very deliberately added a wink that rocked her nice, safe world. Adelia actually thought her heart might have come to a complete standstill for a few seconds.

And that, she concluded, should be sufficient warning to send her right back to where her day had started, knowing that she needed to avoid this man at all costs.

CHAPTER FIVE

———◆———

Gabe got one whiff of the aromas coming from Adelia's kitchen and decided that any interrogation that might lie ahead would be well worth it, as long as he was invited to stick around for dinner. Adelia must have noticed that he was practically drooling, because she chuckled.

"Let me put you out of your misery," she said. "Would you like to join us for dinner?"

"Yes," he said so quickly that it immediately brought a deepening smile to her lips.

"You haven't even met my mother yet," she reminded him. "Are you sure?"

"Not a doubt in my mind."

"Either you're sick of pizza or you're a very brave man."

Gabe laughed. "Probably a little of both with some curiosity thrown in."

"Curiosity?"

He nodded. "I find myself wanting to meet the woman who can fill this house with such incredible aromas and yet make grown men cower. That's an impressive combination. It'll be interesting to discover if you two are anything alike."

Just then the very woman in question, diminutive in size but with the regal bearing of a matriarch used to respect, came out of the kitchen.

"I thought I heard voices," she said, regarding Gabe speculatively. "I don't believe we've met."

"Mother, I'd like you to meet Gabe Franklin," Adelia said.

Mrs. Cruz's eyes narrowed. "I believe my son has mentioned you."

"Uh-oh," Adelia murmured under her breath.

"He probably has," Gabe said easily. "Elliott and I had dinner just the other night."

Mrs. Cruz's eyes lit with amusement at his interpretation of the encounter. "I hardly think my son's choice of a dinner companion would have stuck in my mind. I believe it was his comment that we needed to keep an eye on you around Adelia. Do we?"

"Mother!" Adelia said, blushing furiously. She turned to him. "I warned you. There's still time to make a run for it."

"Not a chance," he replied. Since Mrs. Cruz didn't seem to harbor any particular biases toward him, Gabe figured he'd passed some sort of test with Elliott, if not yet with her. He was eager to see how the evening might play out. He couldn't help it. Challenges always caught his interest.

"Gabe is here to check out the work I want to have done on the house," Adelia explained quickly. "I've invited him to join us for dinner."

"If it's not an imposition," Gabe told the older woman, drawing on manners he'd picked up from watching the way civilized people behaved, rather than any examples that had been set in his home.

"It's not an imposition at all," Mrs. Cruz said. "I have a large family. I cook accordingly. There's always more than enough for company. Dinner will be ready in a half hour, if that will give you time to look around at the renovations my daughter has in mind."

"Absolutely," Gabe said, relieved to have passed the initial screening at least.

Somehow, though, he wouldn't be one bit surprised to find Elliott and heaven knew how many other members of the Cruz family joining them at the table.

Adelia took one look at her mother's face and decided that giving Gabe a personal tour to go over her notes would be preferable to the cross-examination she was likely to receive if she joined her mother in the kitchen, even long enough to apologize for bringing home a last-minute guest. She realized there was a certain irony in the fact that she was more intimidated by the thought of answering her mother's penetrating questions than Gabe was. Of course, she'd had experience that he didn't share.

"Let's start outside," she suggested to Gabe. "I think I saw a ladder in the shed, if you want to check out the roof. Mother, you don't need my help, do you?"

Her mother gave her a knowing look. "Of course not. The girls are helping. It's time they learned their way around a kitchen. I left Selena stirring the sauce for the enchiladas. Knowing how distracted she gets by those text messages she receives every couple of minutes, I'd better check on it before it burns."

Adelia frowned. "She's not supposed to be using her cell phone these days."

Her mother looked startled. "I see. She didn't mention that."

"I'd better go in there and deal with this," Adelia said.

Her mother waved her off. "I can handle it."

"Thanks," Adelia said, relieved not to have to force yet another confrontation with her daughter or get caught in her mother's crosshairs.

Adelia avoided Gabe's gaze as she led the way to the backyard. When she finally risked a glance, she found his eyes sparkling with barely concealed mirth.

"When did I become the lesser of two evils?" he asked.

"In the past five minutes," she said, not even trying to pretend he hadn't hit the target with his observation. "If I'd had any idea she and Elliott had been chatting about you and me, you wouldn't have gotten within a hundred yards of this place while she was here. I don't need the aggravation."

A smile spread across his face. "You're scared of your mother," he taunted.

"Terrified," Adelia admitted, seeing little reason to deny it. "Why do you find that so amusing?"

"Because you're a pretty formidable presence in your own right."

"Formidable? Me?" she said, laughing. "Hardly. As you just heard, not even my own daughter takes my rules seriously."

"Maybe you need to see yourself from where I'm standing," Gabe said, his expression turning serious.

"Seems to me you could hold your own with anybody, even Selena. She's just testing the limits."

Adelia wished she could see herself that way. After years of Ernesto's criticism and neglect, she had a very low opinion of her own worth. She was determined to get past that, but she wasn't there yet.

"So, what is it about your mother that intimidates you?" Gabe asked.

Adelia gave the question a moment's thought before responding. "She has some very rigid and old-fashioned ideas about the role of women, the sanctity of marriage and in general about the relationships between men and women. I've been a disappointment."

He looked skeptical. "I didn't hear even a hint of judgment in her voice, just concern."

"You haven't had the practice I've had at reading between the lines," Adelia told him. "It's ironic really, because on many levels, I don't even disagree with her."

"So you're an old-fashioned woman at heart?"

She considered the label. It actually fit better than she'd realized. She might chafe at it, but she'd done nothing in her life that would indicate she'd broken that particular mold. Until very recently she hadn't even been sure she wanted to. It was only lately that she'd come to appreciate the value of independence and self-sufficiency.

"In some ways, I suppose I am old-fashioned," she said. "I liked being a stay-at-home mom and wife. I thought marriage vows meant forever." She shrugged. "I've just come to accept that some marriages can't be saved."

She shuddered at the memory of the day she'd broken the news of her intention to divorce Ernesto. "You have no idea how much courage it took for me to tell my devoutly Catholic mother that I was leaving my husband. That brought on a huge family intervention that entailed quite a bit of yelling and a host of recriminations about how I'd failed the test as a dutiful wife."

Gabe regarded her with surprise. "She disapproved, even under the circumstances?"

"At first I was too humiliated to admit the reason, so she vehemently disapproved. When I was finally persuaded to tell her everything, it took some adjustment on her part, but she actually turned out to be surprisingly supportive."

"And the rest of the family?"

"Elliott and his wife have been incredible," she said. "The others, not so much." She held up a hand. "Could we drop this? It's more than you ever really wanted or needed to know about my personal life, I'm sure."

Gabe looked as if he wanted to argue about that, but he nodded and gestured toward the shed. "The ladder's in there? Is it locked?"

"No, it's open."

She took a deep breath and fought for composure while he got the extension ladder and put it against the side of the house. No sooner had he started up to the roof, than Tomas spotted him and came running across the yard.

"Who's that?" he asked, staring after Gabe. "Can I go up on the roof with him?"

He already had one foot on the bottom rung when Adelia clamped a hand on his shoulder. "Not now," she said firmly. "Let Gabe do his job."

Tomas stared up at the roof, his disappointment plain. "But what's he doing?"

"Looking to see what kind of shape the roof is in and what it will take to fix it," she said.

Tomas frowned. "Do we know him?"

"I do," she said. "You remember Mitch Franklin?"

"The man who's fixing all those stores on Main Street," Tomas said. "He's married to the cupcake lady."

Adelia smiled at the characterization. Clearly baking cupcakes was more memorable to Tomas than Lynn's name. "Exactly. Gabe is his cousin. He works for Mitch."

"Is he gonna do anything else here?" he asked, his curious gaze still fixed on Gabe, who was scrambling over the steep roof with the agility of a mountain goat.

"Lots of things," Adelia said. "He or the people who work for him are going to do all those things on that list we made."

"Like paint my room?"

She smiled at his sudden eagerness. "That's definitely on the list," she agreed.

"Will he let me help? Mitch let Jeremy help when he was working at Raylene's."

"I'm sure he'll try to find some things you can do," Adelia said, hoping that would be the case. She was sure Tomas would start to feel better about this new home if he had even a tiny role to play in making the necessary improvements. "You have to promise, though, to do exactly what Gabe or any of the other professionals tell you to do and never to do anything involving tools without supervision."

"Promise," Tomas said, his attention already wandering as he saw Gabe descending the ladder. He scampered over to wait for him.

"Hi," he said, startling Gabe so badly he almost missed his footing. "I'm Tomas."

Gabe steadied himself, then held out a hand. "I'm Gabe," he said. "Are you the man of the house?"

Tomas looked surprised by the question, but Adelia saw his chest swell just a little as he realized that was exactly what he was. "Since my dad's not here, I am."

"Then I'll be sure to talk things over with you when I start working around here," Gabe promised him, winking at Adelia over his head.

"I don't imagine he'll give you much choice," she told Gabe. "Tomas wants to be part of your crew, that is, if you can find anything for him to do that isn't too dangerous."

"Mom! I'm not a baby," her son protested.

"Of course not," Gabe was quick to say. "But you are inexperienced, or am I wrong about that? Have you built a house before?"

Tomas giggled. "No."

Gabe nodded solemnly. "Then in that case, you'll learn on the job."

"I can do that," her son said with enthusiasm. "I'm a quick learner. I get really good grades in school and I hardly have to study at all." He made a face. "Except spelling. I'm bad at spelling."

"We've all struggled with that on occasion," Gabe said.

Tomas looked surprised. "Even you?"

"Even me," Gabe said. "Why don't you show me these things that are on your mom's list? This is man's work, after all."

Adelia might have taken offense at that if Tomas

hadn't looked so excited at being included among the men on this particular job.

Smiling, she said, "I'll leave you to it, then. Make sure you're in the dining room for dinner in fifteen minutes," she told them both. "*Abuela* doesn't like dinner getting cold."

Tomas nodded at once, then confided to Gabe. "*Abuela* makes the best food ever!"

"I'll bet she does," Gabe said. "I'm looking forward to it." He glanced at the list, found the next item—painting the bedrooms—and suggested that Tomas lead the way.

As they went into the house, she heard her son chattering away, sounding happier than she'd heard him in weeks.

Left with no other alternative, she went into the kitchen and found all three of her girls dealing with various assignments while her mother watched over them. Natalia was putting rice into a bowl almost as big as she was. Juanita, her tongue caught between her teeth and a frown of concentration on her forehead, was carefully pouring steaming, fragrant black beans into another bowl.

"Sounds to me as if you just made Tomas's day," her mother said, regarding her approvingly. "What do you know about this man? Is he a good role model?"

"I can't really say," Adelia admitted. "But he was very kind to Tomas just now. If he hadn't been, if he'd shown any hint of impatience, I wouldn't have left them alone."

"And is he equally kind to you?" her mother asked quietly, the question spoken low enough that she wouldn't be heard over the girls' squabbling.

"He doesn't need to be kind to me. He just needs to get the work done," Adelia replied.

"I spoke to your brother just now and mentioned that Gabe was here."

"Thanks for that," Adelia said dryly. She should probably expect a visit or call from her protective brother no later than tomorrow.

Her mother ignored the hint of sarcasm in her voice and told her, "Elliott still seems to think there might be more to his interest than any work he might do around here."

"My brother has stars in his eyes these days," Adelia said in a tone that made light of Elliott's opinion. "Karen has made him very happy with their life as a family."

"One thing has nothing to do with the other," her mother insisted. "He's concerned for your happiness. We all are."

"I'm happier than I have been in years," Adelia said. Even as the words tumbled out just to divert unwanted attention, she realized they were actually true. Her life might not be perfect, but it was a whole lot better than the lie she'd been forced to live with Ernesto. Better yet, her happiness was within herself and not tied to any man.

Gabe couldn't ever recall having a meal that came with quite as much commotion as the one he was sharing with Adelia and her family. The good news was that it was impossible for them to share a single private word. That was the bad news, as well.

Still, he liked seeing her up close like this with her family. Her daughters, well, the younger two, anyway, had plenty to say, talking over each other in an attempt to get not only their mother's attention, but his. To do that, though, they had to compete with Tomas, who'd managed to sit beside Gabe and asked more questions than Alex Trebek in a year's worth of *Jeopardy* episodes. Gabe noted that Adelia seemed amused and showed not the slightest inclination to rescue him.

Mrs. Cruz, however, did chime in from time to time to remind her grandson to give Mr. Franklin time to breathe.

Tomas regarded her blankly. "He is breathing," he said, looking puzzled. "Wouldn't he die if he wasn't?"

Adelia laughed, and the light sound echoed in the room in a way that drew the attention of even Selena, who looked as if she hadn't heard that laugh in a while. The teen stared at her mother with evident surprise, then turned a scowl on Gabe, as if she didn't like him being even indirectly responsible for her mom's brighter mood.

Selena started to push back from the table, but at a pointed glance from her grandmother, she hesitated. "May I be excused?" she asked.

Adelia frowned at the request. "You haven't finished your meal."

"I'm not hungry. Please."

"Let her go," Mrs. Cruz said.

After Selena had run upstairs, Adelia turned to her mother. "Any idea what that was about?"

Mrs. Cruz looked in his direction. "I have some idea."

As her implication registered, shock settled on Adelia's face. "But there's nothing…" She regarded him with dismay. "Gabe, I'm sorry."

"Maybe I should go," he said, not wanting to be the cause of dissension between Adelia and her daughter, even inadvertently. Maybe it was time for him to go, anyway. He'd been enjoying the whole meal—and the company—a little too much. It would be easy to get comfortable here, a little too alluring to experience how real families interacted. With his cousin's recent warning still echoing in his head, he knew what a bad idea that would be.

"Not before you've had dessert," Mrs. Cruz said adamantly.

"*Abuela* made flan," Natalia said excitedly. "She hardly ever makes it anymore. It's the best. And she let us help."

Gabe could see how proud she was of herself. "Do you think it'll be as good as if she made it herself?" he teased.

"It'll be even better," Juanita said firmly. "We made it with love."

Gabe had to hide his desire to chuckle at her repetition of something she'd obviously heard often.

"And do you think I haven't always made it with love?" Mrs. Cruz inquired with feigned indignation.

"Uh-oh," Adelia said. "Do you think you might have hurt your grandmother's feelings?"

Juanita studied her grandmother closely, then shook her head. "No, she's just teasing," she declared.

"I think so, too," Natalia chimed in.

Gabe laughed at their solemn expressions. "Then I think I definitely have to try this flan you've made with such love," he said. He turned to Adelia with what he hoped was a believably quizzical expression, then whispered, "What is flan?"

Mrs. Cruz and Adelia both chuckled at the question. Even the girls giggled.

"Girls, clear the table and let *Abuela* bring in the flan, so Mr. Franklin can find out for himself why it's your favorite dessert," Adelia said. "The best way to learn about flan is to experience it."

Tomas pulled on Gabe's sleeve until he leaned down.

"It's like custard with caramel," Tomas confided. "You're gonna love it."

"I'll bet you're right," Gabe said, glancing across the table at Adelia. "There's been nothing about this meal so far that I haven't loved."

And that just about scared him to death.

It was late on Monday afternoon before Gabe had time to sit down with Mitch and go over his estimates for the work Adelia wanted done. There'd been one crisis after another all day long on the Main Street job. Add in his cousin's distraction thanks to some other job he was handling across town and they hadn't exchanged more than a couple of words all day.

He was sitting at his makeshift desk on the construction site when Mitch wandered in after six.

"You look beat," Gabe said, frowning. "Why don't you go on home? This can wait."

"I need to unwind a little before I head home," Mitch said. "Going over those figures with you should do the trick."

"Are you sure? I don't want your wife on my case for making you late for dinner."

"It'll be at least another hour before we eat. Lynn's gotten in the habit of taking a nap once she closes the bakery and gets home. Being up at the crack of dawn is wearing on her more than she wants to admit." He managed a weary grin. "She doesn't think I know about the naps, but I've caught her a time or two."

"She doesn't know that?"

Mitch shook his head. "I slip right back out the door. She wants to believe it's her little secret. If I say something, then we'll wind up fighting over whether the bakery's too much for her or when she needs to think about hiring some help. It's her business and her decision. Anything I say is bound to come off as interference."

Gabe regarded his cousin with surprise. "How'd you learn so much about women? It's not as if you dated a ton of them. You went from that secret crush you had on Lynn in high school—"

"It can't have been much of a secret if you knew about it," Mitch grumbled.

"Please, you started wearing your heart on your sleeve in junior high," Gabe said. "Then you married Amy. Where did all this profound knowledge of yours come from?"

Mitch laughed. "Observation and self-preservation. Any man intent on staying married has to figure out all the clues to keeping his wife happy. Unfortunately, a whole lot of them are left unsaid. It complicates things."

Gabe could believe that. He'd failed to understand a whole lot of women over the years. He'd never had the will to work on getting it right with a single one of them. He had a feeling Adelia could be an exception.

Mitch beckoned for Gabe's notes on Adelia's renovations. "Looks as if you've got everything covered," he said.

"Except labor," Gabe pointed out. "I didn't know if you were figuring on bringing in one of your crews, assigning a single guy for most of it or what?"

"It'll be cheaper if it's done by one person," Mitch said.

"But it'll take longer," Gabe replied.

"Has she said anything about being in a hurry?"

"No, but people usually are," Gabe said.

"Maybe that's something you should discuss with her before we finalize this," Mitch said, then gave him an innocent look. "Of course, with the exception of the roof, a lot of this could be handled in your spare time. Not that you wouldn't get paid," he added hurriedly. "I'm just saying, it might be a project you wouldn't mind tackling."

Gabe knew exactly what Mitch was up to. "Don't you think I have my hands full keeping up with this Main Street project?"

"Sure you do," Mitch said at once. "Especially since I've seen the way you throw yourself into your work. I'm just saying that this primary job doesn't have the same perks."

"Perks?"

"Adelia," Mitch said, unsuccessfully fighting a smile. "Meals with the family."

Gabe stared at him incredulously. "How did you know about my staying for dinner the other night?"

"Tomas told Jeremy all about it," Mitch said, laughing.

"Who knew little boys could spread gossip that fast," Gabe complained. "I thought that particular trait was reserved for the adults in town."

"Tomas already has a bad case of hero worship," Mitch said. "I remember what that was like. Jeremy followed me around more than once when I was working at Raylene's. Boys their age need role models, Gabe. Even ignoring the way he treated Adelia, I doubt Ernesto Hernandez was much of one."

Gabe had the same impression. Tomas was a little too hungry for someone to teach him guy stuff.

"I'm not sure I'm cut out for the role," Gabe said.

"Sure, you are. If you weren't, Tomas wouldn't have been telling Jeremy all about you. Obviously you handled the situation just right."

"Sure, I answered his questions. I taught him a couple of basic things, but that's not the same as being a role model for an impressionable kid," Gabe argued. "Heck, even some of the jerks my mom dated were nice to me when they thought they had something to gain from it. That doesn't mean I should have aspired to be like a single one of them."

"Definitely not," Mitch agreed readily. "But you learned from that, Gabe. You'll try real hard to be a good influence on Tomas."

"Why do I have the feeling that you think the kid's going to be as much of an influence on me as I am on him? Do you think I'll stay on the straight and narrow because of him?"

Mitch frowned at that. "To my way of thinking, you've never been that far off the straight and narrow in anyone's mind but your own, but, yes, I think you'll be good for each other. I think you need to start to see yourself as more than a rolling stone. You seem to have this crazy idea that you don't deserve to find real happiness, the kind that can last."

Gabe couldn't deny that Mitch had nailed it. He'd never seen himself as a good bet for happily-ever-after. The only examples he'd had—Mitch's side of the family—had certainly never given him much reason to believe in himself.

"And Adelia? How do you see her fitting in?" he asked his cousin.

Mitch gave him a considering look before saying, "Any way you want her to, I imagine."

Unfortunately, the way Gabe envisioned her fitting into his life had a little too much to do with toppling into his bed than it did with the straight and narrow.

CHAPTER SIX

For some reason it seemed as if every woman in Serenity had chosen today to shop at the boutique. Many of the women were contacts Adelia had made through her school committees. They'd come to rely on her fashion sense, more than doubling the boutique's business since she'd started working there.

Adelia closed the register after the last sale just past lunchtime and drew in a satisfied breath. She was exhausted, but it had been an excellent morning. Raylene was going to be over the moon when she saw the receipts.

Of course, today all those sales had come with a surprising number of questions about Gabe Franklin. Apparently word had already spread that Adelia had the inside scoop on the sexy construction guy who'd just returned to town. Since most of the women asking questions were married, she was a little surprised by the level of curiosity.

She'd managed to skirt the most intrusive questions by diverting attention to a new line of accessories and liberally tossing around compliments about the way

the outfits being tried on fit perfectly or suited the customer's coloring. Because she'd developed a knack for
sincere flattery and a reputation for her own personal
style, which she'd always achieved on a budget, her
tactics mostly worked.

"Nice job," Raylene said, startling her by emerging
from the office in back.

"How long have you been here?" Adelia asked.

Raylene grinned. "Long enough to realize you
could qualify for work at the State Department with
those diplomatic skills you possess."

Adelia laughed. "I was dancing as fast as I knew
how. Who knew that even the married women in this
town were so interested in the latest gossip?"

Raylene gave her an incredulous look. "Oh, please,
it's the town hobby," she said. "Fed by Grace Wharton
and, though I'd never say it to her face, by Sarah over
at the radio station. She and Travis do their part to stir
the pot by announcing some of the juiciest tidbits on
the air. Heck, they even invite Grace to drop by just
to make sure their listeners always know the latest."

"Doesn't anybody ever consider going to the
source?" Adelia asked in frustration. Of course, she'd
been relieved at one time that no one had come directly
to her when her marriage was crumbling.

Raylene looked amused. "Are you suggesting that
people just ask Gabe whatever they want to know
about him?"

"Well, he is the one with all the answers," Adelia replied. "I'm an innocent, uninformed bystander."

"But it's so much more fascinating to see how
many of those answers you're already privy to," Raylene explained. "Were you really bothered by it? You

know most of these women adore you. They're not just being nosy. They'd really like you to be happy after all you've been through."

"And they think Gabe is the answer?" Adelia asked. "Even though they profess to know nothing about him? One or two even seem to recall something about him being a troublemaker back in the day."

Raylene chuckled. "Who doesn't love a bad boy?" she asked. "Who cares what happened back then, anyway? The man is a serious hunk. He has a smile that makes women weak in the knees. I'd say that makes him a good candidate."

"For what? A fling?"

Her boss winked at her. "No woman I know deserves to have fun more than you do. Why not?"

Adelia gave her a horrified look. "I have children. I have responsibilities. Flings were Ernesto's thing, not mine."

"Do not tell me the thought of letting a sexy man show you just how desirable you are has never crossed your mind," Raylene said. "You'll disappoint me."

"Never," Adelia said staunchly, then thought of the way that smile of Gabe's made her toes curl. "Well, hardly ever."

Raylene laughed. "Thank goodness. I was getting a little worried there."

"But it's a fantasy," Adelia insisted. "I'd never act on it. My children need one parent with a sense of decorum. And if I did happen to lose my head and my self-control, I'd certainly never spread the news all over Serenity."

"Not even to rub it in Ernesto's sorry face?"

The thought of retribution did hold a certain appeal,

Adelia thought, then immediately dismissed the idea. The momentary satisfaction wouldn't be worth the potential humiliation of having her children hear about it.

"Not even then," she said, though she couldn't keep a tiny hint of regret out of her voice. Determined to change the subject, she studied Raylene. "You're actually glowing. Pregnancy obviously agrees with you. How are you feeling?"

"The morning sickness seems to be over with, knock on wood. I feel pretty darn amazing." Her expression brightened. "We're going to find out the sex of the baby next week. At least I am. Carter's on the fence. He claims he wants to be surprised."

"You don't believe him?"

"Maybe I would if he hadn't bought four gallons of paint in various colors for the nursery this past weekend. If ever a man needed to have an idea whether he's having a son or daughter, it's my husband," she said, then confided, "I think he's secretly hoping for a boy."

"What makes you think so?"

"Three of those four gallons of paint were in different shades of blue," Raylene said with a smile. "It makes sense, too. He's been guardian to his two younger sisters for several years now. It would be natural for him to want to raise a son."

"How about you? Do you care?"

Raylene shook her head. "I'm just so thrilled to have a man like Carter in my life after the disaster of my first marriage and to be having a child I'd never expected to have, I honestly don't care. The girls were already in their early teens when Carter and I met, so it's not as if I've had baby girls in my life. But Carter's so amazing with all the kids in town. He spends a lot of his spare time helping Cal Maddox and Ronnie Sullivan coach all the sports teams. I'd love to watch him teaching his own son how to do all those little boy things."

Adelia smiled at Raylene's wistful expression. Then her friend sighed.

"The girls are rooting for a niece," Raylene admitted. "They came home the other day with a tiny pink outfit that they'd bought with their babysitting money. When I suggested perhaps they should have waited till we know for sure, they looked as if I were betraying them by even considering the possibility it could be a boy. They love that women are the dominant force in our household. They don't want to see the odds evened, not even a little bit by a kid who won't even be able to talk for a year or so."

Adelia could hardly relate to the excitement in Raylene's voice. She wished she'd shared that sort of excitement with Ernesto during her pregnancies. His daughters had been a disappointment to him. By the time Tomas had been born, he'd lost all interest.

"I am so happy for you," she told Raylene. "You deserve this."

Raylene laughed. "I really do, don't I? It took a long time to get past my ex's abuse and the agoraphobia that kept me a prisoner in my own home." She shook her head. "My gosh, I sound like I lived through my own personal soap opera."

"You did," Adelia said. And every time she thought of what she'd been through with her cheating husband, considering Raylene's past helped her to put it into perspective. No matter a person's own difficulties, there was always someone who'd been through something just a little worse and survived. It was good to remember that.

"You know what?" she said. "I think we deserve a little celebration. Why don't I run next door and get some decaf or tea, if you'd prefer, and a couple of cupcakes?"

"I'm all in favor of cupcakes, but what are we celebrating?" Raylene asked.

"Survival," Adelia replied at once.

Sometimes, she thought, she didn't give herself half enough credit for that.

At Sweet Things, Adelia was studying the cupcake display case, trying to make a decision, when Sarah McDonald came in.

"I need caffeine," she announced with an edge of desperation in her voice. "I just finished a double on-air shift at the radio station." She sighed heavily, then retracted her order. "Make it decaf."

"You need more than coffee, with or without caffeine," Lynn told her. "I'll bet you haven't eaten all day. Pick out a couple of cupcakes on the house." She glanced at Adelia. "You, too."

"You can't be giving away your inventory," Adelia protested, her business instincts kicking in.

"Of course I can," Lynn replied. "Especially if it means I can put a sign on the door that says I'm sold out for the day and can go home."

Adelia and Sarah exchanged a worried look.

"Are you okay?" Sarah asked. "Now that I look closely, I can see the circles under your eyes. You're a woman in serious need of sleep."

"Thanks so much for noticing," Lynn replied wearily.

"Just an observation," Sarah said. "I know for a fact you're in here before dawn every day because I see the lights on when I go into the station for my morning show. And the lights are usually still on right up till dinnertime when Travis and I go for our walk before he goes in to do his stint on the air."

Lynn sighed. "For so long I dreamed about how wonderful it would be to have my own bakery, but I never believed it would happen. Then Mitch and Raylene and the Sweet Magnolias started pushing and convinced me I could pull it off. Baking's always been second nature to me. Running a business is not. If you say a word about this to my husband, I'll call you a liar, but I don't know how much longer I can keep up this schedule, especially now."

Adelia studied her intently, then gasped as she recognized the signs. "You're pregnant!"

Sarah's eyes widened. "You are, aren't you? Oh my gosh, it's like an epidemic. Raylene, you." She blushed furiously. "Me."

"You, too?" Lynn said, her expression brightening. "We're all going to have babies? That's amazing."

"Okay, that does it," Adelia said. "Bag up a half dozen or so of those cupcakes, put the closed sign on the door and come with me. We're having a party."

"A party?" Lynn echoed.

"Right this second," Adelia confirmed, a little surprised by her own spontaneity. She couldn't recall a single time in her adult life when she hadn't had to consider a million things before moving forward on something fun. This was just one more indication that she was carving out a new path for her life.

"Next door," she told the two women. "Raylene's over there waiting for me to get back. We were just going to celebrate survival, but this will be so much more fun, like an impromptu baby shower."

"Without the presents," Sarah said, feigning disappointment.

Adelia laughed. "There will be plenty of time for the real thing, complete with lots and lots of presents," she promised. "This is just for us, and anyone else who wanders by."

Lynn nodded happily. "I'll just bring a whole tray of cupcakes. And I have a pot of decaf I just made."

"Then we have ourselves a party," Adelia declared.

"You know," Sarah said, her expression thoughtful. "The only other people I know who are so eager for parties at the drop of a hat are the Sweet Magnolias. Adelia, you'd fit right in. You get right into the spirit of a celebration."

Lynn's eyes immediately lit up. "You would, you know." She turned to Sarah. "We'll have to work on making that happen."

"You don't have to do that," Adelia protested. "I wasn't angling for an invitation."

"Of course not," Lynn said. "But these are women you know, women who know what it means to be friends. Surely you're not telling us you have all the friends you need."

"Not possible," Sarah answered for her. "You may not know you need these women in your life, but you do. Alone, every one of us may be pretty amazing, but together..."

"We could run the world," Lynn chimed in, completing the thought.

"Or at least Serenity," Sarah amended.

Adelia couldn't deny that the prospect of having strong bonds with women who'd always have her back held a lot of appeal. She knew the original band of Sweet Magnolias—Maddie Maddox, Dana Sue Sullivan and Helen Decatur-Whitney—had been there for her sister-in-law even before Elliott had come into Karen's life. Raylene credited them with all but saving her life, too.

But Adelia didn't want to push herself into a clique where she might not be welcomed.

Sarah nudged her. "I can practically hear those wheels in your head going round and round. This is not some exclusive secret society, I promise. You'll see. Of course with all these pregnant women these days, our wild margarita nights have gotten pretty tame. Everybody's drinking virgin cocktails."

"Frozen limeade," Lynn confirmed. "Amazingly, it seems to have the same effect as the alcohol-laced variety. We all get a little crazy. I think it's about knowing we can say absolutely anything and nobody's going to judge us."

"Exactly," Sarah said. "Adelia, we'll make sure you know the next time we're getting together." She gestured toward the display case. "Pack up those cupcakes, Lynn. I'm starving."

Adelia marveled at the way her trip to pick up coffee and a couple of cupcakes had suddenly turned into a special occasion. And when they trooped into the boutique, Raylene didn't seem to be the least bit flustered by the impromptu party.

"I'm calling Annie and telling her to get over here," she said at once. "Since we're going to be talking babies, she's going to want to be in on it." She glanced at Sarah. "Does she know about you yet?"

Sarah shook her head. "Not even Travis knows, so I'm swearing you all to secrecy right this second."

"But it's okay if we let Annie in on the secret, right?" Raylene said. "How cool is it that we were best friends growing up and now the three of us are all having kids at the same time? Plus Lynn."

Adelia sat back and listened to their excited chatter. Not once when she'd been pregnant with any of her children had she been surrounded by girlfriends like this. She'd counted on her sisters, instead. While they'd all been great back then, it hadn't been the same as this. If that invitation to get together with the Sweet Magnolias truly did come her way, she wasn't going to hesitate. She felt a surprising longing deep in her soul for what these women had found together. Maybe real sisterhood wasn't about biology at all.

Gabe walked past Chic after six and was surprised to find the lights still on and laughter drifting from inside. He paused long enough to glance inside and see Adelia, Lynn and three other women he didn't recognize sitting on an assortment of chairs and stools with a large pastry box, napkins and Styrofoam coffee cups scattered across the counter. Judging from the tossed aside cupcake papers, the women had been having themselves a little party.

It was the laughter, though, that got to him, especially Adelia's. He'd been under the impression that she didn't have a lot of friends. Perhaps he'd based that on his own tendency to go through life alone.

Taking one final glance inside, he smiled to himself and walked on.

At the Serenity Inn, he showered, changed into clean jeans and a fresh shirt, then headed for his usual lonely dinner at Rosalina's. For once, though, the comfortable rut he'd carved out for himself bothered him.

As soon as he was settled in his regular booth, Debbie brought his soda. "Let me guess. A large pepperoni pizza," she said.

"Not tonight," Gabe said, startling them both. He gave a quick glance at the menu, then said, "How about the lasagna and a salad?"

A smile broke across her face. "Well, hallelujah! It's about time you started experimenting."

Gabe chuckled. "I take it you recommend the lasagna."

"I recommend anything other than pizza," she replied. "Not that there's a thing wrong with our pizza. It's excellent, but not as a steady diet. Who knows? Next time maybe you'll really cut loose and try the eggplant Parmesan."

"One step at a time," he said.

Debbie glanced across the restaurant just then and another smile lit her face. "Well, well, well, this is definitely a night full of surprises. There's Adelia and it looks as if she's all alone." She glanced at him. "You want some company?"

Gabe shook his head. "Skip the matchmaking and bring my dinner, please," he said, even though he couldn't quite take his gaze off Adelia. She was glancing around nervously. When her gaze fell on him, she actually looked relieved.

Gabe stood as she crossed the room. "You looking for somebody?"

"Not really. My mom has the kids, and when I left work, I didn't feel like going home, so I decided to stop by here for dinner. Then I walked in the door and realized I haven't eaten a meal by myself in a restaurant in years. I also realized I didn't much like the idea of it."

Gabe laughed. "Well, unless you were putting yourself to some sort of a test, you're welcome to join me. I wouldn't mind the company. I'm pretty sick of my own." He leaned closer and whispered, "It will make Debbie very happy. She thinks I have no life."

"And you care what your waitress thinks?" Adelia said, clearly amused.

"No man likes being the object of pity," he told her.

"No woman, either," she confessed. "If you really don't mind, I'd love to join you." She hesitated. "It's not a date, just so we're clear. I'll buy my own meal."

"How about we negotiate that?" he suggested. "It might be even worse for my image if Debbie thinks I'm a cheapskate on top of everything."

No sooner had Adelia slid into place than the waitress reappeared. She gave Gabe a subtle thumbs-up, but Adelia caught it. He could tell she was about to launch into an explanation about this being a chance encounter, not a date, and decided that was a whole lot more than Debbie needed to know. He jumped in before she could speak.

"Debbie, can you hold back my order till Adelia's is ready?"

"Already done," she said, giving him a look that told

him she was proud of her intuitiveness. "Hon, what can I get you?" she asked Adelia. "Gabe's breaking with his pizza tradition and having the lasagna and a salad. How about you?"

"Lasagna sounds excellent," Adelia said. "A small salad, too."

"Perfect. I'll be back in no time," Debbie promised.

Gabe met Adelia's nervous gaze. "Since you've made it abundantly clear that this isn't a date, why are you so nervous? Or are you just on a sugar high?"

She looked startled by the question. "A sugar high?"

"I passed the boutique on my way home and it looked as if you and some friends were gorging on Lynn's cupcakes."

She laughed. "Guilty as charged. I had three." Her expression sobered. "What on earth am I doing ordering lasagna after that? I should tell Debbie just to bring me the salad."

"Did you want the lasagna?"

She nodded. "It sounded wonderful when she mentioned it. I haven't had it in ages."

"Then you'll have a couple of bites if that's all you want and take the rest home," he said.

"Thank you for not making me feel guilty."

There was something in her voice that made him frown, a hint of an unspoken apology. "What would you have to feel guilty about?"

It was clear the question flustered her, but he couldn't imagine why. "Adelia, why would you feel guilty about ordering whatever you wanted?"

"You didn't know me a few years ago," she said softly, not meeting his gaze. "I was a mess. I'd gained some weight with each of the kids. Ernesto—"

"The man who cheated on you," Gabe said, not even trying to hide his disgust. "Was that his excuse, that you'd gained weight?"

She gave him a rueful look. "He didn't think he needed an excuse. But he did like to throw my weight in my face. If I'd just admitted to him I'd had three cupcakes and then ordered a big meal, I'd hear about it for days."

"Your ex-husband was a pig," Gabe declared forcefully, not even remotely inclined to censor himself.

A startled expression spread across her face. "Do you know him?"

"No, but I've heard enough to know the type. Don't waste a single minute worrying about his opinions. He doesn't deserve that much respect."

To his surprise, she frowned at his vehemence. "You won't say anything like that around the kids, will you? Ernesto is still their father."

"Of course not," Gabe said. "It's not my place, though maybe they should know the truth about the kind of man he is."

She shook her head at once. "Selena knows and it's tearing her apart. I don't want the younger ones to be disillusioned. One day they may figure things out for themselves, but I'd like them to remain innocent as long as possible. They love their dad."

"That's more generous than he deserves," Gabe said.

She smiled. "I know that. I get to feel all noble. Maybe that's better than spending as much time as I'd like wanting to rip out his heart."

Her comment startled him, but as the heartfelt sentiment registered, he chuckled. "Now you're talking."

"You sound like my brother. He'd love it if I'd give him permission to beat the daylights out of my ex, but I won't do it."

"Nobility's not all it's cracked up to be," he said. "Sometimes plain old revenge is awfully sweet."

She studied him curiously. "You sound as if you know that firsthand."

Gabe sighed. "To be honest, I do, and those memories are not among my proudest moments."

"I'm sorry to have sent you back there, then."

He shrugged. "Protective instincts die hard."

"Who was it you were protecting?"

"My mother."

"What made you think she needed your protection? She was the grown-up, after all."

"She was older," he corrected. "That didn't make her mature. She got mixed up with too many guys like your ex-husband. She had a reputation around town as what you'd probably call a party girl." He shrugged. "Or maybe worse. By the time I was in my teens, I knew she deserved the label, but that didn't mean I liked hearing it."

"So you fought," Adelia concluded.

"And got kicked out of school eventually. I was a troublemaker back then, no question about it."

"Have you reformed?"

"I'd like to think so, which is probably the only thing that makes your ex-husband safe."

"You do know I don't need you to fight my battles for me," she said. "Any more than I want Elliott fighting them."

Gabe nodded. "But you'll let me know if that ever changes, right?"

"Probably not," she said softly. "But I appreciate the thought, Gabe. It's been a long time since any man other than my brother wanted to look after me. It's a little disconcerting."

"Come to think of it, it's been a long time since I offered to be anyone's knight in shining armor," he told her. "That's a little disconcerting for me, too."

She smiled. "Then it's a good thing this isn't a date."

"Oh?"

"No obligations or expectations when it comes to shining up that armor."

But for reasons he didn't want to examine too closely, Gabe found that he was more disappointed than reassured.

Despite her nervousness, Adelia enjoyed dinner with Gabe more than she'd expected to. And somehow he'd managed to pay the check for both of them, probably when she'd made a visit to the ladies' room. Her protests had fallen on deaf ears, as had her perfectly reasonable arguments that he didn't need to walk her home.

"This is Serenity, for goodness' sake," she said as they stood on the sidewalk in front of Rosalina's. "The Serenity Inn is in the opposite direction from Swan Point."

"And I just ate a huge meal. A walk is just what I need," Gabe said, his jaw set stubbornly.

"I'm not going to win this debate, am I?" she asked in frustration.

"Not a chance," he agreed cheerfully. "Give in gracefully."

It was a pleasant night with a soft breeze and the

scent of honeysuckle in the air. A tiny sliver of a moon lit the inky sky.

They'd stayed at Rosalina's much later than Adelia had intended. She was grateful that the kids were spending the night with her mother, so there wouldn't be the endless round of questions that would have ensued if she'd arrived so late to pick them up.

She and Gabe walked in companionable silence for a couple of blocks. She was very aware of the man next to her. Masculinity radiated from him in alluring waves. It was a little scary—no, a *lot* scary—that she was so aware of him. And when he tucked a steadying hand under her elbow when she stepped off a curb, the touch, rather than helping, almost caused her to stumble. It was like a jolt of electricity to her system.

Gabe glanced at her curiously. "You okay?"

"Of course," she said, though there was an unmistakably breathless note in her voice that belied that.

Another touch had her pausing in her tracks. She looked up in alarm to see his gaze on hers.

"Adelia," he said, his voice like a soft caress.

"Uh-huh," she murmured, lost in his eyes.

"I think I'm going to have to kiss you," he said, his lips curving slightly. "Tell me now if that's going to freak you out."

She swallowed hard. "It's going to freak me out," she whispered. Then, keeping her gaze locked with his, she added, "But I want you to."

He seemed startled by her candor. "You do?"

She blinked. "Unless you've changed your mind. I mean, if you have, it's okay. I really have no idea how to do this, Gabe."

"Do what? Kiss a man?"

"Uh-huh."

A smile spread across his face. "I'll bet you do," he said. "Let's see."

He lowered his head slowly until his lips were so tantalizingly close she could feel his breath whispering across her cheek. Her pulse jumped. Anticipation and heat built low in her belly. If he didn't do it soon, if he didn't put his mouth on hers, she thought she very well might cry.

As if he sensed her nerves were at their limit, he closed that last bit of distance, touching his firm lips to hers. That tantalizing heat she'd been feeling exploded into a demanding fire. She put her hands on his shoulders, not just to steady herself, but because she needed to touch him, to feel his muscles bunch, telling her that he was as affected by this moment as she was. She needed to know she wasn't just some pitiful woman desperate and hungry for a man's touch and that he wasn't kissing her because he'd sensed that and felt sorry for her. She needed reassurance that the desire she was so sure was simmering between them went both ways.

The kiss, so gentle at first, deepened in a way she only vaguely remembered. That desperation and hunger curling inside her seemed to be matched by a similar intensity in Gabe. There was a moan low in his throat as their tongues tangled and he pulled her even closer.

Adelia couldn't think after that. Nothing mattered except that extraordinary demanding heat inside her and the wonder of discovering she was still desirable.

The sound of a car in the stillness of the night seemed to shock them both. Gabe reluctantly drew back. Adelia even more reluctantly let him go.

"That was…" Words failed her.

"Unexpected," he said, looking as shaken as she felt. He smiled. "We might have to try it again sometime."

A profound relief spread through her. "We might," she agreed solemnly.

He ran a finger along her cheek as if he wasn't quite ready for the moment to end. "Soon."

Though a part of her wanted to demand that soon be, say, a half hour from now, she managed a teasing grin instead. "We'll see."

To her surprise, he laughed.

"What?" she demanded.

"Sweetheart, you haven't forgotten how to kiss or how to flirt."

Adelia couldn't think of a single thing he might have said that would have pleased her more. She was beginning to think her brother and Raylene might have been right, after all. Maybe Gabe was going to turn out to be the best thing to happen to her, the right man at the right moment in her life…even if nothing lasting ever came of it.

CHAPTER SEVEN

"How dare you!" Carolina Cruz Losado demanded of Adelia.

With her hands on her broad hips, her black hair windblown and the color in her cheeks high, she practically radiated indignation as she faced down her sister in the boutique.

Caught off guard by the unexpected attack in the middle of her workplace, Adelia gasped. Then her own temper flared. It was one thing for her family to feel compelled to question her choices and criticize her at home, but not here, not at Chic where anyone could wander in at any minute. It had taken her a long time to achieve professional respect and she wasn't about to let her judgmental sister destroy that.

"Whatever you have on your mind, Carolina, this is not the place to discuss it," she told her youngest sister. Though she kept her voice soft, but firm, she was more than ready to march her straight out the door if need be.

"Afraid you'll get fired if your boss hears what you've been up to?" Carolina taunted, her voice raised deliberately, obviously in the hope that Raylene would be in her office in the back.

Thank goodness Raylene had left for the bank just minutes earlier, Adelia thought. Not that Raylene would be shocked by anything Carolina might have on her mind, but Adelia didn't want her exposed to the kind of scene her sister was trying to cause.

"What about Mama?" Carolina pressed. "Does she know the kind of woman you're turning into?"

Adelia wasn't sure how to answer any of that since she had no idea what had brought Carolina into her workplace in such a mood. She was the more volatile of Adelia's sisters, but this was extreme even for her.

"I know that Mama taught us both better manners," she responded, still keeping her tone surprisingly calm. "We don't attack family with no provocation and we certainly don't do it in public."

"You're in no position to tell me how to behave," Carolina retorted. "It wasn't enough that you disgraced us all by tearing your family apart, but now you're making a spectacle of yourself."

"I have no idea what you're talking about," Adelia said. "And, for the last time, whatever it is, we're not discussing it here. I want you to leave."

"Well, I want you to stop humiliating us," Carolina countered.

Adelia could see that she wasn't going to get her sister out of the shop without resorting to unseemly bodily force, at least not before she'd had her say. Sighing heavily, she said, "Okay, Carolina, out with it. What is it you think I've done?"

"It's not speculation. I saw you kissing that man,

right in the middle of Main Street. Do you even know him? Or did you pick him up in some bar?"

Adelia flinched. So this was about that impulsive kiss she and Gabe had shared. She should have known it would come back to haunt her.

"Gabe is a friend," she said quietly. "I'm divorced. He's single. We weren't doing anything wrong. And just so you know, Mama and Elliott both know him. They approve. In fact, they've encouraged me to see him." That might be a bit of a stretch, but desperate times and all that.

The comment seemed to have the desired effect. It appeared to take the wind out of her sister's sails. "Mama knows you have a new man in your life when the ink's barely dry on your divorce papers?" she asked, her skepticism plain.

"The ink may barely be dry," Adelia said wryly, "but the marriage has been over for years. And I'm not the one who broke my wedding vows, Carolina. Ernesto did. Again and again. You know that. How can you continue to take his side?"

Her sister faltered at the hurt in Adelia's voice. "I wasn't taking his side," she murmured.

"It sure seems that way to me. You've done nothing but criticize me since I found the courage to walk out on a man who repeatedly betrayed me."

To her shock, tears filled her sister's eyes.

"I should go," Carolina said.

Adelia stepped around the counter and put a re-straining hand on her sister's arm. "You started this. Let's finish it. Maybe it's past time we get all this anger and resentment out in the open."

"No," Carolina said in the same petulant tone she'd

used as a little girl when she didn't want to do something.

Adelia smiled. "Now there's the sister I recognize. You sound like you did when you were ten and Mama asked you to do some chore that didn't appeal to you."

For the first time, a faint smile touched her sister's lips. "Spoiled and stubborn?"

Adelia nodded. "Pretty much." She brushed a strand of hair from her sister's cheek. "Talk to me, please. Why are you so angry with me because I walked away from an impossible situation? Staying would have destroyed every last trace of self-respect I possessed."

Carolina swallowed hard, her gaze avoiding Adelia's. "Maybe I was jealous," she admitted, her voice barely above a whisper.

The response all but confirmed Adelia's guess that her marriage, too, was on shaky ground.

"Is Ricky cheating on you?" she asked. Her opinion of Enrique Losado was almost as low as the one she held of her ex-husband, even without her sister's confirmation that he was cheating. He had the kind of macho, dismissive attitude that no self-respecting woman should tolerate.

"No," Carolina said a little too quickly. "At least I don't have any proof that he is."

"Because you don't want to know the truth?" Adelia suggested gently.

"Maybe," she said evasively. "Look, I've got to go. The kids will be home from school soon. They'll be expecting snacks." She finally dared to meet Adelia's gaze. "I'm sorry I came in here hell-bent on making a scene. I just saw you last night and lost it."

"Apology accepted," Adelia said. "And, sweetie,

if you ever need to talk, I'm here. I'll always be here. And, believe me, I've learned not to make judgments. We all did it when Elliott brought Karen home, but now that I've had some serious problems of my own, I totally get why Karen made the choices she made. Lesson learned."

"I'll try to remember that," Carolina said. "You won't say anything to Mama or Elliott about this, will you? Not about me coming here or about my life being such a mess? Ricky and I will be fine." There was, unfortunately, more resignation in her voice than real conviction.

"Not a word," Adelia promised. "But just so you know, they'd be on your side, unconditionally."

"Probably, but I'm still hoping I'll never have to test that."

Carolina wrapped her arms around Adelia in an impulsive hug. "Thanks for not tossing me out the door. I know you wanted to."

"I kept imagining Mama's reaction," Adelia told her. Then she warned, "Next time, I might not let that stop me."

"There won't be a next time," her sister promised. "I'll think twice before throwing around accusations."

Adelia gave her a squeeze. "I plan to hold you to that."

She watched as her sister left and walked away, her shoulders slumped. She'd never seen Carolina looking so miserable. Adelia's heart ached for her. One thing she'd learned from her own experience, though, was that the only person who could make Carolina's life better was Carolina herself. And she clearly wasn't ready.

* * *

"You kissed Gabe!" Raylene emerged from the office and regarded Adelia with delight.

"You were eavesdropping?" Adelia said, humiliated. "I thought you went to the bank."

"I did, but I got back for the big show," Raylene said. "And I didn't intentionally eavesdrop, but you know how thin these walls are and your sister's voice wasn't exactly on mute. I knew you were aware I might get back at some point, so you could have insisted she leave or take her accusations outside or whatever."

Adelia regarded her with amusement. "Or once you realized she was determined to have her say, you could have slipped out the back door to give us some privacy."

"After I heard her mention that kiss?" Raylene asked incredulously. "Come on. I'm only human. So, how was it?"

"I am not discussing that kiss with you."

"Hot, I'll bet," Raylene said, undeterred. "It must have been if you didn't even notice there were witnesses."

"It was late. The street was empty," Adelia corrected. "Except for one car that came along." She groaned. "What kind of bad luck was it that my sister happened to be in that car? It had to have been her, since she claimed to see us."

"Oh, so what if she did?" Raylene said. "You're entitled. Too bad she wasn't half as indignant when Ernesto was flaunting his affairs all over town."

"Yes, that is too bad," Adelia agreed. "But I think she had her reasons."

"You mean that it was hitting too close to home?"

Raylene guessed. "It sounded like that to me, too, not that I know your sister all that well. And that said, I will now butt out of your business, especially if you're not going to spill all the juicy details about that kiss."

"I'm not even confirming there was a kiss," Adelia said. "You didn't witness it. You can't prove it. And anything else you might have heard in here just now is hearsay."

Raylene laughed. "Helen should hear you right now. She'd insist you go to law school." She held up a hand. "Not that I'm saying a word to her. You're indispensable around here."

"Thank you for that." She gave her boss a speculative look. "Maybe this would be a good time to ask for a raise."

"I just gave you a raise. If those commissions of yours keep mounting up, pretty soon I'll have to make you a part owner just to keep my costs down." As soon as the words were out of her mouth, Raylene's eyes lit up. Her expression turned thoughtful. "You know, that might not be a bad idea."

Adelia simply stared at her. "You'd consider letting me buy part of the business?"

Raylene nodded. "It might be a smart move for both of us."

"I don't have the cash to pay you," Adelia said, though she couldn't help being intrigued by the idea. Wasn't that exactly why she'd studied business, with the hope of owning her own retail store someday? But was she anywhere near ready to claim such a dream?

Raylene waved off her concern about money as if it were of no consequence. "Let's keep mulling this over," she suggested. "We'll talk about it again after

I have the baby. If I need to cut back my hours dramatically, this could be the perfect solution. For now, though, I'd better get back to that mountain of paperwork on my desk."

Adelia hesitated, then said, "I could start learning how you handle some of that. If it would help you out, that is. I'm familiar with the accounting program you use."

"I hired you to sell pretty clothes," Raylene reminded her, though her expression was hopeful. "Are you sure you want to deal with something that boring?"

Adelia laughed. "What can I say? I like making sure numbers add up."

Raylene threw her arms around her. "Bless you, bless you, bless you. This partnership idea is sounding better and better."

Adelia held up her hand. "You need to give it a lot more thought."

"Oh, believe me—I will," Raylene said.

The bell over the front door tinkled merrily.

"Go," Raylene said. "I'll deal with the paperwork for now. We'll have another talk about all the rest later."

Adelia stared after her. A part owner of her own business? How astonishing would that be? Even if it never happened, that the idea had even crossed Raylene's mind meant the world to her. Sure, she knew she was a good saleswoman. And the committees she'd organized for the schools had always run smoothly. But this was something else, proof that she was truly capable of making a real life for herself and her kids, that she'd been right all those years ago when she'd studied so hard and envisioned a shop just like this one for herself.

A morning that had started out leaving her shaken and questioning her actions by sharing that impulsive kiss with Gabe had turned around dramatically to boost her self-esteem.

"Yay for me!" she murmured, then went out to wait on the customer who'd wandered in.

After she'd sold the stranger an expensive handbag, she went back to straightening a display of colorful cashmere sweaters she'd encouraged Raylene to order. More than half had already sold in less than a week, yet more proof of her business instincts.

She sighed. If only she were half as confident about the personal choices she was making.

"Well, as I live and breathe, if it isn't Gabe Franklin," Grace Wharton exclaimed, putting her hands on her hips and regarding Gabe with a surprising amount of affection.

"You aren't planning to kick me right back out the door the way you used to, are you?" he asked, only half in jest.

"That depends. You here to start trouble?"

He laughed. "My days of stirring up trouble are behind me," he assured her.

She didn't look as if she entirely believed him, but she nodded. "Then you can stay."

"I'm glad because I've had a hankering for one of your burgers ever since I got back to town."

She regarded him skeptically. "There's that charm I remember. Too bad you didn't use that to talk your way out of trouble back then, instead of using your fists."

"I have to agree with you," he said. "I'm glad to see you still don't hesitate to speak your mind, Grace."

"Never saw any point to it," she replied. "What would you like to go with that burger? Are you ready now or will Mitch be joining you?"

"He's on his way," Gabe told her. "You can put my order in when he gets here, but I'll take a large soda now."

"Will do." She started away, hesitated, then turned back, her expression filled with sympathy. "I'm real sorry about your mama, Gabe. I wanted to tell you that when she died, but you took off before anyone could let you know how much we cared. A lot of folks in town did."

Funny, he didn't remember much evidence of anyone caring, not about either one of them. Grace's expression suggested she knew exactly what he was thinking.

"It probably didn't seem that way to you," she told him. "People talk, sometimes without thinking. I'm one of them. It's a curse as much as it's a blessing. You'll always know what's on my mind, even when I should be wise enough to keep my mouth shut. It was one thing to say cruel things about your mama. She chose her own path. It was quite another to say them openly where a young boy would hear them. I regret that. I really do."

The sincerity of her words resonated in a way they might not have years ago. "I appreciate your saying that," he told her.

"None of the gossip was meant to be malicious," she told him. "But it must have seemed that way to you."

"Grace, I know you mean well now, and maybe you

did back then, but not everyone was the same as you. Even as a boy, I recognized the joy some people took in spreading rumors about my mom. She did plenty to cause talk, but I always wondered if things would have been different if anyone had reached out to help her. The only ones who did were after what she had to offer them, a willing body."

Grace might pride herself on being candid, but she looked uncomfortable at his straight talk. "I'm sorry," she said again.

Gabe merely nodded. "I'd like that soda now, if you don't mind."

"Right away," she said, clearly eager to have an excuse to leave.

Mitch showed up in time to note her relieved expression. He frowned at Gabe. "What was that about?"

"Just catching up," Gabe claimed.

Mitch didn't look as if he bought that, but he let it go. When Grace returned, he ordered his own burger, then sat back in the booth with a sigh.

"Problems on the job?" Gabe asked him. "I mean other than those I already know about."

"Not on Main Street," Mitch said. "I may have mentioned, though, that I have a customer in town who's changed his mind at least once a week about what he wants done. Then he goes crazy when I tell him the change is going to cost him." He shook his head. "My bad. I should never have taken the job. I've regretted it practically from day one."

"Anyone I know?"

"Ernesto Hernandez," Mitch admitted, his expression rueful. "And you don't need to say a word. I've already gotten an earful from my wife and every one of her friends."

Gabe bit back his own indignation since Mitch looked as if he'd already paid a heavy price for his decision. "Why'd you take the job?" Gabe asked curiously. "You don't need the work."

"The call originally came from Mary Vaughn Lewis. She said she had a client who wanted some renovations done and she'd told him I was the best. You know how persuasive Mary Vaughn can be when she wants something."

"You let a little flattery get you to take a job working for a piece of slime like Ernesto Hernandez?" Gabe made no attempt to hide his incredulous reaction. He'd never thought his honorable, upstanding cousin could be flattered or bought.

"I told you, it was Mary Vaughn who got me to take the job. She took me to look at the house, told me what the client wanted and that money was no object. It wasn't until I saw Ernesto's name on the contract that I realized who I'd be dealing with. By then, it was too late to back out. I'd given Mary Vaughn my word."

"Didn't it occur to you that it was odd that the Realtor was setting up the deal instead of the client? Hernandez must have known you'd never agree to work for him."

Mitch flushed. "Of course it occurred to me," he said. "Unfortunately, though, not till after I'd agreed to do the job."

Gabe frowned, still confused about how a smart man like Mitch could have been taken in. "You didn't realize it was Ernesto's house when you went there to check out what he wanted done?"

"It's not his house," Mitch revealed. "To top off a lousy situation, it belongs to his mistress. He apparently wants to get top dollar when she sells it and moves in with him."

Gabe could only think about how that scenario must feel to Adelia, knowing that her husband's mistress was about to move into her old home. His opinion of Ernesto sank a little lower, which he'd thought was pretty much impossible.

"I suppose you could take some comfort by charging him an arm and a leg for everything you do," Gabe suggested.

Mitch laughed. "Believe me, that would give me a great deal of pleasure, but it's not in the cards. The man's a cheapskate. He wants a top-dollar renovation on a shoestring. Apparently Mary Vaughn was overly optimistic about cost being no object."

"I see the dilemma," Gabe told him. "Better you than me." He gave his cousin a long look. "No one would blame you if you tore up the contract and walked away from the job. Sounds as if he's given you plenty of cause. I imagine Helen Decatur—isn't she the best lawyer in town?—could find a loophole for you."

"I'm sure she could and she'd be eager to do it, too," Mitch conceded. "But I don't do business that way. Once I give my word, I like to keep it."

Gabe nodded. It had been a long time before anyone took his word. He understood, perhaps even more than Mitch, how important that kind of respect could be and why a man would do anything he had to in order not to violate that trust. Sure, people might understand or even cheer if Mitch halted his dealings with Ernesto, but Mitch would find it hard to live with himself.

"Let's talk about something else," Mitch pleaded. "Have you gotten together with Adelia to go over those cost estimates?"

Gabe shook his head.

His cousin's expression turned puzzled. "Didn't I hear you had dinner with her at Rosalina's just last night? The subject of the renovations never came up?"

Gabe could tell his cousin was fishing for details that had absolutely nothing to do with any home renovations. "Nope. Forgot all about it."

Mitch didn't even try to hide his amusement. "Then what was the topic that was so fascinating it kept the two of you there till closing?"

A frown spread across Gabe's face. "Do you have some sort of pipeline to what's going on at Rosalina's?"

He was half joking, but Mitch apparently took him seriously.

"Well, let's see," Mitch said. "You got there about seven-thirty, the way I heard it. Adelia came in right on your heels and joined you. You were huddled over lasagna and salad for at least a couple of hours. Then you ordered pie. She turned down dessert."

"You mean to tell me you missed out on the kind of pie I ordered?" Gabe inquired sourly.

"Apple with ice cream on top," Mitch said. At Gabe's incredulous expression, he added, "That was just a guess. I happen to know it's your favorite."

"Well, thank goodness the gossips left out a few of the details," Gabe muttered.

"Did I forget to mention the kiss?" Mitch asked innocently. "Word on the street is that it looked pretty memorable."

Gabe groaned. "I have to leave town," he muttered. "Who can live like this?"

"Most of us survive," Mitch said. "The reports about Lynn and me flew around town pretty quickly, too. I learned to ignore it. Lynn had more trouble with it than I did, because her ex-husband got worked into a frenzy every time he heard we were together, never mind how he reacted when he spotted me with his kids."

"I now have an inkling of what my mom must have gone through," Gabe said wearily. "No wonder she drank herself to death."

Mitch looked alarmed by the bitterness in his voice. "Different situation entirely," he said firmly.

"Really? You think so? You think she deserved to have people in her business?"

"No, of course not. People, especially family, should have been more understanding. We should have stood up for her."

Gabe closed his eyes against the pain that washed over him just thinking about how all that talk had eaten away at his mom. Sure, it was the alcohol that had killed her, that and a long string of bad choices, but being picked at by everyone in town certainly hadn't helped. She'd had no one but him on her side, and he'd been a kid who hadn't really known how to help. Bailing him out of scrapes at school had just added to her downward spiral.

"Words hurt," he said softly. "I wonder if some of the gossips in this town understand that. They may think that it's all harmless fun, but it's not. Sometimes careless words can destroy lives." He met Mitch's gaze. "I won't subject Adelia to that."

Once more his cousin looked startled by the ferocity of his words. "Gabe, if you like this woman, don't back off, not unless she asks you to. Both of you are tough enough to weather a little gossip. She's certainly been through worse, thanks to Ernesto."

"Then she deserves a break," Gabe said. "Find someone else to oversee that job at her place, Mitch."

Just then Grace arrived with their meals. Gabe held up a hand. "Could you make that to go, Grace? I have someplace I need to be."

She looked from him to Mitch and back, then nodded. "Give me a minute. Mitch, are you staying?"

Mitch nodded. She set his plate in front of him.

When she'd gone, Mitch regarded Gabe with real concern. "I'm not putting anyone else in charge at Adelia's," he said, his tone unyielding. "Not until you've had time to think this through or unless she asks me herself to make a change."

"Don't do this," Gabe pleaded, determined to do the honorable thing. "It's for the best."

"I don't see it that way," Mitch said. "And last time I checked, you were working for me."

Gabe frowned at his cousin pulling rank. "That could change in a heartbeat," he said angrily.

Fortunately Grace returned just then with his meal. He took it, turned and walked out before he could lash out further at Mitch. He had a hunch if he said what was on his mind, he'd live to regret it. He already had enough regrets on his plate for one day. That amazing kiss he'd shared with Adelia was suddenly right at the top of the list.

CHAPTER EIGHT

Adelia had no sooner walked in the front door than Selena stormed out of the kitchen, her expression sullen.

"What's wrong?" Adelia asked. "Has something happened? Are your sisters and brother okay?"

"*They're* just fine," she replied sourly. "Maybe I'm just tired of babysitting."

Selena had suggested that she be responsible for watching her younger siblings after school since she was confined to home, anyway, so Adelia wasn't sure what to make of her sudden change of heart. One thing she was sure of, she didn't like the attitude.

"I don't know where this mood of yours is coming from, but I don't appreciate it," she told her daughter.

"Well, I don't like a lot of things," Selena retorted.

"Okay, that's it," Adelia said, pointing to the living room. "In there right now."

Though she didn't look happy about it, Selena went into the living room and sat down. Only when they were both seated on the sofa, albeit with a good bit of distance between them, did Adelia ask, "What is going on with you? You were perfectly fine when you left for school this morning."

"I want you to lift my grounding," Selena said.

Something in her tone suggested she thought she had the upper hand. "And why would I do that?" Adelia asked. "We agreed that a month was appropriate for leaving school without permission."

"Well, I don't agree anymore," her daughter replied, her expression belligerent. "Not after what you did."

"Watch your tone with me, young lady." Adelia looked into Selena's increasingly stormy eyes and went still. "What is it you think I've done?"

"You made a spectacle of yourself, that's what," Selena said angrily. "Just like Dad. Why should I respect anything you say after that?"

Given her choice of words, Adelia had a pretty good idea where Selena had gotten her information. "Since you were in bed at your grandmother's last night when I made this so-called spectacle of myself, I suppose your cousin is the one who filled you in." Jose, Carolina's oldest son, would happily spread bad news. Only a year younger than Selena and possessing a surprisingly mean streak, even at twelve he had a knack for trying to make her life miserable. "What did he tell you?"

"Joey saw you kissing that Gabe person right on Main Street. He was with Aunt Carolina coming home from shopping at the mall in Columbia. He said it just proved you were no better than Dad." Suddenly there was more hurt than anger in Selena's expression. "Is it true? Did you kiss Gabe?"

"Sweetie, you're my daughter and I love you, but I don't have to keep you posted on my actions, much less justify them to you. And this is nothing like what your dad did. Men and women sometimes kiss. It's very different when that kiss is between two single people who haven't made vows to other people. What your dad did was a betrayal." She watched Selena's face closely to see if her words were registering. "You do understand the difference, right?"

Tears welled in Selena's eyes and she sighed heavily. "I guess," she admitted.

"Then what is it you're really upset about?"

"Do you like him?" Selena asked, her tone plaintive. "Gabe, I mean. It looked like you might when he was here for dinner."

"We hardly know each other," Adelia said honestly.

"But you were on a date. You must have been if you kissed him."

Though she chafed at having to explain herself to her thirteen-year-old daughter, Adelia wanted Selena to understand. She'd already seen too much for a girl her age. It was little wonder she was angry and confused so much of the time.

"It wasn't a date," she said. "Gabe and I ran into each other at Rosalina's. He invited me to join him. Then he walked me home. I told him he didn't have to, but he insisted. That's the way a true gentleman treats a lady." It was behavior both of them had far too little experience with, and she wanted Selena to learn to watch for and appreciate such gestures.

"But what about the kiss?" Selena persisted. "Was that some kind of weird coincidence? Your lips just accidently locked?"

Adelia smiled. "It was…" She thought of the word Gabe had used the night before. "It was unexpected."

Selena frowned. "Did you like it? Are you going to do it again?"

"It was a nice kiss," she said, her voice softening as she remembered. "I don't know if it will happen again. Would you mind so very much if it did?"

"Yes," Selena said forcefully. "You said it yourself. We don't even know him. Things are already changing too fast."

"Does it feel to you as if I'm betraying your dad?"

The troubled expression on Selena's face answered the question, but her words came more slowly.

"I know you're divorced," Selena replied carefully. "And I totally get why. I'm even glad about it."

"But you miss your dad."

"I don't!" Selena all but shouted, clearly agitated by the suggestion that she missed a man she'd sworn to hate forever.

"Of course you do," Adelia soothed. "And, sweetie, it's okay to miss him. No matter what happened between your father and me, it's okay for you to love him. And he will always love you."

"Like I believe that," Selena said, her voice radiating skepticism and pain.

"Well, I believe it," Adelia told her. "He might not always show his love in ways you might like him to, but I remember the look on his face when you were born. You were this tiny little bundle with the most amazing lungs on any baby ever. Your face was scrunched up and red. You were screaming your head off, but he looked as if he'd just seen the most perfect angel."

That story—and the snapshot commemorating that exact moment—had always calmed Selena. At one time, when she was struggling to accept her father's actions, she'd clutched that photo and asked to hear the story over and over as if she needed reminding that at one time they'd been a happy family and she'd been the center of it.

"Not anymore," Selena said wearily. "He hates me now."

"Never," Adelia said.

"Mom, I know you're trying to make me feel better, but you can just stop. I'm not a little kid. I know the kind of man Dad is. Why would I still want anyone like that in my life?"

"Just because someone we love has flaws, we don't always stop loving them. There's even a part of me that can remember the good times I had with your dad. We've talked about that."

"Well, I don't love him, not anymore," Selena said fiercely. "Not after what he did to you. And I don't want anyone else to hurt you like that again."

"No one will," Adelia told her. "I'd like to think I'm smarter now. I certainly have more self-respect." At least she was working on that, she amended to herself.

Selena studied her intently. "So you're not going to let Gabe hurt you the way Dad did?"

"Not the way your father did, no. But, sweetie, falling in love comes with risks."

Alarm immediately crossed Selena's face. "You're falling in love already?"

"Of course not. It's much too soon. But I hope I'll be open to the possibility someday, whether it's with Gabe or someone else," she said, aware of the irony that she was echoing Elliott's words to her, advice she hadn't been interested in hearing. Her brother would be thrilled by her apparent change of heart. She knew, though, she was saying them for her daughter's benefit. She didn't want Selena to grow up bitter and jaded, always keeping herself safely protected against any pain love might bring.

"But no matter when it happens," Adelia continued when she was sure Selena was listening, "it won't come with any guarantees that I won't get hurt. That's just life."

"Then why would you take a chance? You have me, Juanita, Natalia and Tomas. Aren't we enough for you?"

Adelia smiled at her naïveté. "You all are the very best part of my life," she said. "But when relationships work, they can be wonderful. You'll find that out for yourself someday." She gave her a meaningful look. "A long, long time from now. Maybe when you're thirty."

Selena giggled, but her expression sobered quickly. "Do you think this thing with Gabe can be wonderful?"

"I have no idea. We're just starting to get to know each other. I don't even know how long he's going to be in town."

"So it might not get serious?" Selena asked, sounding a little too hopeful.

"It might not," Adelia confirmed.

"Isn't kissing supposed to be serious?"

Adelia hid a smile. It was a refrain she'd repeated to her teenage daughter a million times, hoping to keep her from making a mistake when she was still so young. "Yes, it is," she said. "But this was just one kiss and, like I said, it was unexpected."

"Well, I'm going to be keeping an eye on him," Selena declared.

"You do that," she said. It would be just one more person keeping him under close scrutiny.

"Do I have to like him if you do?"

"No, but just remember that we should always give people a chance to prove themselves. And we're nice to everyone, no matter what reservations we might have about them. Understood?"

Selena nodded, though she didn't seem entirely happy about it. Adelia realized that the reminder was one she needed to heed, as well.

Her conversation with Selena was still very much on Adelia's mind when she opened the boutique in the morning. She told herself that was the only reason her pulse scrambled when she looked up as Gabe opened the door and walked inside. She was feeling guilty that she was glad to see him, she told herself. That's all it was.

"You shopping for a gift?" she asked, aware that her voice betrayed her nerves.

He shook his head. "I came to see you."

"Oh."

She studied him closely and realized he looked just about as nervous as she felt. "Everything okay?"

"I'm not sure," he said candidly. "Did you catch as much flak yesterday over that kiss as I did?"

She laughed, oddly relieved that his feet had apparently been held to the fire, as well. "Probably more," she told him. "My sister accused me of making a spectacle of myself. Her son filled my daughter in on my unseemly behavior, and then I had to answer a whole lot of questions about relationships, kissing and betrayal. Oh, and did I mention that my boss wanted to hear all the juicy details?"

His jaw dropped as he listened. "I thought it was bad enough that Mitch put me on the hot seat."

Adelia shrugged. "It's just Serenity."

"You seem to be taking the gossip in stride," he said, seeming surprised.

"Have you forgotten that I was married to a man who was having serial affairs for years? I had to tune out the gossip to survive."

He shoved his hands in his pockets. "Well, I don't want to be the one to put you through anything like that again. I told Mitch I thought he ought to assign someone else to handle your renovations."

The sensation that washed over Adelia caught her by surprise. She realized it was disappointment. "If that's what you think is best," she said stiffly.

He frowned. "Don't you?"

"I suppose it depends on why you're suggesting it. If you think you're protecting me, I don't need it. If you don't want to do the job, that's something else entirely. I liked the ideas we discussed the other night when you were at the house. I suppose another man could handle the work, but I'm comfortable that you and I are on the same page." She smiled at him. "And I'm not sure anyone else will want my eight-year-old son on his crew."

"What about the gossip, though?"

"Like I said, I'm used to it."

"And it doesn't bother you? Honestly?"

She suddenly realized she wasn't the only one whose name was going to be spread all over town amid speculation, disapproval and who knew what else. "Gabe, does this bring back too many bad memories for you? If that's it, I totally understand. I don't remember the talk about your mom all those years ago, but you've told me how painful it was."

"It was a long time ago. I should be over it by now."

"But are you?"

He paused a moment. "I guess I'm not. I still remember how helpless I felt and how angry I was at the whole world. I don't want to be the guy who brings that kind of unwanted attention to you. I'd hate to have to start punching people out again."

"And you think you'd be tempted to do that?"

"If I thought what they were saying might be hurtful to you? I'd like to think I'd find a more mature way to handle it, but I can't swear to that. Old habits die hard."

"How about this? We can keep things strictly professional, if that's what you want," she suggested. "No more impulsive kisses."

He gave her a disbelieving look. "You and me under the same roof for days on end," he said. "There are going to be more kisses, Adelia. Right this second it's taking every ounce of willpower I possess to keep from dragging you into my arms and we're smack in the middle of a conversation about what a bad idea that would be. Just imagine what might happen if we stop telling ourselves it's a bad idea."

She felt a little frisson of relief just knowing that he was struggling with the same impulse that she was. The fact that he was trying so darned hard to do the right thing for her made him even more appealing. Frustrating but appealing.

She met his gaze. "What did Mitch say when you

told him you wanted someone else to take over the renovations?"

"That he disapproved of the idea and expected me to do the work. He reminded me that he was my boss."

She laughed, though it was evident he found no humor in the situation. "Maybe we should trust his judgment. He's lived here his whole life, too. He knows a thing or two about the Serenity grapevine and how to live with it."

"You honestly think I'm making a big deal out of nothing?"

"Not out of nothing," she corrected. "I'm just saying I think we can handle it. Most of the time the talk isn't meant maliciously. It's just curiosity and some crazy need to be the first to know what's going on around town."

He didn't look as if he was entirely pleased by her conviction. "Okay, then," he said, relenting. "I'll be by tonight with the cost estimates and a timetable."

"Come for dinner," she said on impulse. "It won't be anything like my mom's cooking, just burgers on the grill."

For a minute it looked as if he might refuse. Instead, though, he shook his head as if unsure what to make of her. "I'm told I can grill a pretty mean burger myself," he said at last. "If you'll let me cook and bring dessert, it's a date."

"A date? Really?"

He frowned at her teasing. "Not that kind of a date. Not the boy–girl kind. Just a professional appointment at a specified time that happens to include food."

She bit back a grin. "Duly noted."

But no matter what he insisted on calling it, she found that her pulse was skipping merrily in anticipation.

* * *

Tomas was like a little shadow from the instant that Gabe arrived at Adelia's. Natalia and Juanita were a bit more reserved, and Selena was downright hostile. Gabe realized he was going to have his work cut out for him trying to win her over, not because he needed her approval, but because it was going to be awkward doing the work for Adelia if Selena set out to make the situation intolerable.

"Is it just me she doesn't like?" he asked Adelia when he'd slipped into the kitchen and caught her alone.

"She wouldn't approve of any man hanging around right now," Adelia reassured him. "As I mentioned this morning, she got word of the kiss, though, and that definitely didn't help. She may not want me back with her dad, but she doesn't want me with anyone else, either."

"I guess the divorce was hard on her," he said.

"Not the divorce so much as the reason for it. She knew all about her dad's infidelity. Not only didn't he work very hard to hide it, he actually flaunted it toward the end."

Gabe frowned. "What kind of a man does that to his kid?" he said, then winced. His mom had been no better. He'd been well aware of all her affairs. She hadn't cared enough to keep them secret. And she'd made him her shoulder to cry on when things had gone south, as they had each and every time. He doubted she'd had any idea of the damage she'd done to him.

"Never mind," he said. "I think I know just how she must have felt. Discovering that your parents have feet of clay is never easy."

Adelia studied him intently. "Did you swear off of love because of what your mom did?"

"Pretty much. I've dated over the years, but not once have I allowed things to get too serious. Anytime I sensed they might, I broke things off and moved on. I didn't want to be responsible for hurting anyone the way my mom's lovers hurt her."

"So no string of brokenhearted girlfriends for you," Adelia said lightly.

"Nope."

"But what about you? Were there any of them you were sorry to leave?"

Gabe frowned at the question. "What are you asking?"

She looked directly into his eyes. "I'm asking if it was always so easy to keep things light and casual or if you ever fell in love along the way, but then broke things off because that was the pattern you were determined to follow?"

"I never let myself get that serious," he insisted.

"I find that a little sad," Adelia told him.

Gabe shrugged. "It was for the best. I'm not the kind of man who puts down roots."

She held his gaze. "So, fair warning? Now that you've made yourself clear, you're off the hook if I get any crazy ideas?"

"I didn't mean it like that," he said, not liking the implication that he was looking for a cop-out. "You asked a question. I tried to answer it honestly."

She gave him a bright smile that seemed a little forced. "No need to get defensive. Message received." She turned to stir the mayonnaise into the big bowl of potato salad on the counter.

"I wasn't sending a message," he said impatiently. "Adelia, look at me."

She turned slowly, the spoon still in her hand.

"I was *not* sending a message."

She smiled slightly, though her eyes looked a little sad. "Sure you were. Now, maybe you'd better get those burgers going. Everything else is just about ready."

Gabe wanted to stay right there and argue, tell her she'd misunderstood, but the truth was, she probably hadn't. He just didn't happen to like the conclusion she'd reached. It didn't say anything good about him, and, for reasons he didn't care to examine too closely, he wanted her to think well of him.

Dinner had been a little tense, at least between her and Gabe, but the chatter of Tomas and the younger girls had overshadowed their awkward silence. Adelia was furious with herself for pressing him earlier, for getting a little too deeply into his personal business. He was here to do a job. One kiss didn't give her the right to start questioning his behavior and his motives with women.

After she'd sent the younger children off to their rooms to settle down for the night and managed to discourage Selena from standing guard over her and Gabe, Adelia sat across from him at the dining room table. Her lists were spread between them, along with his notations and cost estimates.

"Gabe, I owe you an apology," she said.

His head snapped up. "For what?"

"I had no right cross-examining you earlier. If I made you uncomfortable, I'm sorry. I know how much

I hate it when people start asking me about stuff I don't want to discuss."

He met her gaze. "I only hated it because you might have hit a little too close to the truth. I do keep women at a careful distance to protect myself, as much as I do to be fair to them. It's an ingrained habit." He paused. "But I don't regret it. I figure it's saved me a lot of pain."

"It's also kept you from loving deeply," she suggested.

He looked startled by her words. "Are you such a big proponent of love after everything Ernesto put you through?"

"Right this second, not so much," she told him candidly. "Elliott's been on my case about that. So has Mama. I even told Selena she shouldn't let what happened between her dad and me discourage her from giving her heart to someone someday."

"But you're not ready to take that chance?"

"Not today," she said. "Maybe not even tomorrow or the next day. But I hope someday I'll change my mind and open my heart again. I don't want to give Ernesto the power to rob me of a full and rich life. That's what I'd be doing if I never took another chance on love."

"And you think I let my mother's bad experiences cost me this full and rich life you're talking about," he said, looking skeptical.

"Did you?"

"Maybe I just think my life is full and rich as it is," he replied.

She smiled. "You only say that because you've never experienced what it could be. It's like saying you love mashed potatoes and could live on a steady diet of them your whole life, but never having discovered a great enchilada or a pizza with everything, the claim wouldn't mean all that much."

Gabe laughed. "You're comparing love to food?"

"In a way. Think about it. Bland food may sustain you, but life is better with lots of spices. You can survive without love, but you'll miss all that heat and excitement."

Even as she spoke, she realized that she herself had come up with the most convincing reason of all to let love back into her life. She'd had heat and excitement once. Sure, it had died a long time ago, but deep down she knew that she'd only be living a half life if she didn't reach for that again. Someday. That kiss she'd shared with Gabe had reminded her of that.

She looked into Gabe's eyes and saw the spark of amusement there. "Heat and excitement, huh?"

"Definitely," she said, daring to hold his gaze.

"I could get behind that," he said softly.

Adelia felt her cheeks burn. "I wasn't... I'm not..."

"What?" he asked, his grin spreading. "You're not talking about sex?"

"No. Well, yes. I mean that's a part of it, of course," she said, rattled.

"I happen to like sex," he said.

"What's not to like?" she said impatiently, then blushed even more furiously. "We need to change the subject. Show me those cost estimates."

He held her gaze for another beat, then dutifully pushed the papers across the table. His hand deliberately grazed hers, sending heat rushing through her veins. Blast the man. He was heat and excitement all wrapped up in one sexy, contradictory, infuriating bundle. But she knew without a doubt that he possessed the power to drag her back into the world of the living. She just wasn't sure she was entirely ready for it.

CHAPTER NINE

Adelia came home from work two days after her touchy conversation with Gabe and found a half-dozen men swarming all over her roof. A Dumpster was overflowing with the old roofing materials and it looked as if more than half the roof had already been replaced with new shingles. Tomas was standing wide-eyed at the bottom of a ladder, practically dancing with excitement.

"Mom! Mom!" he shouted when he saw her. "Gabe's fixing the roof and I'm helping."

"Are you really?" she said, tousling his black hair, loving the way it curled around her fingers. If he had his way, he'd have a crew cut, but Adelia couldn't bring herself to have those beautiful curls shorn. Someday soon, though, she wouldn't be able to fight him.

"What's your assignment?" she asked. Thankfully it didn't appear to include scampering around two stories aboveground.

"First, I was supposed to pick up stuff if it didn't go into the trash when it got tossed off the roof. Now I have to wait right by the ladder to make sure it's there when they need it to get down. Gabe says that's really important because otherwise the guys could get stuck up on the roof and have to jump and maybe even break a leg."

"Then it's definitely an important job," she acknowledged, appreciating Gabe's cleverness in making the menial task sound so critical while keeping Tomas on solid ground.

"Gabe says if I do it really well, he'll take me up on the roof later so I can see what they've done up close," Tomas told her excitedly. "He promised to explain how they put on the new shingles and maybe even to let me do one myself."

She frowned at that, glanced up and caught the eye of the man who'd told her son he could climb onto the roof. "Did he now?"

Tomas must have heard the dismay in her voice and seen the direction of her gaze, because he patted her arm. "It's okay, Mom. Really. Gabe will be with me."

Just then the man in question climbed down the ladder and put a hand on Tomas's shoulder. "Good job today, buddy. How about you scout around the yard and make sure everything's picked up while I speak to your mom? Take the big magnet and use it like I showed you in case there are any nails around."

The second they were alone, Adelia looked Gabe in the eye. "You promised him he could go on the roof? Are you nuts?"

He laughed. "It's not as if I'm giving him a hammer and nails and putting him to work up there unsupervised. I gave him an incentive to stay safely on the ground while we worked. And now, with me hanging on to him for dear life, he can go up for a couple of minutes and check things out. It's a fitting reward for a job well done."

"He said you were going to let him put on a shingle, so he could learn how to do it himself. Doesn't that involve a hammer and nails?"

"And very, very close supervision," Gabe reminded her.

She sighed. "You think I'm overreacting."

"Maybe just a little."

"But, Gabe, what if he decides he likes it up there and goes up on his own later?" she said, knowing how her son's mind worked.

"There won't be a ladder in sight that he can get to," Gabe promised. "I bought a big combination lock for the shed and the ladders and tools will all be stored in there when we're not here working."

Even as he spoke, the crew was scrambling down the ladder and taking their tools to the shed. Adelia finally released the breath she felt as if she'd been holding ever since her child had made his big announcement. "I guess that's okay then."

"Adelia," Gabe said softly, tucking a finger under her chin and forcing her to meet his gaze. "I'm not going to endanger your son. Not ever. That's a promise."

"I know that," she said, relenting. "And I keep forgetting that he's growing up and has an inquisitive mind that should be encouraged, not stomped on by an overly protective mother. In some ways, I felt better that he had a dad like Ernesto. Ernesto wasn't the sort of man who'd put himself into dangerous situations, much less Tomas."

"Roofing isn't dangerous if you know what you're doing," Gabe reminded her.

She smiled. "And you do."

"And I do," he confirmed. "Okay? You can stand right here at the bottom of the ladder and hold on tight every second we're up there if it'll make you feel better." A grin lit his eyes. "Or you could come up there with us."

The dare in his voice actually had her glancing up and considering the idea, but only for a second. "I think I'll wait right here and be prepared to catch him if he slips."

"And me?" he asked, amusement sparkling in his eyes. "Will you catch me if I fall?"

"I've seen you on the roof. You're as agile as a mountain goat, but, yes, if you slipped, I'd try to catch you, too."

"The view's pretty amazing from up there," Gabe said, deliberately continuing to tease her. "I can see all the way to the park. I'll bet it's beautiful when there's a full moon. Maybe you'll sneak up there with me then."

Adelia got lost in his eyes for just a heartbeat and temptation licked through her. "Maybe I will," she said softly.

Gabe winked at her. "I'll hold you to that." He raised his voice then. "Tomas, you ready to hit the roof?"

Tomas came around the house at a run, his eyes bright with excitement. "You bet. Mom, are you gonna watch?"

"I am," she said, smiling at him. She'd be watching both of them like a hawk until they were safely on the ground again.

"I'm not sure I'm going to survive this renovation," Adelia told Lynn when she stopped by the bakery for

coffee a couple of days later. For once neither Gabe
nor Mitch were there. Lynn said they'd been called to
a job site where there were ongoing problems with a
difficult client.

Lynn sat across from her, flour on her cheeks and
circles under her eyes. "I heard about Gabe taking
Tomas up on the roof. You didn't approve."

"Once Gabe explained his theory, I actually got it,
but that doesn't mean I wasn't scared out of my wits
the whole time they were up there."

"I can imagine," Lynn said. "When I found out
Mitch was letting Jeremy use power tools, I flipped
out. He finally got me to see that it was better he try
things with strict supervision than sneak in there on
his own and try them with nobody looking."

"That's pretty much what Gabe said, too. What is
it with little boys and danger?"

Lynn laughed. "They want to be like the big boys,
especially the ones they admire. It's a guy thing. Since
neither of our sons had especially good role models
as dads, at least when it comes to that sort of thing, I
think it's natural that they gravitate to guys like Mitch
and Gabe."

"You're probably right," Adelia said, trying to re-
sign herself to accept reality. "And I certainly don't
want to turn my son into some sort of sissy who's
scared of his own shadow, but I'm not sure if I can
live with my heart in my throat every time I walk into
my own yard."

"The roof is done now, right? The worst is over."

Adelia laughed at her friend's naive comment. "And
now the demolition starts inside. Oh, boy! Sledge-
hammers and saws. Fun stuff." She shuddered at the

thought. "Okay, enough about me. Are you okay? Are you getting enough sleep?"

"No, and Mitch has noticed. He's caught me napping when he comes home at night, but so far he's pretending not to see it. I know he's just waiting for me to say something, and that almost makes it worse. He's so blasted determined to let me make my own decisions."

"How is that a bad thing?"

"Because I'm stubborn," Lynn said, her expression rueful. "I almost wish he'd take this one decision out of my hands and tell me I need to cut back or hire help or something."

"But he wants you to reach that conclusion on your own," Adelia said.

Lynn nodded. "When we were first dating, I really appreciated his letting me get back on my feet on my own. I needed to know I was strong enough to handle things."

"But now you wouldn't mind leaning on him just a little?" Adelia guessed.

"Something like that," Lynn said. "I know he'd step up in a heartbeat if I told him I needed help, but to me that feels like conceding defeat."

Adelia understood the dilemma. "It's not, you know. It's being smart. You're having a baby. If you want a healthy baby, you can't wear yourself out."

"But I wasn't this tired when I was pregnant with Lexie and Jeremy," Lynn complained. "Do you think there's something wrong with me?"

Since there was real worry in her voice, Adelia held back a chuckle. "Nothing more than that you're a few years older now," she said gently. "And trying to run a demanding business."

Lynn gave her a chagrined look. "Oh, that."

"You're not Superwoman. You're just human."

"But I want Mitch to think I'm Superwoman," she said plaintively.

Adelia did laugh at that. "Honey, I think he knows better, and you know what's best about that?"

"What?"

"He's crazy in love with you, anyway."

Lynn's expression brightened at last. "He really is, isn't he?"

"Seems that way to all of us watching the two of you enviously."

"You envy me?" Lynn asked, looking surprised.

"Of course. You're my role model. You went through a crappy marriage just like me, and look at you now. You have your own very successful business. Your kids are happy again. You have a baby on the way. And then there's Mitch, who adores you. It can't get much better than that."

"I predict you'll have all that, too," Lynn said. "Your kids are already doing better. They come by after school every now and then on their way to see you next door. They're chattering away with their friends and laughing. It's really good to see."

"All of them except Selena," Adelia corrected. "I think it's going to take a while for her to get over what her father did."

"But she will," Lynn said. "And I have it on good authority that Raylene is considering making you a half owner in the boutique. Your life is definitely turning around."

Adelia regarded Lynn with surprise. "Raylene told you about that?"

"She mentioned it. She said it made a lot of sense, that she'd be making a decision once the baby's here and she sees how demanding he or she is." Her eyes narrowed. "She also said you seemed hesitant. Why?"

"Only because I don't have the money to invest right now," Adelia admitted. "Well, mostly that, anyway."

"Trust me, that's the least of your worries," Lynn said as if it were of no significance at all. "The Sweet Magnolias have a way of making things happen. They did that for me. They did it way back with The Corner Spa, when Helen and Dana Sue put up the cash and Maddie put in the sweat equity. Your own brother got his interest in Fit for Anything the same way."

"I know about that, but I don't want to feel beholden to anyone," Adelia told her. "After being under Ernesto's thumb all those years, I want to make my own way."

"Accepting a helping hand does not make you beholden," Lynn corrected. "I had to learn that lesson myself. You'll find ways to pay it forward. We all have. If Raylene brings this up again once the baby's here, don't even hesitate, Adelia. You've earned the right to be more than just an incredibly good salesclerk."

When Adelia remained silent, Lynn studied her intently. "You said it was mostly about the money. What's the rest?"

"I know that so far my instincts about the business have been pretty decent—" Adelia began.

"More than pretty decent to hear Raylene tell it," Lynn said.

"But I'm not really experienced," Adelia said. "Not with running a company, that's for sure."

Lynn laughed. "Honey, do you think any of us had

a ton of experience when we got started? Dana Sue knew she could cook, but she'd never run a restaurant. Look at Sullivan's now. It's listed in guidebooks all over as one of the best in the state. As for The Corner Spa, when Helen, Maddie and Dana Sue opened it, they didn't even like to exercise. They just believed this town needed a gym that catered to pampering women. This bakery's the same for me. I'm flying by the seat of my pants most of the time. You'll be just fine, the same as the rest of us."

Apparently satisfied with her pep talk, Lynn stood up then. "Break's over. At least for me," she said, pouring more coffee into Adelia's to-go cup. "I've got cookies in the oven that should be ready."

"And I need to get to work," Adelia said. "Thanks for the company and for the advice."

"Back at you," Lynn said. "Maybe one of these days you and Gabe will come over for dinner."

Adelia immediately frowned at the suggestion. "I'm not sure… I mean we're not…"

Lynn grinned. "I'm no fortune-teller, but I predict one of these days you will be all those things you can't bring yourself to say," she said confidently.

"What things?"

"Dating. A couple." She laughed at Adelia's expression. "I know," she soothed. "Now I get why everybody had so much fun listening to me protest that there was nothing between Mitch and me."

Adelia couldn't think of anything to say to that, so she took her coffee refill and left. While it was great to have someone she could bounce her worries off of, in some ways she was leaving with more on her mind than she'd had before.

* * *

Gabe studied Ernesto Hernandez and wondered how a woman like Adelia could have given him the time of day, much less years of her life. Successful people in Serenity dressed well enough, but none of them put on the show that Ernesto did with his fancy watch, Italian shoes and a suit that had evidently been custom-tailored. His silk-blend shirt even had monogrammed cuffs, for goodness' sake. Most men in town figured they were dressed well enough if there was a little starch in their collars when they got their oxford cloth shirts back from the laundry.

"I gave you a budget for sprucing up this kitchen," Ernesto complained to Mitch. "Now you want to charge me double what we agreed on."

Gabe watched as his cousin struggled to hold on to his temper. Gabe wondered if Mitch would be able to pull it off. The pulsing vein in his forehead seemed to be working overtime. Gabe was tempted to step in and help him out, but this was Mitch's company and his call.

"It's not a matter of *wanting* to charge you double," Mitch corrected, his voice surprisingly quiet. "I *have* to charge you double because you've upgraded everything we talked about. You're the one who decided only granite countertops would do and that the appliances ought to be stainless steel."

Ernesto sighed. "Not me. That's all Kendra."

"If you're going to let her start calling the shots, then you have to pay for the changes," Mitch said. "Or we can go back to the original plan and stay on budget."

"We're selling the blasted house. I don't know why she even cares," Ernesto grumbled.

Without ever having laid eyes on Kendra, Gabe had his own theory. He had a hunch the woman wanted the house upgraded her way just in case things didn't work out with Ernesto. If he'd cheated on his wife, he was likely to cheat on her. She wanted a nice place to go home to, that is, if the relationship even lasted long enough for her to move out. The woman might have the morals of an alley cat, but she was clearly smart enough to see Ernesto for the lousy bet he was.

Mitch sat at the kitchen table, his gaze on Ernesto. "What's it going to be?" he asked eventually.

"Do the upgrades," Ernesto said after a pause.

Mitch nodded and pushed a piece of paper in his direction. "Then I'm going to need you to sign this change order."

Ernesto frowned. "My word's not good enough."

Now there was a minefield, Gabe thought as he awaited Mitch's reply.

"It's standard procedure to have a change order when the original contract is amended in any way."

Ernesto glanced toward Gabe. "Are witnesses necessary, too?" he inquired sourly.

"Gabe's my second-in-command," Mitch said easily. "He oversees a lot of the work. It's just smart business to have him aware of any changes we're making."

Ernesto's frown deepened. "You're the man I hired. I thought you were overseeing this yourself. That's the impression Mary Vaughn gave me."

"I oversee all my company's work," Mitch explained patiently. "And I stand behind it. But I learned to delegate a long time ago. Gabe's taking over a lot of the details and he's very good at what he does."

"No way," Ernesto said heatedly. "I won't have a man who's been hanging around with my wife in charge of a job I'm paying for."

Gabe stilled at his words. Instinctively his hands balled into fists. Just like the old days, he was ready for a fight. Only out of respect for Adelia and Mitch did he manage to control the urge to use them.

"Excuse me," he said softly. "Are you referring to Adelia? Isn't she your ex-wife?"

"Technically," Ernesto said, not looking one bit happy about the concession to reality. "But she's bound to influence how you feel about me. I know she doesn't hesitate to tell everyone how mistreated she was, even after I gave her everything she could possibly need."

"Except fidelity and respect," Gabe snapped before he could stop himself. He glanced at Mitch. "Sorry."

Mitch sat back, barely restraining a smile. "Not a problem," he said, clearly happy to let Gabe say all the things he'd managed to keep himself from saying.

Ernesto stood up and squared his shoulders, radiating indignation. He scowled down at Mitch. "Are you going to let him speak to a client in such a disrespectful way?"

Mitch stood up, as well. He might not be wearing outrageously expensive business attire, but he towered over Ernesto. There was little question who was the more intimidating presence in the room.

"I believe you started it," he said calmly. "I don't think this is going to work out, Mr. Hernandez. I'll return your deposit. Get another company to do the job."

"I'll sue you for breach of contract," Ernesto warned.

"Try it," Mitch said, waving the unsigned change order under his nose. "You wanted to make changes to that contract but didn't want to pay for them. That nullifies the contract. I'm pretty sure Helen Decatur-Whitney can counter any claim you want to make. She did a pretty good job for your wife in the divorce. Do you really want to tangle with her again?"

"Get out!" Ernesto said. "I want you off my property."

"I don't believe the property is yours," Gabe said as they were on their way out. "And if your girlfriend is even half as smart as I think she must be since she convinced you to do all these fancy renovations for her, eventually you'll be the one who's escorted from it by the police."

Ernesto blinked at Gabe's words. "You don't know what you're talking about."

Gabe grinned, surprisingly satisfied to let words win this particular battle. "Sure I do. I always recognize a good con when I see one. Now you have yourself a nice day."

Mitch didn't say a word until they were in his truck and on their way back to town. Gabe studied him, worried that he'd gone too far and cost his cousin this job.

"I'll go back and apologize if you want me to," he offered. Then he added, "Though I'd probably choke on the words."

Mitch chuckled then. "No, absolutely not. You said everything I'd been dying to say. I told you days ago I didn't want to do this job. Thanks to you, Ernesto finally gave me the perfect way out."

"Then you're not furious with me for what I said back there?"

"Nope. I just wish I'd guessed what his girlfriend was up to the way you did. I never look for devious motives."

"Because you're a nice guy," Gabe told him. "You never see the bad in anyone. Me, I've seen more than my share of good cons over the years."

"Do you really think his girlfriend is just after a sugar daddy to fix up her house before she calls it quits?"

Gabe shrugged. "I've never laid eyes on her, so who knows, but I can't imagine she thinks the man who cheated so openly on Adelia would be a good bet for a long and happy life. I imagine she'll take him for whatever she can, then shed very few tears when she sends him on his way."

"Well, apparently Ernesto just realized that's a real possibility, too, because he looked pretty shaken when you said it." Mitch glanced over at him. "Seemed to me as if he knew there might be more to your relationship with Adelia than renovating her house for her. Any thoughts about how he knew that?"

Gabe barely contained a groan. That kiss was going to haunt them forever. "There might have been a little talk around town recently," he said eventually.

"About the kiss," Mitch suggested, his amusement plain.

"Yes, about the kiss," Gabe responded ruefully. "Apparently that's been a hot topic."

"It certainly has been at my house," Mitch said. "Lynn's convinced she should start polishing the silver."

Gabe stared at him. "Why would she do that?"

"Wedding shower," Mitch said, then chuckled when Gabe's jaw dropped. "You might want to hold off on any more kissing in public if you want to limit that kind of speculation."

"It was a stupid kiss," Gabe grumbled. "Nobody caught us naked."

Mitch's expression sobered at once. "Well, let's hope when the two of you do get naked, it won't be in the middle of Main Street."

"Nobody's getting naked," Gabe retorted.

Mitch laughed then. "Yet," he corrected. "Never say never, Gabe. Sooner or later you'll wind up eating those words."

Gabe was very much afraid he was probably right about that. Getting naked with Adelia was on his mind way too much lately. It had been ever since he'd discovered the power of a single kiss.

Gabe was atop a ladder painting Natalia and Juanita's room with pale pink on the walls and lavender on the ceiling when Adelia got home from work.

She stood in the bedroom doorway, a smile on her face. "Don't you look cute all splattered with pink and purple. Very princessy."

Gabe gave her a disgruntled look. "You should have seen me with the tiara on my head."

Her eyes widened. "Excuse me?"

"They thought we ought to have a tea party before I started painting. Juanita persuaded me to wear this shiny tiara thing. She said something about princesses always being in charge and I had to do what they said.

Since I wanted to get this room finished sometime before midnight, I cooperated."

Adelia tried to swallow a laugh, but she couldn't pull it off. A giggle slipped out. "I am so, so sorry I missed that."

"I believe there are pictures," he said, his expression disgruntled but his eyes twinkling. "Selena actually smiled while she was snapping them. I consider that worth it."

He climbed down from the ladder and crossed the room in three long strides. "And because of all that, I think I earned this."

He leaned in and stole a kiss. It didn't last more than a heartbeat, but it tripped her heart into overdrive.

He winked at her. "Thanks."

He climbed back on the ladder and went back to work while Adelia still struggled to catch her breath. When she remained silent, he turned back around.

"You okay?" he asked eventually.

"You just caught me by surprise," she said. "Again."

"Well, I've been told that kisses in the middle of Main Street stir up too much talk, so this is my last resort." He grinned. "Since I doubt you came up here just in case I decided to lose my head and kiss you, was there something on your mind? Or were you just checking on today's progress?"

"I came looking for you because I heard you told off my ex-husband this morning. And that he fired Mitch because of it. I didn't even know Mitch was working for him."

Gabe suddenly looked uncomfortable. "Mitch only took the job because Mary Vaughn somehow tricked him into it. If you know Mary Vaughn at all, you can understand how that sort of thing can happen. She's sneaky. Mitch didn't realize Ernesto was the client until it was too late to back out. And technically Ernesto didn't fire Mitch. Mitch fired him. Pretty happily, I might add."

Adelia felt a lot better about that. "Seriously?"

"He definitely had a good time doing it."

"And you? Did you have a good time telling him off?"

"I have to admit, I enjoyed it," Gabe said. "I figured I owed it to you to get in a couple of good shots." He gave her a lingering look. "I'm not sure what came over me, but I cut him down with words instead of punching him out. I consider that progress in my evolution. You must be a good influence on me."

She didn't entirely buy his claim. Knowing his history, she felt compelled to warn him. "While I can't say I don't appreciate the protectiveness, please stay away from him, Gabe. Ernesto has ways of getting even with people he perceives as enemies. It's better just to stay out of his path."

"How about this? I'll promise not to do or say another thing to the man as long as he doesn't give me cause to."

"I'm not sure I like the loophole you left for yourself."

Gabe shrugged. "Take it or leave it. That's the offer."

"He's not worth it, Gabe."

"No question about that, but if I think he's doing anything to hurt you or your kids, I'm not going to ignore it. Not my nature."

"We're not talking about a school-yard bully throwing insults about your mom," she told him.

For an instant she thought she'd gone too far. Gabe's expression went hard.

"A bully is a bully, Adelia," he said flatly. "It doesn't matter where he is or how old he is. And nobody hurts the people I care about. Not ever, if there's a single thing I can do to stop it."

"I don't want or need you to fight my battles for me," she argued, worried that things that had been dismissed as the actions of a troubled teen could turn into something else entirely when two grown men were involved.

Gabe studied her for a minute. "You're not worried about me embarrassing you or causing more trouble for you, are you? You're actually afraid for me."

"Somebody has to worry about you," she said, not denying it.

His expression immediately softened. "Nobody ever has before," he said very, very quietly.

She heard something in his voice that reached in and touched her soul. She heard the pain of a kid who'd spent too many years trying to protect someone only to pay a heavy price for it without ever getting so much as a word of thanks. She couldn't help wondering if all those years ago when he'd been fighting his mom's battles if anyone at all had ever fought his. It didn't sound like it.

She straightened her shoulders and met his gaze. "Well, now you have me. I'll have your back." She smiled to lighten the moment. "But you probably ought to know, I'm not much good in a brawl."

He laughed at that. "I'll keep that in mind and try to stay out of trouble."

She nodded. "All I'm asking."

CHAPTER TEN

Adelia hurried downstairs to keep herself from crossing the bedroom and dragging Gabe into her arms for a hug he seemed to desperately need. Or maybe that was her need, to show him that he was no longer alone. She couldn't help thinking about how long it had been since any man had needed her. Ernesto certainly hadn't, at least not for anything other than being able to claim he was respectably married to a woman who was a terrific mother to his kids.

Downstairs, Adelia found Selena at the kitchen table, along with Natalia, Juanita and even Tomas. To her shock, their homework was spread out on the table.

"I'm impressed," Adelia told them. "And the casserole I left for dinner is in the oven?"

Selena nodded. "I put it in when I heard you come in. I waited till then, because I didn't think you'd want to eat the second you walked in. I figured you'd be a while with Gabe."

Since Selena didn't sound especially distraught by that, it was evident something had changed. Adelia wondered how much it had to do with that impromptu tea party and the tiara.

She leaned down to give her two younger girls a hug. "I hear you had a tea party. That must have been fun."

Selena actually giggled at that, filling Adelia's heart with hope. If her teen's sense of humor was back, perhaps she was finally emerging from the dark place she'd been in ever since she'd discovered what Ernesto was up to.

"It was dumb," Tomas said, his voice radiating masculine disgust. "They made Gabe wear this shiny crown thing. He did it, too. I don't get it. Guys shouldn't do stuff like that."

"And why is that?" Adelia asked.

Tomas looked confused by the question. "Just because," he said stubbornly.

Adelia kept her tone even as she told her son, "Someday you'll understand that men will do a lot of unpredictable things for women they like."

"Well, not me," Tomas said. "Daddy wouldn't have done something stupid like that."

"No, he probably wouldn't have," Adelia agreed quietly. "But personally I think it says a lot about Gabe that he would do something silly to make your sisters happy." She turned to Selena. "What do you think?"

"I think he looked pretty cute," she said. She frowned at her brother. "And it was cool that he went along with it." She held her cell phone out to Adelia. "Want to see?"

Sure enough, the younger girls were seated at the kitchen table with Gabe, doll-size teacups in front of all of them. Natalia and Juanita were wearing their favorite princess costumes. Gabe was adorned not only with that ridiculous tiara, but a pink feather boa. Neither could do a thing to take away from his potent masculinity, though. If anything, he looked sexier than ever, at least to her.

Adelia chuckled at the image. She really did owe him big-time for going along with her girls' request. It had clearly been an attempt to win her daughters' approval. And judging from the broad grins just now, it had worked, even with Selena, at least temporarily.

"Looks like a lot of fun. I wish I'd been here," she told the girls. She gave Selena a measured look. "So, how many people have you texted that picture to?"

"A few," she admitted, then added with a touch of defensiveness in her voice, "Come on, Mom. It's a great picture. Gabe knew I was taking it."

"I imagine he also knew you'd delight in making him a laughingstock all over town."

Selena flushed guiltily at the gently spoken accusation. "Do you think he's going to be mad?"

"No," Adelia told her. "I think he knew exactly what your intentions were and went along with it to try to win a couple of points with you. He wants to get along with you, you know."

"Maybe he's not such a bad guy," Selena conceded.

Adelia patted her shoulder. "Remember that the next time you see him. Cut him a little slack."

"Is he staying for dinner?" Selena asked.

"I didn't mention it to him."

"Can I ask him?" Selena requested.

Relieved by Selena's willingness to make more of an effort with Gabe, Adelia nodded at once. "I think he'd really appreciate that."

"We'll come, too," Natalia said, jumping up.

"No," Adelia said, stopping her. "Let Selena do this."

She could see from her oldest's expression that Selena understood not only just how much this gesture meant to Adelia, but how much it might matter to Gabe.

Selena wrapped her arms around Adelia's waist and gave her a fierce hug. "I'll try harder, Mom. I promise."

Adelia tucked a finger under her chin. "It makes me very happy to hear you say that. All I'll ever ask of you is that you be open-minded."

"Because everybody deserves a chance," Selena said, echoing what Adelia had said only a few days earlier. She glanced at the photo still on the screen on her cell phone. "Gabe might really, really deserve one."

She gave Adelia another grin and headed upstairs. Watching her go, Adelia breathed a sigh of relief. She didn't need her daughter's approval for whatever might happen between her and Gabe, but it was nice to know it might not be withheld. Things between her and Gabe were complicated enough without having to fight that particular battle. Of course, she was wise enough to recognize that winning one battle did not win this particular war. Selena's mercurial moods could change on a dime.

Gabe had finished painting the ceiling and was working on the trim when he noticed Selena standing hesitantly in the bedroom doorway.

"Hey," he said. "Everything okay?"

"I thought you might want to see the picture I took earlier," she said, then grinned. "Or maybe not."

Gabe chuckled. "I have a hunch I'll be begging you to delete it."

She shook her head at once. "Not a chance."

"Good blackmail material?" he asked.

A smile tugged at her lips. "Really good."

He beckoned for her to come closer. "Let me see."

He took in the tiara, the pink boa and the miniature teacups and barely contained a groan. Sadly the picture was clear as a bell. Too bad it wasn't so blurry no one would be able to identify him.

"Nice shot," he commented.

"That's what everyone thinks," she said, then winced, her expression filled with guilt.

"Everyone?"

"I might have texted it to some people. Sorry." She tried to look contrite, but failed at it.

"If I had a picture this good, I'd want to share it, too," he said.

She looked surprised by that. "Really?"

"Sure."

"You aren't humiliated that it's probably all over town by now?"

"Was that your intention, to humiliate me?"

"Maybe," she confessed. "At least until I thought about it."

"And then?"

"I realized it was really nice what you did, going along with Natalia and Juanita. My dad would never have done something like that. He'd be too freaked out about his image." She made a face. "As if his is all that great in the first place," she added.

There was real anger in her voice. Or perhaps it was disappointment Gabe heard. Either way he wasn't about to go down that road with Selena. "Well, if you promise not to tell anyone," he said, "I'll tell you a secret."

She looked intrigued. "I won't tell. Cross my heart."

He leaned closer. "I had fun. I'd never been to a tea party before. Or worn a tiara and whatever that feathery thing was."

"A boa," she said, giggling. "You liked it?"

"I liked that it made you laugh and it made your sisters happy," he corrected.

To his surprise, his words seemed to cause tears to well up. Unsure of what he'd said to bring them on, he regarded her worriedly. "Selena, what did I say? I didn't mean to upset you."

"I'll bet you wouldn't have made a big deal about going to a father–daughter dance with your daughter, would you?" she blurted, the question seemingly coming out of nowhere.

Gabe regarded her with confusion. "I don't understand. What's a father–daughter dance got to do with this?"

Her expression turned sad. "I asked my dad to take me to one at school a while back. He said he'd go, but at the last minute he tried to bail, just like always when something was important to me. He said he was too busy. My mom made him go, but he didn't want to be there. It was awful. My uncle Elliott took Daisy and he loved being there. That made it worse."

Gabe heard the misery in her voice and added yet one more reason to dislike Ernesto to his rapidly growing list. "I'm sorry," he said.

She swiped angrily at the tears on her cheeks, then asked, "Would you have gone?"

There had never been an opportunity for such a thing in Gabe's life, but he was pretty sure he'd never disappoint a child the way Ernesto had disappointed Selena. "If I had a daughter, there's nothing I'd be more honored to do than to take her to a father–daughter dance if she wanted me to be there."

"That's how Uncle Elliott felt, too." She sighed. "I guess some people can't change who they are and how they feel about stuff, huh?"

No, but they ought to try, especially if their actions were going to hurt their kids, Gabe thought. "People can always change," he said carefully.

"You're nice," she said, as if that was a huge surprise to her.

"Not always," he confided just to see another smile on her face. She rewarded him with a bright one.

"Yes, you are." She stuffed her phone into her pocket, then regarded him hesitantly. "I came up here to see if you want to stay for dinner. We're having Mom's enchilada casserole. Actually it's *Abuela*'s recipe, but Mom's getting pretty good at making it. It'll be ready in about ten minutes."

"I would love to stay," Gabe said, not just because the promise of good food was tempting, but because she'd made the unexpected overture. "Thanks, Selena."

"Okay, I'll tell Mom." She got to the door and turned back. "Mr. Franklin?"

"You can call me Gabe, if that's okay with your mother."

"Okay, Gabe. Do you like my mom?"

"I do," he said.

"I mean a lot. Do you want to date her and stuff?"

Gabe wasn't sure what sort of "stuff" Selena had

in mind, but he knew admitting to it was probably a very bad idea. "We're getting to know each other," he said, choosing his words carefully.

"That's what she says, too."

"Are you okay with that?"

"I'm not really sure."

Gabe nodded at her honest reaction. "You don't have to be sure right this minute. Nobody's on a timetable here."

Her expression brightened again at that. "That's good then. Thanks."

"No thanks necessary," he said, watching as she left.

While the whole conversation seemed like a giant step forward, it was also a very big reminder that the situation was a whole lot more complicated than he'd ever imagined. If he did decide to see where things might go with Adelia, he needed to remember that there were a lot of other people who'd be affected by their actions. Was that a risk he was willing to take? Especially when he'd already made it clear, to Adelia at least, that he didn't do the whole happily-ever-after thing?

"You were awfully quiet during dinner," Adelia said as she and Gabe cleared the table and put dishes into the dishwasher. He'd insisted on helping, so she'd let the younger kids go outside to play and allowed Selena a half hour of phone time with her friends.

"Seriously?" she'd asked, looking shocked at the special dispensation from the rules of being grounded.

"Seriously," Adelia had told her. "I think you showed some signs of real maturity today. I think you deserve a break, just this once." She'd given her a stern look. "Though from now on, would you please remember that no phone includes no texting. You seem to be having a little trouble with that."

"I know. I'm sorry," Selena said, sounding suitably contrite. A genuine smile had broken across her face then. She'd thrown her arms around Adelia. "Thanks, Mom." Then she'd grinned at Gabe. "Thank you, too."

Gabe had regarded her with bewilderment. "Me? What did I do?"

"You've made Mom all mellow," Selena responded, then darted off.

Now Adelia focused her attention on Gabe, who seemed to be avoiding not only her comment, but her gaze. "What's going on, Gabe?"

"I have a lot on my mind, that's all," he said, an oddly defensive note in his voice.

"About work? Is it getting to be too much, doing my renovations after hours?"

"No."

"Am I going to have to play twenty questions to get the truth out of you?"

His lips quirked up at that. "No. It was something Selena said earlier. It got me to thinking."

"What did she say?" Adelia frowned. "She wasn't rude, was she? I told her she could call her friends because I thought she'd made amends with you."

"She never needed to make amends with me, but, no, she wasn't rude. Nothing like that. It's just that some of the things she said made me realize that what's going on with us…" He glanced at her quickly. "Not that anything is."

"Right. Not that anything is."

"It's just that the decisions we might make down the road don't just affect us."

Adelia began to understand. "You're absolutely right. I will always have to think about my kids and put them first."

"Which means I have to think about them, too," he said. "I've never had to look beyond my own wants and needs before."

"Of course you have," she said impatiently. "For years you put your mom's needs first."

"Since then," he said, conceding the point. "And let's just say it—that situation was all upside down. I was a kid. She was the parent. I'm not sure what I took away from that, maybe just an understanding that I didn't ever want to be responsible for anyone's happiness or well-being again."

"Which is why you don't do relationships," she said. "Yes, you've mentioned that."

"I just want to be up front with you."

"And you have been. You're doing it again right now, making it clear that I shouldn't have any expectations where you're concerned."

Gabe frowned. "You make that sound like a bad thing. Would you prefer me to start something with you and then take off with no warning when the situation gets to be more than I can handle?"

Adelia sighed. She knew that wouldn't be better. But what made the most sense of all was to never start anything in the first place, not with a man who'd declared very clearly that there would be no commitment, not ever. It didn't matter that she thought he was selling himself short. It only mattered what he thought.

And while she might not be anywhere near ready

for a commitment herself, she wasn't so sure she was cut out for a flirtation that had absolutely no potential for going anywhere.

"Gabe, are we crazy for spending even a single second with each other?" she asked.

"What do you mean?"

"We both know there's some kind of attraction thing going on. Heaven knows, I liked kissing you."

"Right back at you," he said.

"Then it seems to me we're playing with fire. I don't think I'm capable of having some sort of passionate fling without expecting it to go somewhere. And you're very clear about where you stand on anything more than a fling. One of us is bound to get hurt, and, frankly, I've had about all of the misery I can handle."

"It would kill me to know I'd made you miserable," he said, gently cupping her cheek with his hand. "It really would. I don't ever want to give you a reason to lump me in any category in which a man like Ernesto is the star offender."

She smiled at that. "I doubt I'd ever compare you to him. You've already shown me more thoughtfulness and consideration than he had in years."

"Still, it's not a risk I'm willing to take."

"So, where does that leave us?" she asked, already knowing the sensible answer. "Do we agree just to be friends? Do we avoid each other entirely?"

Gabe looked genuinely taken aback by the limited options she'd presented. "Friends isn't going to work, Adelia. Not for me. That attraction thing isn't going to go away. Sooner or later one of us will cave in to it. I'm betting it will be me." He gave her a self-deprecating grin. "And given my excellent powers of persuasion…"

She couldn't help smiling at that, too. "Really?"

"Oh, yes. I'll be very persuasive. You'll give in and then you'll wind up hating me for it."

She understood his logic and bought the argument. Even now, if he reached for her, she knew she'd be unable to resist.

"Then I suppose we have to avoid each other," she said with real regret. She drew herself up, though, and said with resolve, "We can do that. I know when you're likely to be at the bakery. I'll go in at a different time or not at all. As for the work here, I can call the kids and let them know when I'm heading home. They can alert you and you can be gone by the time I get here. That should be easy enough."

"Or I could insist that Mitch replace me on this job," he said.

"That's not fair," she protested. "I don't want you to lose the income and I like the work you're doing. I'll just make sure to limit the times we cross paths."

Gabe sighed, clearly reluctant to agree to her plan. "I have to tell you, Adelia, I hate this."

"I'm not wild about it, either, but it's the only sensible way to handle things so they don't get out of hand," she said.

"Preventative medicine, so to speak."

She nodded. "Exactly."

Even as she managed to sound determined, her heart was aching. The thought of not seeing Gabe anymore like this, of not witnessing the growing bond between him and Tomas or the laughter he stirred with her girls, made her incredibly sad. Sure, this was the smart decision, perhaps the *only* decision, but that didn't mean she had to like it.

Just when she was trying to mentally congratulate herself for making the tough choice, Gabe stepped closer. His heat drew her the way that giant magnet he had Tomas using in the yard drew metal. She swayed toward him, just as she'd predicted she would.

He put his hands on her shoulders and held her in place, his touch gentle but firm.

"One last kiss?" he said.

It was posed as a question, but there was a quiet urgency, a command to the words, too.

Adelia nodded, her heart in her throat.

His hands—his big, strong hands—left her shoulders to frame her face. His gaze held hers, his eyes darkening with desire.

And then his lips were on hers. This wasn't a tender, exploratory kiss like the one they'd shared on Main Street, or the teasing kiss he'd bestowed on her earlier. This was passion and heat and longing all wrapped up in a moment that seemed to last forever. It stole her breath and left her pulse racing.

And it filled her with a longing she'd never expected to feel again.

I just ended this, she thought to herself incredulously. *I just declared this man off-limits? Am I nuts?*

The kiss stopped too soon and yet not nearly soon enough. It had lasted long enough to give her second thoughts, maybe even third thoughts. From the dazed and hungry look in Gabe's eyes, it had done the same to him.

"No second thoughts," he said, as if he'd read her mind. "We've agreed that this is for the best."

"It is," she managed to say, even though she found

it hard to believe that anything this good could possibly come to a bad end.

He caressed her cheek one last time, then regarded her with unmistakable regret. "Good night, Adelia."

The regret in his eyes was almost her undoing. Then she steadied her resolve. "Bye, Gabe," she whispered as he walked away, closing the back door oh so quietly but emphatically behind him.

If this was so right, she thought, why did it feel as if she'd just given up the best thing to come into her life in years?

CHAPTER ELEVEN

It had been a slow morning at the boutique. None of the new merchandise Adelia had helped Raylene select had turned up. Customers had been few and far between. Adelia had straightened up all the displays, dusted every surface and looked through half a dozen catalogues for potential new stock. Raylene always took her recommendations seriously, which had given her self-confidence a much-needed boost.

Typically on a day like today, she'd lock up for a ten-minute break and head next door for a pick-me-up cup of coffee, maybe even one of Lynn's tart lemon-blueberry bars. Ever since her most recent encounter with Gabe, though, she'd grown more skittish than ever about dropping into her friend's bakery. She and Gabe had an agreement, and while he was rarely at the bakery in the middle of the day, she couldn't take a chance on running into him, not while this agreed-upon separation of theirs was so new. It would be far too easy to backslide.

At the sound of the bell over the door, she bounced up eagerly and walked into the front of the store.

"It's just me," Raylene called out. "I thought you might be ready for a break, so I brought coffee."

"Thank goodness," Adelia said, accepting the cup.

Raylene grinned. "Quiet day?"

"You have no idea. It's as if everyone in town is all shopped out. I suppose that's to be expected after the crazy busy days we had last week."

"You should know by now that it's feast or famine in retail," Raylene said, not sounding particularly upset by the decline in business.

Adelia couldn't make herself be so blasé. She'd spent the morning thinking of ways to generate more customers. "Maybe we need to have a sale," she suggested. "Or send out an announcement about the new lingerie line. We have email addresses for all our customers. I could do that this afternoon."

"And that is why you're going to make an excellent business partner," Raylene said. "Ever since you came to work here, you've been coming up with ways to build the business. I hope you know how much I value your input. If you want to do an email blast to our customer base, go for it."

"I'm going to blunder sooner or later," Adelia warned.

Raylene laughed. "No doubt about it. You weren't working here at the time of my great Christmas sweater catastrophe."

"What was that?" Adelia asked, intrigued.

"I ordered a ton of what I thought were really fun Christmas sweaters before I realized that my customers were looking for style, not things that would be passed around at parties as the year's worst gifts. I'll bet you would have steered me away from that disaster."

"Absolutely," Adelia said. "This shop has become the fashion trendsetter in town. Those sweaters sound as if they might have been just a bit off the mark."

"And there's that diplomatic skill of yours again," Raylene said, laughing. Her expression sobered as she held Adelia's gaze.

She studied Adelia over the rim of her own take-out cup of decaf. "Is there some particular reason you're so jittery today?"

"I'm not jittery," Adelia said. "I'm bored. It's ironic really. Before I started working full-time for you, I was on so many committees for the schools that I never had a spare minute. Now it feels as if I'm at loose ends, even when I'm here on days like today."

"That's not boredom, my friend," Raylene said, her eyes twinkling with mirth. "I'm guessing this has something to do with Gabe Franklin."

Startled by the assessment, Adelia stared at her. "Why on earth would you jump to that conclusion?"

"Because Lynn told me you've stopped coming by in the morning to pick up coffee. She has the feeling you're avoiding him." Raylene gave her a penetrating look. "Are you? Did the two of you have a fight?"

Adelia sighed. It was useless to try to pretend with Raylene. She'd keep poking and prodding till she got the answers she wanted. In recent months, Adelia had discovered it was something friends did. She still wasn't sure how she felt about the habit.

"There was no fight," she told Raylene, then tried to minimize the situation that had left her more shaken than she'd expected to be. "He's still doing the work at the house. It's all good."

"Then why do you sound so unhappy and why is Gabe storming around as if someone stole his favorite power saw?"

Adelia actually took some comfort from hearing that Gabe was no happier than she was. Of course, neither of them had genuinely wanted this separation. They'd just agreed it was for the best.

"I can't explain Gabe's moods," Adelia claimed. "As far as I know, everything's just fine."

"I'm not buying it," Raylene said. "You're saying all the right words, but the look in your eyes says something else entirely. What really happened between you two? He didn't cross a line, did he? I certainly know the two of you kissed."

"Everybody in town knew the two of us kissed," Adelia said wryly.

"Well, I thought it was something you were into," Raylene said. "Was I wrong? Gabe wasn't making unwanted advances, was he? Was he pressuring you?" Indignation immediately laced through her voice.

"Absolutely not," Adelia said quickly. She certainly didn't want the full weight of a bunch of riled up women coming down on him, not when he'd done nothing to deserve it. "He'd never do anything like that."

"And the kids like him okay?" Raylene prodded, clearly determined to find the missing piece to the puzzle she was trying to unravel. "I know Tomas is like his little shadow, but the girls? How do they feel about him?"

Adelia regarded her with exasperation. "You need a hobby, something other than my life."

"Probably so," Raylene said unrepentantly. "But for right this second, you're all I've got. Were things okay with Gabe and the kids? You didn't dump him because of them, did you?"

In a way that's exactly what had happened, Adelia thought, but she wasn't prepared to admit it. Instead, she said, "You're absolutely right that Tomas thinks he hung the moon, or at least he did before Gabe went along with Natalia and Juanita and attended one of their tea parties. He's struggling a bit with why a real guy would do that."

Raylene chuckled. "Yeah, that picture made the rounds. I thought it showed a lot about the kind of man Gabe is. Not many men could pull off a tiara and a feather boa and still look sexy as sin."

"Not many men would be willing to try it just to make a couple of little girls happy," Adelia commented.

"So, we have a man who puts a blush in your cheeks, is a good role model for your son and makes your girls happy," Raylene assessed. "I'm not seeing the downside. What am I missing?"

Adelia finally gave up on keeping the situation under wraps. "It was never going to work," she confided.

Raylene stared at her incredulously. "And you knew that after a couple of weeks and not even one real date? How?"

"It just wasn't. We have very different ideas about what we want in life. Better to end it before it got started and anyone got hurt, especially my kids."

Understanding dawned in Raylene's expression. "Now I get it. You did call it off to protect your kids, just not the way I was talking about."

Adelia shrugged. "Pretty much."

"But he's still at the house. He's still in their lives on a daily basis. How is this helping to protect them?"

"They won't get any ideas about the two of us," Adelia said. They'd miss any displays of affection, any stolen kisses.

"Ah," Raylene said, nodding. "And what about you? Do you feel all safe and secure now, too?"

"I did what I had to do," Adelia said defensively. "Gabe agreed with me."

"Well, that is just plain wrong," Raylene said.

"How is it wrong to want what's best for my family, especially after all they've gone through with the divorce?"

"Putting your family first is always good," Raylene agreed. "It's what mothers do. But smart *women* know that sometimes what's best for a happy family is taking care of their own needs, too. Remember that expression, 'If Mama ain't happy, ain't nobody happy'?"

Adelia smiled. "A simplified slogan isn't necessarily the best motto for living your life."

"I think this one has merit," Raylene said. "Happiness is contagious. Even in the very limited time you and Gabe have been acquainted, I've seen a change in you. You were happier, Adelia. Don't even try to deny it. This job may be giving your self-esteem a boost when it comes to your professional skills, but with Gabe you were rediscovering your worth as a woman."

Adelia didn't bother trying to deny it, because she knew it would be a lie. "It wouldn't have lasted," she said instead. That wasn't a lie. It was the inevitable truth.

"Gabe doesn't do forever," she revealed to Raylene. "How could I get involved with someone who openly made that clear from the outset? I've already been with one man who was incapable of sticking to his wedding vows. Gabe was pretty clear he'd never even take the vows."

Raylene scowled at the comment. "Don't you dare compare him to Ernesto. It's not fair."

"That's not what I'm doing. Gabe said—"

Raylene cut her off. "Men say stuff. They even believe it to be true. It gives them an easy out if they decide down the line that they need one. It's very rare for anyone to fall head over heels in love in a minute. It takes time. People have to get to know each other, to trust each other. Look at Carter and me. We had enough issues and past history to scare off any sane person. But we hung in there. Actually I should say that he did. He was persistent even in the face of all my doubts. In the end, love won out."

"If it were just me," Adelia began, unable to keep a wistful note from her voice.

"You'd take the chance," Raylene said triumphantly. "That right there tells you that you're giving up too easily."

"My kids," she protested.

"Your kids deserve to have a happy mom who has a wonderful man in her life. He's already won over Tomas, Juanita and Natalia, right?"

"Even Selena has fewer reservations," Adelia admitted. "That whole tea party thing, even though it was for the benefit of the younger girls, made an impression on her, too, probably because it was such a contrast to anything Ernesto would have done to please her or her sisters."

"Well, there you go."

"But if Gabe and I can't make it, I'll be dragging them through a whole big drama all over again," Adelia said. "I can't do that. I won't."

"You're scared," Raylene assessed. "And who can blame you? This is a man who flirts, who makes you feel like a woman, who makes you feel alive. That's scary stuff after too many years of being dismissed as unworthy and competing with a string of mistresses."

"Okay, yes. I'm finding it hard to trust that Gabe's even attracted to me, but I swear that is not why I called it quits. It was the sensible thing to do." She gave her friend a defiant look. "And I'm not changing my mind."

"Okay, this calls for an intervention by a higher authority," Raylene said.

Adelia stared at her, surprised. "You think I should pray about it?"

Raylene grinned. "Well, that probably wouldn't hurt, either, but I was thinking that what you really need is a margarita night with a bunch of women who've been there, done just about everything."

"The Sweet Magnolias," Adelia guessed, then shook her head. "I don't know."

"Come with me," Raylene ordered, pointing to the back room. "Let's think about this." She led the way into the tiny office. "Sit."

"I don't want to," Adelia said, then chuckled. "What is wrong with me? I sounded like Selena then, just like a sullen teenager."

"Want to know what I think?" Raylene asked, then continued without waiting for Adelia's reply. "I think of all the women I know, nobody deserves the chance to flirt and feel like an attractive woman again more than you do. Ernesto took that skill set away from you. He played havoc with your self-confidence by going after all those other women. You're entitled to have a little fun. Flirt with Gabe if you want to. Let him make you laugh. Let him make you blush. It doesn't have to lead to anything more, not if you don't want it to."

"I have to concentrate on being a good mom right now," Adelia argued yet again, even though it seemed her words were falling on deaf ears. Raylene was nothing if not stubborn. "The kids need me more than ever to make sure they feel safe and loved."

"And who's supposed to make you feel that way?" Raylene asked.

"Not Gabe Franklin," Adelia said.

"Maybe not," Raylene agreed. "But there is a man out there who is right for you. Think of Gabe as practice, if you want to."

Adelia frowned at the suggestion. "That hardly seems fair."

"Sweetie, I don't know Gabe that well yet, but something tells me he can take care of himself. Worry about what you need for a change."

"And you think what I need is to flirt outrageously?" Adelia asked skeptically.

Raylene gave her wicked grin. "Couldn't hurt. And if you don't trust my opinion, then come over to my place tonight. The Sweet Magnolias are getting together for a margarita night. You can run the idea past everyone. And before you get all crazy and say something about the Sweet Magnolias being some secret society, let me assure you that everyone is on board with you joining us. Karen will be there. So will Lynn and Sarah. You'll know all the others, too. You should at least give us a chance."

Adelia had to admit that the prospect of forming a bond with other women, many of whom had been through what she'd been through and, in some cases, even worse, held a lot of appeal. She'd already promised herself that if she ever had the chance to get to know them, she'd grab it.

And she needed a night like this, not so much to kick up her heels, but to do something for herself. It had been all about the kids lately, especially the decision to walk away from Gabe before they got too attached or misinterpreted why he was around. It was one thing for Tomas to idolize Gabe as a role model. It would be quite another for him to start thinking of Gabe as potential dad material.

"Okay, I'll come," she said at last. "What can I bring?"

"Nothing this time," Raylene told her. "But next time we're going to want you to bring one of your mother's famous Mexican dishes and maybe that secret mole sauce I've been hearing so much about."

Adelia laughed. "Not even I have that recipe, but I'll talk Mama into making it for us. Maybe Dana Sue can dissect it and figure out the ingredients since she's such a great chef. My sister-in-law is pretty good at that, but Karen hasn't been able to figure it out. It's driving her a little nuts."

"So, you'll be there," Raylene pressed.

"I'll be there," Adelia agreed.

"Perfect. I'll see you tonight around seven," Raylene said. "If you need someone to stay with the kids, I can send Carrie or Mandy over. Babysitting gigs on margarita nights keep them in pizza money. Or is Selena babysitting them these days?"

"I don't mind leaving her in charge after school, but nights are another story. I'll check with my mother. The kids could use a night with their *abuela*. If she's not available, I'll let you know."

She watched as her boss left the store without asking a single question about anything work related. She'd even left it to Adelia to decide about sending out those email alerts. Surprisingly, that felt wonderful. She realized it demonstrated just how much Raylene trusted her to be on top of things. Being invited to a margarita night was just the icing on the cake.

"I brought coffee," Mitch said, settling onto a folding chair across from Gabe. He handed over a super-sized to-go cup from the bakery.

"Thanks. To what do I owe this?"

"I thought maybe the caffeine would improve your mood," Mitch said. "I've had half a dozen complaints today that you're behaving like a bear with a thorn in its paw."

Gabe studied his cousin with narrowed eyes. "Is that so? Who's running to you to tattle?"

"Not the point. Is it true? And before you try to deny it, you should probably know that I have to believe it must be true because of all those reliable sources."

"Then why even ask?"

"Because I wanted to give you a chance to explain."

Gabe regarded Mitch curiously. "And if I have nothing to say?"

"Then I will be forced to remind you that I am the boss and that I don't like dissension on my work sites, especially when the man responsible for it is my cousin and my second-in-command."

"There you go, pulling rank again."

"Frankly, I don't like doing it," Mitch said, looking surprisingly uncomfortable. "I shouldn't have to."

Gabe sighed. "No, you shouldn't. And I'll apologize to, well, everybody, I guess, since you refuse to be specific about whom I've offended."

"Just correct the attitude," Mitch suggested. "And talk to me."

"About what?"

"Whatever put you in this mood."

Gabe regarded him incredulously. "Do you honestly want to have some long talk about my feelings and that sort of stuff?"

Mitch looked horrified, just as Gabe expected.

"Absolutely not," Mitch said at once. "Lynn just thought I ought to try to get to the bottom of it." His eyes narrowed. "She doesn't think it's a coincidence that Adelia seems to be making herself scarce at the bakery."

Gabe avoided his cousin's penetrating gaze. "I wouldn't know about that."

"Because the two of you had some sort of falling out?"

"Mitch, please do not go there. My personal life is just that, personal."

"So this is about Adelia," Mitch concluded, looking pleased with himself. Or maybe he was just happy at the proof that his wife had nailed the problem. "Want to talk about that?"

"No!" Gabe said emphatically.

Mitch tried to hide a grin but couldn't pull it off. "Interesting."

"Go to blazes!"

His cousin's laugh echoed through the work site. "And there's the attitude I've been hearing about."

At Gabe's sour look, Mitch's expression sobered. "Okay, here's the deal. The women are all getting together for one of those Sweet Magnolia things tonight. I imagine they're going to roast you for whatever you did."

"I didn't do anything," Gabe protested.

"Doesn't matter. Perception is everything. My point is that when they get together like that, the men play hoops. Frankly, my knees are giving out, but it's nice to hang out, work up a little sweat and tell tall tales with a bunch of the guys. You're coming along tonight."

"Was that an invitation or a command?" Gabe grumbled.

"Call it whatever you want, as long as you're on the court in the park by seven. Want me to pick you up?"

"I can find it," Gabe said.

Actually the idea of a little physical exertion sounded good. Maybe if he was sweating hard, gasping for breath and making a few baskets, he could push all the thoughts of Adelia out of his head. Of course, that might be asking an awful lot of a casual basketball game with the guys. He was pretty sure his steamy thoughts about Adelia weren't going to go away so easily.

When Gabe turned up at the basketball court that night at seven, he was surprised to find several men he remembered there, including Ronnie Sullivan, who now owned the hardware store on Main Street, high school baseball coach Cal Maddox and Adelia's brother, Elliott Cruz. A lot of the others were new to town, proving that Serenity had provided a draw to men from very diverse backgrounds. It made him look at the town with a new perspective.

Perhaps most surprising were Travis McDonald, a former pro baseball player who now owned the country music station, his cousin Tom, who was the town manager, and Carter Rollins, the police chief who Mitch said had moved to town from Columbia in search of a quieter place to raise his two sisters after their parents had been killed in an accident. These were men who could have settled anywhere, but they'd chosen Serenity, seen its potential.

Before the game started, Elliott pulled Gabe aside. Expecting a lecture or worse, he tensed. Instead, Elliott merely asked how the work was coming along at Adelia's.

"The roof's solid now and the demolition is mostly completed. I'm trying to get all the kids' rooms painted so they'll feel settled," Gabe reported.

A smile tugged at Elliott's lips. "I'm surprised you've had the time to accomplish all that, what with the tea parties you've had to attend."

Gabe groaned. "You saw the picture?"

"Oh yeah," Elliott confirmed. "Selena sent it to my daughter. Naturally she shared it with her mom and me and heaven knows how many other people."

Ignoring yet more evidence of how far that blasted picture had spread, Gabe focused on the rest of what Elliott had said. "I didn't think you and Karen had been married long enough to have a daughter Selena's age."

"Daisy's actually a little younger. She was my step-daughter, but we started adoption proceedings a while back. She and her brother, Mack, will be my kids officially before long."

Something in his voice suggested there was a story behind that, but Gabe didn't pry.

"Are you guys ready to get on the court?" Carter called out. "I, for one, could work off a little steam. I had to deal with the mayor today, and that usually tests my patience."

"Amen to that," Tom McDonald said in heartfelt agreement.

The men chose sides and hit the court. It didn't take long for Gabe to realize that most of them played for blood. He was panting in no time, but he felt as if he was holding his own as he blocked a shot by Travis McDonald, then took the ball down the court and dunked it to score the winning points.

Mitch was bent over, but there was pride in his voice, when he said, "And, gentlemen, that is how it's done. Now, if you don't mind, I need water and maybe some oxygen."

Tom followed Mitch to the bench and sank down beside him, then handed out water bottles all around.

"I hate to admit it," Ronnie Sullivan said, "but I might be getting too old for this."

"Join the club," Mitch said, clearly commiserating with him.

"If you guys suggest we quit this and take up golf, I swear I'm going to have to leave town," Travis said. "I can't be surrounded by a bunch of wimps."

"Say that when you're my age," Ronnie countered.

"Or mine," Mitch said.

Travis shook his head. "Pitiful. Just plain pitiful."

"Oh, cut them some slack," Cal suggested. "Old geezers deserve our respect."

Gabe laughed at the indignant expressions that spread over Ronnie's face and his cousin's. Since Mitch was only a couple of years older than Gabe was, he probably shouldn't be laughing at all.

"Maybe we should change the subject," Carter said, "before I have to call in deputies to break up a brawl." He turned to Gabe. "So what's this I hear about you dating Adelia Hernandez?"

Gabe flushed at suddenly having all the attention focused on him. If they'd been asking about the Main Street renovations or even his work at Adelia's, it would have been one thing, but this was clearly a trap he'd fallen into.

"I have no idea where you got your information," he said carefully, only to see Elliott's expression darken.

"I had the impression you were seeing my sister," Elliott said.

"Were, past tense," Gabe said, aware that silence had fallen and all the men were listening attentively to his response. "She and I agreed we should stick to being friends."

That was a bit of a stretch, but it was better than revealing the truth, that they'd called it off before it really got started, mostly because he'd made it clear they had no long-term future.

"I warned you," Elliott said, his voice low, his scowl firmly in place.

Gabe leveled an even look on him. "Her decision," he said quietly. "Ask her if you don't believe me."

"Oh, I will," Elliott assured him. "And if I don't like the answer—"

"Guys, guys!" Carter said, intervening again. "I think we could all use a time-out and something cold to drink."

"Beers at my place," Ronnie said. "Or more water, if that's your preference. And the pizza will be delivered by the time we get there. I've just called the order in to Rosalina's."

Gabe turned to Mitch. "Maybe I should take off."

Mitch shook his head. "No need. These are good men. They're a little protective of their women, but they're not unfair. You need to stand your ground." He held Gabe's gaze. "That is, if you've done nothing wrong."

Gabe wanted to believe Mitch was right. He'd never had buddies like these men appeared to be. It had been nice to feel like a real part of something, even if it had been a casual basketball game.

He nodded eventually. "I'll hang out and see what happens."

After all, he really hadn't done anything wrong. All he'd done was let himself be tempted for just a minute by a strong, beautiful woman. Not a one of these men, all of whom were happily married from what he knew, could possibly believe that was a crime.

CHAPTER TWELVE

The Sweet Magnolia women gathered in the new family room at Raylene's, with its high ceiling and soaring windows, were all people Adelia had known most of her life in one capacity or another. Two or three were even friends.

She was really looking forward, though, to getting to know the original trio of women who'd formed the group. Dana Sue Sullivan, the owner of Sullivan's restaurant, and Maddie Maddox, who ran The Corner Spa, were practically legends in town.

In a way she already knew Maddie as Elliott's boss and an indirect partner in the men's gym he'd created with some of the husbands of the women in this room. Their brief exchanges when Adelia had gone to the spa to try to get fit in a last-ditch effort to save her marriage had been mostly casual, though. She also knew that Maddie had coached Lynn through making her business plan for the bakery. She was obviously generous and kind. Like all the Sweet Magnolias, she was someone worth knowing.

Adelia already knew the third member of that original

group, Helen Decatur-Whitney, professionally. Helen had been her divorce attorney, and she'd fought to ensure that Ernesto provided well for her and for the children. Adelia was determinedly setting most of that support money aside for college for the kids. Some of her lump-sum alimony would go toward the house renovations. Beyond that, she wanted to prove they could live on what she was able to provide on her own these days. Amazingly, thanks to her budgeting skills, which she'd practiced even when living under Ernesto's roof, they were making it. She headed in Helen's direction to thank her yet again for her support. She wondered if a lifetime would be long enough for her to convey the depth of her gratitude for Helen's fierce loyalty.

"You look incredible," Helen said, studying her outfit. "I wish I had your sense of style."

Adelia laughed. "You must be kidding. I recognize that blouse you're wearing. It's from the new designer collection I saw in a boutique when I was over in Charleston a couple of weeks ago. And your shoes are Jimmy Choo." She leaned down for a closer look. "Stunning."

Maddie joined them just then. "We *all* know those are Jimmy Choos, even if we don't have a lick of style. Helen's expensive taste in shoes is her trademark. Before she had a daughter and college expenses to worry about, she indulged in shoes. Lots and lots of shoes."

Helen held out a foot and regarded it with a sorrowful expression. "These are beautiful, aren't they? Sadly, these days I seem to spend a lot of time in sneakers, trying to keep up with my daughter."

Maddie turned to Adelia. "I'm so glad you were able to come tonight. I'm looking forward to getting to know you better. I've watched your progress at the spa and listened to your brother bragging on you."

"Elliott brags about me?" Adelia asked, surprised.

"He takes personal credit for turning you into an exercise junkie," Maddie reported.

"No way," Adelia said adamantly. "I show up. I work out, but I hate every second. I'm there in spite of my brother, not because of him. That's why he's not my personal trainer."

Maddie chuckled. "Working out with your brother might be counterproductive. If I know anything about sibling relationships, I can guess you'd probably do the opposite of anything he suggests."

"Exactly," Adelia confirmed.

"Well, I know Raylene thinks the world of you," Maddie said. "She says she can take time off to be with the baby when it comes, because she knows the boutique will be in excellent hands. She says she really lucked out the day you walked in the door looking for a job."

Though she'd heard the same thing from Raylene herself, it was praise Adelia never tired of hearing. Raylene's confidence in her had been the first step on her path toward rebuilding her confidence in herself. "I certainly intend to try hard not to let her down," she told Maddie.

Raylene came over just then. "No way could you let me down. My business doubled after you came to work for me." She turned to Maddie. "Adelia has this amazing eye for what women should wear and she has this soft-sell approach that always works. Nobody walks out without buying something and they usually buy a lot more than they intended to. Earlier today she sent out an email to our top customers about a new line of lingerie. By the end of the day most of it was sold."

"And this coming from a woman who traveled in very chic social circles in Charleston once upon a time," Maddie said, then winced. She gave Raylene's hand a squeeze. "Sorry, sweetie. I know that time of your life doesn't bring back such good memories, but I wanted Adelia to understand that coming from you, what you said was high praise."

"It's okay," Raylene said. "There are some days when I can actually remember the positive things about that time of my life." She focused on Adelia. "Maddie's right, though. You need to take me seriously when I tell you how good you are."

Adelia flushed at all the compliments. "Thank you."

Helen gave her a sympathetic look. "Okay, fair warning. All this sweetness and light ends now. This group is notorious for asking inappropriate, intrusive questions. You are always free to tell us to butt out."

"But we'll hate you for it," Dana Sue said, joining them. "We pride ourselves on knowing the inside scoop about everything."

"Only Grace Wharton knows more gossip than we do," Helen said with a resigned sigh. "I don't know how she does it, but it's annoying."

"I'm afraid I'm way out of the gossip loop," Adelia apologized. "If that's the card that grants me entry, you're all going to be disappointed."

"Maybe you're not current with *everything,* but the way I hear it, you have the inside track on at least one thing," Dana Sue said, her expression mischievous. "I hear you're getting tight with the sexiest man to hit Serenity this year, Gabe Franklin. What's the scoop with him? He was a couple of years younger than Maddie, Helen and me, but I remember him from years ago. He had quite a reputation as a troublemaker back then. He was nothing at all like Mitch."

Adelia blinked and tried to scramble for an answer that wouldn't reveal much of anything about how Gabe rattled her. She knew instinctively that she shouldn't jump in to defend his past behavior, no matter how great the need. A quick, fierce defense would be far too telling.

"I don't really know much about him," she said evasively, glancing frantically around the room until her gaze landed on Lynn. "Ask her. Gabe is her husband's cousin."

"Which means Gabe doesn't flirt outrageously with her," Maddie said. She glanced at Lynn and grinned. "At least I hope he doesn't."

"Of course he doesn't," Raylene chimed in. "Mitch would kick him out of town if he so much as looked at Lynn." She cast a sympathetic look toward Adelia. "Nope. You're the one he has in his sights. We've all heard the stories."

"Which stories and from whom?" Adelia said, another fiery blush heating her cheeks. Did she have to steer completely clear of the bakery—or maybe even all of Serenity—to put an end to the already rampaging gossip?

"I believe Grace was at Rosalina's on a recent Saturday night when you were there with Elliott and your kids. She says she caught a glimpse of something," Sarah McDonald explained as she joined the group. "She couldn't wait to tell me the next morning. And if she told me, you can bet she told every single customer who walked into Wharton's."

"But nothing happened that night at Rosalina's," Adelia protested, dismayed. "We never even spoke to each other. I didn't meet Gabe till a couple of mornings after that at the bakery."

"Grace thinks of herself as being intuitive about these things," Sarah said. "She says she can spot a budding romance a mile away. Surely having grown up in Serenity, you know that."

"I was probably one of the few kids in town who didn't hang out at Wharton's as a teenager," Adelia explained. "My mother was pretty strict back then. She was worried to death about my sisters and me getting into trouble. She considered a teen hangout to be trouble just waiting to happen."

She grinned as she recalled the lectures about spending time at the local soda fountain. Of course, those lectures had made it sound even more alluring. "Forbidding us to go there was probably a big mistake," she told them. "As it was, I was pretty inexperienced when I met Ernesto in college. Believe me, if I'd dated or hung out at Wharton's the way most other girls in town did, I might not have fallen for him. I might have recognized the sort of macho cheater he turned out to be."

"Ernesto is in the past," Helen declared forcefully, dismissing her ex with a wave of her hand. Then she grinned. "Let's get back to Gabe instead. We've all heard about the kiss." She glanced around as the other women nodded. She used her best interrogator's voice on Adelia. "Care to tell us about that, Ms. Hernandez?"

So this was what friendship was like, Adelia thought, suddenly feeling completely out of her depth.

Being surrounded by women who thought they had the right to ask about her innermost private thoughts was beyond disconcerting. Maybe she'd misjudged the value of the whole friendship thing.

"Careful," Raylene warned Helen. "She's starting to look a little pale. Remember, Adelia's not used to being cross-examined by people she barely knows."

Before Adelia could thank Raylene for trying to intervene, Helen merely smiled and came at her from a different, more subtle direction. At least Adelia assumed Helen considered it more subtle.

"Gabe's definitely a good-looking man," she said casually, then gave Adelia a sly look. "Don't you think so?"

"I wouldn't kick him out of my bed," Dana Sue commented, drawing a shocked look from Helen and Maddie. "Oh, get over it. I'm alive, aren't I? Ronnie's the man for me. Always has been. Always will be. But I can have the occasional fantasy. That's perfectly healthy. And don't either of you dare tell me that you haven't had your share of daydreams about someone other than your husbands."

Helen and Maddie exchanged guilty looks.

"Okay, maybe, from time to time, I fantasize about Brad Pitt," Maddie conceded. "Even if he is way, way out of reach. And even if Cal is the perfect husband."

That drew a few dreamy sighs from around the room. Adelia laughed, finally relaxing. "You all are a little bit crazy," she said, then added apologetically, "If you don't mind me saying so."

Raylene put an arm around her shoulders and gave her a comforting hug. "And now you know our dirty little secret. We are all a little nuts and a little delusional. Have another margarita."

Adelia held out her glass. "I believe I will."

She just hoped the drinks weren't like truth serum. She didn't want to find herself an hour from now spilling her guts about her own unwanted fantasies about Gabe Franklin. Of course, given the speculative looks she'd been receiving, she doubted a single woman in this room would be surprised to hear anything she had to say. They'd probably respond with a fervent "Amen!"

The morning after his night with the guys, Gabe found himself taking a break from the work site at nine-thirty. He swore to himself that he was heading to the bakery at that hour because he hadn't had time to stop there earlier for his usual cup of coffee. He needed a solid caffeine fix.

The fact that he'd chosen the precise time that Adelia tended to get to Chic to open up was purely coincidental. He'd stick to that claim with his dying breath, if need be.

Sure enough as he stepped outside, he saw her at the door to the boutique. She seemed to be fumbling with the key. He frowned as she dropped it, then struggled again to get it in the lock with fingers that were clearly shaking.

Making up his mind, he walked quickly down the block, stepped up behind her and placed his hand over hers. She jumped a good foot in the air, panic on her face.

"Sorry," he said. "It's just me. You looked as if you were having a little trouble with the lock."

Color flooded her cheeks. "I'm a little shaky this morning," she confessed. "I have no idea why. Well, I do know why. It's probably the three margaritas I had last night. Everybody warned me to quit after two, told me they don't call them lethal for nothing." She gave him a shy, almost bewildered look. "They were really good, though."

Gabe bit back a smile. "But you don't drink much."

She frowned. "Are you implying I'm a lightweight who can't hold my liquor?"

He laughed. "Are you?"

She held his gaze with a defiant look, then sighed. "I must be if I can't even unlock a stupid door this morning."

"How's your head?"

"I believe a jackhammer has taken up residence," she admitted.

Gabe pushed open the door to the boutique and handed her the key. "Go on inside and do your thing. I'll be back."

When she seemed about to protest, he held up a hand to cut her off. "I'll be back, Adelia. Leave the door unlocked, okay?"

"Okay," she said, sounding surprisingly meek.

That meek response alone told him just how off-kilter she was feeling.

He headed straight for the bakery and told Lynn, "I need two coffees, both large, one with lots of sugar."

"You drink your coffee black," she said, looking startled.

"It's not for me."

"Then who?" she said, then went perfectly still. "Adelia?"

He nodded. "She's feeling a little under the weather. What the heck did you women do last night? She mentioned three margaritas."

Lynn winced. "I think it was actually four. She might have lost count. That happens."

"Sweet heaven," he said. "I don't imagine they're watered down as the evening goes along."

Lynn looked horrified. "I think Helen would rather give up her entire wardrobe of designer shoes than water down a margarita. Most of us have learned to pace ourselves. And, of course, those of us who are pregnant stick to frozen limeade so we at least look as if we're fitting in. Then we jealously keep count of the drinks the others are consuming."

Gabe thought of what Mitch had told him about these Sweet Magnolia get-togethers. "Not to sound egotistical, but did my name come up last night?"

She chuckled. "Oh yeah."

Gabe groaned. "And you all were on Adelia's case about me and our relationship, that sort of thing?"

"We might have asked a few intrusive questions," Lynn confessed. "All in the spirit of sisterhood, of course. We wanted her to know she has backup." She hesitated, then added, "We might have been a little too inquisitive about any juicy details she might want to share."

No wonder the woman had been downing margaritas like water, Gabe thought. "Maybe you should tell these so-called friends to butt out," he suggested. "Not everyone wants to have their private business hung out like laundry for everyone to see." He gave her a stern look. "And don't you think Adelia might have had more than enough of that with the whole Ernesto fiasco?"

Lynn flushed guiltily. "We didn't think of it like that," she said. "And if you must know, we were all encouraging her to give you another chance. You should be thanking us."

Gabe understood that Lynn at least meant well, but he suspected their efforts had been counterproductive. "Adelia and I are perfectly capable of figuring things out for ourselves."

Lynn leveled a disbelieving look at him. "Are you still seeing each other?"

"No, because—"

She cut him off. "Because you are not capable of figuring things out. She's vulnerable and scared. You're…" She hesitated, then blurted, "Okay, I'll just say it, if you let her go, you're an idiot."

"You don't know what you're talking about," Gabe said.

"Of course I do. I was just as stubborn and stupid about Mitch, that's how I recognize all the signs. And every one of those women there last night has been through something similar. We're experienced with putting up defenses and pretending that we don't need or want some man in our lives. And we don't *need* a man, not a one of us." She held his gaze. "But we'll all tell you now that we're better off for deciding to take a chance."

Gabe sighed at the heartfelt conviction in her voice. "Lynn, I appreciate what you're saying, but could I just have those coffees and maybe a couple of pastries? Whichever ones Adelia likes."

She gave him a long look, but she poured the coffees and put several pastries in a box. "Tell her to call me if she needs anything."

Gabe nodded. "Will do."

"And I don't care what you say, I think it's sweet that you're looking after her."

Gabe frowned. Sweet was the last thing on his mind. He'd taken just one look at the state Adelia was in this morning and felt his heart plummet. No matter how he looked at it, he couldn't help thinking he was responsible for it. If Elliott got wind of this, he was going to punch Gabe's lights out and Gabe wouldn't do a darn thing to try to stop him. A good thrashing was probably just what he deserved.

The simple act of opening the cash register was almost more than Adelia could manage. And the familiar sound the drawer made to signal it was being opened seemed to echo in her head.

This is so wrong, she thought. Women her age should not be suffering from a hangover. They were supposed to have better sense.

The bell over the door rang and she clamped her hands over her ears at the sound and groaned. If this was going to happen every time a customer came in today, she might die. Or at least wish she could.

This, though, was Gabe returning and the look on his face was filled with pity or sympathy. She looked closer and thought she saw just a tiny touch of amusement that he was trying valiantly to hide.

"Head hurt?" he asked lightly.

"You have no idea."

"Here," he said, holding out his hand. "It's just aspirin. That and the caffeine and sugar in the coffee might help."

"I don't like sugar in my coffee. Lynn knows that."

"She made an exception today at my insistence."
He shoved the container a little closer. "Drink up."

Adelia thought about arguing, taking a stance, in
fact, but the thought of caffeine held a little too much
appeal. As did those aspirin he'd set in front of her.
She took those, then a sip of coffee.

"Why are you being so nice to me? We're not even
supposed to be speaking."

"I feel a little responsible," he admitted.

She stared at him incredulously. "Why? You weren't
there shoving margaritas down my throat."

"Might as well have been," he said. "At least the
way I hear it."

She frowned at that. "What did you hear?"

"Lynn says we were a hot topic last night." He held
her gaze. "Adelia, I never meant for you to be in that
position."

He looked so apologetic and dismayed, Adelia
found herself taking pity on him. "Gabe, you don't
know these women. Heck, I don't even know them
that well, but even I could tell that they make a hobby
out of butting in. They're all happily married. We've
just provided them with some new fodder. Sooner or
later some other couple will come along and they'll
meddle in their lives."

"But in the meantime, you shouldn't have to deal
with this. That's what I told Lynn, too."

"You told Lynn that everybody needed to back off?"

"Yep. In no uncertain terms."

Adelia started to laugh, but it hurt, so she settled for
saying, "You're delusional if you think she's going to pay
a bit of attention to you. If anything, she's probably more
convinced than ever that there's something between us."

He looked thoroughly, charmingly confused. "How? Why?"

"Because you immediately leapt to my defense. And because you went over there to get me coffee and pastries and aspirin."

"Why is that a bad thing?" he asked. "And, for the record, I didn't get the aspirin from Lynn. I had them in my car."

She gave him a pitying look. "That is so not the point."

Gabe sighed. "You're going to have to explain this to me. Clearly I, a mere man, am not privy to the way women's minds work."

"What you did for me just now is not a bad thing at all," Adelia explained patiently. "It is, however, exactly the kind of thing that Lynn will report to all the others and they'll sigh happily and conclude that they were exactly right to try to push us straight into each other's arms."

"Are all women this crazy or do these Sweet Magnolias have some kind of a lock on that?" Gabe asked.

Since Adelia had wondered almost the same thing the night before, she shared the conclusion she'd reached. "I think it's these women. They care about their friends. They're intrusive and a little crazy, but they're well-meaning. That makes them more dangerous, I think."

Gabe frowned. "Dangerous? How so?"

"They're all so sweet and normally trustworthy that they make you want to believe them, to make them happy."

"What are you saying? That we ought to take another look at this thing between us?"

She hesitated, because that was exactly what she'd

been thinking by the time she'd left Raylene's the night before. Now in broad daylight with her head pounding, she was having second thoughts. "No, of course not. We decided…"

He held her gaze. "Adelia, do *you* think we made a mistake? Do you want to go back to the way things were? You know, hanging out, just seeing how things develop?"

"What do you think?" she asked, not wanting to crawl out on that shaky limb all by herself.

"I think we made the decision for all the right, sensible reasons," he said.

She fought to hide her disappointment, not just because it was humiliating, but because she didn't want to admit even to herself that she felt so much as a tiny bit of regret. "Yes, of course we did."

He leaned across the counter and tucked a finger under her chin, his eyes locked with hers. "But if we want to change our minds, to maybe reassess, that's up to us, too."

Hope spread through her. "Is that what you want, to reassess?"

He drew in a deep breath, then nodded. "To be honest, this separation hasn't been working as well as I'd hoped it would. If anything, it's just made me think about you more. I can't seem to get you out of my head."

"Me, too," Adelia said softly.

Gabe studied her, then nodded. "Okay then. Dinner tonight?"

She took a deep breath. "Sure, why not. I left another casserole with Selena," she said. "There's plenty for one more."

Gabe shook his head. "Not this time. I think maybe you and I need to go on an actual date, just the two of us."

"Not Rosalina's," she said at once. "There seems to be a direct pipeline from that place to gossip central. And, of course, Wharton's *is* gossip central."

"I've been hearing a lot about Sullivan's since I got back to town," Gabe said. "Everybody says it's the place to go for a nice meal."

"The food's amazing," Adelia confirmed, then thought of the implications of the two of them being seen in the town's best restaurant together on what couldn't possibly be mistaken for anything other than a date. "It'll be like tossing a teaser morsel to a lion, though. Everyone's going to pounce. It might be even worse than Rosalina's."

"But at least we'll have had an excellent meal." He grinned. "Or we can always hope they'll be too busy congratulating each other to bother messing with us."

She thought about it and laughed. Since Dana Sue, who owned the place, would probably have the news of their arrival all over town within seconds, that's probably exactly what they'd be doing.

"Either way," she told him, grinning herself, "I don't think I care."

"That's the spirit."

Of course by the time tomorrow morning rolled around, she might be facing all sorts of regrets. Come to think of it, though, they couldn't be any more uncomfortable than the regrets she'd had this morning after drinking all those margaritas. She glanced at Gabe and allowed herself a brief moment of pure feminine satisfaction. And just look at how well today was turning out.

CHAPTER THIRTEEN

"Mommy, Gabe left again!" Tomas complained when Adelia arrived home from work. "I liked it when he was staying for dinner. I asked him to stay, but he said no."

"Gabe has plans for tonight," Adelia told him.

"What about tomorrow night?" Tomas persisted. "Can he stay then?"

"You'll have to ask him," Adelia said. "Selena, could I speak to you upstairs?"

Her daughter regarded her with suspicion but followed Adelia up to her room. It was still filled with boxes from the move. She'd seen no point in unpacking until her room had been painted. She'd told Gabe to leave it for last, so the kids would start to feel better about their new home by having their rooms decorated just the way they wanted them to be.

"What's going on?" Selena asked her, sitting on the edge of the bed as Adelia opened her closet door and looked at the few outfits she'd pressed and hung up, mostly for work.

"I'm going out for dinner tonight," she announced,

keeping her tone casual. "I won't be late, but do you mind being here alone with your sisters and brother, or would you prefer me to call someone to come over?"

Selena regarded her suspiciously. "Where are you going? You were just out last night."

"I'm having dinner at Sullivan's."

Selena's eyes narrowed even more. "But that's for special occasions," she said slowly, clearly trying to make sense of her mother's unusual behavior. "Is this a special occasion?"

"It's just dinner with a friend," Adelia said evasively.

Selena looked even more skeptical. Then her eyes widened. "You're having dinner with Gabe tonight, that's why he's busy, too. It's a date, isn't it?"

"It's just dinner," Adelia repeated.

"It's a date with Gabe," Selena said again. She didn't seem that unhappy about her conclusion, just puzzled. "I thought you weren't gonna see him anymore, not like that, anyway. I thought that's why he'd made such a big deal about leaving before you got home."

"Well, tonight's an exception," Adelia said, then sat down beside her daughter, clinging to a simple black dress. She met Selena's gaze and sighed. "It's a date. How do you feel about that?"

Selena was silent for a long time. "Do you really need to date somebody?"

Adelia held back a smile at the plaintive question. "I don't have to," she said. "But I do enjoy Gabe's company. It's nice to have another grown-up to talk to."

"You have *Abuela*," Selena said, then sighed. "That's not the same, though, is it?"

"No. Someday you'll understand the difference.

You'll much prefer being out with a boy instead of home with your sisters, brother and me."

"First, I'd have to not be grounded," Selena replied ruefully.

Adelia laughed. "Yes, that would be a requirement." She brushed a strand of hair from her daughter's face. "So, can you accept it if I go on this one date with Gabe?"

"I suppose," Selena said grudgingly, then glanced at the dress Adelia was holding. "But you can't wear that! No way. Mom, you'll look like a nun."

Adelia studied the simple dress and saw her daughter's point. "Maybe that's not such a bad idea."

"No, no, no," Selena protested, jumping up and diving into the closet. "Here," she said, tossing a filmy flowered skirt at Adelia. "And this," she said, adding a low-cut sleeveless top. "You look fantastic in this."

Adelia studied her with increasing surprise. "You sound like you're okay with this, after all."

Selena shrugged. "I told you a while back that I'd decided Gabe wasn't so bad. I guess if you have to go out with a guy, he's okay. I liked it better, though, when you were avoiding each other." She gave Adelia a very grown-up look. "But you weren't happy. Neither was he. It was nice when he made you laugh. You and Dad hadn't laughed in a long time."

"I liked that, too," Adelia confided. "But this is just one date, sweetie. Don't say anything to your sisters or brother. I don't want them to make too much of it. You shouldn't, either."

"I won't ask him if I can call him Daddy, if that's what you're worried about," Selena said.

Adelia regarded her with stunned silence. When she could find her voice, she said, "I certainly hope not."

Selena laughed. "I was just kidding."

Adelia caught the sparkle in her daughter's eyes and realized that maybe she wasn't the only one in the house who was better off with Gabe being in their lives. It seemed he was having much the same effect on Selena, at least when it came to brightening her mood. And that had to be a good thing, worth every one of the butterflies that were currently fluttering crazily in Adelia's stomach.

"What did the kids say when you told them we were having dinner?" Gabe asked when they were settled in a quiet booth at Sullivan's, albeit under Dana Sue's speculative, delighted gaze. She'd been darting out of the kitchen, peering in their direction every few minutes, a cell phone pressed to her ear. There was little doubt every Sweet Magnolia in town knew about this date by now.

"I just said I was having dinner with a friend," Adelia replied. "Selena knows it's you, though."

"And?"

"She approves."

Gabe looked as surprised as she'd been. "Really?" he said.

"Don't count it as a ringing endorsement," Adelia warned. "She doesn't actually want me to date at all, but if I have to go out with someone, she seems okay with it being you. It was a nice change of heart on her part. It was especially nice to have her teasing me rather than berating me."

"But you're still worried about how the others will

react," he guessed. "That's why you insisted on meeting me here instead of letting me pick you up. You didn't want Tomas, Natalia and Juanita getting any ideas."

Adelia nodded. "I still believe we need to be very cautious, at least until we know how this is going to go. You should know, though, that Tomas intends to ask you to stay for dinner again tomorrow."

Gabe studied her. "What should I tell him?"

"That's up to you."

He held her gaze. "Not entirely. What do you want me to tell him?"

Flustered under his penetrating look, she could barely manage a whisper. "That you'll stay."

A smile spread across his face. "Okay, then. And, Adelia, we need to be clear about one thing."

"What's that?" she asked, worried about his suddenly serious tone.

"When it comes to how much time I spend with your kids or what we tell them, you're in charge. I don't want to mess with their heads any more than you want me to."

"You're good for them," she admitted. "You treat them like real people. I can see them blossoming under all that attention, Tomas especially. I don't want to take that away from them. I just don't want them to get too far ahead of themselves when it comes to us. I don't want them to be hurt."

Gabe nodded. "It's a fine line," he agreed. "But we'll figure it out." He reached under the table, laced his fingers with hers and gave her hand a squeeze. "Could we focus on us now?"

She shivered under the intensity of his gaze. "I guess so," she said, not sounding very certain.

He smiled. "You're not used to having the attention focused on you, are you?"

She shook her head. "Not like this."

"Did you and Ernesto ever have date nights?" he asked.

Adelia knew that was something a lot of married couples did. It was a way to solidify their relationship and keep the romance alive without all the demands of being parents, at least for an evening. She knew it was something Elliott and Karen credited with getting their marriage back on track after a rough patch. She'd suggested it once to Ernesto and he'd looked at her as if she were nuts.

She shook her head. "Never."

"Why not?"

"He didn't see the point," she said, then shrugged. "I suppose he figured he'd already paid for the rings and the fancy house. Why bother courting me?" She winced at the bitterness in her voice. "Sorry."

Gabe frowned. "Why are you apologizing? The man should have been down on his knees every night thanking you for making a nice home and taking such great care of his kids."

"He was too busy chasing other women to bother with that."

Her reply seemed to anger Gabe.

"You do know that reflects badly on him, not you, right?" Gabe said. "I may not think I'm a good candidate for marriage, but I do know that a husband should treat his wife with more respect than that. He shouldn't be taking her for granted."

"Maybe it was me," she ventured, voicing the fear that she still hadn't totally overcome.

Now there was no mistaking the heat in Gabe's eyes. "Absolutely not," he told her.

"You don't know. You didn't know me then. I've gotten myself together in the past year or so."

"Meaning what?"

"I did what I thought Ernesto wanted. I went to the spa and lost weight. I tried to compete with those other women."

"You shouldn't have had to compete with anyone," Gabe told her. "And in a matchup with any woman who'd get involved with a married father of four, you'd come out way, way ahead in all the areas that matter."

He said it with such conviction that Adelia sat a little taller. "You really mean that, don't you?"

"I really mean it," he said quietly. "And if you doubt me, let me tell you that everyone I've met since I got back to town feels the same way. If your name comes up, it's always said with respect. Don't let one idiot make you question yourself."

"Even if that one idiot was my husband, who knew me better than anyone?" she said wryly.

"Not even then. It just shows what poor judgment he has."

He'd just carved another big chunk out of her wall of defenses. "You know something, Gabe Franklin?" she said lightly.

"What?"

"The kids aren't the only ones you're good for."

Now it was his turn to blush. "Just calling it like I see it," he said. Then, clearly flustered, he opened the menu. "Maybe we should order. Any suggestions?"

His sudden nervousness actually served to calm her own nerves. "Everything I've ever had here is great," Adelia said, more than willing to go along with the change in topic. "The meat loaf is a specialty. So is the fried catfish."

Gabe's expression turned nostalgic. "My mom used to make meat loaf. It was terrible, but it was the one thing she thought she could cook, so she made it for special occasions."

"Well, Dana Sue's version takes it to a whole new level," Adelia told him.

"Then I think I'll have that, for old times' sake."

Adelia studied him closely. "There were good times with your mom, weren't there? Mostly you make it sound as if it was all bad."

For a moment, she thought he might not answer. He looked as if he'd gone someplace far away, or more likely just back in time.

"There were good times," he said eventually. "Christmas, my birthday. Those were the occasions when she tried to do something special. Of course, at Christmas she went crazy with decorations and a big meal, not because the holiday meant much to her, but to take her mind off the fact that whatever man was in her life was home with his own family that day."

Adelia winced at the stark pain in his voice. "I'm sorry things weren't better for you."

"Hey, I survived it, didn't I? I just wish her life had been better, but I was way too young to know how to help."

"That didn't stop you from trying, though. Remember that."

"I went about it in all the wrong ways," he said. "At

least that's what a lot of people in town would have said back then, including my aunts and uncles and grandparents. They just lumped me in with her and considered us both a lost cause."

"Mitch, too?" she asked, shocked.

"Mitch was just a kid himself. I don't blame him or any of the other cousins. He's more than made up for it now by giving me a fresh start."

Dana Sue arrived at the table just then, clearly in search of hot new information to impart. "Have you all ordered yet?" she asked, studying them with amusement. "Or have you been too engrossed with each other?"

Ronnie Sullivan appeared at her side almost immediately and tucked his wife's arm through his. "Leave them alone," he told her firmly.

"I'm just checking on my customers," Dana Sue protested, though she flushed guiltily.

"No, you're being nosy," Ronnie said, giving them an apologetic look. "Sorry. She can't help herself."

Gabe chuckled. "Maybe you can send over our waitress," he suggested.

"Now there's a thought," Ronnie said. "Darlin', as the owner of this fine establishment, why didn't you think of that? Go get their waitress, then get back in the kitchen and make something delicious."

Dana Sue gave Ronnie a mock scowl, then kissed his cheek. "You stay and ask questions," she suggested.

Ronnie looked after her with tolerant amusement, then called out, "Nobody's asking questions." He winked at Gabe and Adelia. "You should be safe for an hour or so, but I'd suggest you get dessert to go. I'm not sure how long I can keep her in the kitchen. I'm sure she's back there texting half the town right now, even though she has very little to report."

Adelia chuckled. "Thanks for the tip."

"Maybe we should get the whole meal to go," Gabe said.

Ronnie shook his head at once. "And have the whole town speculating about where you went to eat it?"

"They would, too," Adelia confirmed with a resigned sigh.

"Then let's just wolf down our meal and take off," Gabe said.

"Wolf down one of Dana Sue's meals?" Adelia asked. "That's practically sacrilegious."

"She's right," Ronnie said. "The only thing worse than keeping my wife in the dark about your relationship would be insulting her food."

Gabe shook his head. "Who knew that eating out in Serenity could get this complicated?" He turned to Adelia. "Next time we're going to Charleston."

Ronnie chuckled, but one look into Gabe's eyes told Adelia he was 100 percent serious. Since the thought of a night on the town in Charleston sent a shiver of anticipation straight down Adelia's spine, she didn't find anything even moderately amusing about the prospect.

"You went awfully quiet when I mentioned going to Charleston," Gabe said to Adelia after they'd savored every bite of their dinner and even shared a dessert.

"It's a long way to go just to have dinner," Adelia said carefully.

"Might be worth it, though, to avoid all these prying eyes in Serenity."

She gave him a long look. "And it would just be about dinner?"

He regarded her with confusion. "That's what I said, isn't it?" Understanding dawned. "Oh, I see. You thought I meant, well, something more than dinner."

"Like I said, it's a long drive for a meal."

"Adelia, I honestly wasn't suggesting we go off for some intimate overnight rendezvous." He studied her. "Or am I getting this all wrong? Were you hoping that was exactly what I was suggesting?"

She blushed furiously. "Don't mind me. I don't know what I was thinking. You made the suggestion and I guess I let my imagination run wild."

He smiled at that. "Well, I'm certainly open to negotiation. I didn't think you were ready for anything more than dinner."

"I'm not," she said firmly. "At least I don't think I am."

"But you're tempted."

She didn't meet his gaze but gave an almost imperceptible nod. "I might be tempted," she conceded, then buried her face in her hands. "What is wrong with me? Just a few days ago I was telling you we should stop seeing each other and now here I am practically throwing myself at you."

"I don't mind," he said. "You're not saying a thing I haven't fantasized about myself."

She glanced up. "You have?"

"Of course. I'm not sure we wouldn't be jumping into something we're not ready for, but I've thought about making love to you about a million times since the first night I saw you at Rosalina's."

A tiny self-satisfied smile tugged at her lips. "About a million times, huh?"

"At least."

Her smile spread. "Good to know. Maybe that'll hold me for now."

"So no secret overnights to Charleston?" he asked, not even trying to hide his disappointment.

"Not just yet," she said, though she sounded even more intrigued by the possibility.

Even though he doubted he'd be able to get the idea out of his head so he could sleep tonight, Gabe was glad she'd gone there. She'd taken a tiny step out of her shell by admitting that the thought of sleeping with him had crossed her mind. Actually doing it might take a little longer, but anticipation was going to be half the fun.

Adelia was surprised to find her mother waiting for her in front of the boutique when she arrived the morning after her dinner with Gabe.

"Mama, what are you doing here so early?" she asked as she led the way inside. "Do you have a wardrobe emergency?"

Her mother gave her an as-if look. "I came to see you, since I can't seem to catch up with you in the evening. You dropped the kids off the other night and took off before I could ask you a single question."

Adelia smiled. "Did you ever think that maybe that was on purpose?"

"Of course it was. I know how skilled you are at evading my questions. I tried again last night, but when I called the house, Selena said you were out. Then I heard from my friend that you were with a handsome man at Sullivan's. Were you on a date?"

Adelia sighed. It had been too much to hope that her mother would be far removed from the gossip loop. "I was."

"With that Gabe Franklin person?"

"You say that as if you'd never laid eyes on him or as if you disapproved of him," Adelia said. "Have you suddenly changed your mind? You seemed to like him well enough when he stayed for dinner and you got to cross-examine him to your heart's content."

"That was before," her mother said.

"Before what?"

"Before I thought you were going to jump into something with both feet and parade your indiscretions around town the way Ernesto did."

Adelia froze at her words. "Excuse me? You did not just compare what I'm doing with what Ernesto did."

At the scathing, furious note in her voice, her mother backtracked at once. "Of course it's not like that. I just mean that it's awfully soon after your divorce to be seen all over town with someone. People might make too much of it."

"People? Or is this Carolina again? She's already told me that she thinks I'm making a public spectacle of myself. And Joey said the same thing to Selena."

That last had the desired effect. Shock registered in her mother's eyes. "Joey said something like that to your daughter?"

Adelia nodded. "Clearly he's under his mother's influence."

"I'll speak to Carolina and to Joey," her mother said with grim determination. "It won't happen again."

"Mama, you can't control them. Let it go. I've dealt with them. I just don't like hearing the same sort of judgmental comments from you. I thought we'd established a different relationship the past few months."

Her mother sighed. "I'm just worried."

"About me? I can take care of myself."

"I'm not so sure that you can after years of letting Ernesto erode your self-confidence, but actually I'm more worried about your children. They can't stop talking about Gabe."

Now it was Adelia's turn to sigh. "I know. I worry about that, too. That's why Gabe and I decided to take a break."

"And dinner last night was part of this so-called break?"

Adelia smiled at her mother's incredulous expression. "Not exactly. We had second thoughts and decided to keep seeing each other. We're taking it slowly, though, because of the kids. Neither of us wants them to get the wrong idea."

"The wrong idea being that you might have a future with this man?"

Adelia nodded.

"That's a big risk," her mother warned. "And this time I'm not talking about my grandchildren. Are you ready to take such a risk?"

Adelia thought of the way Gabe made her feel. "Apparently I am," she said softly. "I enjoy being with him, Mama. He makes me feel special."

Her mother's expression softened at that. "You deserve that. You *are* special, and I am so sorry that Ernesto caused you to think otherwise for even a single minute."

"Me, too," Adelia responded. "I'm not deluding my-self that this is going to lead to some big thing, but it's right for me now."

"Then I'll focus my prayers on that," her mother said. "That Gabe will be exactly what you need in your life right now."

Adelia understood what a concession that was for her rigidly moral mother. "Thank you, Mama."

"Of course, I might also say a prayer or two that he'll be wise enough to make an honest woman of you."

Adelia laughed and gave her mother a fierce hug. "Of course you will. Thank you for that, too."

"Perhaps he'll join us for Sunday dinner one of these days," she suggested slyly.

Adelia choked at that. "No way," she said. "We are definitely not ready for that."

Her mother shrugged. "In time then. I only want what's best for you, for all my children. Sometimes I credit myself with knowing what that is, but the truth is each of you must decide for yourself. I'm adjusting to that concept."

"Keep trying, Mama. I think you're pretty darn close to getting it exactly right."

Her mother looked pleased by that. "Now I'll leave you to your work."

"Not without looking at these new sweaters that just came in," Adelia told her, leading her to the display. "Feel how soft they are. Pure cashmere."

Her mother put a tentative hand on the sweater, then stroked it gently. "It is soft."

"And look at this red one," Adelia encouraged her. "It's your favorite color."

Her mother looked at her, amusement dancing in her eyes. "Now I see why everyone says you have a magic touch as a saleswoman. I'll take it, even though it's far too indulgent."

"I'll give you my discount," Adelia told her, already heading for the register.

"It's still an indulgence, but given the joy I'll get wearing it, it will be worth it." She touched Adelia's cheek. "And seeing the color here, that makes me even happier."

Adelia watched her mother leave, then realized a tear was rolling down her cheek. No matter how grown-up and independent she thought she was, receiving her mother's unequivocal approval was an unexpected blessing.

CHAPTER FOURTEEN

Gabe was grabbing a burger at Wharton's when he overheard one of the men in the booth behind him mention Mitch's name. He wasn't in the habit of eavesdropping on conversations, but he couldn't help it since the tone of the remark had been derogatory. He put his burger down. Though he didn't turn around, he did tune in.

"Well, I'm not buying it," another man responded. "Mitch Franklin is one of the most honorable men in this town. He'd never cheat a customer. And look at what he's doing for downtown. Main Street's going to be revitalized once he's through with the renovations. It's already showing more signs of life than it's shown in years."

"You can thank Ronnie Sullivan for that," the other man said. "He bought that old hardware store and got things started."

"And Raylene Rollins opened her boutique not long after that," a third voice added.

"But she and Mitch bought up all those other neglected properties and are fixing them up," Mitch's defender argued. "We're already hearing from a few businesses that are interested in locating downtown."

By now Gabe had recognized that the man who was standing up for his cousin was Howard Lewis, the mayor, one of the town's biggest boosters and a proponent of improving the economy of Serenity. After a glance over his shoulder Gabe still couldn't put a name to the other two.

"If you ask me, whoever's been spreading those lies has an ax to grind with Mitch," Howard said. "I'd say it was Ed Morrow, but I thought he'd learned his lesson when he tried it before and most of the town sided with Lynn and Mitch."

"I can't name my source, but it wasn't Ed," the first man revealed.

"That leaves Ernesto Hernandez then," Howard said, his voice filled with disgust.

"Makes sense," the more neutral of the other men said. "I did hear that Mitch tore up the contract he had to do some renovations for Ernesto. I imagine Hernandez didn't like that one bit. This sure sounds like payback. Walter, you should know better than to listen to anyone like that."

"I'm not confirming that my source was Hernandez, but it sounded like he had the facts to back up what he was saying," Walter said defiantly. "I believe him. I think somebody ought to take a long, hard look at what Franklin's up to on Main Street. And we all remember that cousin of his, Gabe. The kid was nothing but trouble, and now he's back here and in the thick of that whole scam."

"Walter!" Howard said, casting a warning glance

at him. Clearly he'd caught sight of Gabe in the next booth.

Walter, however, didn't take the hint. "Who knows how many shortcuts they're taking with building materials and such?" he continued. "The whole dang thing could fall down a year from now."

That brought Gabe out of his seat. Temper barely leashed, he moved swiftly to stand beside their table. He put his hands down and leaned in. First he directed a look at Howard. "Mr. Mayor. Nice to see you," he said pleasantly.

Howard looked even more uncomfortable. "Son, no need to get worked up," he told Gabe, clearly hoping to avoid a scene, no matter how justified he might think Gabe was in causing one. "Walter here didn't mean anything by what he was saying. And you must have heard me tell him he was way off base."

"I did hear what you said, and I appreciate that," Gabe replied, then turned his attention to the man who'd just been identified as Walter. "But this gentlemen just suggested my cousin and I might be doing something illegal by skirting around regulations or using questionable materials." He looked the man in the eye. "That is what you were saying, isn't it?"

"It's what I heard," he said, his face bright red now.

Gabe gave him an incredulous look. "And you heard this from a man who cheated on his wife and then tried to hire my cousin to renovate his mistress's house, correct? Did he mention he kept asking for changes and upgrades, then wanted Mitch to shave his costs down to nothing? That's the kind of man you find believable? What do you suppose that says about you?"

Walter clearly wasn't ready to give up yet. "He said

he had proof," he countered, a triumphant note in his voice.

"Did you see any? Because if you did, it was phony. Mitch doesn't cut corners. Neither do I. And if I find out you're spreading those lies, I'll encourage Mitch to sue you for slander." He gave him a hard look. "But first I might forget that I'm no longer the town trouble-maker and deal with you myself."

"Your gripe's with Hernandez, not me," Walter responded, though he looked shaken by the threat of a lawsuit or worse, just as Gabe had intended.

"Oh, believe me, I'll deal with him," Gabe said readily. "But you're the one doing his dirty work by spreading it all over town, so right now I'm concentrating on you. Are we clear?"

"He won't be saying another word about this," Howard promised. "I'll see to it."

"I can speak for myself," Walter said belligerently.

"Then do it," Howard said. "Or I'll encourage Mitch to sue you myself. I'm not sure I'll even bother with discouraging Gabe from getting even, either."

The two men locked gazes, but it was Walter who blinked first. "Not another word," he said grudgingly.

Though Gabe didn't entirely buy that this would be the end of it, he gave a nod of satisfaction, then turned to Howard. "Thanks for backing me up and for defending Mitch."

"No problem," Howard said, clearly relieved to have the matter settled without a single punch being thrown. "And just so you know, this project of Mitch's has my full support. The town manager's, too. Main Street's already looking better than I ever imagined it could."

"It'll look even better when we're done," Gabe said, appreciative of the vote of confidence.

His appetite gone, he tossed some bills on his own table and left without touching the rest of his burger. Mitch needed to hear about this, but maybe not till after Gabe could have a few words with Ernesto Hernandez.

The carpet in Ernesto's fancy suite of offices was a light beige. Coming into the suite from a sudden downpour that had left him soaked, Gabe took a certain amount of delight in tracking mud across that pristine carpet as he headed for Ernesto's office. He waved off the secretary who jumped up and tried to block his path.

"This won't take long," Gabe told her, pushing open the office door without bothering to knock.

Ernesto had removed his jacket, but that was his only concession to being all alone in his office. He was in another one of those stiff fancy shirts, a silk tie knotted at his throat. Gabe harbored a strong desire to tighten that knot until it made the man squirm. Instead, he took a seat across from Ernesto, settling in as if he had all the time in the world. He couldn't help hoping that his rain-soaked clothes would ruin the fancy upholstery.

"How're you doing, Ernesto?" he inquired casually.

Ernesto's eyes narrowed. His secretary hovered uncertainly in the doorway. Apparently aware that anything Gabe was likely to say wouldn't be anything he'd want the woman to hear, Ernesto waved her off.

"It's okay. I'll handle this," he said tightly. "Close the door."

"Are you sure?" she asked worriedly.

Ernesto nodded, his gaze never leaving Gabe. "Okay, what do you want?" he demanded when they were alone.

"I want you to stop spreading lies about Mitch," Gabe said, his voice quiet but unyielding.

"No idea what you're talking about."

"Yet another lie," Gabe said. "But I can refresh your memory if you like. You've been telling people that he's cutting corners, using faulty materials."

Ernesto shrugged. "I might have mentioned to a couple of friends that I had my suspicions about the quality of his work. If that happened to get around town, that's on them."

Gabe stood up, then leaned down until he was just inches from Ernesto's face. Adding this latest offense to everything Ernesto had done to Adelia made him want desperately to plant his fist squarely in Ernesto's smug face. Only the thought of Adelia's reaction and the reminder that this man was the father of her children kept him from acting on the impulse.

"First of all, I think I can safely say that you have no friends in this town, not after what you did to Adelia and your kids. Second, the instant those deliberate lies came out of your mouth, you were guilty of slander. The law has reasonably stiff penalties for that. I think my next stop will be Helen Decatur-Whitney's office to check into just how long you might rot in jail if we pursue charges."

For the first time a tiny hint of panic flickered in Ernesto's eyes. "Who's going to believe a man who was in trouble with the law as much as you were in this town?" he said with pure bravado.

Gabe allowed himself a faint smile. "There's not

a thing on my record but a string of warnings about fighting back against some bullies who were talking about my mom. I may have mishandled things back then, but I was standing up for someone I care about, the same way I'm doing right now. And if you know anything at all about those incidents, you probably also know that I know how to use my fists when I'm worked up. Right this second, I'm getting pretty worked up."

"Are you threatening me?"

"I suppose you could test me and find out for sure," Gabe said.

Suddenly a smirk settled on Ernesto's face. "I wonder how much time you'll be spending around my ex-wife and my kids once a judge hears about this. Two can play at this game."

Having Adelia and the kids dragged into this fight nearly got the best of Gabe. He wanted desperately to wipe that smug look off Ernesto's face, but once again he restrained himself. He knew nothing good would come of it.

"I thought that might shut you up," Ernesto said, obviously pleased with himself.

"It is only out of respect for Adelia that I'm not wiping the floor with you right this second," Gabe told him. "But don't push me too far, Ernesto. And stop with the mudslinging about Mitch. If I hear one more word that's attributed to you, we'll both see you in court."

He walked out of the office without looking back, aware that the secretary went rushing in, probably to make sure her boss was still in one piece.

He was just exiting the building when a patrol car

pulled up out front. Carter Rollins gestured for him to come over, then nodded in the direction of the building.

"Everything okay in there?"

"Ernesto's pretty face is untouched, if that's what you're asking."

"Too bad," Carter muttered, then regarded him sternly. "You did not just hear those words come out of my mouth."

Gabe bit back a grin. "Never heard a thing. I imagine I can thank his secretary for alerting you that trouble was on the horizon."

"She said you'd stormed in without an appointment and she'd heard raised voices. I decided given the complicated dynamics of the situation, I'd better check it out myself."

Gabe's expression sobered. "I threatened him," he told Carter.

"I do not need to hear that," the Serenity police chief said.

"Yes, you do. You also need to understand why." He explained about the campaign Ernesto had been waging to undermine Mitch's reputation. "My next stop is Helen's office. I want her to be aware of this, too. I don't know that Mitch will want to take action, but I need to know what the options are." He nodded toward the building. "And just so you know the whole ugly story, since he wasn't real happy with me, Ernesto threatened to find a way to keep me away from Adelia and his kids."

Carter groaned. "Gabe, I know you're in the right here, especially since you gave him a warning and didn't lay a hand on him, but watch yourself. I wouldn't put anything past him. Ernesto may not have many supporters around here, but the courts have to be above that. If a judge sees you as a threat, he'll have no choice but to order you to steer clear of the kids. He probably can't do the same when it comes to Adelia, but you know what it would do to her. If she's forced to make a choice, you'll lose."

Gabe sighed. "I know that. I'm just praying it won't get to that point."

"Warn her, okay? Ernesto's unpredictable and he's angry. You don't want Adelia to be blindsided by any of this."

"Got it," Gabe said. "Thanks, Carter."

"I'll have your back as long as you don't cross any lines. Understood?"

Gabe nodded. "Understood."

For the first time ever in this town, he felt as if he wasn't totally alone when it came to standing up to a bully. And when it came right down to it, that's what Ernesto was, nothing more than a grown-up version of the sort of thugs Gabe had seen far too much of as a kid.

Gabe's conversations with Helen and with Mitch to fill them in went reasonably well. Helen was ready to start legal proceedings right away, but Gabe told her to hold off, that it was Mitch's call whether he wanted to go that route.

To his surprise, Mitch laughed off Ernesto's underhanded campaign against him. "Gabe, people in this town know me. He's not going to be able to say a thing that will hurt my reputation. All I have to do is say, 'Consider the source.'"

Gabe thought he was being naive. "That kind of talk is insidious. Once he plants the idea that you do shoddy work, if a single shingle falls off a roof anywhere in town, people will start to wonder."

Mitch's expression sobered at that. "Okay, you may be right. It is dangerous to let his lies circulate without fighting back, but a lawsuit might be overkill. I'll just have Helen send some kind of cease and desist letter just to let him know that I'm taking the matter seriously. That ought to put him on notice to shut his mouth." He held Gabe's gaze. "Will that suit you?"

Gabe nodded. "I just saw red when I overheard Walter in Wharton's. Who knows how many other people heard him?"

"They also heard the mayor standing up for me. And you," Mitch reminded him. He smiled. "Thanks for that, by the way. As for Howard, he's respected in this town. He's been reelected time and again. He may be a figurehead for all intents and purposes, but his faith in my work will carry a lot of weight."

"I suppose."

"I'm not worried," Mitch insisted. "You need to let it go for now. Take off and go over to Adelia's. You need to fill her in sooner rather than later."

Because he knew both Mitch and Carter were right, Gabe agreed. "I'll make up for all the time I missed this afternoon," he promised.

"Not to worry," Mitch said. "You were on company business." To Gabe's shock, Mitch pulled him into a bear hug. "Thanks for standing up for me, Gabe."

"Hey, it's what family does."

"I didn't, not back when you needed someone on your side," Mitch said.

"We agreed that's in the past," Gabe told him.

At Adelia's a few minutes later, he found Tomas sitting glumly in the middle of his bedroom, awaiting Gabe's arrival. He glanced up when Gabe walked in.

"Hey, buddy," Gabe greeted him. "Something wrong?"

"You're late. I thought you weren't coming."

"I told you I'd be here, didn't I?" Gabe said, sitting on the floor beside him. "I'll always keep my word."

"Like I believe that," Tomas said. "Nobody does."

Gabe had a sick feeling he was being tarred for someone else's neglect. He had a pretty good idea who that might be.

"Somebody let you down?" he asked. "Besides me, that is?"

"My dad said he was going to get me today and play catch with me in the park."

"He didn't show up?"

Tomas shook his head, fighting tears. "I called him when he wasn't here when he said he would be. He said he didn't have time, that he had a lot of important work to do. It's what he always says," Tomas said in a resigned tone.

Gabe muttered a harsh curse in his head but refrained from saying a word against Ernesto aloud. "I'm sure he does have a pretty busy schedule at work," he suggested instead.

Tomas brushed impatiently at the tears on his cheeks. "He's not at work. I called there first. He's with that lady, the one he picked over Mom. I heard her telling him to hurry up and get off the phone."

"I'm sorry," Gabe said, unable to think of a single

comforting thing he could possibly say, much less any defense he could offer for Ernesto's behavior.

"It's not like it's the first time," Tomas said. "I should be used to it, huh?"

His plaintive words took Gabe straight back to his own childhood when he'd struggled time and again to prepare himself to be let down by his mom.

"It's not the kind of thing you should have to get used to," he told Tomas honestly. "But the truth is that sometimes adults make choices kids don't understand. It is hard, but one of the important lessons of life we need to learn is that we have to find some way to accept that people we love have flaws. It takes a real grown-up to understand that. Do you think you can try? Personally I think you're pretty mature for a kid your age."

Tomas sat a little taller. "I can try," he said.

"Good for you. Now, are you going to help me get this room painted?"

For the first time the boy's eyes lit up. "I get to help?"

Gabe wasn't sure how much help Tomas would be, but he nodded. "Put on some really old clothes, so you don't ruin what you're wearing, and you can help," he confirmed. "And later on, if it's okay with your mom, I'll take you to the park and we can play catch."

"Cool," Tomas said, racing over to dig through a box of things still packed from the move. "Mom says these are ready to be turned into dust cloths," he said, holding up a pair of shorts that looked practically threadbare and a faded T-shirt.

"Those look perfect to me," Gabe said.

When Tomas ran off to the bathroom to change,

Gabe drew in a deep breath. As sleazy as Gabe thought Ernesto was, he still couldn't grasp how he could so easily dismiss the needs of a great kid like his son. Gabe might not be the best person to make up for a dad's attention, but he sure as heck intended to try.

Adelia waited until dinner was over, Gabe and Tomas had returned from their game of catch and all the kids had gone upstairs to bed before she walked across the kitchen to Gabe and kissed him firmly on the lips. Shock and a quick flash of desire lit his eyes.

"What was that about?" he asked, his expression incredulous.

"To thank you for the way you handled Tomas earlier this afternoon."

"You were here? I thought you were still at work."

"I would have been, but Selena called me and told me what Ernesto had pulled and that Tomas was really upset. By the time Raylene could get in to cover for me and I got home, you were with him."

"Why didn't you say something?"

"Because you were already saying all the right things," she told him. "And, to be honest, it made me cry."

Gabe looked dismayed. "I made you cry?"

"You were so sweet, exactly the kind of man my son should have as a father. Instead, he has this thoughtless, careless jerk in his life, a man who will always put his own needs ahead of his son's."

Gabe seemed uncomfortable with her praise. "You might not feel that way when you've heard about what I've been up to today," he suggested direly.

"Gabe, you put a smile back on my son's face and

made him feel as if he matters. You took him to the park for a game of catch, when I know you must be beat. I can't think of a thing you could tell me that would negate that."

"Don't be so sure," he said and described what had apparently been quite the confrontation with Ernesto.

Adelia heard him out. "Of course you had to stand up for Mitch," she said.

"That's not all of it, though."

She stood silently as he described Ernesto's reaction.

"He threatened to go to court to keep me away from you and the kids," he concluded.

Adelia laughed. "It's all bluster," she said. "He wouldn't dare set foot in that courtroom again. The judge wasn't any happier than Helen that I let him off as easily as I did when we divorced. He's not going to listen to anything Ernesto has to say, especially when it comes to throwing mud on someone who's been as great with my kids as you've been. Don't you get it, Gabe? You're everything that Ernesto's not. That's why he's so upset."

"He could complicate things for us," Gabe countered.

"Not a chance," Adelia insisted. "You don't know him like I do. It took me a very long time, but I finally realized that despite the way he behaved when it came to honoring our wedding vows, Ernesto craves respect. He liked the image he presented of being this terrific family man with a big house and four kids who excelled in school and a wife who was involved in all sorts of community activities. He didn't give two hoots about us, but he did like what it said about him. We mattered to him just a tiny bit more than his designer suits and his Rolex watch."

"But the whole blasted town knows now that it was a lie, that your kids are great because of you, that you were the person to be admired."

Adelia didn't even try to deny it. In fact, the knowledge satisfied her need to feel a sense of pride in the way she'd lived her life despite Ernesto's philandering. "But he's not going to want to have any of that mud slung in his face again. He won't risk it by attacking you."

"He's already attacking Mitch," Gabe countered.

"Not the same thing, at least as he sees it. That's all about business. This would be personal, and he wouldn't come out smelling like a rose. More like a pile of manure."

Gabe regarded her with surprise, then shook his head and chuckled. "You really do see him clearly now, don't you?"

"If I didn't, shame on me," she said, then cautioned, "That doesn't mean I want my kids disillusioned about him, at least not until they figure out what he's all about on their own. I think Tomas made that discovery today." Sadness settled over her. "His awakening came a little sooner than I might have liked, though."

"I'm sorry if I contributed to that," Gabe apologized.

"Don't go there. I meant what I said before. You said all the right things. You put a smile back on his face." She grinned then. "How'd the painting go, by the way?"

He gave her a rueful look. "The painting went great," he claimed. "The cleanup, not so much."

"So you're saying my son probably doesn't have a career as a housepainter in store."

"Not unless someone's after a decor that looks as if it was painted by Jackson Pollock. Tomas can splatter with the great modern artists of all time."

"Maybe I'll get him some canvases and some washable paints for his birthday and nudge him in that direction," she said, laughing. "Though personally I prefer to know what I'm looking at when I see a painting."

"Oh, you will when you see his," Gabe said. "Chaos."

She let her gaze linger on his face. "You just did it again," she said.

"What?"

"Put a smile on someone's face after a difficult day. Thank you for that."

He ran his thumb over her lips, lingered at the up-turned corner of her mouth. "Glad to help. I wonder if I can do the same thing without words."

Even before he lowered his mouth to claim hers, Adelia murmured, "I'll bet you can."

In fact, just as she'd anticipated, Gabe turned out to be very good at silent communication, too.

CHAPTER FIFTEEN

Because it was a family tradition and because her children begged to go, at least the younger ones, Adelia agreed to return to her mother's for Sunday dinner that week. Even so, when she arrived, she wasn't anxious to face all the judgmental looks from her sisters and their husbands. Instead, she urged the kids toward the backyard, where their cousins were already playing.

Karen, who'd never been comfortable—or, to be honest, welcomed—in the kitchen with the other women, was sitting on the patio with the baby in her arms. Elliott, as usual, was in the thick of the games the kids were devising. Adelia sat beside her sister-in-law, then nodded toward her brother.

"He really is just a big kid himself, isn't he?" she said, amused.

Karen laughed. "I know that's why Daisy and Mack loved him from the instant they met him. It takes a man with real confidence to risk looking silly." Karen turned her gaze on Adelia. "You must feel the same way about Gabe. I saw the picture from the tea party."

Adelia laughed. "That picture is destined to haunt him forever."

Karen studied her worriedly. "Adelia, are you deliberately hiding out from your mother and sisters?"

"How'd you guess?"

"I recognize the signs," Karen said. "I tend to avoid the house and head straight back here. It gives me time to prepare for all that Cruz togetherness."

"It's not the togetherness that bothers me," Adelia confided. "It's the way my sisters and their husbands still look at me as if I'd committed a sin. I'm tired of defending my actions to them."

"Welcome to my world," Karen replied lightly.

"Why do you keep coming back?" Adelia asked, genuinely wanting to know. She was well aware that for months she'd been part of the problem, no more understanding with Karen than her sisters were being with her now.

"For Elliott's sake, of course. And I want my children to be part of this family. I have no issues with your mom. Not anymore, anyway. And I can tolerate the judgment and unwelcoming looks from the rest of them. They'll either come around to give me a chance as you and your mother have, or they won't." She shrugged. "I can't control that. I've given up trying to. As long as there's nothing overt said that might hurt my family, I can deal with whatever they might direct at me."

Adelia regarded her with deepening respect. "I hope I get to that point. As disappointed as I am in them, I'd still like us to be as close as we once were."

"I can understand that," Karen said. "It's different for you. You've had a lifetime of being close to your mother and sisters. It has to be incredibly hard to feel they've turned on you."

Once again, Adelia thought, Karen had surprised her. "That's exactly right," she admitted. "It feels as if I don't even know the people I've loved and trusted my whole life. Or as if they don't know me. Either way, I feel uncomfortable in the house I grew up in. It's hard, too, seeing Mama caught in the middle. She's doing her best to be supportive of my decisions, but I don't think she can quite bring herself to call Carolina and Maria to task, because on some level she agrees with them."

"Same with me," Karen said. Her expression brightened. "But we have Elliott and we have each other, at least if you want my backing."

Adelia reached over and squeezed her hand. "I count on it," she said, realizing it was true. "Now, hand over my nephew. I need to hold a sweet, innocent baby and forget all about this complicated family drama."

Karen shifted the baby to her. He whimpered but then settled trustingly in Adelia's arms. "I've missed this," Adelia whispered, eyes closed as she drew in the baby powder scent and felt the weight of the child in her arms. She'd never really aspired to be anything more than a great mom. While she was discovering that she had strong business skills, her real passion was her family.

"It's not too late to have another one," Karen said, regarding her with amusement.

"Are you nuts?" Adelia asked, her eyes snapping open. She handed the baby back as if pregnancy could be brought on by the power of suggestion. "I have four children already and no man in my life."

Karen grinned. "That sure wasn't the way it sounded

at margarita night. By the time you left Raylene's, I thought you were ready to give Gabe a second chance."

Adelia glanced around to be sure her brother wasn't close enough to overhear her. "I have," she told Karen in a hushed voice, unable to stop the smile that spread across her face at the admission.

"Well, there you go," Karen said. "He's most definitely all man. Seems like he might make good daddy material."

Elliott walked over just in time to overhear his wife's comment. A frown settled on his face. "Did you just suggest that my sister and Gabe have a baby?"

Karen didn't seem the least bit intimidated by Elliott's scowl. "I was merely suggesting that if she wanted another baby, there was a candidate who might prove helpful."

Elliott turned his disapproving gaze from his wife to Adelia. "I told you to give the man a chance, not to let him father your children."

Adelia bit back a smile. "Nobody's going to father any children with me," she soothed, then allowed herself a grin. "At least not right this minute. And this conversation is exactly why I discouraged Mama from asking Gabe to join us for dinner."

Elliott looked as if he wanted to launch into a protective, brotherly lecture, but just then the back door opened and their mother announced that dinner was ready.

"Time to face the music," Adelia said, getting to her feet.

Karen handed the baby off to Elliott, then put an arm around Adelia's waist. "Come on. I'll protect you."

"And who's going to protect you?" Adelia asked.

"You, of course. And that big, strong man carrying my baby. Nobody in church heard it on the day we got married, but one of his vows was to stand between me and his family."

"I've got your back," Elliott confirmed, giving her a doting look. He winked at Adelia. "Yours, too, if you'll let me."

"You already have your hands full, little brother. I can take care of myself," Adelia told him.

She allowed herself just a moment of envy at the bond between Elliott and Karen. She wondered if she'd ever have that sort of bond again. While she was starting to trust Gabe around her kids, she wasn't quite ready to trust him with her heart. After all, she'd known Ernesto for years and never suspected he was a serial cheater. How could she possibly trust any man after just a few weeks?

In Cruz family tradition, the children had all been served at their table. Now the adults said grace and began passing around the familiar bowls of rice and beans, fried plantains and fragrant pork. Adelia absorbed the temporary calm and goodwill and almost allowed herself to relax.

Within minutes, though, she realized that there was an underlying tension in the room and that, for once, it had nothing to do with her. She glanced across the table and saw that Carolina was fighting tears while her husband sat back in his chair with a dark expression on his face. This time there was no ignoring her gut feeling that something wasn't right there.

Since everyone else was studiously avoiding the obviously angry couple, Adelia did, as well, but she resolved that after dinner she'd make another attempt to reach out to her sister, despite the harsh words they'd exchanged on their last encounter.

Maria tried to fill the silence with idle chitchat, but no one seemed interested in helping her out. Adelia glanced at her mother and realized that she was clearly at the end of her rope. She didn't like dissension in the family in general and especially not at these Sunday gatherings.

"Carolina, could you help me in the kitchen?" their mother said, suddenly standing up.

"But, Mama—" Carolina started to protest, only to be cut off.

"Now!"

Adelia started to stand, as well, but her mother gestured for her to stay.

When mother and daughter had gone into the kitchen, all eyes turned angrily on Enrique.

"What's going on, Ricky?" Elliott demanded of his brother-in-law.

"Nothing but hormones," Ricky replied, as if his wife's mood were of no consequence. "You know how women get."

Adelia almost came out of her seat at that. "Don't take that condescending tone about my sister," she snapped, sitting down only because Karen reached out, then shook her head. Confronting Ricky about his attitude would only stir the pot. And Adelia knew, as did Karen, that little good would come of that, not with these old-school men who believed their wives were more possessions than partners.

"Let your mother get to the bottom of this," Karen whispered.

Elliott looked as if he was no more inclined to listen to that advice than Adelia was, but he sat back in his chair, as well.

"For now," he said, a heated warning in his voice as he stared hard at Ricky, who was fingering an unlit cigar as if nothing at all were wrong in his world.

Adelia turned to her brother. "I have no idea what's going on between those two, but I would give anything to wipe that smug look off his face," she said, speaking in an undertone she hoped wouldn't be overheard.

"Don't tempt me," Elliott replied.

Just then their mother returned to the dining room alone. She turned a gaze on Ricky that startled Adelia. She looked as if she was furious and fighting to contain it.

"Your wife isn't feeling well," she said tightly to her son-in-law. "She's waiting in the car. I suggest you take her home. The children will be staying here."

Ricky looked as if he might balk at what could only be interpreted as an order, but after a quick glance around the table, during which he obviously spotted no allies, he finally shrugged and stood.

"Lovely as always," he said sarcastically.

Elliott was on his feet before the remark was finished, but after a stern look from his mother, he didn't go after Ricky.

"I believe we've had enough drama for the moment," his mother said. "Leave the two of them to work this out."

Elliott didn't look happy, but he nodded. "Whatever you say, Mama."

Maria glanced at her husband, but Marco seemed to be avoiding her gaze. For once, without an ally in the room, he apparently had nothing to say, either. Adelia couldn't help thinking that he must have a good idea about what was going on, but he'd never betray Ricky, any more than either of them had revealed Ernesto's secrets. It was as if the three brothers-in-law had taken a pact of unity.

Adelia kept her own thoughts to herself until after dinner, when she volunteered to help her mother clear the table and deal with the dishes. Alone with her mother in the kitchen, she asked quietly, "Is Carolina okay?"

Her mother sighed heavily. "She's more troubled than I imagined," she admitted. A tear spilled down her cheek. "What is happening to my family?"

Adelia gave her a fierce hug. "Nothing you are responsible for, Mama. We all made our own choices, and each of us must decide how we want to move forward."

"I've always believed marriage vows to be sacred, that it should be forever. I harbored what was apparently an illusion, that problems could always be worked out," her mother said, a plaintive note in her voice. "That's the way it should be. It's the way I taught all of you to live your lives. Now you're divorced." She met Adelia's gaze. "And rightfully so. As for Carolina..." Her voice quavered and she sat down, then lifted her sad gaze to Adelia. "There are bruises. Ricky hit her, Adelia. That man hit my child."

Adelia was indignant. Beyond indignant. She wanted to rip into Ricky herself. "And you let her leave here with him?"

"I didn't let her. She insisted."

Now Adelia was actually stunned. "Carolina wanted to go home with him after that?"

Her mother nodded, her expression helpless. "Did I teach her too well? About honoring her vows, I mean. Is it my fault that she won't walk away from a man who abuses her?"

Adelia thought it might, indeed, be about that, at least to some extent. She knew firsthand how eager they all were for their mother's approval. She also knew that some women couldn't make that break from an abusive man for far different reasons.

"What did she say?" she asked her mother. "Did she admit that he was responsible for the bruises?"

"Yes, but she said they were her fault, that she'd upset him and that he'd apologized. Over and over, she said, as if that made up for it."

Adelia knew that was the classic response of far too many women. "I'll talk to her," she told her mother. "Better yet, I'll have Raylene talk to her. Raylene knows how that kind of abuse can escalate. Maybe she can get through to Carolina that it's never okay, not even the first time." She was struck by a terrible thought. "Was it the first time?"

"I don't know," her mother responded. "I couldn't get her to open up. I swear I wanted to walk into the dining room and swing a cast-iron skillet straight at his head myself." She held Adelia's gaze. "I had it in my hand. I've never felt that kind of rage before. I wanted to send my girl upstairs and tell her she was grounded and not allowed to leave this house."

Adelia smiled at that. "Carolina's thirty-eight, a little old for grounding, but I totally understand your wanting to do just that. I want to go over there and snatch her out of that house myself. God help us if Elliott gets wind of this. I've kept him from laying a hand on Ernesto, but I doubt there's anything any of us could say to keep him from going after Ricky."

"Which is why we won't say a word to anyone," her mother said. "Not unless it becomes necessary to protect Carolina."

"Well, I'm going over there now," Adelia said. "Who knows how Ricky might react if he finds out Carolina's told you the truth?"

"You can't," her mother protested. "What if that makes him even madder?"

"Then he'll have two of us to deal with. May my children stay here? If you already have too much on your hands, I can ask Elliott to take them, or call Gabe to pick them up."

"No, no. They'll be fine right here. Looking after them will help to take my mind off of all this. I'll bake them cookies."

Adelia knew that baking was her mother's best stress reducer. That worked out nicely for her appreciative, always hungry grandkids. She leaned down and gave her a hug.

"I'll be back soon," she promised. "Hopefully I can persuade Carolina to come with me."

"I'll pray for that," her mother said, but her sorrowful expression suggested she didn't believe that particular prayer would be answered.

Adelia slipped out of the kitchen door, hoping that no one would notice her departure. The fewer explanations she had to offer, the better. She doubted she could contain the anger she was feeling toward Ricky right now or the pity she felt for her sister.

Though she'd suspected that Carolina's marriage

was in trouble, she hadn't guessed something like this. When Adelia had suggested he might be cheating, Carolina had even let her believe she'd gotten it right. Obviously she'd been too ashamed to admit that it was even worse than that. While Ernesto's behavior had been its own form of abuse that she'd tolerated for far too long, Adelia had always believed that she'd have the strength to walk away the first time any man ever laid a hand on her. From talking to Raylene, though, she knew that wasn't always the case, that the situation could sometimes be too complex for a quick, easy solution.

Adelia drove into Carolina's neighborhood of modest but well-kept homes. Her sister's passion for gardening was evident in the small, lushly landscaped lawn that was edged with fragrant roses in full bloom. Baskets of bright flowers hung from the porch ceiling and more pots lined the steps. The cheerful riot of color was a far cry from what Adelia expected to find inside.

On the way over, she'd come up with a reason for the impromptu visit, one that might be believable to both her sister and Ricky. Pressing the doorbell, she drew in a deep breath and prepared to sell her hastily devised story.

When Carolina opened the door, her eyes were puffy from crying, her expression dismayed. "This isn't a good time," she said, stepping outside and closing the door behind her.

Relieved to be able to speak to her sister alone, Adelia kept her voice low. "Mama told me," she said. "Come with me, Carolina. Please don't stay here."

"This is my home," Carolina said stubbornly. "It's where I belong."

"Just for tonight," Adelia pleaded. "Stay with me if you don't want to go to Mama's. The kids, too."

Her sister regarded her miserably. "I can't. It will only make him angrier."

"Who cares how angry he gets?" Adelia said. "And if your visiting your sister is all it takes to set him off, you don't belong here."

"How can you possibly understand? You had a man who gave you everything. You had a beautiful home. Your children had whatever they needed. You could spend your days at home. Your life was perfect, and you threw it away. For what?"

Adelia held her gaze. "My self-respect," she said softly. "That's more important than any of the rest."

"And do you have your precious self-respect now with your reputation ruined because of a man you've known for, what, a few weeks?"

"My reputation isn't ruined, except, perhaps, in your eyes. Gabe's a good and decent man. I can't say the same about Ernesto." She dared to touch her sister's cheek. "This has nothing to do with me, Carolina. I'm here because of you. This situation isn't acceptable. Please let me help you."

Carolina shook her head. "I don't need your help. Ricky was angry. He didn't mean it." She said it almost by rote, as if she'd repeated it to herself a thousand times to justify what was happening to her.

"And how many times has he told you that?" Adelia asked her, holding her gaze. Her sister blinked and looked away. "I thought so. This isn't the first time, as Mama had hoped."

"It will get better," her sister argued. "It always does. I just have to try harder."

"And how long will things be better? How many weeks or days or hours does it take before he finds another excuse?"

"Stop it," Carolina said angrily. "It's not his fault. It's mine."

Adelia felt her temper flare at the way Ricky had managed to manipulate Carolina into believing that she'd done anything to justify the abuse. "You're being abused," she told her heatedly. "That is never, ever okay, Carolina. Will you at least go with me to talk to Raylene? She's been through this. There are people ready and willing to help you. If you don't want to talk to her or me or even Mama, there's a wonderful counselor who can help. Don't let this escalate. Don't let yourself be a victim for a second longer. Think about what happened to Raylene."

Since everyone in town had heard Raylene's story and was aware that her ex-husband had come to town to try to kill her after his release from jail on abuse charges, Carolina did flinch at the mention of Raylene's name.

"It's not the same," she insisted to Adelia. "Ricky's a good man. He just has a quick temper."

"And a willing target, apparently," Adelia said, hoping to provoke her sister. Maybe straight talk would snap her out of this destructive, accepting attitude she seemed to have adopted.

Carolina regarded Adelia with real heat in her eyes. "That's not fair. You don't know what it's like."

"Thank God for that," Adelia said. "But you shouldn't know what it's like, either. You shouldn't be living like this, in constant fear of your husband's moods. This isn't a marriage."

Just then Ricky bellowed from inside. "Carolina, get back in here! Tell that troublemaking sister of yours to mind her own business."

Panic immediately spread across Carolina's face. "I have to go."

"Come with me," Adelia repeated. "Get away from here."

A faint smile touched her sister's lips, but it was gone in a heartbeat. "Do you think I'd be safer at your house or Mama's?" she inquired. "Never. I'd just be putting you in danger, too."

Her words were more alarming than anything she'd said before. Adelia regarded her with growing dismay. "All the more reason to leave. If Ricky's that dangerous, you have to get away. We can protect you. Elliott, Gabe, there are others, too, who'll see to it that no more harm comes to you. Carter Rollins can arrest Ricky. You know he has no tolerance for domestic violence."

"What about my children?" Carolina asked. "What would they think if I sent their father to jail?"

"That you'd stood up for yourself." She looked her sister in the eye. "And for them," she added.

"Ricky would never touch them," Carolina responded, looking genuinely shocked by the suggestion. Once more, she was clearly deluding herself.

"Are you so sure?" Adelia asked more gently, seeing an opening that might make Carolina see reason. "And even if he never lays a hand on them, how do you think it makes them feel to know their father is abusing you?"

"They don't know," Carolina insisted.

Adelia regarded her incredulously. "Maybe not the younger ones, but I'll bet Joey knows," she told Carolina. "And sooner or later he will either get dragged into the middle of it to protect you or he'll wind up believing that it's okay for a husband to hit a wife."

Carolina looked deeply shaken by Adelia's words, but she backed away just the same. "I have to go inside."

"Please don't," Adelia pleaded one last time.

"I have to," Carolina said, her expression defeated.

She darted inside, leaving Adelia standing on the porch, tears streaming down her cheeks and fury burning in her heart.

CHAPTER SIXTEEN

Gabe had never had a problem with loneliness before. After years of the chaos of living with his mom, he'd craved a peaceful lifestyle. He'd lived mostly on his own for years now, found female companionship when he wanted it or created distractions that kept him occupied whenever he had time off.

Since coming back to Serenity, though, he'd discovered that Sundays seemed endless. Mitch flatly refused to let him work at the Main Street site. He claimed the churchgoers in town wouldn't approve, that Sundays were meant for church and family.

Though he considered himself to be a man of faith, Gabe hadn't set foot in church since the one time his mother had dragged him to a service, only to be subjected to searing looks of disapproval that didn't seem to him to be very Christian or welcoming.

As for family, he figured Mitch had seen more than enough of him weekdays. Though he had a standing invitation to Mitch's, he didn't want to interrupt his cousin's family time just because he was at loose ends.

That left Adelia's. The renovations were coming

along, even with the scant amount of time he had to devote to them. That didn't mean that the occasional Sunday on the job wouldn't help to speed things up. If he caught a glimpse of her or got to spend time with the kids, so much the better.

As he headed to Swan Point, he called to make sure it would be okay with Adelia for him to put in a few hours. He didn't get an answer and assumed she was off somewhere with her family. Since he had a key and her permission to work whenever he could, he went on over.

He'd just pulled into the driveway and was about to go inside when he spotted Adelia's car coming down the street at a breakneck pace. She skidded to a stop in front of the house, at least a foot from the curb. To his surprise, though, while she cut the engine, she didn't get out. She sat where she was, arms braced on the steering wheel, her head lowered onto them. Gabe doubted she'd even taken note of his presence. Something definitely wasn't right.

His heart thudding, he walked over and tapped on the window. She jumped, then regarded him with dismay. He took in her pale complexion and the tears streaming down her cheeks and grabbed the door handle. Opening the door carefully, he kneeled beside her and rested a hand lightly on her thigh.

"What is it? What's happened?" he asked, keeping his tone gentle.

She shook her head, the tears coming harder than ever. Her pain was enough to break his heart.

"Is it one of the kids? Is someone hurt? Is it your mom?"

Again, she could only seem to shake her head.

For a minute he couldn't think what to do. Then it occurred to him that sitting here in the car sobbing where anyone could see probably wasn't something she'd want if she were thinking clearly.

"Is it okay if I take you inside?" he asked, sensing that she was so fragile right now, he didn't dare do anything without her permission.

"Please," she whispered. "I can't seem to move."

He snagged the keys from the ignition, then gently picked her up and cradled her against his chest. It took only a few strides to carry her up the walkway and open the door. Inside, though, he hesitated.

"Living room? Kitchen? Your bedroom?" The last came out on a husky note. "Do you need to lie down?"

"Just hold me," she said, snuggling closer.

Gabe knew she was distraught, that she'd never be all over him if she were thinking straight. He vowed not to take advantage of her while she was in this state, not even if it killed him. He at least had to get to the bottom of her distress first.

Since that was the immediate goal, he decided they'd better steer clear of the bedroom. She was obviously vulnerable, and he'd never been called a saint.

He strode into the living room, sat on the sofa and held her close. Though it was a warm day and the air-conditioning wasn't running in the house, she shivered. He rubbed his hands up and down her arms to try to get the circulation going. She shivered even more, though it was hard to tell if it was from a chill or a reaction to his touch.

"Talk to me," he pleaded. "What's going on?"

She drew in a deep shuddering breath and then the words began to tumble out. He tried to follow, but she was so upset and speaking so quickly, he could barely piece together what had happened.

"Your sister's husband is abusing her?" he asked, to be sure he'd heard right.

"I tried to get her to come home with me, but she won't." She gave him a heartbroken look. "How can she stay there, Gabe? Was I wrong to leave her in that house with him?"

"It sounds like you did everything you could," he said slowly. He thought of the times his mother had tolerated being slapped around just to keep some man in her life for a few more days or weeks. He'd tried intervening with them, even taking a punch himself on occasion. He'd tried pleading with her, but nothing had worked. She'd made her choices. The irony, of course, was that the men had eventually left, anyway, taking her self-respect right along with them. "You can't make her do something she's not ready to do," he said based on experience.

A sudden thought crossed his mind. "Does Elliott know?"

She shook her head. "Mama and I agreed he can't find out. He'd kill Ricky."

"Secrets like this always come out," Gabe warned. "I think you need to fill him in." He held her gaze. "And Carter at the same time. If Carter's aware of the situation, maybe that will be enough to keep your brother from going off the deep end."

"I can't take that chance," she said at once. "And if Carter knows, won't he have to do something? I know if he tries to arrest Ricky, Carolina will deny anything's happened. She's already said as much. She's convinced herself—and tried to convince Mama and me—that this is all her fault."

"What about her kids?" Gabe asked. "Are they in danger?"

"They're at Mama's," Adelia reported. "Hopefully Carolina will let them stay there."

"And your kids? Are they at your mother's, too?"

She nodded. "I called when I left my sister's and told Mama that I hadn't had any luck changing Carolina's mind. My kids are fine with Mama for another couple of hours. She's baking cookies. They get to lick the bowl and eat the cookies straight out of the oven. I doubt they're even aware I'm gone. I needed some time to pull myself together before they come home. I'll pick them up later or she'll bring them home."

Even in her distressed state, she'd thought of her children, made sure they were okay. Gabe tried to imagine what his life would have been like if his mother had ever put him first.

"Is there anything I can do?" he asked Adelia, wanting to share this burden with her, to ease it if he could.

"Stay here with me, Gabe. You don't need to be mixed up in this. You don't even know my sister."

"She matters to you, so she matters to me," Gabe said without hesitation.

She regarded him with wonder. "You really mean that, don't you?"

Gabe was almost as surprised by that as she was, but it was true. It might not be his problem to resolve, but he hated what it was doing to this woman he cared about. If he could pummel Ricky and solve anything, he'd do it in a heartbeat. It was ironic really how many people he'd wanted to punch out on Adelia's behalf or Mitch's lately, but he'd managed to resist the urge. Maybe he really had grown up and realized there were always better choices.

"I really mean it," he told her.

"I've never had a hero before," she murmured, her eyes drifting closed as she finally relaxed in his arms.

"Oh, darlin', I'm nobody's hero," Gabe protested, but she was beyond hearing him. She'd fallen asleep, obviously worn-out by the day's traumatic events.

As he sat there holding her, Gabe realized something else. The loneliness he'd felt earlier in the day had vanished. Even with Adelia asleep and a very real crisis threatening to erupt, he felt more at peace than he had in a long time, maybe ever.

When Gabe was satisfied that Adelia was sleeping soundly, he covered her with a soft blue afghan that was on the back of the sofa and slipped away. First, he went out and pulled her car closer to the curb to lessen the risk of it being struck by another driver. Then he considered going upstairs to work, but he was afraid any noise he made would wake her. Instead, he went into the kitchen to see if there was anything basic that he could fix for dinner.

He'd just pulled salad ingredients and hamburger meat from the refrigerator when Selena came in. Her eyes widened when she saw him.

"You're making dinner?" she asked.

He smiled at her incredulous expression. "I thought I'd give it a try. Want to help me?"

"Sure," she said, taking over with the salad ingredients. "Mom's asleep in the living room. How come?

She left *Abuela*'s early and never came back. Is she sick?"

Sick at heart more likely, Gabe thought. To Selena he said only, "I think she was tired."

"She does work awfully hard," Selena said. She gave Gabe a worried look. "Do you think it's too much for her? I know she was determined not to take any help from my dad, except for the money he gives her for us. She puts that into a college fund, though. Maybe she should be spending it, instead, so she doesn't have to work so hard."

"I may not know your mom very well yet, but I think she wants to provide for you guys. I think she takes a lot of pride in it."

"I guess," Selena said, setting aside the bowl she'd filled with lettuce, peppers, grape tomatoes and croutons. "But if she's worn-out, that can't be good."

"I think it just hit her today," Gabe said. "I don't think it's anything you need to worry about. Where are your sisters and brother? I thought you were all over at your grandmother's."

"We were, but we wanted to come back here. *Abuela* wanted us to stay, but I told her I could look out for the kids." She flushed guiltily. "I guess maybe she knew Mom was here resting or with you. I probably should have listened to her, but Uncle Elliott was leaving and he said he'd drop us off."

Gabe smiled. "It's good you're home. I think your mom will be glad to see you when she's awake. Where are Tomas and your sisters now?"

"Out back. When I saw that Mom was asleep, I sent them outside to play. Tomas didn't want to go, because he saw your truck. He wanted to come in and help you."

"He can help me with the burgers on the grill," Gabe said. He gave Selena an approving look. "I hope you know what a big help you are to your mom by looking out for Tomas, Natalia and Juanita."

She blushed at the compliment. "I'm grounded. What else do I have to do?"

He smiled at that. "It's more than that. You're mature enough to see that your mom could use a little help and you've stepped up."

"Does being mature mean I have to keep doing this, like, forever? Even after I'm not grounded?"

Gabe laughed. "Oh, I imagine your mom will reward you with some time off for good behavior."

"I hope so, 'cause I really, really miss hanging out with my friends."

He studied her for a minute. "Are you allowed to use your cell phone yet?"

"Only for emergencies," she said despondently. "And for maybe fifteen minutes, if Mom thinks I've been extra good."

"If she were awake, I think she'd let you use it for fifteen minutes right now," he said. "The salad is made. You have a little time before the burgers will be ready."

Her eyes brightened. "Really?"

"I think so."

"But what if you get in trouble for letting me?" she asked worriedly.

"My problem," he said, then grinned. "Maybe she'll ground me, too."

Selena laughed at that. "Thanks, Gabe."

"Fifteen minutes," he warned. "Not a second longer."

"I promise," she said and ran from them room, already making a call.

He was about to go outside when he saw Adelia standing in the doorway, hands on hips and what he hoped was a mock scowl in place. "Did I just hear you give my daughter permission to use her cell phone?"

He winced. "Sorry. She'd been really helpful." He gestured toward the counter. "She made the salad. She shooed the younger kids outside so they wouldn't wake you. And she admitted she wasn't allowed to use the phone except when you gave her permission." He shrugged. "I made an executive decision."

"And what if I did decide to ground you for it?" she asked, her lips twitching. "How do you see that working?"

"I'd have to stay here," he told her solemnly. "For as long as you want."

Her eyes sparkled. "For some reason, when you say it, it doesn't sound so much like a punishment."

"That depends on where you let me sleep," he teased.

"Gabe!" she protested, giving a quick glance around to make sure none of the kids were nearby.

He stepped closer. "Any thoughts about that, Adelia?"

She swallowed hard. "I can't think about anything when you're this close."

He grinned. "Exactly what I was going for," he said. "That and getting some color back in your complexion. Mission accomplished."

She touched a hand to his cheek. "I meant what I

said earlier, you know. You are my hero. And I won't let you deny it now, the way you did then."

"I thought you were asleep and didn't hear me."

"No, I heard you, but it wasn't worth arguing about. I know the truth and that's what counts."

For the first time in his entire life, Gabe actually realized what it felt like to be someone's hero. He wasn't sure he deserved the label, but it felt darn good just the same.

Adelia did her best to put her sister's situation out of her mind and to focus on her own family for the remainder of the evening. She smiled when Selena bounced back downstairs after exactly fifteen minutes and put her cell phone down on the kitchen counter with a dramatic flourish.

"Right on time," Selena announced, then regarded her mother worriedly. "Gabe's not in trouble for letting me use it, is he?"

"No, I think he showed good judgment," Adelia told her. "You've been a huge help to me lately. You deserved a break. And the fact that you acknowledged to him that you weren't allowed to use the phone without permission showed me something, too."

"What?"

"That you respect my rules, even if you don't always agree with them," Adelia told her. "You're growing up, Selena." She grinned. "A little too fast for my taste, but I do appreciate the maturity you've been demonstrating lately."

To her surprise, Selena gave her a fierce hug.

"I don't want to let you down, Mom." She glanced around. "Where's Gabe?"

"Outside cooking hamburgers, or trying to. Last time I looked, he was trying to keep Tomas from flipping them onto the ground."

"Dad was never patient enough to let Tomas do anything," Selena said. "I think it's cool that Gabe is."

"So, you really have changed your opinion of him?" Adelia asked carefully.

"He's a good guy," Selena conceded, then frowned. "I just don't know how I feel about him being with you. It's still kind of soon."

"Remember that feeling when I try to tell you who you can date," Adelia said, deciding it wasn't worth some long and serious discussion since things were far from settled between her and Gabe. One official date was hardly a relationship, though he did seem to be increasingly a part of their lives.

Selena grinned at her comment, just as Adelia had intended. "Good point," she said. "How about I promise not to butt into your life and you don't butt into mine?"

Adelia laughed. "Nice try, but I'm the mom. I get to butt in anytime I want to." She tugged gently on a strand of her daughter's hair. "And you have to listen."

"Not fair," Selena declared, but her eyes were shining. "Do you think Gabe will want to do game night with us?"

Adelia regarded her with surprise. "We haven't had a game night in a long time." It had been a Sunday night tradition for years, though Ernesto had rarely joined in the games. With all the commotion of the past few months, the tradition seemed to have died.

"I know," Selena said. "I kinda miss it. We could play team Scrabble. I could play with either Juanita or

Natalia, you could play with the other one and Tomas could play with Gabe. It might be fun."

"Why don't we bring it up at dinner?" Adelia suggested. "We can see if everyone wants to play that or something else."

"As long as it's not Candy Land," Selena said, rolling her eyes. "I think I played that about a million times."

Adelia laughed. "I think maybe everyone's beyond that now. You should be safe."

Just then the younger girls came running inside, announced that the burgers were ready, then raced off to wash their hands.

Gabe was right on their heels with the platter of hamburgers, toasted buns and, to her astonishment, some grilled vegetables, as well.

"Gabe says everything tastes better when it's cooked on the grill," Tomas announced. "We did peppers and squash and even some onions." He wrinkled his nose at that.

Gabe caught his expression and chided, "But we're all going to try everything, right? Because that's the only way to know if we really like it or not."

"I guess," Tomas said, his expression doubtful. "But I don't have to eat it if it's yucky. That's the deal."

Gabe nodded, fighting a smile. "That's the deal."

"It's a better deal than I ever got," Adelia told him as he set the platter on the table. She turned to Selena. "Bring in the ketchup and mustard, please. I forgot those."

As soon as they were seated, Adelia realized she was starving. She'd lost her appetite at her mother's earlier and eaten very little of the food on her plate.

Now, surrounded by her laughing kids and with Gabe across the table, she finally let herself relax.

As the platter was passed, she noted that Gabe put a little of everything on Tomas's plate. She hid a grin as her son reluctantly tried tiny bites of each vegetable. He looked up at Gabe with a shocked expression. "They're really good," he announced.

"Told you," Gabe said.

Her son's reaction had the desired effect and she noted that everyone's plate was quickly piled high with grilled veggies. She met Gabe's gaze. "Miracle worker," she mouthed.

He laughed at that.

When everyone was starting to slow down, Selena announced, "I told Mom I think we should have a game night. How about it?"

Juanita and Natalia immediately bounced eagerly in their chairs and shouted their agreement. Tomas looked skeptical.

"Daddy hated game night," he said.

"Oh, so what?" Selena said. "It's fun. I thought we could play team Scrabble." She gave her brother a sly look. "You could play with Gabe."

Tomas immediately looked more interested. "Are you gonna play, Gabe?"

Adelia waited almost breathlessly for his response.

"Sounds as if I've been drafted," Gabe said. He leaned toward Tomas. "But you're going to have to teach me. I haven't played a lot of Scrabble."

"I can do that," Tomas agreed. "My spelling's not so good, but I know strategy and stuff."

"Then we should make a good team," Gabe told him. "I got A's in spelling."

"Seriously?" Tomas said, wide-eyed. "Daddy always said it didn't matter, that that's what spell-check on the computer was for."

"Well, in my day, we had to learn to spell the old-fashioned way," Gabe told him. "We practiced and practiced."

"Could you practice with me sometime?" Tomas begged. "I get new words every week."

Gabe nodded. "Get your list. Maybe we can use them in the game."

"Okay, it's settled then," Adelia said. "Kids, I want to see your homework before we start to make sure it's ready for school tomorrow. While you get that, I'll clean up the kitchen."

Gabe automatically picked up dishes and carried them into the kitchen. Adelia frowned at him. "You don't need to do that. You cooked, after all."

"Maybe I'm looking for a few more points," he said solemnly. "Or a couple of minutes alone with you away from prying eyes."

She flushed at his teasing. "Why would you need to be alone with me?"

He backed her up toward the counter, then braced his hands on either side of her. "For this," he said, brushing his lips over hers. "And this." He settled in for a longer taste, then stepped away at the sound of footsteps running in their direction.

"Guess that'll have to do for now," he said, pulling away. He winked at her. "Fair warning, though. If I win at Scrabble, I expect a really, really nice reward."

She laughed at the impudent comment. "Winning should be its own reward."

"You might be able to convince your kids of that,

but I know there are things that matter more. There's a whole lot I'd do for a few more stolen kisses."

"Gabe Franklin," she said a little breathlessly, "if you keep this up, you're going to turn my head. Is that your intention?"

He seemed surprised by the idea, but then a smile stole across his face. "You know, I think maybe it is."

Adelia was shaken by the intensity she heard in his voice. How long had it been since any man had wanted her? Even more, how long had it been since one had openly put his heart on the line? After so many years of being viewed as the woman who raised Ernesto's kids and kept his house spotless, but little more, it was heady stuff to be seen as a desirable woman.

Suddenly she couldn't wait to put this Scrabble tournament behind them. In fact, she might even throw a game or two Gabe's way just so she could see how clever he was about claiming his rewards.

CHAPTER SEVENTEEN

The Scrabble board had been put away. The exhausted kids had gone to bed. Gabe could see that Adelia was completely drained, but there was a brightness in her eyes as she held the score sheet up for him to see.

"This tells me you bamboozled us," she accused. "You know a whole lot more about playing Scrabble than you let on."

"Just luck," he claimed. "I got great letters and your son has killer instincts about how to make the best use of them."

"He might have the instincts, but you're a very good coach. I actually have high hopes that he might pass his spelling test this week."

Gabe gave her a long, speculative look. "So, you're saying I not only won, but that you're pleased with how I got Tomas to study for his spelling test?"

"You have a definite knack for both," she agreed.

He stepped closer. "So, any thoughts about what sort of reward I deserve?" He ran a finger along the curve of her jaw and down her neck. He felt her pulse jump and her skin heat.

She gave him a surprisingly innocent look, though there was an unmistakable twinkle in her eyes. "I'll buy you an extralarge coffee in the morning," she offered.

Gabe shook his head and traced her lower lip with his thumb. "Not quite what I had in mind."

She swallowed hard. "Pastry?" she suggested in a choked voice. "I'll buy your pastry, too. Two, if you want. Even three."

"Nope. I want something sweeter," he said softly, his gaze holding hers. "And more immediate."

"What if..." Her voice shook. "What if that's not available?"

"Isn't it? What I want, what I need is standing right here, right now." He lowered his head and claimed her mouth. After barely more than a heartbeat of hesitation, she surrendered to the kiss, parting her lips, taking him in. Gabe lost himself in the sweetness of the moment. This woman who'd been through so much, not just today, but for months now, was trusting him, welcoming him. He suddenly felt ten feet tall.

Still, this wasn't the time or the place to claim all he wanted from her, not with her children right upstairs and her so exhausted she might not be thinking clearly. Reluctantly, he took a step back, still holding her lightly.

"I want even more than that, Adelia," he told her candidly. "Not because of some game, but because I don't think I'll ever get enough of you."

She looked as if she desperately wanted to believe him, but he could see the doubts crowding in and wanted, yet again, to curse Ernesto for planting those seeds in her head. If he were being honest, he'd probably added to those doubts with his repeated warnings that he didn't do the whole forever thing. Since he couldn't take back his words, he focused on her shaky self-confidence.

He brushed her thick dark hair back from her face and kept his hands gentle on her cheeks. "You don't believe me now, but you will," he told her. "I'll make sure you start to see yourself as I do."

"And then what?" she blurted, then covered her mouth with her hand, obviously embarrassed.

"Then we'll see," he said, his expression sobering as she called him on the very thing he'd been trying to avoid. "I won't make false promises to you, Adelia. Not ever. This is new to me, too. I'm not sure I know how to do a real relationship. I don't know if I can."

"Oh," she whispered, looking shaken by the repeated warning.

"Look at me," he commanded. When she dared to lift her eyes to meet his, he said, "But you make me want to try, Adelia. No woman's ever done that before. Lately, spending time with you, with your family..." He fell silent, almost afraid of the thought, much less of expressing it. Nights like tonight had been nonexistent in his past. He'd never known how happy being with a family could make him. On the rare occasions when he and his mom had been included in family events, any joy had been overshadowed by anger and recriminations and judgment. Tonight had given him a taste of something far different, something he found himself longing to claim.

When he was about to say more, she touched a finger to his lips. "It's okay, Gabe. There's no rush. I'm not exactly ready to jump into anything too serious, either."

Perversely, that made him want to do the opposite, to jump straight into wherever this might be taking them. Instead, though, he let her have the last word on the topic.

"You need to get some sleep," he said. "You've had a long and stressful day."

"You made it better," she told him. "You really did. Thank you for being here for me and for being so good with my kids."

"Anytime, darlin'. And that really is a promise."

He left then, because he didn't entirely trust himself not to make more promises or to ask for more from her as he'd just been so tempted to do. If he did either of those things and then bailed, as he feared he someday would, he'd never forgive himself for disappointing her.

Adelia took a late morning break, put a sign on the boutique's door and ran next door to the bakery for coffee. She could barely keep her eyes open. Between worrying about her sister and thinking about Gabe, she'd barely slept a wink the night before.

Lynn took one look at her and poured her a large cup of coffee to go. "If you don't mind me saying so, you look beat, and that's coming from a woman who knows a thing or two about exhaustion." Lynn studied her speculatively. "Is it too much to hope that you had a late night with Gabe?"

"Gabe was over, but it wasn't like that," Adelia told her. "We played Scrabble with the kids. It was a relatively early evening."

To her surprise, Lynn grinned. "Ah, so that's it. Frustration is what kept you awake."

Adelia laughed. "What is it with you Sweet Magnolias? Your minds are always on romance and sex."

"Because we have men who make us very happy," Lynn said, her own contentment plain. "We want that for everyone. And maybe since we're all settled into our old married ruts, we want to live vicariously through the courtship rituals."

"Well, there's no courting going on," Adelia insisted, though she feared the heat she could feel in her cheeks would give her away.

"Not buying that," Lynn said, dismissing the claim without a second's hesitation. "Gabe's no fool. I also think he's the kind of man who'll go after what he wants. And all the signs point to his wanting you."

"What if I'm not sure I can handle what he wants?" Adelia asked, unable to keep a plaintive note from her voice.

Lynn's teasing expression sobered at once. "Do you know what he wants?"

"Well, he says he wants me, but I think he means in an uncomplicated, casual fling sort of way. Last night he was tossing around all sorts of warnings about not making promises. It was nothing he hasn't said before, so I have to believe he means it."

"He probably thinks he does," Lynn said, looking exasperated. "I suppose he's trying to play fair, the idiot."

Adelia smiled at the disgust she heard in her friend's voice. "Being fair doesn't make him an idiot. It probably makes me the idiot for wanting to plunge in head-first, anyway."

Lynn's expression brightened at that. "You want to plunge in?"

"Well, sure. The man can kiss like it's an Olympic event and he's going for the gold. And the way he is with my kids, well, let me just say that after the way Ernesto all but ignored them, seeing Gabe with them fills my heart with happiness. So, yes, I start fantasizing just a little about what the future could be like. But down that road disaster's waiting to happen, so I've put my defenses firmly in place."

"Oh, boy," Lynn said. "I thought you might have a little crush, but it sounds to me as if you're way beyond that."

"Absolutely not," Adelia said hurriedly. "Expecting anything more would be crazy. Gabe's warned me again and again about that."

"I didn't say you expected it, but I do think you want it."

Adelia sighed. "Maybe I do. And, given all the signs that it will never happen, that definitely makes me an idiot."

"Just because he warned you off?" Lynn asked, clearly trying to follow her logic.

"No, because men like Gabe don't fall for women like me. Not in some forever kind of way, anyway."

Lynn stared at her incredulously. "That is absolute hogwash!" she said emphatically. "Women like you? What does that even mean? Are you talking about bright, beautiful, sexy, caring, generous women? Any man would be lucky to have you. Gabe might be oblivious to what he needs in his life, but he's not oblivious to the fact that you're incredible."

Adelia let the praise sink in, then stood up. Between the pep talk, overly optimistic though it may have been, and the coffee, she felt much better.

"Thank you, Lynn," she said. "Maybe you should get a degree in psychology and dispense wisdom with your coffee and pastries."

"And exactly when would I fit those classes into my day?" Lynn asked, laughing. "Maybe I could do that instead of, say, laundry. Or dusting." Her expression brightened as if she might actually consider that. "I really hate dusting."

"Ditto," Adelia said. "I'm just saying I came in here feeling wiped out physically and emotionally, and now I feel as if I just might be able to cope with the rest of the day."

"Okay, then. Happy to help," Lynn told her. "For you the advice is always free."

Adelia's step was lighter when she went back next door, at least until she saw her brother leaning against the wall, obviously waiting for her. Since she knew Elliott wouldn't willingly set foot in a place as girlie as the boutique unless he was on a mission, her heart plunged. Still, she forced a smile.

"Well, this is an unexpected surprise," she said as she unlocked the door and led the way inside.

"Really?" he said, his expression dark. "I would have thought you'd be expecting me."

"Why is that?"

"Because something was going on at the house yesterday and you and Mama were doing everything in your power to keep me from finding out what it was."

"If you believe that, then what makes you think I'll tell you anything now?"

"Because I've taken the afternoon off and I can sit here all day until you decide to open up."

When he deliberately settled his tall, muscled frame onto a dainty little chair as if to prove his intentions, Adelia had to fight a smile.

"I'm surprised you aren't more worked up over finding Gabe at my house when you brought the kids home from Mama's," she said in an attempt to deflect his attention.

"We'll get to that," he said direly. "First I want to know what you're keeping from me."

"Nothing you don't already know," she claimed. "Carolina was having a bad day. Mama and I were worried about her."

"Is she sick?"

Adelia considered lying and saying yes, but the lie wouldn't hold up for more time than it took Elliott to rush over to their sister's.

"No, not the way you mean."

"Then her marriage is in trouble," he guessed. "I'm right, aren't I? I should have punched Ricky yesterday, when I wanted to."

Adelia saw little point in denying that much. "Yes, but she insists she wants to work it out herself," she told him. "You punching out her husband wouldn't solve anything."

Though she genuinely regretted that she couldn't tell him the rest, that comment about starting a fight proved she was right to remain silent. That was for his protection as well as their sister's. The last thing Carolina needed was to have Elliott taking on Ricky in what was bound to be a messy and likely public brawl. For now the situation needed to be dealt with in a calm way, at least until that was no longer safe or reasonable.

"Show her that respect," she advised her brother.

"Is that what you were doing when you went over there?" he asked. "And don't even pretend that wasn't where you headed when you snuck out Mama's back door."

She managed a weak smile. "But that's because I'm the calm, rational one. You'd go in there ready to start something and only wind up making things worse." Come to think of it, she wasn't entirely sure she hadn't done the same thing. She should have called Carolina first thing this morning to be sure she was okay. She resolved to do that the instant Elliott left.

"I'm not buying any of this," he told her. "If I find out you're hiding something serious from me, something I should have handled, I swear, Adelia…" His voice trailed off.

"What will you do, Elliott? Yell at me? Berate Mama? How come you're not over there asking her all these questions?"

"Because she's already told me to stay out of it," he admitted, his expression chagrined. "Once yesterday afternoon and again earlier today."

"And you thought I'd be made of weaker stuff?" Adelia asked, amused. "I am my mother's daughter, after all. You can't bully me into talking."

Her brother sighed heavily. "I just want to help." He held her gaze. "Does Carolina need my help, Adelia? The truth?"

"Not yet," Adelia said, praying it was true. "But the minute she does, I promise you I'll come to you. Can you let that be enough for now?"

"You swear it?"

She sketched a mark across her chest. "Cross my heart."

"Okay, then."

He stood up, and Adelia thought she might be home free, but he turned back. "Is this thing between you and Gabe getting serious?"

"I haven't even confirmed there is a thing with Gabe."

"I'm not blind or stupid," he said. "And as long as he's good to you, I'm in your corner."

"That's very sweet," she told him. "But you have nothing to worry about. Just concentrate on your own family."

"You're my family, too. So is Carolina. I have plenty of time to worry about all of you."

She walked over and gave him a hug. "And that's why you'd win brother of the year in this town every single time if we had such a contest. In fact, I think that's why no one's ever suggested it. It wouldn't be fair to have the same winner over and over."

Elliott gave her a wry look. "The flattery's nice, but I see through it, you know. You just want me gone."

She grinned. "How'd you guess? I have work to do. Love you."

"Te amo," he said.

How lucky was she? she thought as he walked away. It seemed she had two men in her life she could count on in a crisis. The only thing worrisome was how soon she—or Carolina—might need them.

Once Elliott had gone, Adelia started worrying in earnest about Carolina. She couldn't shake off the feeling that she ought to check on her, not by phone but in person. It would be far too easy to lie over the phone.

She went into the boutique's office and called Raylene. "Are you busy?"

"Not unless you count sitting around with my feet up to try to make the swelling in my ankles go down as work," Raylene said, then lamented, "I used to have such nice ankles."

"And you will again," Adelia assured her. "In just a few more months."

"I suppose. So, what's up? Did you need me for something?"

"Could you come in for an hour? I need to check on someone."

"Absolutely," Raylene said eagerly. "Give me fifteen minutes to walk over there."

Adelia hesitated. "Raylene, I'm not taking advantage, am I? This isn't the first time I've called you to cover for me lately."

"Who else should you call?" Raylene said. "It's my business. I count on you to handle way more than you should have to. Covering for you when something comes up will never be a problem, unless I'm in labor or something."

"Well, thank goodness you're not in labor just yet," Adelia told her.

While she waited for Raylene to get there, she totaled her receipts for the day so far and made a note of that. Raylene would need the figures if Adelia turned out to be gone longer than she expected to be.

The second her boss came in the door, Adelia grabbed her purse. Raylene stopped her before she could leave, her expression worried.

"You don't have to tell me if you don't want to, but is everything okay? I never thought to ask on the phone if there was some sort of crisis."

"I hope there's not," Adelia told her, then drew in a deep breath. "Actually it is something I'd like to discuss with you, but could we do it when I get back?"

"Of course," Raylene said. "Do you need backup? I could call someone to go along with you. Or to stay here, so I could go. Any of the Sweet Magnolias would be happy to help."

"Thank you so much, but I'll be fine. It's just a bit of a family situation. I won't be gone long. I promise."

"Take as long as you need," Raylene said, her expression still concerned.

"I'll call if I'm going to be gone more than an hour," Adelia promised.

Grateful that she'd driven her car to work this morning, rather than walking, she headed for Carolina's. Her sister's car was in the driveway, but when Adelia rang the bell, no one answered the door. Adelia pulled out her cell phone and called her sister, first on the house phone, then on her cell. Both went to voice mail. Adelia tried the cell phone again.

"What?" Carolina finally snapped.

"Where are you?" Adelia asked, keeping her own voice level. "Your car's in the driveway."

"Maybe I went for a walk."

Since her sister's aversion to exercise was even greater than Adelia's own, the response didn't ring true. "Did you?"

"What do you want, Adelia?"

"I want to see you."

"It's not a good time."

"That's what you said yesterday. I understood then that you were trying not to anger Ricky, but what about now?"

"Just go away, Adelia. I'm not your problem."

"You're my little sister. You will always be my problem. And in case there's any doubt in your mind, our brother is worried about you, too. You're a whole lot better off dealing with me than you would be with Elliott. If he finds out what's going on, Carolina..." She drew in a deep breath. "Well, I don't have to tell you what will happen then."

"Elliott can't find out about any of this," Carolina said, real panic in her voice.

"Then let me in," Adelia said emphatically. "Once we've talked and I'm satisfied that you're okay, I'll do what I can to keep Elliott out of this."

"What if I'm not okay?" Carolina asked, her voice barely above a whisper.

Now Adelia was the one in a panic. "What do you mean you're not okay? Let me in this minute, Carolina, or I swear I will call Carter Rollins and have him break down the door. That will put an end to all of this. Maybe it's what I need to do, anyway."

"No, please," her sister pleaded, opening the door a crack. The chain on it remained in place. "Let it go, Adelia."

"Sweetie, I can't do that. You know I can't."

"Okay, but don't freak out. Promise me you won't freak out."

The plea wasn't enough to stop Adelia's gasp when the door opened and she caught a glimpse of the black-and-blue marks on her sister's face. "Oh, my God," she whispered, even as rage tore through her. "Ricky did this to you? Because I was here yesterday?"

"No," Carolina said at once. "I thought about what you'd said. I told him that I wasn't going to take it anymore. It's because I listened to you and tried to stand up for myself. He lost his temper. He said he wouldn't have you interfering in our marriage, that you needed to learn your place." Fresh tears spilled down her cheeks. "He said Ernesto was lucky to be rid of you."

"And then he hit you?" Adelia whispered. "To teach you a lesson, so you'd know what to expect if you tried to leave?"

Carolina nodded.

"And you stayed after that?" Adelia asked incredulously.

"What choice did I have?" Carolina asked, her tone flat and defeated.

"What about this morning, after he'd left for work? You could have packed up then and taken off."

"Where could I go like this?" Carolina asked. "To Mama? It would kill her. She flipped out over a couple of bruises on my arm when she caught a glimpse of them yesterday."

"You could have come to me," Adelia said, brokenhearted that her sister didn't realize that.

"And listen to you gloat?"

Adelia merely stared at her, wondering how things between them had deteriorated so badly. There'd been a time, when they were young, that they'd been so close. She'd dried Carolina's tears when she'd scraped her knees falling off her bike, when her first boyfriend had broken up with her.

"I'm so sorry you feel that way," she told her sister. "Do I seem to be gloating now? Carolina, I love you. It tears me apart to see what's happening here. I just want to help."

"Then go away. That's the only way to help. Stay out of it."

"You know I can't do that, not after this. Come with me. Raylene's at the boutique. She can tell us how to get help. Or we can go straight to Carter. With pictures of your injuries and your statement, he'll handle Ricky. Your husband will never hurt you again."

"You're so naive," Carolina said. "My marriage is all I have. I'm not strong like you. I don't have job skills. Ricky would fight me for custody of the kids and he'd probably win. I'd be all alone."

"Never," Adelia said fiercely. "Helen would make sure you have sole custody. No judge would award those children to a man who's beaten his wife."

"Okay, let's say you're right," Carolina said. "Then what? Should we all move in with Mama?"

"We can figure all of that out," Adelia assured her. "The first step is to leave."

"I can't."

"Of course you can. You must. You have children," Adelia reminded her. "Do this for them. Walk away, while you still can. They need their mother."

"They need both parents," Carolina contradicted. "The way it was meant to be."

Adelia was struck by a sudden sickening thought. "What exactly has Ricky told you would happen if you tried to leave him? Did he threaten to kill you, Carolina?" she asked, thinking of Raylene's ex-husband, who'd gone beyond threats to actually trying to kill her.

"No, of course not," Carolina replied unconvincingly.

"I don't believe you. He hit you last night. Tell me the truth. Has he threatened to do worse?"

"It doesn't matter," Carolina said, sounding thoroughly defeated. "I'm staying."

One of the blessings and, it seemed, curses of being born a Cruz was pure stubbornness. Adelia knew she was fighting yet another losing battle. She reached out and gently stroked a finger along the bruised and swollen curve of her sister's jaw.

"It makes me physically ill that you're allowing him to do this to you," she said softly. "You're too good to be treated this way, Carolina." She sighed. "But if you don't want to go, I can't drag you away from here."

Carolina didn't reply, but she held the front door open a little wider, as if to encourage Adelia to leave.

Adelia hesitated on the front stoop. She faced her sister and took a risky but necessary stance. "I will warn you about one thing, though. If I ever see another bruise on you, I will unleash the hounds of hell on Ricky myself."

Alarm flashed in her sister's eyes. "You wouldn't dare."

"Oh, yes, I would," Adelia told her. "I'm already terrified that I'm waiting too long as it is. Next time I won't ask you first. I won't plead with you to leave. I'll just make sure that Ricky gets what's coming to him. I don't know if you're staying out of fear or some twisted idea of love, but either way, perhaps you'll reconsider and get out before he winds up in jail or you wind up in the hospital. Those are only two of the potential consequences of staying."

Carolina frowned. "What could possibly be worse than sending my husband to jail?"

"Letting him take out his anger on one of your children," Adelia suggested. "Or letting our brother in on what's going on in your marriage."

"Ricky would never hurt the kids," Carolina said again, but she didn't sound quite as convinced as she had the day before. "And you would never tell Elliott about any of this."

"Wouldn't I? Try me."

"But if Elliott did something crazy to defend me, he'd be the one in jail. You wouldn't take that risk."

"I think Elliott might agree with me that it would be worth it," Adelia said. "Don't test me, Carolina. If you won't accept help from me, ask someone else. But don't let this escalate. Please. Think about your kids. Think about Mama. But most of all think about yourself."

It took every bit of resolve Adelia possessed to turn and walk away then. She still wanted desperately to throw her arms around her sister and forcibly drag her from the house. Since that would be only a temporary solution, good only as long as it took Carolina to break free and go back home, Adelia resisted the temptation.

What she needed now was Raylene's advice on the next step. Thankfully that was waiting for her just a couple of miles away.

CHAPTER EIGHTEEN

Gabe wandered into the boutique hoping to catch Adelia, but found Raylene there instead.

"Looking for a special gift?" Raylene taunted, her eyes filled with mischief. "Or were you looking for a special someone?"

"I had a few things to discuss with Adelia," he improvised quickly. "About the renovations at her place."

"Really?" Raylene asked, her skepticism plain. "And these things came up out of the blue overnight?"

He frowned at her. "What are you suggesting?"

"Just that I happen to know you were over there last night. Were the two of you especially busy, too busy to discuss these important things?" There was an unmistakable and worrisome twinkle in her eyes when she said it.

Even though Gabe recognized that Raylene was deliberately baiting him, he reacted with exactly the sort of exasperation he knew she was hoping for. "And how would you know a thing like that? Were you out spying on your friends?"

Rather than taking offense, she chuckled. "Carter

and I went for a long walk, just like we do every night. We strolled through Swan Point," she explained, then added pointedly, "just like we do every night." Her smile spread. "And your truck was parked in Adelia's driveway, the same as it has been on a lot of nights lately." She gave him an innocent look. "Or did it just break down there?"

Gabe's scowl deepened. "How is this any of your business?"

It seemed his annoyed tone finally registered with her. Her expression sobered at once.

"Adelia's my friend," she said with a hint of defiance. "As are Lynn and Mitch. I'd like to think we'd be friends, too, if I knew you a little better. So, yes, I pay attention."

"And you feel entitled to poke around in our lives?" he concluded.

Her winning smile returned. "Pretty much."

Gabe shook his head. "I knew this would happen sooner or later. This town is going to drive me nuts. This is exactly why I left all those years ago. People didn't know how to mind their own business."

Somehow all those years of moving from place to place had lulled him into thinking that maybe Serenity hadn't been as bad as he'd thought, that his memories were tainted by the pain of a kid constantly in trouble for defending his mom against gossip. Since it had been the last place he'd had any family to speak of, he'd wanted to give the town another chance. It occurred to him now that he'd been yearning for family even before he'd met Adelia and fallen for hers.

The gossip and meddling, though? He hadn't been yearning for that.

"Maybe I need to start thinking about moving on again," he said, not even trying to hide his frustration.

"Don't say that," Raylene protested urgently, clearly regretting having pushed him too far. "There are great people here, Gabe. You have family here. And Adelia's here."

"Sometimes I have to wonder if that's enough," he said. "Just tell her I dropped by, okay?"

"You don't want to wait?"

"And let you pry some more? I don't think so."

The bell over the door tinkled merrily as he left, the sound oddly jarring given his suddenly sour mood.

This was the Serenity he remembered, a town where people poked their noses where they didn't belong. Things were already complicated between him and Adelia. How could they possibly figure anything out, if everyone started interfering?

Gabe could respect the fact that Elliott cared about his sister. He could even deal with Mitch and Lynn and their questions. They were family, and he actually believed they might want the best for him.

But everybody else? Didn't they have better things to do than dig around in his personal life? Pressure wasn't going to help anything. He was already stressed out enough over feelings he didn't quite understand and wasn't sure he wanted to be experiencing. If he and Adelia were constantly under a microscope, no matter how well-meaning, he figured they were pretty much doomed.

He worked himself into a real lousy mood just between the boutique and the bakery. He should have turned right around and gone back to the work site down the block, but instead he opted for coffee. With any luck, he could pour himself a cup, leave some money on the counter and get out before Lynn was even aware of his presence.

Naturally that was not the way it went. When he opened the door, Lynn was standing right there, a phone in her hand and a speculative gleam in her eyes. She carefully returned the cell phone to her pocket.

"Raylene says she's sorry," Lynn reported, her eyes narrowing. "What does she have to be sorry about?"

"Nothing," he said tightly, unwilling to open that particular can of worms.

Lynn nodded knowingly. "It must have had something to do with Adelia then."

"Don't go there," Gabe warned.

"Why? Because you can't take being teased?"

Gabe was about to snap back a quick denial, when he realized the evidence would contradict him. Whatever Lynn had heard or guessed clearly suggested that he'd lost it over something that had only been spoken in jest. And he'd overreacted, because he was suddenly very sensitive on the topic of Adelia.

"I'll go next door and apologize," he muttered.

Lynn tried unsuccessfully to hide a grin. "There may be hope for you yet."

"What's that supposed to mean?"

"You recognize that you went a little crazy just because a friend dared to tease you."

"I barely know Raylene."

Lynn rolled her eyes. "That's the part of what I said you want to focus on?"

Gabe scowled. "Okay, yes. I went a little crazy. Maybe even a lot crazy."

"I wonder why," Lynn said, studying him speculatively. "Did she hit too close to home, suggesting that you and Adelia are a couple?"

"It wasn't that," he said, accepting the coffee she'd finally poured for him without his needing to beg. He drew in a deep breath. "Suddenly I was a teenager again and people in this town were dissecting my mom's life. I know I came back here to try to put all of that behind me once and for all, but suddenly it smacked me right in the face." He met Lynn's suddenly worried gaze. "To tell you the truth, I'm not sure I can do this."

"Do what?"

"Stay here."

Now there was real alarm in Lynn's eyes. "You want to take off? You didn't just say that to provoke Raylene?"

"I do and I don't," he said candidly. "And here's the real kicker, either way it's about Adelia."

Lynn waved him toward a table. "Maybe Adelia was right," she mumbled as she followed him.

"Adelia was right about what?" he asked, confused by the odd remark.

"She suggested I get a degree in psychology and start holding my sessions right here. Since you're my second client of the day, she might have been on to something."

"Who was your first?"

"Adelia, of course. She's as confused as you are, by the way." She leveled a look at him that held his attention. "And do you know what that tells me? It tells me that whatever's between the two of you matters. Otherwise neither of you would be wrestling with it. You'd give in to the attraction, settle for a fling and then move on."

"I'm not having a fling with Adelia," Gabe said heatedly, outraged by the suggestion. He had more respect for her than that. He frowned at Lynn. "After everything she's been through, don't you think she deserves better than a fling?"

"Absolutely, and I'm thrilled that you recognize that," Lynn said approvingly. "And what do you deserve, Gabe?"

"Not a woman like Adelia," he said at once.

"Oh, for heaven's sake, do I have to sit here and list all your attributes the way I did for her?"

"You were trying to sell her on my good points?"

"No, on her own," Lynn said impatiently. "Neither of you seems to have a lick of self-esteem, and, frankly, I think that's just pitiful."

"I imagine there are a few people who'd tell you my ego's in pretty good shape," he replied.

"Well, they're not here, and I am. From where I'm sitting, you don't seem to be giving yourself half enough credit for the decent, honorable man you are. Let me ask you something, and I want you to think about the answer for a minute."

"Okay, shoot," he said agreeably, though there was little doubt that he couldn't stop her if he wanted to.

"You think Adelia is an admirable woman, correct?"

"Of course."

"Smart?"

"Absolutely." His eyes narrowed. "Where are you going with this? Do you want me to realize she's too good for me?"

Lynn merely rolled her eyes. "No, my point is that she likes you. She's been spending time with you. She seems to be at least a little bit infatuated. Maybe you should trust her judgment about how worthy you are. She obviously sees something in you that you don't see in yourself."

She'd gotten Gabe's attention at last. "Okay, let's say I'm a great guy, in her eyes, anyway. And we know she's terrific. That still doesn't mean we're a good match."

"No, it doesn't," Lynn agreed.

Her candid reply caught him off guard. "I thought you were a big booster of this relationship."

"Not exactly. I'm a big booster of the two of you getting out of your own way and finding out if you're a good match. She needs to stop throwing up her defenses and you need to stop looking for ways to bail." She stood up and held his gaze. "And that is all I intend to say about that. Mull it over."

Gabe sat where he was and let Lynn's advice sink in. It didn't take long for him to realize she had a point. Maybe more than one. So maybe he wouldn't leave Serenity just yet. Maybe he'd hang around and see how things played out, at least for a little while longer. The grand prize—marriage and a family he'd never dared to envision—just might be within his grasp after all.

Adelia had barely walked in the door at the boutique before Gabe stuck his head in.

"Hey," she said. "You coming in?"

He looked uncomfortable. "I was looking for Raylene."

"I'm here," Raylene called out, stepping out of the office.

"I just wanted to apologize for jumping down your

throat before," he said. He glanced at Adelia. "I'm sure Raylene will explain. I'll see you at the house later?"

"Sure," Adelia said, though she was thoroughly confused and wanted answers now.

Gabe nodded. "Later, then."

"Well, that was odd," Adelia said, watching him back out and take off down the block.

"Not from where I'm standing," Raylene said, a grin on her face.

"What on earth happened while I was gone?"

A guilty expression passed over Raylene's face. "I might have freaked him out just a little."

"How?"

"By teasing him about whatever's going on between the two of you," Raylene admitted. "I don't think he was quite ready for the full-on Sweet Magnolia treatment. You know, prying inappropriately."

Adelia shook her head. "I can imagine. I'm still having a tough time with that myself." She waved off the situation with Gabe. Right this second it wasn't that important. "Do you need to leave right away or can we talk?"

Raylene regarded her with immediate concern. "Of course we can talk. Sounds as if we should have some privacy for this. Not that the office is all that private, but it's better than out here where anybody could walk in and overhear something they shouldn't."

When Raylene was seated at her desk, Adelia had no choice but to sit on the folding chair next to it. There was no room for the nervous pacing that might have made the conversation easier.

She filled Raylene in on what was going on with Carolina, then concluded, "She needs help, but she doesn't want it. I'm way out of my depth here. I don't know what else to do."

"The sad reality is that there's not a lot you can do," Raylene said. "If your sister won't admit what's going on to Carter or agree to press charges, his hands are tied. I think if he got a call to the house and saw evidence of the abuse, he could act, even if she denied it, but she's not going to call, is she?"

"I don't think so," Adelia said. "She keeps saying it's all her fault, as if she's triggering Ricky's rage and, therefore, his reaction is acceptable."

"Been there, done that," Raylene said wearily. "My husband was very good at isolating me, making sure I understood that no one would listen to me, the little nobody from Serenity. Because he had this sterling reputation in Charleston and an important family, I believed him."

"I think that's exactly what Ricky is doing," Adelia said.

"Well, sadly it took losing the baby I was carrying before I finally had the courage to get out and to file charges," Raylene said. "I didn't think there was a chance the charges would stick given his reputation and ability to wiggle out of tight spots, but some doctors stood up and testified about what they'd seen, not just that awful night, but on other E.R. visits. Not even his expensive lawyers and doting parents could save him at that point. These were respected colleagues speaking out, not just me."

"I don't want it to take something terrible for Carolina to wake up," Adelia said.

"Then be there for her as much as you can be. Don't let her push you away. Keep reminding her that help's available, that she has family who loves her, that her kids deserve a mother who doesn't tolerate abuse, that she needs to set an example for them."

Adelia nodded. "That's what finally did it for me with Ernesto. I realized Selena was losing all respect for me because I stayed after finding out about his affairs. And I didn't want Tomas to grow up thinking that men had some inalienable right to cheat. It's surprising how much strength you can find when you see how your decisions are affecting your children."

She thought about Joey and his tendency to lash out with hurtful comments. "I think the situation is taking more of a toll on her oldest than I realized," Adelia said. "I've thought for some time that Joey was just a brat, but now I wonder if he's not acting out either because he's hurting or, even worse, because he's mimicking his father's attitude."

"Give me an example," Raylene suggested.

Adelia described his deliberately mean remarks to Selena about the kiss Adelia and Gabe had shared.

"Maybe you need to tell Carolina about that," Raylene suggested. "Or did you?"

"No. I let it pass. I was more concerned with Selena's reaction."

"I think you need to tell Carolina," Raylene said. "It's a concrete example of how her son is being affected by what's going on. She's a mother first. That instinct to protect her kids is strong."

"She doesn't think they're in danger," Adelia lamented.

"Maybe they're not, physically," Raylene said. "But that doesn't mean the situation isn't harmful to them.

Just what you described about her oldest suggests that much."

"I'll try bringing that to her attention," Adelia said. "Thanks."

"Don't thank me," Raylene said. "I owe a lot of people for standing by me. If I can do even half as much for someone else, it'll go at least a tiny bit toward paying back that debt." She held Adelia's gaze. "Don't stay away, no matter how hard Carolina tries to push you out of her life. When things get worse, and there's little doubt in my mind that they will, she'll remember that she can come to you."

Adelia sighed, thinking of her conversation earlier, the one in which her sister had expected her to gloat. "I hope so," she said softly. "I really hope so."

For the second day in a row, Adelia went home exhausted and emotionally drained. Just inside the front door, she paused and listened to the laughter coming from the kitchen. The happy sound washed over her, easing just a little of the tension she'd been feeling ever since her visit to Carolina.

She walked into the kitchen and found the girls once more around the kitchen table doing homework. Selena jumped up and hugged her, then bounced toward the refrigerator.

"I'll put dinner in the oven now," she said. "I've set the dining room table already."

"Mama, look at the A I got on my book report," Juanita said, interrupting them.

"And I got a B plus on my math test," Natalia chimed in, eager to share her own success. "It's the first time ever!"

Adelia smiled at them. "Then we need to celebrate." She turned to her oldest. "And how did you do on your history test?"

Selena made a face that had Adelia's heart dropping. Then her daughter grinned.

"An A minus," Selena said, then confided, "It's because Gabe helped me."

"He helped us, too," Natalia said.

That came as a surprise to Adelia. "How did he help?"

"He came up with a way for me to remember all those dates," Selena said. "While he was working, he'd play this game he made up, sort of like *Jeopardy* only just about history. For the first time ever, history was actually fun."

"He showed me what I was doing wrong on my math problems," Natalia revealed. "He never once said I was dumb for not getting it."

Adelia's temper stirred. "Who told you that you were dumb?" she asked. "You know that's not a word I like you to use."

"The teacher," Natalia said.

"She actually said that you were dumb?" Adelia pressed, increasingly infuriated.

"Kinda," Natalia said, backing off a little. "The other kids laughed."

Adelia vowed to have a talk with that teacher first thing in the morning. Nobody should be telling a student, any student, that they were dumb just because they were having trouble grasping a concept.

Biting back her annoyance, she turned to Juanita. "Did Gabe help you, too?"

Juanita nodded. "He asked me to tell him what my

book was about," she explained. "Then he told me I should write the report just the way I'd told him. So that's what I did. The teacher said it was the best book report she'd heard all day."

How had she not been aware of any of this, Adelia wondered. She joined her children at the kitchen table. "So maybe we should have more than a celebration," she suggested. "Maybe you could think of some way to thank Gabe for his help."

"We already did," Juanita said, bouncing in her seat. "Show Mom, Selena."

Selena rolled out a banner they'd made: Gabe, you're the best! The colorful letters were decorated not just with bright drawings of balloons and streamers, but with an assortment of tools. There was even a sparkling tiara over his name.

Adelia touched a finger to that tiara and smiled. "Nice touch."

She glanced around. "Where's your brother, or do I even need to ask?"

"Helping Gabe, of course," Selena said.

"And his homework?"

"He did that first. Gabe said if he didn't get it finished, he couldn't help. Now Gabe's working on his spelling words with him."

Amazing, Adelia thought. She couldn't recall a single time when Ernesto had even asked to see homework, much less helped any of the kids with it. That, he'd insisted, was her responsibility.

"What's Gabe working on today?" she asked as she rose to go upstairs and check on him.

Selena smiled. "I think it's a surprise. You should probably stay here. I'll go check."

Though Adelia wanted to argue, a part of her couldn't resist the prospect of a surprise, especially one that put a smile on her daughter's face. Most of the surprises that had come her way lately had been less than positive.

"I'll check the freezer for ice cream while you're gone," she told Selena. "Then we can celebrate after dinner."

"There isn't any," Selena said. "I checked." She regarded Adelia hopefully. "Instead, maybe we could walk to Wharton's after we eat."

"Yes, please," Natalia said. Her plea was echoed by Juanita.

Adelia looked into their happy, expectant faces and realized how far they'd come in just a few weeks. "Wharton's it is," she agreed.

"Great. I'll tell Gabe," Selena said, bounding off.

Shaking her head at her daughter's burst of enthusiasm, Adelia wondered if Gabe had any idea of the role he'd played in the miracle that was happening in her home. He still thought he wasn't cut out for family life, but around here, it sure seemed he was slowly becoming the center of hers.

Gabe looked around Adelia's bedroom worriedly. He'd tried to put it together in the way he thought she'd want it, but he was a guy and he was pretty sure she'd have her own ideas. Selena walked in the door and uttered a gasp. He turned to look at her.

"Was that an 'oh my gosh what a mess' gasp?" he asked, frowning.

"No, it was a 'you got it exactly right' gasp," she said, grinning at him. "Mom's going to love it."

"I hope so. She did pick out the color."

"It's not just about the paint," she told him. "It's all the stuff you got, the pretty pillows, the new comforter." She gestured toward the nightstand. "The flowers. I can't remember Mom ever getting flowers before."

Gabe didn't find that especially reassuring. Sure, Ernesto was a jerk, but maybe she was allergic. Maybe she didn't like flowers.

"She doesn't have an allergy to flowers, does she?" he asked worriedly.

"No, she loves them," Selena said. "You should have seen our garden at the old house. She was out there all the time. Sometimes she'd pick this huge bouquet and make a centerpiece for the dining room table. It was as pretty as anything I've ever seen in a magazine."

"Maybe this won't seem like much, then," he said, unable to stop himself from fretting. It was ridiculous. It was a bouquet of flowers, not a declaration of some kind.

"Gabe, she's going to love them," Selena reassured him. She glanced around the room. "Is everything ready? Can I let her come up?"

He surveyed the room one more time and concluded it was as ready as he knew how to make it. "Send her up."

Selena nodded and beckoned for Tomas. "Come downstairs with me."

"But I want to be here when Mom sees the surprise," he protested.

"It's Gabe's surprise," she said emphatically. "Let him show Mom. Otherwise, I'll tell her you don't deserve to go with the rest of us for ice cream after dinner." She glanced at Gabe. "That's one reason I came up here, to tell you we're going out to celebrate all the good grades we got. You have to come, too."

Gabe chuckled at her enthusiasm. "Absolutely."

Though he was tempted to tell her Tomas could stay, just to have a buffer, he let Selena coax her brother from the room.

Gabe walked around after Selena and Tomas had gone, checking things that didn't need to be checked again, his nerves shot. What had made him think he could pull off something like this? He had no idea what sort of frilly things women liked.

"Gabe!"

He whirled around at the stunned tone of Adelia's voice. "Is it okay?" he asked, annoyed at how insecure he sounded. "I have all the receipts if you want to take anything back. Selena gave me some ideas, but I've never shopped for stuff like this before. She unpacked all the boxes and put all your clothes in the closet. I think she even ironed a few things. She wanted to be part of the surprise."

"It's perfect," Adelia whispered, tears filling her eyes. "Nobody has ever done anything this sweet for me before."

"Then you like it?" he asked again, just to be sure. "And you're not mad because I overstepped or something?"

"I love it. And if there weren't a bunch of kids downstairs desperate to know if I like it, I'd show you just how much."

Gabe's lips curved at that. "Really?" He crossed the room and stood in front of her. "You sure we couldn't take just a minute?"

"It would be a risk," she said, a twinkle in her eyes. "They're very anxious."

"We could call Selena's cell phone and bribe her to keep them down there," he suggested hopefully.

"First, she's not allowed to answer her cell phone," Adelia said, struggling to keep her expression stern. "Second, I do not want my teenage daughter wondering what you and I might be doing up here. And, third, if we try it, I sense there will be a rebellion. Tomas was already putting up a struggle about having to be downstairs and missing the surprise. He's probably sitting on the top step right this second."

Gabe sighed dramatically. "Another time then?"

"Most definitely," she said.

There was a heated promise in her eyes that left him a little bit desperate.

"Maybe after dinner—"

"And a walk to Wharton's for ice cream," she reminded him, not shooting him down exactly but postponing any reward even longer.

"Right. I forgot all about the celebration. Maybe after that, if either of us can even keep our eyes open, we can steal a little alone time to talk about things."

"Things?"

"Us. Our days. You know, the stuff I assume couples talk about at the end of the day."

She regarded him with obvious surprise. "We're a couple?"

"I'm beginning to think we might not have a choice in the matter," he said, his tone resigned.

"You sound so cheery about that," she teased. "It makes me all warm and fuzzy."

"Hey, I'm just getting used to the idea, but something Lynn said finally got through to me."

"What was that?"

"That we needed to get out of our own way."

Adelia smiled. "She said much the same to me. Something tells me tomorrow I'll owe her a very big tip."

Gabe laughed. "Let's see how her advice works out first."

She gestured around the bedroom. "It's already resulted in this. I'm obviously a lucky woman."

"No, sweetheart. I'm the lucky one," Gabe said. And he had no idea what he'd done to deserve it.

CHAPTER NINETEEN

When Adelia, Gabe and her children walked into Wharton's, Adelia didn't miss the speculative look Grace cast at them. She wondered just how long it would take before word of this outing spread through town.

"Well, this looks like it might be some sort of special occasion," Grace said.

"We're celebrating," Tomas piped up. "'Cause we all got good grades in school and Gabe helped us."

Grace's eyes lit up. "Is that so?" she said, regarding Gabe with approval. "Times surely have changed."

Adelia wasn't sure she cared for Grace's implication, but Gabe didn't seem to be taking offense, so she, too, let it pass.

"What does this celebration call for?" Grace asked. "Cones? Hot fudge sundaes?"

Tomas's eyes lit up. "I want a hot fudge sundae," he said eagerly. "Or a banana split."

"That's too much for you," Adelia told him. "You'll never finish it."

"Gabe can share with me," he said, then turned to his newfound hero. "Wanna?"

"Sure," Gabe said, then looked to Grace. "Do you still make those small banana splits?"

"I sure do," she said.

"But I want a big one," Tomas protested.

"A small one that you share with Gabe or none," Adelia told him firmly.

Though he wore a pout on his face, Tomas grudgingly agreed.

The girls ordered cones and then Grace turned to her.

"How about you, Adelia?"

She thought of how hard she'd fought to take off the pounds she'd gained after carrying each of her babies. Ice cream had been off-limits for months now. As if he were reading her mind, she realized Gabe's gaze was on her.

"I think you deserve a hot fudge sundae," he told her solemnly.

"But—"

"I'll eat what you don't finish."

She laughed at his hopeful expression. "Are you thinking that half a small banana split won't fill you up?"

He leaned closer and whispered in her ear, "No, I'm thinking of how much I'm going to enjoy watching you savor every bite of that sundae. Maybe I'll even get to lick a little hot fudge off your lips later."

Adelia felt an instant rush of heat into her cheeks. She quickly turned to Grace. "A very small hot fudge sundae," she requested, a breathless note in her voice.

Grace chuckled. "Good choice."

Because there were six of them, they took two booths, with the girls seated in the one behind Adelia, Gabe and Tomas. Apparently her disappointment at not being alone with Gabe showed in her face, because within seconds after their ice cream had been served, Gabe put down his spoon with a dramatic sigh.

"That's it for me," he announced. "Tomas, you can take the rest and finish it up with your sisters."

Adelia saw the storm clouds darkening her son's eyes, but before she could second Gabe's suggestion, he held her son's gaze. "Please," he said quietly. "I need a few minutes to speak to your mom alone."

"Okay," Tomas grumbled, his tone resigned.

She studied Gabe with a sense of wonder as her son took his ice cream to the neighboring booth. "Do you have some kind of magic touch? I was expecting a full-blown tantrum."

He shrugged. "He usually listens to me."

"Because you have something he wants," she realized.

Gabe looked confused. "What?"

"Tools," she said. "And the willingness to spend the time to teach him how to use them. I imagine to Tomas that's a pretty good bargaining chip."

"I've never resorted to bribing your son," Gabe protested with a touch of indignation.

"Haven't you? I heard that just this afternoon you told him he couldn't help you till his homework was done. Well done, by the way."

Gabe regarded her with a startled expression. "I was just trying to be responsible."

"An excellent parental attitude," she commended him. Before she could lose her nerve, she asked,

"Gabe, you've told me you didn't think you were any good at relationships. Didn't you ever want kids?"

He seemed taken aback by the question. "I never thought about it," he claimed.

"Why?"

"Because I didn't have a very good example in my life. My mom did her best under the circumstances, but her best wasn't so great. I never even knew my dad, and the men who paraded through her life weren't exactly role models. I didn't want to take any chances about messing up some kid's life."

"You're certainly not doing anything to mess up my kids' lives. They're happier than they have been in months. They're doing well in school, something I'd despaired of seeing this school year. A lot of the credit for that goes to you. And in my book that makes you great parent material."

Gabe looked shaken by the comment. "Adelia, I don't know. I'm still grappling with whether I can give you what you need, much less your kids."

"First of all, you're already giving them what they need, your love and attention. Second, we're a package deal. You can't separate me from my kids."

"No, of course not," he said at once. "I guess I was just compartmentalizing."

"How so?"

"I thought maybe we could figure out the whole relationship thing. Then if that's going okay, we'd start thinking about the rest."

She laughed at his naïveté. "Then I think you've done things backwards. You already have my kids thinking you hung the moon. Even Selena has come around a lot more quickly than I'd anticipated." The implications of that suddenly had her sobering. "I wonder if that's been a mistake."

Gabe frowned. "What do you mean?"

"What if this thing between us doesn't go anywhere?" she asked. "What is wrong with me? I never should have let this happen. I just saw how the kids seemed to be blossoming under your attention and stood by and let them start to care about you. Even when you and I split up so they wouldn't get ideas about us, I still let them spend time with you. Naturally they were going to get attached."

Gabe reached for her hand and gave it a squeeze. "I won't let them down," he promised. "No matter what happens between us."

"I don't think it will work that way," she said. "If we can't figure things out, they're bound to be crushed."

"So, what are you saying?" he asked, a frown on his face. "Do you want to call it all off, after all?"

Before she could respond, he added, "If you do, just say the word. I can probably rearrange things with Mitch so I can work while they're at school. Or with most of the work already done, someone else could finish up. I can ease out of their lives, if that's what you think is best."

"It's not best," Adelia said, thoroughly frustrated by his willingness to end things before they even got started. Was he really that skittish? Or was she that unimportant to him? Or was this another one of those misunderstandings that could easily spiral out of control and have them making decisions they'd come to regret.

She sighed, determined not to let that happen. "It's already too late to do what's best, Gabe. They adore you. I don't know about the younger ones, but Selena's already getting ideas about the two of us. You should have seen how excited she was helping me get dressed for our date and that was before she fully approved of me being with you at all. Then again today when you'd planned that surprise for me, I think she was almost as excited as you were."

Gabe regarded her with confusion. "Help me out here, Adelia. I'm getting mixed signals. What exactly do you want me to do?"

She'd never felt so utterly helpless in her life. Anything she suggested would wind up hurting someone she loved. Her kids. Gabe. Even herself. "I honestly don't know."

"Is this one of those times when we should be listening to Lynn's advice?" he asked. "Are we getting in our own way, complicating something that doesn't need to be that complicated?"

"I have to think about my kids," she said stubbornly.

But wasn't that the rub? If she pushed Gabe away now, her kids would be miserable. If she let him stay in their lives and they grew even more attached and he left eventually, they'd be devastated.

Gabe shoved a hand through his hair, his expression filled with obvious frustration. "This sure wasn't how I envisioned tonight going," he told her.

"Me, either." She studied him, sensing she didn't have the whole picture. "I know about the reward thing you were hoping for later. Was there more?"

He nodded. "After listening to Lynn and putting up with Raylene's commentary, I was ready to make it official."

Adelia's heart thudded. "Official?"

"To tell you I wanted us to be a couple, or at least to try to be. I figured we could go on more dates, hang out in public." He gave her a rueful smile. "Let those Sweet Magnolia friends of yours have a field day."

She knew exactly what it was costing him to express a willingness to submit to all that well-meant teasing and interference. And here she was suggesting they take not just a step back, but maybe call it off entirely. Talk about crossed signals.

Her dilemma must have showed on her face, because he leaned forward and kept a tight grip on her hand. "What do you want, Adelia? Forget the kids for a minute. Forget all the potential complications that may or may not happen. What do you really want?"

She thought of the kisses they'd shared, the way Gabe made her feel, as if she were incredibly special. "You," she said, her voice barely above a whisper. She dared to meet his gaze. "I want you."

"Are you sure?"

She nodded. "But what if—"

A smile broke across his face. "Too late for what-if," he declared, cutting her off. "You've already said you want me. I heard you."

"But—"

"Nope, too late," he said again. "We're in too deep for what-if. Your kids are already invested. We need to play this out. If we don't, if we cut and run because you're scared for them or because I'm just plain terrified, it would be wrong. We're going to do the adult thing and see where this goes."

He sounded so sure, so confident, but Adelia could see the uncertainty in his eyes. Ironically, it was that uncertainty and his willingness to rise above it that gave her the courage to nod. "We'll do the adult thing, then," she said softly. "At least we can be terrified together."

He nodded. "Sounds like a plan."

Despite all her reservations, despite the panic that she was barely keeping at bay, she had to agree. It sounded like an amazing plan.

"I warned you!"

Gabe's head snapped up at the threatening tone. Ernesto Hernandez was just inside the doorway at the construction site, his voice echoing across the cavernous room. Every worker in the place had gone silent. Gabe gestured for them to resume working, but they ignored his words and kept a careful gaze on Ernesto as Gabe crossed to stand in front of him. Apparently his maturity was about to be tested again, because he wanted like crazy just to slug the man.

Instead, refusing to let the scene escalate if he could help it, he said mildly, "Something I can do for you?"

"You can stay away from my kids," Ernesto said. "You don't get to parade them around town as if they're yours."

"When have I ever done that?" Gabe asked, barely restraining the desire to remind the man that he wasn't exactly filling up the hours of their days with his attention.

"Last night," Ernesto said. "I heard all about your little outing to Wharton's. What was it you were celebrating? A few good marks at school? The kids are supposed to make good grades. That's their job. There's no need to reward them for it."

"Their mother doesn't seem to agree," Gabe said.

Ernesto shrugged off the comment. "She'll ruin them before she's done. I have half a mind to get Tomas out of her house."

Gabe's temper kicked up another notch at the threat. "Adelia is a wonderful mother. No court would take that boy away from her."

"Are you so sure about that? Even after they hear about the kind of man she's allowing to influence him?" He pulled his cell phone from his pocket. "I have my lawyer on speed dial. Maybe we should ask him."

"Be sure to remind him why you're divorced in the first place," Gabe suggested.

The remark hit home. Now Ernesto looked as if he wanted to throw the first punch. A part of Gabe actually hoped that he would. It was plain, though, that even Ernesto recognized that doing it in front of witnesses wouldn't help his cause. Gabe's crew, led by Henry Davis, had moved a little closer just in case Ernesto dared to start something. Or maybe they'd moved so they could hear better. Either way, their presence kept things from turning even uglier.

"This isn't over," Ernesto warned him. "I can still make Adelia's life hell."

"Worse than you have already?" Gabe inquired.

Ernesto leveled a cold look straight at him. "Watch me." He turned then and left, leaving Gabe both shaken and furious.

One of his men edged closer. Gabe turned to meet Henry's worried gaze.

"Boss, you don't want to mess with him," Henry warned. "He's a nasty, self-important son of a gun."

"I've noticed," Gabe said.

"He'll get to Adelia by going after you," Henry said. "I know his type. It took a strip out of his pride when she left him. He's been waiting for a chance to get even."

Gabe had figured out that much for himself. "Thanks, Henry. I'll watch out for Adelia."

The older man smiled. "I don't doubt that, but who's going to be watching out for you?" He held Gabe's gaze. "You might want to sit down with Helen Decatur-Whitney. That woman has a good head on her shoulders. She tangled with Hernandez once and I'm pretty sure she'd be eager to take him on again."

Gabe nodded. "I think I'll do just that. Can you handle things here for an hour or two?"

"I've got it," Henry said at once. "And I know how to reach you or Mitch if anything comes up I can't handle."

Gabe walked the few blocks to Helen's office, using the time to try to cool down. He was not going to let a slime bag like Ernesto make Adelia miserable or ruin what they'd just agreed to try to build together.

Unfortunately, when he walked into Helen's waiting room, it was packed. Her secretary, a woman he thought he recognized from working in the high school office years ago, scowled when she saw him.

"I know you don't have an appointment, Gabe Franklin," Barb told him. She gestured to the crowded waiting room. "Helen doesn't have time for you. You might just as well turn around and leave."

Since he didn't want everyone in the waiting room in on his business with Helen, he leaned down and tried to practice some of that charm he was supposed to possess. "Darlin', I know I don't have an appointment, but this is a little bit of an emergency."

"Are the police on your heels?" she asked. "It wouldn't surprise me a bit."

Gabe bit back his annoyance. "No, but they could be my next stop. Ernesto Hernandez is making threats about trying to take Adelia's son from her. I thought Helen ought to know about it."

Barb's expression went from annoyance to dismay in a heartbeat. "He wouldn't dare."

"Not if he has half a brain," Gabe agreed. "Do you think he does?"

"Hardly," she said, clearly concluding that whatever her beef might be with Gabe, he was the lesser of two evils. "Give me a minute and I'll squeeze you in."

"Thank you, darlin'."

"Stop calling me that. It won't work on me."

Gabe gave her an innocent look. "No idea what you mean."

She shook her head, but for an instant, he thought he saw her expression mellow just a little.

He stood off to the side and waited. The second Helen's current client exited her office, Barb stood up and headed in. In less than a minute, she was beckoning for him.

"Fifteen minutes," she warned both Gabe and Helen. "Not one second more or I'll have a rebellion on my hands out there."

Helen's serious expression reflected Gabe's mood. "Tell me," she said.

Gabe described the incident and the threat. "It's the second time he's warned me to stay away from his kids and suggested he'd take Adelia to court to make sure I couldn't be a bad influence on them."

"He doesn't have a leg to stand on," Helen said. "I know all about the trouble you got in back then. It was kid stuff. I'll check, but you never spent a single night in jail or even had a charge against you that stood up, right?"

"Not a one," Gabe said. "It doesn't mean I didn't cause my share of trouble. I don't want that to be used against Adelia."

To his surprise, Helen grinned. "Spoken like the honorable man I've been hearing a lot about recently. Stop worrying, Gabe. I'm on this."

He didn't believe it could be as easy to keep Ernesto in check as she was making it sound. "But—"

"Gabe, I am very, very good at what I do," Helen assured him quietly. "And what I do, among many other things, is neutralize threats against my clients, especially when it comes to their kids."

Gabe saw the fire in her eyes and realized this was not a woman he'd want to go up against in court, not when she thought she was on the side of right and justice.

He nodded, satisfied. "I'll leave it in your hands then."

"By the way," she said, a smile on her lips. "Good job in not punching the guy's lights out. It might have been satisfying, but it wouldn't have helped."

"I figured as much. If he hurts Adelia, though, I can't promise I'll show the same restraint."

"Try," she said. "But if you do lose control, and frankly I could hardly blame you, call me. I'll bail you out and represent you pro bono for doing what a whole lot of us would like to do to that man."

Gabe chuckled. "Now you're just tempting me."

She held up a hand. "Last resort, okay? Promise."

"Last resort," Gabe confirmed. Somehow knowing the kind of friend Adelia had on her side made it a whole lot easier to swear to that and mean it.

At the sound of the bell, Adelia glanced up from the catalogs she'd been marking while waiting for any customers to turn up at the boutique. To her surprise Selena stood hesitantly in the doorway, her expression dark. It had been weeks since Adelia had seen that particular look on Selena's face.

"What's wrong?" she asked at once.

"Is it okay that I'm here? Are you busy?"

"It's fine. I've told you before that you can come by here whenever you want to. Where are your sisters and brother?"

"Next door at the bakery," her oldest reported. "It'll take them forever to pick out cupcakes. I needed to talk to you when they're not around."

Adelia beckoned her in. "What's going on? Did something happen at school today?"

Selena nodded. "Daddy was waiting outside of school when I got out," she said. "He was with that woman again."

Adelia wanted to utter a curse, but she refrained. "What did he want?"

"He said we needed to get to know each other because she'd be our stepmother and we'd all be living with them soon."

Adelia's control vanished. "He said what?" she asked, stunned by what she was hearing.

"Mom, he was lying, wasn't he?" Selena asked, real panic in her voice. "He can't make us come and live with them. I'll run away if he does that. I swear I will."

"You're not going to live with your father," Adelia said flatly, already reaching for her phone.

Selena's eyes widened. If anything, she looked even more frightened. "You're not going to call him, are you? I don't want you fighting again."

"I'm not calling him. I'm calling Helen."

Selena immediately looked relieved. "She'll fix it, won't she? She'll stop him before he says anything to Tomas and the girls, right? I know they're supposed to spend the day with him Saturday, but he's never shown up before." Her panic suddenly returned. "What if he does this time and gets them all worked up? Or even worse, what if he won't bring them home?"

"Not going to happen," Adelia said fiercely. She held up a hand to silence Selena when Barb answered the phone in Helen's office. Adelia quickly explained the situation and was put right through.

"Blast it all!" Helen said when Adelia had filled her in. "I was afraid of something like this. I thought I had time to deal with it before Ernesto did something stupid. I guess I underestimated how angry he was."

"Angry? What are you talking about?" Adelia asked.

"Gabe was here earlier. Apparently Ernesto confronted him at work earlier."

"Why?"

"He was furious about your outing last night to Wharton's," Helen explained. "It must have triggered some sort of macho pride thing because he told Gabe he was going to take Tomas away from you. He didn't say anything about the girls as far as I know. Obviously after giving it more thought, he concluded that Selena would be a great target to stir things up even more. He knows she's never forgiven him. By going to her, he's escalated the situation and gotten her to panic."

"You have no idea," Adelia said, as Selena leaned into her side, tears on her cheeks. She kept a firm arm around her daughter's waist. "What can we do?"

"You said his mistress was with him when he spoke to Selena?"

"That's what she said."

"I know this is personal, but have you and Gabe slept together? I know it's what we've all been hoping for you, but it could complicate this situation."

"Not yet," Adelia said, cheeks flushed.

"Keep it that way for now. I want to be able to use the way Ernesto flaunts his mistress in front of his children. I'm calling the judge's office now to set an emergency hearing. Try not to worry, okay? He's not going to take your kids. He hasn't even exercised the right he was granted for visitation, has he?"

"Not more than a couple of times way back at the beginning. He doesn't even call, as far as I know."

Selena nodded. "He's never called me. Not even once."

Adelia started to repeat it, but Helen said, "I heard. I'll let you know the minute I have that hearing scheduled."

Adelia uttered a sigh of relief. She knew she was in good hands. Helen's reputation as a barracuda in the courtroom wasn't an idle designation. She'd tear

Ernesto apart if he tried to hurt Adelia's kids. In fact, she'd probably do a better job than Adelia could ever do on her own.

When she hung up, she looked into Selena's worried gaze. "Helen's going to fix this?" her daughter asked.

"Absolutely."

"Mom, is this because of Gabe? Did I hear Helen say something about Dad going after him?"

"It's nothing for you to worry about," Adelia insisted. "Helen's got it."

"But it's not fair that Dad would try to hurt Gabe," Selena protested. "All he's done is be nice to us and to you."

"I know, sweetie. You don't need to worry about Gabe. He can take care of himself."

"But he shouldn't have to," Selena protested.

No, Adelia thought. *He really shouldn't have to.* Perhaps last night's decision had been premature. Perhaps this was just one more sign that their attempt to form some sort of relationship was a really bad idea.

CHAPTER TWENTY

❖

Gabe was stunned when he received a call from Helen just as he was about to leave the work site on Main Street.

"I need you in court tomorrow morning at nine. Can you be there?" she asked.

"This must be about Ernesto."

"Of course. After he paid a visit to you this morning, he waited at school for Selena," she explained, her voice filled with disdain. "He wanted her to get to know her potential new stepmommy. He told her they'd all soon be living together. Naturally that sent her into a tailspin."

Gabe felt his free hand close into a fist. "I can't believe even he would be so insensitive."

"Of course he is. The man's either delusional or an idiot. Either way, it played right into my hands. I intend to prove to the judge that this demonstrates that he's completely unsuited to be a parent. He's using those children as a weapon. If I have my way, he'll be stripped of visitation rights, at least until the kids are old enough to decide for themselves if they want to spend time with him. If I can't convince the judge of that, then I at least want the visits supervised."

Despite the seriousness of the situation, Gabe was reassured by the determination in Helen's voice. Whatever she needed from him, she had it. "What can I do?"

"Just tell the judge about the threats Ernesto made to you," she said.

"Done," Gabe said at once. "And I have witnesses. Would they help? You may not want my whole crew traipsing into court, but how about Henry Davis? He heard every word for sure. I know he'd be willing, maybe even eager, to testify about what he saw and heard."

"Good idea," Helen said. "Henry's a good guy and he'll be viewed as impartial, at least when it comes to the custody matter. I may not need him, but it won't hurt to have backup just in case."

"We'll be there," Gabe promised. "I'll give him a call right now."

As soon as he'd hung up, he tracked down Henry and got his commitment to be at the courthouse before nine.

Gabe had intended to head to Adelia's, but under the circumstances he had to wonder if that was such a good idea, at least tonight. Maybe they should be more circumspect, at least for the next twenty-four hours. He was still debating with himself about that when Adelia appeared on the sidewalk outside the space he was renovating. Gabe stepped out and locked the door behind him.

She studied his expression, then sighed. "You've already heard?"

Gabe nodded. "I'm so sorry that I seem to have triggered this."

"You didn't do anything wrong. Neither did I. This is just Ernesto's way of trying to prove he's still got control of my life. I swear I actually hate him for this," she said, the look on her face filled with loathing.

"Up till now I've managed to stand up for him with the kids." She shook her head. "Why did I even bother? I've even encouraged them to spend time with him, not that he's taken advantage of that. I'm done, though," she declared forcefully. "He's crossed a line. I won't let them be his pawns and I certainly won't let him force that woman on them, not unless it's court-mandated that I have to."

"Good for you," he said, desperately wanting to reach for her but knowing it was a bad idea.

"Are you coming over?"

Gabe shook his head. "I was just thinking we should probably take a time-out, especially with this court date in the morning."

She heaved another sigh, clearly disappointed. "You're probably right. Ernesto probably has a private detective stationed across the street from the house, ready to snap pictures. That would be just like him."

Gabe regretted that he'd already locked up. He wished he could drag Adelia inside and kiss her until she lost that anxious expression. It wasn't something he could do out here on the street, though. That private eye she was so worried about could just as easily be right here on Main Street. He settled for tucking a finger under her chin.

"It's going to be okay," he promised. "Helen's exactly the person I'd want on my side in this situation. She impressed the daylights out of me when I spoke to her earlier."

She smiled a little at that. "No question about it. She kept me sane during the divorce. Nothing rattles her."

"Then don't let it rattle you," he said. "I'll see you first thing in the morning. If you need me before then, call."

"I'm sorry you got dragged into this," she said again.

"Hey, don't you dare be sorry," he replied. "You didn't do the dragging. We can both thank Ernesto for that."

"But you like things easy and uncomplicated."

"Seems as if that's been a lost cause since I met you," he said, then winked at her. "I'm starting to think easy and uncomplicated are highly overrated, anyway."

She laughed, just as he'd intended.

"Night, darlin'." He regretted he couldn't put some color in her cheeks with a kiss, but the endearment seemed to have almost the same effect.

"Maybe I'll call you later just to say good-night again," she said, then added in a low, surprisingly sultry voice, "After I'm in bed."

He swallowed hard at the twinkle in her eyes, then chuckled. "Who knew you were a big ol' tease, Adelia Hernandez?"

"I know," she said, smiling brightly at last. "Who knew?"

To Adelia's surprise just that few minutes with Gabe right on Main Street where anyone could see was enough to settle her nerves over tomorrow's court date. Of course, the realization that she'd been flirting outrageously with him caused its own share of jitters.

What had she been thinking? She couldn't think of a single time in her life that she'd tossed out daring innuendoes the way she had with him.

As she remained standing on the corner after he'd gone, her kids came running out of the bakery to join her. Given the amount of frosting on their faces, she had a hunch they'd be on a sugar high for most of the evening.

"Mommy, we had cupcakes," Juanita announced happily. "I had one with chocolate frosting and sprinkles and one with pink frosting."

"Yes, I can see that," Adelia said, taking a tissue from her purse and wiping away the evidence. She beckoned for Natalia, then wiped her face. "Only chocolate?"

Natalia nodded. "But I had three."

Adelia put her hands on her hips and turned to Tomas. "And you, young man? I see chocolate frosting and vanilla," she said as she scrubbed his face with the tissue. "And what's this?"

"Caramel," he said happily. "Lynn said it was new. I still like chocolate the best, though."

She glanced over his head at Selena.

"Sorry, Mom. I didn't think they had enough money for more than one, but Lynn floated them a loan. I paid her when I got back over there."

"What about you?" she asked Selena. "Didn't you want a cupcake?"

Her daughter, who'd always loved sweets, shook her head. "I wasn't hungry."

Adelia understood exactly why. "How about one to take home? You might feel more like it later."

Selena shrugged off the offer. "That's okay."

"Well, I doubt these three are going to be hungry anytime soon. What about you? Anything special you'd like me to fix for dinner?"

Again, Selena shook her head. Adelia decided to let it drop for now.

At home she sent the three younger children into the yard to run off some of their excess energy, then gestured for Selena to join her in the kitchen.

"Sweetie, I know you're worried, but you don't need to be," she told her.

"How can you say that?" Selena demanded with surprising anger. "Dad's going to ruin everything again."

Startled by her vehemence, Adelia reached for her hands. "Nothing's ruined."

"How can you say that? Gabe's not here, is he? I don't hear him upstairs and his truck's not in the driveway. That's because of Dad."

"In a way, yes," Adelia said, unable to deny it. "But Gabe and I agreed it would be for the best if he stayed away just for tonight. Once we see the judge in the morning, things can go back to normal."

"What if they can't?" Selena asked. "You don't know for sure what the judge is going to say. He could be on Dad's side. He could make us live with him."

"He could, but he's not going to," Adelia said with more confidence than she actually felt. "Helen won't let that happen."

"I know Helen's a really, really good lawyer, but she's not the judge," Selena said, unappeased. "Dad could bribe the judge or something."

While Adelia doubted Ernesto would be above doing just that, she had faith in Helen and, for that matter, in the judge. "I think it would only land your father in a lot of hot water if he tried anything like that," she told Selena. "There are pretty serious consequences for crossing that line."

"I guess," Selena said.

Adelia heard the skepticism in Selena's voice and realized the toll the past months had taken on her daughter. At only thirteen, she was bitter and cynical. Adelia wondered if there was any way at all to recapture just a little of that lost innocence.

"Look, I understand why you find all of this upsetting," Adelia told her gently. "I really do."

"No, you don't," Selena said. "Lately we've been like a real family, or the way a family's supposed to be. We have dinner together. Gabe helps us with homework. We even had game night again. Now it's all messed up. What if Gabe goes away and we never see him again?"

"Not that long ago you didn't want him around here," Adelia reminded her.

"That was before," Selena said.

"Before what?"

"Before he made you laugh again and before he was so nice to Tomas and to me, Natalia and Juanita, too." She gave Adelia a plaintive look. "He reminds me of the way Uncle Elliott treats Daisy and Mack. I was so jealous of that for so long. Then Gabe came along and I thought maybe we'd have someone who treats us like that, like he really cares about us."

Adelia smiled, even though her eyes were stinging with tears she didn't dare shed. "Gabe does care about you," she agreed. She wasn't sure if even he was aware how much.

"You'd hate it if he went away, wouldn't you?" Selena asked.

"Sure I would," Adelia admitted. "But I don't think Gabe plans on going anywhere right now. And he certainly wouldn't take off just because your dad's being a bully."

"He left town once before," Selena said, her voice hesitant. "Joey told me. He said Gabe was always in trouble when he was a kid and that when things got bad, he just took off. Joey says he'll probably do it again."

"Joey doesn't know what he's talking about," Adelia said angrily, though she knew that wasn't exactly the case. For once he did have the basic facts right. He just wasn't taking into account the man Gabe was today.

"Did Joey lie?" Selena pressed.

"Not exactly," Adelia conceded. "There were people who were mean to him and to his mom back then. He got into some fights trying to stand up for her. After his mom died, he did leave Serenity. Who could blame him? Nobody wants to be where they've been mistreated."

"But that's exactly the same as what's happening now," Selena protested.

"But Gabe isn't the same person. I believe he'll stay right here, at least for as long as we need him," Adelia said, aware that she was putting her faith in him. There were so many reasons she needed to believe he wouldn't let them down.

Selena frowned. "What does that mean, for as long as we need him?"

Adelia didn't dare look too far into the future. Now was all she could count on. "It means that he's not going to bail on us because of anything your dad does."

Apparently Adelia wasn't as good at hiding her own

fears as she'd hoped to be. Selena, rather than looking relieved, seemed more worried than before. Apparently she was a little too good at reading between the lines.

"But you think he will leave eventually, don't you?" Selena asked, proving Adelia's point.

"It's a possibility," Adelia admitted reluctantly.

"But I thought he really liked us," Selena said plaintively. "You just said so yourself. And I thought he might even be falling in love with you."

"Sweetie, life's more complicated than that. Even if both of those things are true, it doesn't always mean that things will work out," Adelia said.

"Well, that just sucks," Selena said, pushing away from the table and racing from the room in tears.

Adelia sighed, hating that she'd managed to make things worse for Selena by trying to be honest with her. Selena was right about one thing, though. Sometimes facing reality was the pits.

Lynn's temper stirred as she listened to Helen's description of what was going on with Ernesto and his attempts to wrest custody of his kids from Adelia.

"What can I do?" she asked at once.

"Normally I'd call the Sweet Magnolias myself, but I'm swamped with pulling everything together for tomorrow's hearing," Helen said. "I need a huge show of support for Adelia in the courtroom."

"Consider it done," Lynn said. "I'll start making calls right now."

"Call Maddie first," Helen suggested. "She had her share of tough custody issues back in the day. She'll help you make the calls."

"I'm on it," Lynn promised, then hung up and

turned to Mitch and filled him in. "You might want to look for Gabe. I imagine he's busy blaming himself for this."

Her husband nodded. "Only if you promise me that you'll get your nap the second you've made those calls."

Lynn regarded him with dismay. "You know about the naps?"

Mitch chuckled. "Sweetheart, only a robot could keep the hours you keep without a nap." He gave her a long look. "Maybe it's time we talked about that."

"Not until this mess with Ernesto is resolved," she said. "Then I promise I'll listen to whatever you have to say." She held his gaze. "Have I told you lately how glad I am that you're my husband?"

"Right back at you."

Lynn watched as he left the house to go in search of his cousin, then picked up the phone and made that first call to Maddie Maddox.

Within an hour they'd reached out to every one of the Sweet Magnolias. Adelia would have some of the most prominent women in town in court in the morning. Even if Helen never called a single one of them to the stand, the show of support would speak for itself.

Gabe retreated to his regular table at Rosalina's for a lonely meal, drawing a surprised look from his old waitress.

"It's been a while," Debbie said. "I thought you'd deserted us for good. Word around town is that you've found somebody to share your meals with."

Gabe wasn't about to confirm or deny that. "I just took a temporary reprieve from the pizza," he said.

"Then I suppose you want your usual," Debbie said, clearly disappointed that he wasn't willing to reveal more details.

"Sure. Why not?"

While he was waiting for his order, his cell phone rang. He considered ignoring it, then saw Adelia's name on the caller ID.

"What's up?" he asked at once. "I thought we were going to talk later."

"I think you need to come over here, after all," Adelia said, sounding worried. "Selena's totally freaked out about what's going on. Her cousin, who seems to thrive on taunting her these days, told her you took off from Serenity years ago because you were sick of being bullied. Now she's afraid her dad is going to chase you off again. I tried to be honest with her, but I only made it worse."

"What did you tell her?"

"That I didn't think her dad could chase you away, but that it was always possible that you could leave eventually."

Gabe immediately saw the dilemma. "You know I can't come over there and deny that," he said. "Neither of us has any idea what could happen down the road."

"I know," she said with obvious frustration. "I just don't think Selena was ready for quite that degree of candor. I could shake Joey for planting these seeds of doubt in her head, but he has his own share of issues at home right now. I'll deal with him later."

She drew in a deep breath. "Please, Gabe, can you stop by? I think it would help if Selena could just see you tonight and know that you're not planning to abandon us because of this mess."

"I'll be there in a few minutes," he promised. "I

just ordered pizza. I'll double the order so there will be enough to share."

"That sounds great to me and maybe we can coax Selena to eat, but don't count on the little kids," Adelia warned him. "They overdosed on cupcakes. Right now they're running off all that excess sugar in the backyard. I'm going to take a stab at getting them in bed before you get here, so we can focus on Selena."

He laughed at her optimism. "I'll make it a half hour, then, though I doubt even that will be enough time for you to round them up and herd them into their beds."

"I'll make it long enough," she said with grim determination. "And remind me tomorrow to thank Lynn for caving in to their pleas for all those cupcakes."

"Hey, business is business."

"They didn't even have enough cash on them," Adelia retorted dryly. "She floated them a loan till Selena came back for them. I hope this new baby when it comes doesn't sleep a wink at night for a month."

Gabe stifled a chuckle. "Now that's just mean."

"It's called payback," she said. "It's perfectly fair."

"Remind me not to cross you," Gabe said. "I hate to think what you'd consider to be a fitting punishment."

"I'll have to give that some thought," she said. "If I'm clever enough, maybe I can keep you in town."

Gabe almost admitted that she was close to ensuring his presence for good now, but he had enough remaining doubts to keep silent. "See you soon," he said instead.

Before Gabe could collect his pizza and take off for Adelia's, Mitch walked into Rosalina's with his stepchildren, Lexie and Jeremy. As soon as he caught sight of Gabe, he handed over a bunch of quarters and sent them off to play video games.

As soon as Mitch sat down, Gabe warned him that he was about to leave. "I'm heading over to Adelia's."

Mitch frowned. "After what happened today? I heard Ernesto paid a visit to you and tried to stir up trouble. Lynn just got a call from Helen, who filled her in on the rest. I figured you'd be steering clear of her for a few days till things settled down. In fact, I tried looking for you at the inn and at the work site before I picked up the kids and headed over here. I thought you might want to join us for dinner."

"Not tonight," Gabe said. "Something just came up. Adelia needs me over there."

"Is it important enough to risk getting Ernesto all worked up again?" Mitch asked, his worry plain.

Gabe thought of Selena and what she'd been through today. "It's important enough," he declared. "And if Ernesto tries to stir up more trouble, I can handle that, too. I kept my cool today. I can do it again."

Mitch nodded. "Your crew thought you behaved a lot better than he deserved. Henry said you did go over to Helen's office to fill her in."

"And now Henry and I are going to testify about what happened at an emergency hearing in court first thing in the morning," Gabe told him.

Mitch regarded him with surprise. "Henry didn't mention that."

"He probably didn't know about it when he spoke to you. I just filled him in a little while ago that it would be a help to Helen if we were both there." He met Mitch's worried gaze. "I'm sorry about getting one of your men involved in all this drama."

"Hey, stuff happens. Ed Morrow tried to haul me into the middle of his divorce from Lynn. She was falling all over herself apologizing. What she didn't get was that I'd have done anything for her. Ed's fussing didn't worry me. The only thing I cared two hoots about was whether he could use me to hurt Lynn."

"Same with me," Gabe said. "Helen seems to think Ernesto overplayed his hand. After he caused that scene with me, he took his mistress to see Selena and told her they'd all be a family soon."

Outrage spread across Mitch's face. "I don't think Helen mentioned that part to Lynn. That just proves that as low as I thought Ernesto was, I was overestimating him. He's even lower than slime."

"No doubt about it," Gabe agreed. "By the way, have there been any repercussions from those lies he was spreading about you and the business?"

Mitch shook his head. "Nothing I couldn't handle."

"Meaning there were some," Gabe guessed. "Blast it all, Mitch, you need to sue him."

"I took care of it," Mitch said. "No harm, no foul. In fact, I imagine if anyone lost business over it, it was Ernesto. The guy Ernesto went to had been planning to work with him on a new development outside of town. Once Conway heard the whole story, he opted to go with another developer." Mitch grinned. "And I'll be hiring more men to handle the construction."

Gabe slapped him on the back. "Good for you."

Mitch's expression immediately turned serious. "Which is why it's more important than ever that you stick around, Gabe. With all this work and a baby on the way, I need you right here. I hope you're not getting any ideas about moving on. Lynn said you'd mentioned it."

"I was having a bad day when I told her that. For now, I'm staying," Gabe assured him.

"I'd feel a whole lot more confident about that if you'd start looking for a place to live, instead of staying in that room at the Serenity Inn." His cousin gave him a sly look. "Or are you hoping if you do make a move, it will be into Adelia's house in Swan Point?"

Gabe frowned. "Nobody's suggesting that, least of all me. It's way too soon."

"One thing I've learned over the years is that there's no such thing as a timetable when it comes to love," Mitch told him. "I waited for years before Lynn and I got together."

"And spent a lot of those years happily married to someone else," Gabe reminded him.

"True," Mitch said. "And if Amy hadn't died in that accident and Ed hadn't finally owned up to being gay and asked for a divorce, who knows if Lynn and I would ever have gotten together? I'm just saying that fate works in its own mysterious way. If this thing with Adelia is right, it could be as right after a few weeks as it would be a couple of years from now."

"Well, we're opting for slow and steady," Gabe told him.

Mitch smiled. "Only because anything else terrifies you."

"If you're trying to suggest I'm a coward without saying the word, I'm not denying it," Gabe countered. "I prefer to think of it as old habits dying hard."

"The old habit being to avoid commitment at all costs," Mitch guessed.

"Exactly."

"A piece of advice?"

"As if I could stop you," Gabe said.

"People have a way of clinging to old habits long past the time when they're useful. Something to think about, okay?"

Fortunately Debbie arrived with Gabe's pizzas before he had to respond to his cousin's advice.

"Gotta go," Gabe announced, relieved.

"Have a good evening," Mitch said, a twinkle in his eyes.

Gabe thought of what awaited him at Adelia's, the thankless task of trying to cheer up a teenager. Then again, he'd get to spend some unexpected time with Adelia, so perhaps the night wouldn't be a lost cause after all.

CHAPTER TWENTY-ONE

Gabe wasn't sure what sort of chaos he might find when he got to Adelia's. To his surprise the house was eerily quiet when he used his key to get in. Apparently she'd somehow managed to get the younger children to bed before his arrival.

He carried the pizza into the kitchen and was getting three plates down from the cupboard when Adelia finally came in. Judging from her harried expression, he concluded the kids hadn't gone to bed willingly.

"Everything under control?" he asked, pausing to drop a quick kiss on her cheek before setting the plates on the table. At least that kiss put some color in her face, he thought, satisfied with the effect. It was startling how much he was coming to appreciate the impact of bestowing these little acts of affection. Until recently he'd always considered sex to be the endgame. Lately he'd been developing a whole new fondness for intimate gestures and foreplay.

"I suppose it depends on how you define control," she replied dryly. "Tomas is crying because he heard your truck and I wouldn't let him come downstairs to see you. Juanita just threw up. Natalia is under the covers reading with a flashlight, which is normally against the rules and which she apparently assumes I didn't notice. I was just too tired to start a fight with her."

"Come here," Gabe said, opening his arms. Adelia practically sagged against him, letting her head rest on his shoulder. That she gave in so easily told him exactly how draining the day had been for her. He held her close. "After tomorrow everything will settle down again."

"We don't know that," she said wearily. "The little kids don't have any idea about what's going on. What if the judge rules in Ernesto's favor and I haven't prepared them?"

Gabe took a step back and looked her in the eye. "The only way any judge would rule in Ernesto's favor would be if he concluded I were a worse influence on them than Ernesto is. Helen doesn't believe that will happen, but if it does, I will back off. You can take out a restraining order to make it official if that's what it takes."

Adelia looked shocked. "I could never do that. It would suggest you've done something wrong and quite the opposite is true."

"If it's the last resort, you could," Gabe stated flatly. "I mean it, Adelia. You do whatever you need to do to keep your kids right here where they belong."

"But that would be so unfair," she protested.

"Hopefully it won't come to that, but I do not want to be the reason your kids are not with you. I'll pack up and take off before I'll let that happen."

Naturally that was the precise instant that Selena chose to join them. Alarm spread across her face.

"You're leaving? Just like Joey said you would?" Her eyes filled with tears. "I knew I shouldn't trust you. I *knew* it. I was right all along. I hate you!"

She whirled around and was about to run, but Adelia caught her arm. "Not until you let Gabe explain," she said quietly.

"Explain what? That he's no better than Dad?"

Adelia looked as if she'd been slapped. "You know that's not true," she said furiously. "And I won't have you talking to Gabe or about him like that."

"Then let me leave before I say something even more rude," Selena said, trying to pull free.

Gabe decided it was time to step in and stand up for himself. Adelia had more than enough on her plate without trying to handle his battles.

"Selena," he said quietly. "You're almost an adult and part of being grown-up is giving people a chance to explain, especially when you only heard part of what we were discussing."

"What if I don't want to hear anything you have to say?" she asked angrily. "I'm sick of everybody lying to me."

"I will never lie to you," Gabe said. He gestured toward a kitchen chair. "Please, sit down and listen. Just a few minutes. That's all I'm asking."

"Sweetie, you owe him that much," Adelia said. "Think about everything he's done for you."

"I guess," Selena said sullenly.

"Gabe brought pizza," Adelia added. "Wouldn't you like some? You haven't eaten a thing."

Selena shook her head. Even so, Adelia put the box

on the table and moved one of the plates and several napkins so they were right in front of her daughter.

"Just in case you change you mind," she told her.

"I won't," Selena said stubbornly.

Gabe pulled out the chair opposite her and sat. "What did you hear when you walked in here?"

"That you're going to leave, just like Joey said you would."

"But you didn't hear why I said that, did you?" Gabe asked.

"Because it's what you do—you run away," she said bitterly.

"I did once," Gabe conceded. "But this time I would only go if the judge thinks I'm a bad influence on you kids and sides with your dad. I would only leave town to protect you and make sure you can stay here with your mom."

Selena looked shaken. She turned to Adelia. "But you said the judge would never do that."

"I don't believe he will," Adelia said.

"And I don't think he will, either," Gabe added. "This was a just-in-case promise, a way to make sure nothing in your life changes."

The tension in Selena's shoulders visibly eased. Her gaze hopeful, her voice tremulous, she whispered, "Cross your heart? You won't just pack up and go?"

"Cross my heart," Gabe told her, suiting action to words. "I don't want to leave, Selena."

"But you did once before. Joey told me, and Mom didn't deny it."

"That's true. Have you heard the whole story?"

"It had something to do with your mom," Selena said.

"That's exactly right," Gabe confirmed. "When I

was about your age, maybe even a couple of years younger, kids started making really mean remarks about my mom. To be honest, a lot of it was true, but that didn't mean it didn't hurt to hear them say it. My mom did a lot of bad stuff back then. Since it was just the two of us, I figured it was my job to defend her. I started a lot of fights. Eventually I got kicked out of school. Fortunately that was the worst of what happened. Still, your dad wants to bring all of that up to the judge."

"But that's not fair," Selena said. "You were just worried about your mom. I feel the same way about my mom. That's why I got so mad when I heard you might take off. I thought you were going to hurt her by leaving, and it would be even worse if you did, because I was starting to think you're a really good guy and I know she likes you."

He glanced at Adelia, then back at her daughter. "Would it help if I promise that it's not my intention to hurt your mother?"

She was silent for a long time, then said wearily, "My dad promised to love her for always. He didn't keep his promise."

Gabe's heart ached for the pain he could hear in this young girl's voice. She was learning lessons no one her age needed to know. He couldn't help wondering how those would shape the woman she'd become.

"I know," he said quietly. "Adults always mean their promises when they make them, but they can't always keep them."

"Then why should I trust you?" Selena asked with a touch of belligerence.

Gabe gave Adelia a meaningful look. "Because I

will never make a promise if I don't think I can keep it," he said, the words directed at Selena but meant for her mother, as well. "And I suppose the only way I can prove that is if you'll give me another chance. Can you do that?"

Again, Selena hesitated. "I guess," she said eventually.

"Thank you," he said, relieved because he knew that without Selena's blessing, his chances for making any inroads with her mother would be nil. Adelia would shift gears all over again and want him out of their lives.

Before he realized what she intended, Selena was out of her chair, her arms tight around his neck. "Please don't leave us. Please. It's been so much better since you came here."

Gabe closed his eyes. Here it was, the test he'd dreaded, because the promise she so desperately wanted was one he couldn't guarantee he could keep. His silence finally registered with her apparently, because she pulled away.

"Why aren't you saying anything?" she asked, her gaze accusing.

"I told you I would never lie and that I wouldn't make a promise I didn't think I could keep," he said quietly. "What I will promise you is that no matter what happens, I will always, always care about you and be around anytime you tell me you need me. No matter where I might be, I will only be a phone call away."

"But you could go away," she concluded, her expression resigned.

"I won't want to, but, yes, it could happen."

"Even if the judge doesn't make you?"

Gabe nodded, though his heart ached. "Even then."

Though Selena was clearly fighting tears, a few managed to leak out and dampen her cheeks. "Will you tell me if you have to go?"

"Absolutely," he said, his own eyes stinging. "I promise."

"Okay," she said in a small voice. She sat back down and took a slice of pizza from the box, picking off bits of pepperoni and tearing them into smaller bits.

Gabe and Adelia waited until she eventually turned to her mom.

"I want to come to court tomorrow," Selena said, her voice filled with determination. "I want to testify."

"Oh, sweetie, I don't think that's a good idea," Adelia protested. "Helen didn't ask that you be there."

"I'll call her myself and tell her I'm coming," Selena said stubbornly. "I was the one Dad brought that woman to see. I can tell the judge that he doesn't care about us. And I can tell him that Gabe does, so much that he'd go away before he'd ever hurt us."

Gabe could see that Adelia was torn between trying to protect her daughter and letting her have her way.

"I think you should talk it over with Helen," he told Adelia. "Let her decide."

Selena gave him a grateful look, then turned back to Adelia. "Please, Mom. I have to do this. I have to stand up for our family."

Adelia finally nodded. "I'll ask Helen."

"Now," Selena prodded.

Adelia stood up and regarded Gabe wryly. "I wonder where she gets that stubborn streak from."

He winked at her. "I think we both know the answer to that. You're no slouch in that department yourself."

After Adelia left the room to make the call, Selena regarded him shyly. "Thanks for backing me up."

"I think you've earned the right to have a say," he told her. "Just remember, it's up to Helen. She knows best."

Adelia returned before Selena could even respond to that. "Helen says it's fine if you're there, but she will only call on you to testify if it seems like the right thing to do or if the judge asks to hear from you."

"I can live with that," Selena said happily.

This time when she picked up her slice of pizza, she actually ate it. Two slices after that, she glanced from her mom to Gabe and back again.

"I guess you'd like to be alone, huh?"

Gabe laughed. "I wouldn't mind."

Selena gave her mother a kiss, then gave him a peck on the cheek, too. Gabe held her gaze.

"All is forgiven?" he asked.

She nodded.

"Then get some sleep. I'll see you tomorrow at the courthouse."

"Good night, Gabe. It's all going to work out," she said, sounding surprisingly confident. "You'll see."

Gabe couldn't help wishing he had the same crystal ball Selena seemed to be looking into.

"You were good with Selena earlier," Adelia told Gabe when they were alone on the back patio after Selena had finally gone upstairs to bed.

"I meant what I said to her. I know where she's coming from," Gabe said. "My mom went through some tough times, a lot of tough times, to be honest."

He regarded her curiously. "No one's filled you in on the stories?"

She shook her head. "I only know what you've mentioned."

"I'm surprised. She was certainly the talk of the town back then."

Adelia tried to imagine what it was like for a young man to have his mother at the center of town gossip, then realized that was exactly what Selena had experienced because of Ernesto. She certainly knew the effect that had had. "That must have been so hard on you."

He shrugged. "Thus my reputation as a troublemaker. Just like I told Selena, I was in a lot of fights back then, defending her honor, or at least that's how I viewed it. Maybe she deserved it, maybe she didn't, but I didn't think I had a choice."

"Of course you didn't," Adelia said at once. "She was your mother. Selena feels that same sort of loyalty to me, but thankfully she hasn't felt the need to beat anyone up. I think she was probably tempted to throw a few punches at Ernesto's mistress, but she didn't. I was tempted to do that myself, so I could hardly have blamed her if she had."

"I'm sorry you went through that. I'm sorry Selena did, too."

"It's behind me now," she said, then sighed. "At least I was working on leaving it in the past until this latest mess came up."

"What about the future?" he asked. "Not tomorrow, but way beyond that. What do you see for yourself?"

"I try not to look too far beyond today," she told him. "I'm still at the stage of trying to put one foot in front of the other, making sure the kids are okay, getting this place fixed up." She glanced his way. "What about you? Once you've got your life on an even keel, what's next?"

"I haven't been back all that long," he said. "An even keel feels as if it's a long way off."

"No big dreams, Gabe?"

He met her gaze, held it. "I haven't let myself dream for a long time," he confessed. "I didn't think I deserved to have dreams. Now, since I've met you…"

His voice trailed off, but his meaning was clear. It left Adelia shaken but filled with the kind of anticipation she hadn't thought possible just a few months ago.

She shook off her desire to bask in his words. "I should stop this."

"Stop what?"

"Talking about the future as if either one of us has any control over it. Knowing that a judge could change my life forever tomorrow morning is proof enough that I'm not the one in charge of anything."

Gabe scooted closer and put his arm around her. "Have a little faith. You're a great mom. You've done right by your kids. They're healthy and getting happier by the day. You have a good job and the respect of a lot of people in this town. There's not a judge in the world who would choose Ernesto over you. I'm the complication."

She smiled at his willingness to take responsibility for anything that might not go her way in court. "No, Gabe. You're the good influence. I imagine Selena intends to tell the judge exactly that if she gets the chance. Do you know what she told me earlier?"

"What?"

"That because of you, it feels like we're a real family. I can't argue with that. The past few weeks have been the way I always wanted my family to be. She also said you treat her and my other kids the way Elliott treats Daisy and Mack. Believe me, that's high praise. Even before my brother officially adopted those two, he loved them to pieces. And because he did, even the most judgmental people in my family accepted them, and ultimately Karen, too."

Gabe frowned. "What did they have against Karen? Admittedly, I don't know her that well, but she seems to have an approval sticker from that whole group of Sweet Magnolia women. From what Mitch has said, they're pretty tight-knit."

"Ah, but in the eyes of my family, she has a tragic flaw. She's divorced," she responded.

"But you're divorced, too," he said, clearly confused.

"I wasn't then. And in fact, my sisters think Karen had some sort of evil influence over me. They're no more accepting of me now than they were of Karen back then."

"What about the one whose husband is abusing her? Carolina, is it? Surely she understands."

"Afraid not. If anything, she hates me even more because I got out of a bad marriage and she can't bring herself to leave hers." She waved off the topic. "Enough of that. It's too depressing and it's not anything I can resolve tonight. I have enough on my mind."

Gabe looked into her eyes. "I wish I could stay right here and distract you."

She smiled at the wistfulness in his voice. "Believe me, I wish you could, too."

"But I should go," he said without making a move to do so.

"You should," she agreed.

He glanced around, as if to determine if there were spies lurking in the bushes, then leaned in close. "Not before this," he whispered, then sealed his mouth over hers.

Once again Adelia lost herself in his kiss. How had she never realized what sort of sweet torment a simple kiss could stir up? Not that there was anything simple about the way Gabe kissed. He teased and taunted, coaxed and demanded, until her body was shouting for a whole lot more. It had been a long time since she'd experienced the sweet torment of foreplay.

"If that judge tries to banish me from your life tomorrow, I may have to pummel some sense into him myself," he said with a moan as he pulled away. "I want a whole lot more than kisses from you, Adelia."

Shaken and breathless, she could only nod.

"You, too?" he asked, clearly amused.

"Oh yeah."

"Still going to call me after you put on your sexy nightie and crawl into bed?" he teased.

She swallowed hard, imagining it. "I don't think so," she said with regret. "I'm going to have enough trouble getting to sleep as it is. If I let you get me all stirred up, I'll be awake and frustrated all night long."

Gabe laughed. "Welcome to my world, darlin'."

When Adelia arrived at the courthouse in the morning, she was stunned to find a whole contingent of Sweet Magnolias waiting in the courtroom, along with her mother.

She addressed her mother's presence first. "Mama, I wasn't expecting you to be here."

"Where else would I be? What I want to know is why you didn't tell me yourself what was happening?"

"You have enough on your mind," Adelia said, then lowered her voice. "Have you seen Carolina?"

Her mother frowned at the question. "She won't open the door for me. That alone tells me things are worse. I'm terrified to even think about how much worse. She has one more day and then I'm taking Elliott over there with me."

Adelia recognized that her mother was at her wits' end if she was even considering involving Elliott. "I'll go with you, Mama. We'll go first thing tomorrow. Maybe if we gang up on Carolina, we can make her get out of that house before things get even worse."

"For now let's focus on seeing that Ernesto gets what's coming to him," her mother said, her expression grim. She beckoned for Selena. "You sit with me. We'll say prayers that the judge is a good and decent man."

Selena grinned. "*Abuela,* I hope you have a lot of pull with God."

"I have enough," she replied. "So do you."

Adelia turned then to Maddie, Dana Sue, Raylene and the other Sweet Magnolias. As far as she could tell the only ones missing were Lynn, who had to be at the bakery, and Sarah, who was on the air at the radio station. She regarded the women with tears in her eyes, then faced Helen.

"I see you rallied the troops," she whispered. "Thank you."

"Lynn made the calls. This is what we do any time one of us is in trouble," Helen said simply. "Every one of those women is prepared to tell the judge what an excellent mother you are. Collectively they carry a lot of weight in this town."

Gabe came in just then, dressed in a suit and tie that made him look as if he'd just stepped off the cover of some slick men's fashion magazine. He'd even shaved off that sexy stubble she'd come to love. She stared at him, practically tongue-tied. He caught her eye and winked as he stopped to speak to her mother, who looked almost as stunned as Adelia knew she must.

Beside her, Helen chuckled. "Something tells me you just had a mental flash of what Gabe would look like on your wedding day."

Adelia turned a shocked look on her. "Don't even say something like that. What if Ernesto overheard you?"

"Oh, so what if he did?" Helen said. "It serves him right to have to sit here and see that another man values you the way you should be valued."

"It may serve him right," Adelia agreed, "but is it a good legal strategy?"

Helen grinned. "Anything that rattles him is a good legal strategy," she said, then nodded toward Gabe. "Ernesto didn't expect he'd clean up so well, I'm sure. Just one more lesson in not underestimating the opposition. There's no one in this courtroom right now who looks more respectable than Gabe."

Adelia was taken aback by her assessment. "Did you take him out and buy him that suit first thing this morning?"

"Didn't have to," Helen said. "I just suggested if he owned a suit, this would be a good occasion to trot it out. Sexy as he looks in those tight jeans and T-shirts he usually wears, I told him a suit might give a better impression in court."

"I notice you didn't say the same thing to Henry Davis. He looks as if he came here straight from the construction site."

"Henry's not the one Ernesto is after," Helen reminded her just as the bailiff called the court to order. "He looks exactly like what he is, an honest, hardworking man. That works nicely in our favor, too."

As soon as the judge was seated, Ernesto's attorney was on his feet. "Your Honor, given that this is a custody issue involving minor children, we move that the courtroom be closed to all but those directly involved."

Helen leveled a withering look in his direction. "My apologies, Your Honor, but when my client's family and friends learned of what her ex-husband is trying to pull today, they all insisted on being here to testify on her behalf. I intend to call every one of them, if Your Honor needs convincing that she is the best person to continue to have custody of her children."

"They may stay," he ruled. "Now let's get on with this. I've looked over my earlier ruling in this case." He turned to Ernesto. "What's changed?"

Once again, Ernesto's attorney stood. "We've learned that their mother has been subjecting the children to the influence of a man known to be a troublemaker. It is no longer a safe environment."

"That's nuts!" Selena shouted, standing up and staring belligerently at her father. "Gabe's a better influence than you ever were."

The judge's gavel slammed down. "Young lady, I won't have my courtroom disrupted."

"How about disrespected, then?" she said, fighting

off her grandmother's attempts to pull her back into her seat. "That's what my father's doing. He's in here lying to you."

Helen was on her feet. "I'm sorry, Your Honor. As you can imagine, emotions are running high."

He nodded. He glanced down at the papers in front of him, then returned his gaze to Selena. "You are the oldest child, Selena Hernandez?"

"Yes, sir."

"Come up here," he ordered, then gestured for her to take a seat in the witness box. He glanced at Adelia and at Ernesto. "Any objections?"

Ernesto opened his mouth, but his attorney immediately silenced him.

"Okay, then," the judge said.

Though she looked scared, Selena squared her shoulders and walked forward, casting a defiant look at her father. For once Ernesto actually looked shaken.

Adelia glanced at Helen. "Shouldn't you do something?"

"I don't think so," Helen said. "I think Selena knows exactly what she's doing. I'll intercede if I see a need to."

"Young lady, why do you say that your father is lying?"

"Because he's trying to convince you he wants what's best for my sisters, brother and me. He doesn't. All he wants to do is hurt my mom more than he already has."

"Sometimes children don't know what's best for them," the judge said.

"Maybe not, but I'm not exactly a kid. I may be only thirteen, but thanks to my dad I know a lot about the way people cheat and lie and break their vows. If you ask him, I'll bet he'll try to tell you how much he loves us."

"I'm sure he will," the judge agreed. "Fathers love their children."

"Then why hasn't he seen me even once since the divorce? He'll say it's because I took my mom's side, but so what? And what about my sisters and brother? They didn't take sides. And they wait every weekend for him to show up and spend time with them. He did a couple of times, but I can't even remember the last time he didn't break a promise to them."

The judge's expression darkened as he turned to Ernesto. "Is that true?"

"She," Ernesto began, pointing at Adelia, "has turned them against me. That's why I want the custody arrangement changed, so I can get my kids back before it's too late."

"You're the one who doesn't show up," Selena retorted. "Mom's never said a bad word against you, not one. In fact, she's told us we should spend time with you. It's not her fault that I don't want to be with a liar and a cheat."

Helen did stand then. "Your Honor, I think you can see that Mr. Hernandez's words and actions don't match. If you doubt that Selena is telling the truth, there are other witnesses here who can back her up."

"I imagine they can," the judge said wearily. "That still leaves the matter of this person that Mr. Hernandez says is a bad influence." Again, he glanced at his notes. "Gabe Franklin, I believe." He glanced around the courtroom until his gaze landed on Gabe. "I believe we've met before. Stand up, if you would."

Gabe stood. "We have, Your Honor."

"Under less than favorable circumstances, as I recall," the judge said, causing Adelia to wince, even as Selena looked indignant.

"I'll bet it was because of his mom," Selena said, jumping to Gabe's defense. "Whatever he did, it was trying to protect his mom, so you can't hold that against him."

The judge actually smiled at her fierce reaction. "No, I can't," he told her gently.

"I just thought you should know," Selena said.

"I've heard only good things about you since you got back to town," the judge told Gabe.

"I hope so, Your Honor," Gabe replied.

"He's the best," Selena chimed in. "He helps us with our homework. He makes my mom laugh. He even wore a tiara for my sisters when they had a tea party."

The judge didn't even try to hide his grin. "I believe I saw a picture of that occasion."

"I know he's not our dad," Selena said. "But it's been like having a real family with him around. Please don't make him go away." She regarded the judge with an earnest expression. "He said he'd go if that's what it took to keep us with our mom. That's how much he cares about us."

"Did he now?" the judge said softly, casting an approving look toward Gabe.

Ernesto's attorney was on his feet. "If this show is over, could we get back to deciding the facts of the situation?"

The judge shot him a daunting look. "I think I have all the facts I need. The custody arrangement will remain as is. However, we will readdress this in three months." He turned to Ernesto and warned, "If you continue to neglect your children or try to use them as weapons in your fight with your ex-wife, I'll consider taking away the visitation rights you do have. Am I clear?"

Ernesto was clearly too furious to reply, so his attorney said, "Yes, Your Honor."

"Then we're done here," the judge said. He turned to Selena. "I've seen adults who didn't understand right and wrong as well as you do, young lady. Good job here today."

As soon as he'd left the courtroom, the Sweet Magnolias erupted into cheers. Selena ran straight to her mother's arms.

Adelia felt tears streaming down her cheeks. She couldn't have been more proud of her daughter. "You saved the day."

"I just told the truth." She looked around. "Where's Gabe?"

Adelia glanced toward the back of the courtroom, but he wasn't anywhere to be found. A sinking sensation settled in the pit of her stomach. She had this terrible feeling that she might have won the war with Ernesto today, only to lose the battle to keep Gabe in her life.

CHAPTER TWENTY-TWO

Gabe had been so moved by what Selena said to the judge, he'd practically run from the courthouse to keep anyone from seeing the tears gathering in his eyes. Sure, she'd said much the same the night before, but hearing her declare it in public had shaken him. There was a lot of pressure in trying to live up to the kind of faith she'd so openly placed in him.

How could he even be thinking about trying to take care of a family when he'd spent a lot of his adult years barely taking care of himself? He'd been rebelling, albeit unknowingly until now, against having so much responsibility heaped on him as a kid. He wasn't convinced he was ready—or even worthy enough—to take on more.

After he went back to the Serenity Inn, changed into his work clothes and headed for the construction site, he stopped by the hardware store to pick up a few things.

"How'd it go in court?" Ronnie Sullivan asked, proving that everyone in town was no doubt up-to-date on Ernesto's latest attempt to turn Adelia's life upside down. "I know Dana Sue was there, but I imagine she went straight to work at the restaurant. I haven't heard from her."

Gabe filled him in, figuring the news would be all over town in the blink of an eye, anyway. "Adelia kept custody of the kids and Ernesto got his wrist slapped by the judge."

Ronnie took off the glasses he'd been wearing to read an invoice, then frowned as he studied Gabe more intently. "Then why do you look so down in the dumps?"

"Just some stuff Selena said in court," Gabe told him. "It hit home how much she's counting on me. I don't know if I can live up to all those expectations. It's one thing for me and Adelia to try to work things out and fail, but I don't think I could bear it if I let those kids down." He met Ronnie's gaze. "They're great kids. They deserve the best—you know what I mean?"

Rather than dismissing his worries, Ronnie nodded. "I get that, Gabe. I really do. The truth is, though, that nobody knows if they're any good at being a parent until they're in the thick of it. If someone tells you they know exactly what to do in any and all conditions, they're crazy. Just when you figure you've handled one crisis, another one will crop up and blindside you."

Since Ronnie was a grandfather now and seemed to have a rock-solid marriage, Gabe listened.

"Just look at Dana Sue and me," Ronnie continued. "Our daughter nearly died because we messed up so bad. Thankfully Annie made it through all the terrible side effects of her anorexia. She's married to her childhood sweetheart and a mom now. Dana Sue and I are back together again and happier than ever for having survived that nightmare. I thank God every day for giving all of us a second chance."

"I hadn't heard about any of that," Gabe said, shaken.

"I'm surprised, even though most of it probably happened while you were gone. The day Dana Sue chased me out of the house with a cast-iron skillet is one of those stories the guys like to repeat when they want to get under my skin."

"She didn't!"

"She sure did," Ronnie said, laughing. Then his expression sobered. "Here's the condensed version. I acted like a fool, Dana Sue kicked me out and our divorce rocked Annie's world so badly she developed an eating disorder. She was still in her teens, but she actually had a heart attack."

"Annie? Kids don't have heart attacks," Gabe said, trying to imagine how terrifying that must have been for Ronnie and Dana Sue.

"Well, mine did," Ronnie said. "That anorexia is a nasty business. When I found out about it, I thought my own heart would stop. In fact, I prayed it would if that would keep Annie alive. I discovered that God's not interested in making bargains. He has His own plans. That crisis brought me back to town and reminded me that everything I wanted was right here. I never should have left."

He met Gabe's gaze. "What I'm trying to tell you is that you will make mistakes as a parent if you decide to take on Adelia's family. But if your love is strong enough, you get through the tough times together. I know the worst time in my life while Annie was in the hospital turned out to be the best thing that ever happened to me, too, because Dana Sue and I found our way back to each other."

Gabe absorbed what Ronnie was saying. Though Ronnie had obviously intended his story to make the prospect of parenting a little less scary, Gabe didn't find it reassuring. If a couple as deeply in love as Ronnie and Dana Sue had been back in the day could fail so badly, what chance did he have to get it right?

"You okay?" Ronnie asked, frowning. "I didn't make it worse, did I? Dana Sue will have my hide if I did."

"You just said some things I needed to hear," Gabe told him.

Ronnie's expression turned even more worried.

"Is there something else?" Gabe asked him.

"Just that I had a call from a friend of mine the other day, a man I worked for in construction while I was away from Serenity. In fact, he helped me put together the plans and money for me to get this store up and running again."

Gabe wondered what that could possibly have to do with him.

Ronnie hesitated. "I'm not sure if this is the right time to get into this."

"Why not?"

"Because he's looking for a new construction crew foreman down in Beaufort," Ronnie explained. "He'd heard good things about you and wondered if I knew you."

Gabe stilled at that. Here it was, the chance to move on, perhaps, to get yet another fresh start away from a community that until recently had held only bad memories.

"What did you tell him?" he asked Ronnie.

"That what I've seen of your work is excellent and that you're the kind of man who'd fit right in with the tight ship he runs. But I also told him that you had some ties that might keep you here." He studied Gabe. "Was I wrong about that?"

Gabe thought of Adelia and the unexpected, amazing way she made him feel. He thought of Selena, Tomas, of Juanita and Natalia. If he left, he'd be giving Selena one more reason not to trust the adults in her life. If he left, who would teach Tomas all the things he was so eager to learn about guy stuff? And who, pray tell, would sit in a feather boa and a tiara at a tea party with Juanita and Natalia?

And then he thought of Mitch, who'd taken a chance on him, who was depending on him as backup now with a baby on the way and more work than ever on his plate. How could he bail on him?

None of that, though, seemed to dull the familiar temptation to take off for yet another fresh beginning in a town where he had no ties at all, no responsibilities except to himself.

"Have him give me a call," he said eventually. "It's worth listening to what he has to say."

Ronnie looked disappointed by his response, but he nodded. "I'll tell him to call. His name's Butch. He gets to town every so often to check on this place. He's Mary Vaughan's uncle, too, so he and his wife like to stop by and watch her trying to juggle her booming real estate career and a toddler. Given Mary Vaughan's type A personality, they consider that to be an excellent form of entertainment."

Since Gabe had watched a very frustrated Mary

Vaughan trying to coax her child into her car one afternoon, he totally got that. The kid had more stubbornness than Mary Vaughan, and she excelled at it. She just called it persistence in her own case.

"I appreciate the good word," he told Ronnie.

"Not a problem, but one more piece of advice," Ronnie said as Gabe started to leave. "Think long and hard before you walk away from what you've found here. I didn't think before I left. I let Helen convince me that Dana Sue and Annie needed space, that having me here would only be a reminder of the mistakes I'd made. I came to regret listening to her."

"Believe me, I won't be thinking about anything else," Gabe told him.

He knew what his pattern was. He knew what the old Gabe would have done. There was safety and comfort in that decision. There was nothing safe or comfortable about staying here.

But there was Adelia. There were four kids he'd come to love. And there was family. Was he brave enough to believe in all that and take a chance on something he'd never dared to hope might be in the cards for him?

Dana Sue insisted that the court ruling deserved to be celebrated. "You're all coming to Sullivan's right now," she announced outside the courthouse. "Brunch is on me."

"Who could say no to that?" Helen said eagerly. "I'll get to sneak into the kitchen and hang out with my honey. It'll be like old times."

"Old times?" Adelia asked.

"Erik and Helen got together when I kept finding

excuses requiring her to help out in the kitchen at Sullivan's," Dana Sue explained. "She couldn't cook a lick, of course, and Erik got on her nerves because he rightfully thought he should be the boss. It was fun to watch."

"Boy, was it ever," Maddie confirmed. "The only thing more fun has been watching Helen accept that her mom has a boyfriend and that they're living together."

Helen put her hands on her hips and tried to stare down her two best friends. "Are you two through?"

Maddie and Dana Sue exchanged a look, then grinned.

"Probably not," Maddie said, then gave Helen a hug. "Though we probably shouldn't be teasing the woman who saved the day in court."

"Actually it was Selena who saved the day," Helen said, putting an arm around the blushing teenager.

"I am so proud of you," Adelia told her daughter.

"I just told the truth," Selena said, then regarded her hopefully. "Do I get to come to brunch, too, or do I have to go to school?"

"I think you can be excused for the whole day just this once," Adelia told her, then warned, "But don't get any ideas."

"As if," Selena said. "The last time I cut class, you grounded me, like, forever."

"And I'll do it again if I have to," Adelia said emphatically.

At Sullivan's, where new spins on traditional Southern cuisine were the order of the day, Dana Sue and Erik managed to whip up a feast for the impromptu brunch, even though the restaurant was scheduled to open in an hour for lunch and those preparations already had the kitchen in a frenzy.

"This stuffed French toast with strawberries is amazing," Maddie said, sitting back and patting her stomach. "I think I just gained five pounds."

"You still have two little kids and an amorous husband at home," Dana Sue retorted. "You'll work those calories off in no time."

As the oldest members of the Sweet Magnolias exchanged taunts, Raylene slipped into the seat next to Adelia. "You doing okay?"

Adelia frowned. "Who's covering the shop?"

"I put a sign on the door that we'd be opening at one today. This is more important than selling a couple of dresses or a scarf. Now answer me. How are you doing?"

"I'm worried about Gabe," Adelia admitted. "He took off before I could even thank him for what he said to the judge today. Because of him and Selena, I still have my kids with me."

"I saw him when I went to put the sign on the door at the shop. He was already back in his work clothes and coming out of the hardware store."

"Oh," Adelia said, oddly deflated by the news. She wasn't sure what she'd hoped for, that maybe he'd at least want to congratulate her on today's outcome or share the moment with her. Something told her, though, that he was pulling away. What she didn't understand was why. The judge hadn't even hinted that he was taking Ernesto's claims seriously.

"Stop worrying," Raylene advised, as if she'd followed Adelia's thoughts. "I imagine Gabe hasn't had that many good things said about him in years. He's probably a little shaken by it."

"That's what concerns me," Adelia said. "What if he tells himself that he doesn't deserve any of it? Even though everything turned out okay, he may be blaming himself for the fact that we were in court in the first place."

"Call him," Raylene suggested. "Or stop by the construction site when you leave here. I can handle the store."

Adelia squeezed her hand. "You may be the most understanding boss in captivity."

"I doubt that," Raylene said. "Keep in mind I have an ulterior motive. I need a happy employee to cover for me while I go off and have a baby and then spend a leisurely few months discovering the joys of motherhood."

Adelia regarded her with shock. "A few months?"

"That's what I've been thinking lately. It could be longer if we move forward with the whole partnership thing. Or if I get really infatuated with this new baby of mine and decide Carter and I should have a few more, I might just sell the whole boutique to you."

Adelia waved off that idea. "Forget that. I'm not even sure I can scrape up enough to be your partner."

"Don't panic. It's all down the road," Raylene advised. "I've told you before, with these women in your corner, anything's possible."

Adelia tried putting Raylene's remarks out of her head. Fortunately, she had a bigger worry at the moment. She needed to find Gabe and make sure that he wasn't going to use today's events to bolt on her after all.

* * *

Adelia found Gabe exactly where Raylene had predicted she would, in the cavernous space at the end of the block on Main Street. His crew had apparently gone to lunch, because he was all alone, sitting at that makeshift desk of his in the middle of dust and debris, eating what looked to be a tuna salad sandwich and some fries from a Wharton's take-out container.

When he glanced up at the sound of her heels tapping on the concrete floor, his eyes immediately filled with wariness.

"You shouldn't be in here without a hard hat," he said.

"You're not wearing one," she pointed out.

"Because no one's working right now."

She smiled at that. "Then the rules are different for you?"

His lips quirked slightly. "Sure. I'm the boss. And I'm hardheaded, anyway."

Adelia pulled up a folding chair and sat beside him. "Why'd you take off after court? I didn't even get a chance to thank you."

"You were surrounded by all those women," he said. "You didn't need me butting in."

She frowned at his words. "Gabe, don't you know that I would never consider you an intrusion?"

"I'm just saying that you had plenty of support."

"But you're the one I wanted most to speak to," she said. "Or is that the problem? Did today make things a little too real for you? Did you suddenly realize this thing between us isn't some game, that the kids and I count on you, that it's not your usual cut-and-run flirtation?"

She could tell from his startled reaction that she'd hit on the truth. She sighed. "I guess you did."

He drew in a deep breath, then said, "I always knew you were different."

"Different how?"

"Not the kind of woman I could ever walk away from easily," he told her.

Something in his voice told her, though, that he was going to walk away.

"You're going anyway, though, aren't you?"

"I don't know," he said, looking miserable. "Maybe it's for the best. Complications aren't my thing, Adelia."

"Gabe, there will always be complications in life. Some are good. Some are lousy." She held his gaze. "Crazy me, I thought maybe we were going to be one of the best kind of complications. I'm not saying it would be easy or that there won't be a million times when one of us would prefer to run, but I think the rewards of staying will be worth it." She drew in a deep breath. "But if you can't see that, I can't make you."

He'd been tearing apart his sandwich bit by bit as she spoke, just as Selena had picked apart the pepperoni the night before. The nervous action was almost enough to make her smile, even though what she really wanted to do was cry and shout at him to look at her, to love her enough to stay with her. She had too much pride, though, to say those words, not to a man who was so obviously intent on leaving.

"There's something I need to tell you," he said. "I've had a job offer in Beaufort. Ronnie Sullivan connected me with the guy he used to work for. He just called. I'm going down this weekend to check it out."

Adelia's heart plummeted. "I see," she said, determined to keep the tears suddenly stinging her eyes from leaking out and betraying her emotions. "So that's it, I guess."

"If I were ever going to stay with someone, it would be you," he told her. "I know it doesn't mean much for me to say I love you, but I'm leaving town anyway, but it's the truth, Adelia. I do love you. I'm doing you a favor."

She stared at him in shock. "That's ridiculous! Leaving isn't doing me a favor. It surely isn't doing my kids a favor. The only one benefiting is you." She shook her head as she regarded him with disbelief. "How could I have been so wrong about you? You're a coward, Gabe Franklin, not a hero at all."

She stood up then, spine straight, shoulders squared, and walked away. She was proud of herself for not shedding a single tear in front of him or even on the walk to Chic.

But when she walked inside the boutique and Raylene glanced up from her cell phone, a shocked expression on her face, Adelia crumbled. Tears flowed unchecked.

"You know, don't you?" she whispered brokenly when she could finally speak.

Raylene nodded. "That was Gabe on the phone. He thought you might need me."

"How considerate!" Adelia said bitterly. "You know, it was bad enough finding out that Ernesto was cheating on me and having to hold my head high and pretend it didn't matter." She gave Raylene a plaintive look. "How am I supposed to pretend this doesn't matter?"

"You don't," Raylene said simply. "You cry and

scream and shout and curse the man's sorry butt as much as you want to. The Sweet Magnolias will ply you with margaritas, if that will help."

The offer brought a watery smile to her lips. "If those things almost killed me when I was having a good day, I don't think I'll rely on them now."

"How about the company? I can get everybody together at my place tonight."

Adelia knew they would all come, too, just as they had that morning to be there for her in court. It was an amazing feeling to discover she had real friends. But while they might be able to offer moral support and would willingly listen to her rip into Gabe, that wasn't what she really needed. What she really needed was to go home and find Gabe at her house, the same as he had been so many times recently.

Sadly, though, that simply wasn't in the cards. She needed to accept reality, and then figure out how on earth she was going to explain all of this to her children.

Despite all Adelia's arguments that she needed to stay at the boutique and work, Raylene insisted that she go home.

"You need a long, leisurely bubble bath and a nap," Raylene said. "It's been a stressful day. Take advantage of the couple of hours you'll have to yourself before the kids come home."

Adelia sighed. "You're probably right. Maybe I'll have a brainstorm about what I'm going to say to them, especially Selena. For her I think this will be worse in some ways than anything Ernesto did."

"From what I saw in court today, she's a very mature

girl. She may be devastated, but she'll be more worried about you."

"And isn't that sad?" Adelia said. It was yet more proof that her daughter had had to grow up too quickly.

"Now go," Raylene ordered. "Tomorrow's soon enough for you to be back in here working your sales magic."

Adelia gave in reluctantly and walked home. As she neared the house, she frowned at the sight of her sister's car in the driveway, Carolina behind the wheel. Adelia prayed that she was right about what this meant.

After approaching the car slowly, she tapped on the window. "Carolina?"

Her sister lifted her head, revealing yet another cut on her cheek and bruises that to Adelia's untrained eye seemed fresh.

"Come inside," Adelia said at once, her own worries forgotten.

Carolina climbed out of the car, but when she tried to walk, she could barely limp. Adelia slipped an arm around her waist.

"Come on," she said softly. "I've got you. Do you need to go to the hospital? Is anything broken?"

Carolina shook her head, then asked hesitantly, "Is it okay if the kids and I stay here, just for tonight?"

"You'll stay for as long as you need to," Adelia replied.

"Thank you. After all the things I've said to you, I don't deserve it," Carolina said.

"We're sisters," Adelia told her. "You will always be welcome in my home."

Her sister gave her a weary look. "Don't call Mama, not yet, okay? I'm just not ready to talk to her."

"Whatever you want."

"Is Gabe coming over? I don't think I could bear it if he or anyone else saw me right now."

"You don't need to worry about that," Adelia said, her tone wry.

Inside, she settled her sister gingerly on the sofa, then took her one small suitcase upstairs. When she came down, she asked, "Is there more?"

"I didn't stop to pack much. What's in there is for the kids."

"Do they know to come here? Do I need to pick them up at school?"

Alarm filled Carolina's eyes. "I didn't think of that. They'll take the bus home from school. I should be there."

"Absolutely not," Adelia told her. "I'll call Helen. She'll know what to do."

"I'm not ready to talk to a lawyer," Carolina said, panic in her voice.

"You don't have a choice," Adelia said firmly. "You have to think about doing what's best for your kids. The only other alternative is for me to call Mama and have her get the kids and bring them here or take them home with her."

Carolina seemed to be struggling between hiding what was happening from their mother or relying on her in this crisis. "Maybe that would be best," she said at last. "You talk to her, though. Ask her to keep the kids with her for a day or two. They have clothes at her house."

"What do I tell her when she asks about what's going on? She will, you know."

"Just that I need a couple of days to think about

things. That will give these bruises time enough to fade some more."

"Haven't the kids already seen what Ricky has done to you? I know Mama has."

She shook her head. "I told Joey I was sick and probably contagious, so I was staying in the guest room. I asked him to keep an eye on his brothers. I couldn't let him see me. He'd have gone after Ricky himself."

Adelia regarded her sister with compassion. "You've done the right thing, Carolina. I know how hard it is to walk out on a marriage, especially after the way we were raised. But God wouldn't want this to go on. I know He wouldn't."

"God might understand, but what about Mama?"

Adelia ran a comforting hand over her sister's head. "She'd want what's best for you, the same way she did for me. It's going to be okay. I promise. You've taken the most important step toward getting your life back."

"It feels more like I've just jumped off a precipice and there's no going back. There's nothing to grab on to going down, either."

Adelia smiled at the first tiny hint of her sister's sense of humor. "Been there, done that," she told her. "But just like me, you're going to land on your feet."

CHAPTER TWENTY-THREE

◆◆◆

Gabe had rushed into a lot of short-term relationships over the years. He'd even had one or two that had lasted well beyond those impulsive first weeks of heat and passion. This long, slow buildup to something with real potential he'd experienced with Adelia was new to him and he didn't mind admitting that it scared him to death. That's why he was going to Beaufort to talk to Ronnie's friend. That's why he thought the only smart thing to do was to leave before anybody got hurt or at least hurt worse than they would be if he bailed now.

Early Saturday morning he drove down to Beaufort to meet with Butch. They talked over a big country breakfast of eggs, bacon and grits and drank about a gallon of coffee to wash it down. He instinctively liked the older man and was intrigued with the construction projects he had going on.

"Do you have time to ride around and take a look at some of the sites?" Butch asked. "I can show you plans, too."

"Sure," Gabe said.

The projects ranged from several historic renovations

to a new development in the suburbs. All were being done with diligent attention to detail, just the way Gabe liked to work. In the end, though, he couldn't figure out why he wasn't more excited by what he'd seen.

After the tour they went back to Butch's office, a far simpler place than that ostentatious building Ernesto had built for himself. Butch, just like Mitch, was obviously a man who put more energy into the work his company was doing than into his own comfort or a pretentious show of success.

"Sorry about the mess," Butch said, as he swept some blueprints off a sofa and gestured for Gabe to have a seat. "I'm never in here long enough to clean this place up. And my secretary reminds me just about daily that it's not what I'm paying her to do."

Gabe chuckled, liking the man more and more. He was a straight shooter, just as Ronnie had described him.

"Now, then," Butch began. "I like what I've seen and heard so far. If you're interested, here's what I'm prepared to offer."

The package of pay and benefits was a good one, more than Gabe could expect to make from Mitch, at least until that new construction project he'd mentioned broke ground. The work sounded challenging.

"What do you think?" Butch asked. "I'll be candid. You're the first person I've talked to, but I have a list of other candidates. Since I need someone who can be on the job in a couple of weeks or a month at the outside, I can't wait around for long while you make a decision."

Gabe told himself he should jump at this chance

that had fallen into his lap, but reservations he didn't totally understand kept him from a quick yes.

"Let me go back to Serenity and think it over," he suggested. "I'll get back to you tomorrow, or first thing Monday morning, if you don't like dealing with work issues on Sunday."

"The sooner the better," Butch told him. "Do you mind telling me what's holding you back from saying yes now?"

"I have some people I need to consider," Gabe hedged. "I'm working for my cousin right now. He's got a baby on the way and he's counting on me."

Butch studied him and nodded. "I appreciate that you want to be fair to him. That's another admirable trait." A gleam lit his eyes. "Something tells me there's more, a woman, maybe. With a decent man as good-looking as you, there's always a woman."

Gabe laughed. "There might be a woman."

"One you're running from or one you're considering staying with?" Butch asked perceptively.

"That is the dilemma," Gabe admitted.

Butch sighed. "I know I'm going to regret telling you this, but one thing I've learned over the years is that a man should never walk away from the possibility of love. Jobs come and go, but the right woman? That's something you should hang on to tight. Given the number of years I've been happily married to the same woman, I think I know what I'm talking about. She'd tell you the same thing."

Gabe felt the knot in his stomach slowly start to ease at Butch's words. It wasn't as if the advice was anything new, or anything he hadn't considered. It just suddenly made sense. Adelia had a hold on his heart. That wouldn't change if he stayed or if he ran.

"Thank you," he said holding out his hand. "I don't think I need to wait after all. I appreciate the offer, but I'm turning it down."

Butch looked disappointed, but he nodded. "Much as I hate to say it, it sounds as if it's the right decision. If it turns out not to be, give me a call."

"I'll do that," Gabe promised.

With luck, though, that would be a call he'd never have to make.

"Can I ask you something personal?" he asked Mitch over coffee on Monday morning. He'd spent the rest of the weekend debating his decision with himself, but not a single one of his many moments of panic had managed to shake his conviction that coming back to Serenity and Adelia was exactly the right choice.

Mitch leveled a look into his eyes. "Maybe first you should tell me about this job offer I hear you've had."

Gabe swallowed hard at the dismay in his cousin's eyes. "I'm sorry. I should have mentioned that I intended to check out another opportunity," he admitted.

"Yes, you should have," Mitch said, his gaze unrelenting.

"My only excuse is that it came up unexpectedly. I felt I owed it to myself to check it out."

"And?"

"I'm staying, Mitch, that is, if you'll still have me."

Relief washed over Mitch's face. "That's good then. We don't have to say another word about it. I assume you had your reasons for even going down to Beaufort."

"Of course I did," Gabe said. "I was running from everything I've been feeling about Adelia."

Mitch smiled. "But you changed your mind and decided to stop running?"

"I did. That brings me back to that personal question I wanted to ask."

"Sure. Shoot," Mitch said.

"How did you know Lynn was the right woman for you?"

Mitch laughed. "You mean back when we were fourteen and the only man she cared about was Ed Morrow? We might be able to chalk that up to teen lust."

"I was thinking about more recently, when you actually got together," Gabe said.

Mitch was silent for several minutes. "I think maybe it was because we did go down those very different paths. When we started running into each other when I was working at Raylene's next door, it just seemed natural to be with her. She was going through hell with her divorce from Ed. I wanted to be the person she leaned on. Not that she did. She was determined to get through that tough time on her own. I think I fell even more in love with her because of that."

"Okay, so there were old feelings, friendship, that leftover lust from when you were fourteen, I assume."

"Oh yeah, there was that," Mitch said, glancing toward the back of the bakery as if to catch a glimpse of Lynn. A smile landed on his lips when she passed by the open doorway into the kitchen. He turned back to Gabe. "What is this really about? Are you wondering if what you feel for Adelia is real?"

Gabe nodded. "We haven't even slept together, if

you can believe it. That's the only sort of relationship
with a woman I've ever known how to have. Despite
that, I feel closer to Adelia than I ever did to those
other women. There's something deeper, even more
intense between us."

He wasn't sure if he was explaining it right, so he
tried again. "Adelia's at the heart of it, though. I feel as
if it's hard to breathe when she's not around. It's like
I found this piece of myself I never even knew was
missing." He gave his cousin a bemused look. "She's
in my blood, you know what I mean?"

Again, Mitch glanced toward the kitchen. "Believe
me, I know. If you're asking what I think about what
you have with Adelia, it sounds real to me, but you
two are the only ones who can really know. How do
you feel about having an instant family?"

Gabe smiled. "Well, I'm not entirely over the panic,
that's for sure. But when Tomas follows me around and
looks at me as if I know all the answers in the uni-
verse, it does something to me. The girls…" He shook
his head. "They scare the daylights out of me. I want
to make sure they avoid all the mistakes my mother
made. I feel so blasted protective, and then I wonder
when that happened."

"It's called being a dad," Mitch said, regarding him
sympathetically. "And girls are definitely different. I
raised two sons. I totally get Lynn's boy, Jeremy, but
Lexie? She's a whole different ball game. She's smart
and sassy and tough, but I'm terrified every time she
mentions going on a date. So far Lynn's insisted that
she only do the group thing, but that won't last much
longer. Then I might consider locking her in her room.

I have a selection of deadbolts in my truck, just in case."

"I can understand that," Gabe said. "I just know that's how I'm going to be when Selena discovers boys." He gave Mitch a surprised look. "But I want that in my life."

"Okay, here's what I see, Gabe. The same instincts that got you into trouble as a kid, being loyal and looking out for your mom the only way you knew how, those instincts have made you into a good man. You'll do whatever it takes to keep anyone from hurting the people you love. And my gut tells me you've learned that brawling isn't the answer."

"Will it shake that belief to know that I still wouldn't mind catching Ernesto Hernandez in some dark alley and punching his lights out?" Gabe asked, not entirely in jest.

"Not a bit, because you haven't done it."

"So you think I wouldn't make a mess of the whole happily-ever-after thing?"

"It doesn't matter what I think," Mitch said. "It only matters what you believe, how willing you are to dedicate yourself to being a good husband and father. You weren't just running from the past all these years. You were running from too much responsibility, too soon. Only you can decide if you're ready to take on the whole passel of responsibility that comes with marrying Adelia."

Gabe sighed. "After what happened the other day, when I told Adelia I was probably leaving, mine may not be the vote that counts. She may not believe I'm ready, no matter what I say now."

Mitch stood up then and gave his shoulder a reassuring squeeze. "But you came to your senses in the nick of time. I have faith in your powers of persuasion. If Adelia's the woman you really, truly want, there's not a doubt in my mind that you can win her over. It may take more patience than you'd like, but I've seen the way the woman looks at you. Play your cards right and you'll have everything you ever dreamed of."

After Mitch had gone, Gabe sipped his cup of coffee and thought about what his cousin had said. He walked over to the counter and called out to Lynn. She came out of the back, wiping her flour-covered hands on a towel.

"I have an idea," he said. "Think you can help me out?"

"Does this have something to do with what you and my husband were discussing?"

"You overheard?"

"I just heard you mention something about Adelia," Lynn said. "It got my hopes up, especially since you're still here in town, instead of down in Beaufort. Thank you for that, by the way. I know Mitch is relieved. He's counting on you."

"I know that. It's one of the reasons I turned down the job."

"And the other is Adelia?"

He smiled. "The other is Adelia," he confirmed. "Now, here's what I'm thinking," he said, watching her face as he described his idea. A smile spread as she listened, so he concluded that just maybe he'd gotten it right.

"It's perfect," she said. "When do you want to do this?"

Now that his mind was made up, he knew waiting would kill him. "How long will it take you?"

Lynn laughed. "So you're going for broke today?"

Gabe faltered. "Do you think that's a mistake? Do I need to lay some groundwork? Mitch said something about patience, but it's not my strong suit."

"Personally, though I've had to practice it a time or two, I think patience can be highly overrated. Come back at closing."

"Perfect," he said. "That'll give me just enough time."

Now that he'd made up his mind to reach for the future he'd never let himself imagine, he wanted to get on with it. The end of the day would give him just enough time to check on things at the work site, then get back to the inn to shower and change into something a whole lot more presentable than his work clothes. A man couldn't very well ask the most important question of his life while covered in dust and wearing denim.

Adelia had just hung the closed sign on the door of the boutique and was about to turn the lock when she saw Gabe approaching wearing that perfectly tailored suit again and carrying a huge pastry box. He beckoned for her to open the door.

"What on earth?" she asked, her eyes wide. "Is it somebody's birthday? Where are you going all dressed up and carrying a cake?"

"Lock the door," he told her, his gaze never leaving her face.

"Gabe?" she whispered questioningly, even as she did as he'd requested. "What's going on?"

He set the box on the counter, then suddenly, charmingly looked as if he wasn't quite sure what to do with his hands. He nodded toward the box.

"Red velvet cake," he began. "Lynn says it's your favorite."

"It is."

"The kids like it, too?"

"Sure."

He swallowed hard. "You and I, we haven't known each other all that long."

"True."

"But I feel as if it's been forever." He hesitated. "Do you know what I mean?"

She drew in a deep breath, suddenly terrified about the direction in which he was heading, yet thrilled just the same. "I do," she said, her voice shaking.

"Your divorce is still new," he said. "So maybe you're not where I am yet." He regarded her questioningly.

"Where are you, Gabe? I thought you were taking off."

"I changed my mind," he said, shocking her.

"Why?"

She waited while he seemed to be struggling with the answer.

"Because I'm in love with you," he finally blurted, as if he needed to get the words out in a rush. "I sure didn't expect it, but that's what makes life interesting, right? The surprises. You were a total surprise, Adelia. The best kind. And those complications we talked about? This is the best kind of those, too."

Relief washed over her. She gave him an encouraging smile. He seemed to need reassurance and suddenly she felt calmer and more composed than she had at any time since she'd left her cheating ex-husband.

"You came as a surprise to me, too," she said. "Definitely the best kind."

He looked as if he hadn't really expected her to admit to the same feelings. She laughed. "You look surprised."

"It's just that I'm not used to getting what I want. I want you, Adelia. I don't mean just in my bed or just for a night. I mean forever. I want to marry you, to be with you and your kids. Who knows, maybe it's not too late for us to have one of our own. Will you marry me? I don't think I'm a bad bet, not anymore. And I'll do everything I can to make sure you're happy. That goes for the kids, too. I won't try to be their dad. They have one. But I think I'm ready to be a good influence on them." He held her gaze and waited, then prodded, "So, what do you think?"

Adelia reached behind her and felt for the stool that was always right behind the counter. She sat down hard at the unexpected question. She hadn't dared to let herself even imagine that marriage was where he was heading.

"You want to marry me?" she repeated to be sure.

Hearing the words, even though she'd been anticipating some sort of dramatic declaration for a few minutes now, stunned her. It was a giant leap from what she'd been thinking. She'd expected maybe a request that they spend more time together, see how it went. Apparently once Gabe made a decision, he was all in. She realized that was something she'd come to appreciate about him. He put what he was thinking, what he wanted, right out there. There were no guessing games about where she stood with him. Even when he'd been thinking of leaving, a move he knew would hurt her, he'd put his cards on the table and told her the truth.

"I do want to marry you," he stated quietly. "More than anything, but I can wait if you need more time. Or if the kids need to adjust to the idea."

"The kids will go a little crazy," she said, then grinned. "But definitely in a good way."

"What about you?"

Her expression sobered. "I need to be clear about a couple of things."

"Okay."

"No more talk about leaving town, getting a fresh start someplace new? Are you really sure you want to stay here in Serenity, crazy gossip and all?"

"Leaving *was* the plan," he said. "I'm apparently a lot more adaptable than I'd realized. *This* is the fresh start I want, Adelia. Right here, with you and your kids, with all those Sweet Magnolia women meddling and their husbands trying to beat my butt in basketball."

"And the red velvet cake? Where does that fit in?"

He grinned, looking more relaxed now that he clearly assumed the conversation was going to go his way. "Answer me first," he countered. "I'm not sure how I feel about being less important to you than a cake."

"Trust me, this cake doesn't hold a candle to you and your proposal," she said. "I just wondered."

"You're stalling," he accused. Then his expression faltered. "Is it because I'm rushing you? I meant it when I said I'd wait till you caught up with me."

She drew in a deep breath, steadied herself, then

walked around the counter until she was standing right in front of this man who'd come to mean the world to her, this man she trusted in ways she'd never expected to trust again. She put her hand on his clean-shaven cheek and smiled.

"You're all dressed up and you even shaved," she whispered as if she'd just noticed.

"It's not the kind of question a man asks when he's covered in drywall dust," he said. "And you're still stalling."

"Just drawing out the moment," she said. "I want to savor it."

"So the answer is…"

"Yes," she said, moving into his arms. Then she was surrounded by all that heat and strength and his lips were on hers in a kiss that stole her breath away.

When she could speak again, she repeated her answer with even more emphasis, "Yes, Gabe Franklin, I will marry you." Then she nudged him in the ribs. "Now tell me about that cake."

He laughed and lifted the lid on the box. "I thought maybe we'd have something to celebrate tonight," he explained. "At least I hoped we would."

In flowing script across the top of the decadent red velvet cake, it said, "Your mom said yes!"

Adelia laughed. "Awfully sure of yourself, weren't you?"

"Darlin', until I met you, I hadn't been sure of anything for a very long time. This, it was just a matter of time. If you hadn't said yes tonight, that cake would have gone in the freezer until you were ready."

"But it's so much better when it's fresh out of the oven," she said. "Let's take it home and celebrate."

As she said it, she smiled. With Gabe by her side, the house she'd chosen for her future really was going to be a home. And they were going to be a family, the kind she'd always dreamed of, the kind Gabe had never had.

Of course, it might be a little crowded for a while now. She probably ought to mention that to make sure the presence of her sister and her kids wouldn't give Gabe cold feet.

"I should probably fill you in about something before we take this cake home," she said.

"Is it something that might be a deal breaker?" he asked worriedly.

"I hope not."

"Then tell me."

"My sister's staying with me."

Gabe's eyes widened. "Carolina finally left her husband?"

Adelia nodded. "I'm still hoping to convince her to file charges against Ricky, but she's not there yet."

"At least she got away from him. How are her kids?"

"They're at my mom's for another day or two, but they could be moving in, too. Carolina needs to be someplace she can feel safe and figure out what comes next. The good news is that Cruz women are never down-and-out for long. I have faith that she's going to find her way, just like I did."

Gabe looked vaguely shaken, but all he said was, "Seems I could be getting even more family than I bargained for."

"And that doesn't terrify you?"

"As long as you're there, I can't think of a thing that would scare me off." He gave her a long, slow look that made her toes curl. "But we might need a very long, very private honeymoon."

Adelia laughed. "That is definitely something I can get behind. I imagine Mama can take over and keep the family on track for a week or two. How soon were you thinking we ought to take this honeymoon?"

He regarded her hopefully. "Well, the minute Mitch's baby is born, I'm going to be busier than ever. And when Raylene's arrives, you're going to have a boatload of responsibility at the boutique. So, I was thinking we'd better get this done before either of those kids gets here."

"And before you can have second thoughts?" she asked.

"Not a consideration," he said adamantly. "It's all about those babies."

"In that case, how about next week? I'm pretty sure at least one of those babies is going to be early, so there's not much time to waste."

To her delight, there wasn't even a flicker of panic in Gabe's eyes at her suggestion.

"Next week is good," he agreed at once.

"The kids are going to complain about not getting to go on the honeymoon," she warned him.

"Too bad," he said, pulling her close for one of his bone-melting kisses. "We'll promise them a family vacation next summer."

Adelia regarded him with approval.

"What?" Gabe asked.

"You're going to be excellent at this parenting thing," she told him. "The promise of a delayed reward can get a parent out of many a tight spot."

"As long as it gets me alone with you for a couple

of weeks on a beach somewhere, I'm good," Gabe told her.

"A beach? You've already picked a spot for the honeymoon?"

"I heard that was one of the groom's responsibilities, but if you want a say, speak up. We're going to be an equal-opportunity couple."

Adelia looked at Gabe with her heart in her throat. How had this man she'd known such a short time understood exactly the right thing to say?

"Thank you," she whispered against his cheek.

"For what?"

"For making me believe in love again."

"I'm going to do my best to make sure you never stop believing again," he promised.

"And I'll do the same," she told him. "I think we're going to be very good together, Gabe."

"I don't have much to compare us to, but I think we're going to be amazing!"

Suddenly Adelia could hardly wait to find out just how amazing life with this man could be, so wasn't it lucky that she only had to wait a week? In no time at all, they'd start an adventure that she was convinced was destined to last forever.

* * * * *

Keep reading for a special sneak peek at
Stealing Home,
a Sweet Magnolias novel
by #1 New York Times *bestselling author*
Sherryl Woods,
coming soon to Netflix as an original series.

CHAPTER ONE

Maddie focused on the wide expanse of mahogany stretching between her and the man who'd been her husband for twenty years. Half her life. She and William Henry Townsend had been high-school sweethearts in Serenity, South Carolina. They'd married before their senior year in college, not because she was pregnant as some of her hastily married friends had been, but because they hadn't wanted to wait one more second before starting their lives together.

Then, after they'd graduated, there had been the exhausting years of medical school for Bill, when she'd worked as an entry-level bookkeeper, making poor use of her degree in business, just to keep their heads above water financially. And then the joyous arrival of three kids—athletic, outgoing Tyler, now sixteen, their jokester, Kyle, fourteen, and their surprise blessing, Katie, who was just turning six.

They'd had the perfect life in the historic Townsend family home in Serenity's oldest neighborhood, surrounded by family and lifelong friends. The passion they'd once shared might have cooled ever so slightly, but they'd been happy.

Or so she'd thought until the day a few months ago when Bill had looked at her after dinner, his expression as distant as a stranger's, and calmly explained that he was moving out and moving on…with his twenty-four-year-old nurse, who was already pregnant. It was, he'd said, one of those things that just happened. He certainly hadn't planned to fall out of love with Maddie, much less *in* love with someone else.

Maddie's first reaction hadn't been shock or dismay. Nope, she'd laughed, sure that her intelligent, compassionate Bill was incapable of such a pitiful cliché. Only when his distant expression remained firmly in place did she realize he was stone-cold serious. Just when life had settled into a comfortable groove, the man she'd loved with all her heart had traded her in for a newer model.

In a disbelieving daze, she'd sat by his side while he'd explained to the children what he was doing and why. He'd omitted the part about a new little half brother or sister being on the way. Then, still in a daze, she'd watched him move out.

And after he'd gone, she'd been left to deal with Tyler's angry acting out, with Kyle's slow descent into unfamiliar silence and Katie's heartbroken sobs, all while she herself was frozen and empty inside.

She'd been the one to cope with their shock when they found out about the baby, too. She'd had to hide her resentment and anger, all in the name of good parenting, maturity and peace. There were days she'd wanted to curse Dr. Phil and all those cool, reasoned episodes on which he advised parents that the needs of the children came first. When, she'd wondered, did her needs start to count?

The day of being completely on her own as a single parent was coming sooner than she'd anticipated. All that was left was getting the details of the divorce on paper, spelling out in black and white the end of a twenty-year marriage. Nothing on those pieces of paper mentioned the broken dreams. Nothing mentioned the heartache of those left behind. It was all reduced to deciding who lived where, who drove which car, the amount of child support—and the amount of temporary spousal support until she could stand on her own feet financially or until she married again.

Maddie listened to her attorney's impassioned fight against the temporary nature of that last term. Helen Decatur, who'd known both Maddie and Bill practically forever, was a top-notch divorce attorney with a statewide reputation. She was also one of Maddie's best friends. And when Maddie was too tired and too sad to fight for herself, Helen stepped in to do it for her. Helen was a blond barracuda in a power suit, and Maddie had never been more grateful.

"This woman worked to help you through medical school," Helen lashed out at Bill, in her element on her own turf. "She gave up a promising career of her own to raise your children, keep your home, help manage your office and support your rise in the South Carolina medical community. The fact that you have a professional reputation far outside of Serenity is because Maddie worked her butt off to make it happen. And now you expect her to struggle to find her place in the workforce? Do you honestly think in five years or even ten she'll be able to give your children the lifestyle to which they've become accustomed?" She pinned Bill with a look that would have withered anyone else. His demeanor reflected a complete lack of interest in Maddie or her future.

That was when Maddie knew it was well and truly over. All the rest, the casual declaration that he'd been cheating on her, the move, none of that had convinced her that it really was the end of her marriage. Until this moment, until she'd seen the uncaring expression in her husband's once-warm brown eyes, she hadn't accepted that Bill wouldn't suddenly come to his senses and tell her it had all been a horrible mistake.

She'd drifted along until this instant, deep in denial and hurt, but no more. Anger, more powerful than anything she'd ever felt in her life, swept through her with a force that brought her to her feet.

"Wait," she said, her voice trembling with outrage. "I'd like to be heard."

Helen regarded her with surprise, but the stunned expression on Bill's face gave Maddie the courage to go on. He hadn't expected her to fight back. She could see now that all her years of striving to please him, of putting him first, had convinced him that she had no spine at all, that she'd make it easy for him to walk away from their family—from *her*—without a backward glance. He'd probably been gloating from the minute she suggested trying to mediate a settlement, rather than letting some judge set the terms of their divorce.

"You've managed to reduce twenty years of our lives to this," she said, waving the settlement papers at him. "And for what?"

She knew the answer, of course. Like so many

other middle-aged men, his head had been turned by a woman barely half his age.

"What happens when you tire of Noreen?" she asked. "Will you trade her in, too?"

"Maddie," he said stiffly. He tugged at the sleeves of his monogrammed shirt, fiddling with the eighteen-carat-gold cuff links she'd given him just six months ago for their twentieth anniversary. "You don't know anything about my relationship with Noreen."

She managed a smile. "Sure I do. It's about a middle-aged man trying to feel young again. I think you're pathetic."

Calmer now that she'd finally expressed her feelings, she turned to Helen. "I can't sit here anymore. Hold out for whatever you think is right. He's the one in a hurry."

Shoulders squared, chin high, Maddie walked out of the lawyer's office and into the rest of her life.

An hour later Maddie had exchanged her prim knit suit and high heels for a tank top, shorts and well-worn sneakers. Oblivious to the early-morning heat, she walked the mile to her much-hated gym, with its smell of sweat pervading the air. Set on a side street just off Main, the gym had once been an old-fashioned dime store. The yellowed linoleum on the floor harked back to that era and the dingy walls hadn't seen a coat of paint since Dexter had bought the place back in the 1970s.

Since the walk downtown had done nothing at all to calm her, Maddie forced herself to climb onto the treadmill, put the dial at the most challenging setting she'd ever attempted and run. She ran until her legs ached, until the perspiration soaked her chin-length, professionally highlighted hair and ran into her eyes, mingling with the tears that, annoyingly, kept welling up.

Suddenly a perfectly manicured hand reached in front of her, slowed the machine, then cut it off.

"We thought we'd find you here," Helen said, still in her power suit and Jimmy Choo stiletto heels. Helen was probably one of the only women in all of Serenity who'd ever owned a pair of the expensive shoes.

Beside her, Dana Sue Sullivan was dressed in comfortable pants, a pristine T-shirt and sneakers. She was the chef and owner of Serenity's fanciest restaurant— meaning it used linen tablecloths and napkins and had a menu that extended beyond fried catfish and collard greens. Sullivan's New Southern Cuisine, as the dark green and gold-leaf sign out front read, was a decided step up from the diner on the outskirts of town that simply said Good Eatin' on the window and used paper place mats on the Formica tabletops.

Maddie climbed off the treadmill on wobbly legs and wiped her face with the towel Helen handed her. "Why are you two here?"

Both women rolled their eyes.

"Why do you think?" Dana Sue asked in her honey-eyed drawl. Her thick, chestnut hair was pulled back with a clip, but already the humidity had curls springing free. "We came to see if you want any help in killing that snake-bellied slime who ran out on you."

"Or the mindless pinup he plans to marry," Helen added. "Though I am somewhat hesitant to recommend murder as a solution, being an officer of the court and all."

Dana Sue nudged her in the ribs. "Don't go soft now. You said we'd do *anything,* if it would make Maddie feel better."

Maddie actually managed a faint grin. "Fortunately for both of you, my revenge fantasies don't run to murder."

"What, then?" Dana Sue asked, looking fascinated. "Personally, after I kicked Ronnie's sorry butt out of the house, I wanted to see him run over by a train."

"Murder's too quick," Maddie said. "Besides, there are the children to consider. Scum that he is, Bill is still their father. I have to remind myself of that on an hourly basis just to keep my temper in check."

"Fortunately, Annie was just as mad at her daddy as I was," Dana Sue said. "I suppose that's the good side of having a teenage daughter. She could see right through his shenanigans. I think she knew what was going on even before I did. She stood on the front steps and applauded when I tossed him out."

"Okay, you two," Helen interrupted, "as much fun as it is listening to you compare notes, can we go someplace else to do it? My suit's going to stink to high heaven if we don't get out in the fresh air soon."

"Don't you both need to get to work?" Maddie asked.

"I took the afternoon off," Helen said. "In case you wanted to get drunk or something."

"And I don't have to be at the restaurant for two hours," Dana Sue said, then studied Maddie with a considering look. "How drunk can you get in that amount of time?"

"Given the fact that there's not a single bar open in Serenity at this hour, I think we can forget about me getting drunk," Maddie noted. "Though I do appreciate the sentiment, that's probably for the best."

"I have the makings of margaritas at my place," Helen offered.

"And we all know how loopy I get on one of those," Maddie retorted, shuddering at the memory of their impromptu pity party a few months back when she'd told them about Bill's plan to leave her. "I think I'd better stick to Diet Coke. I have to pick the kids up at school."

"No, you don't," Dana Sue said. "Your mama's going to do it."

Maddie's mouth gaped. Her mother had uttered two words when Tyler was born and repeated them regularly ever since: no babysitting. She'd been adamant about it then, and she'd stuck to it for sixteen years.

"How on earth did you pull that off?" she asked, a note of admiration in her voice.

"I explained the situation," Dana Sue said with a shrug. "Your mother is a perfectly reasonable woman. I don't know why the two of you have all these issues."

Maddie could have explained, but it would take the rest of the afternoon. More likely, the rest of the week. Besides, Dana Sue had heard most of it a thousand times.

"So, are we going to my place?" Helen asked.

"Yes, but not for the margaritas," Maddie said. "It took me the better part of two days to get over that last batch you made. I need to start looking for a job tomorrow."

"No, you don't," Helen said.

"Oh? Did you finally get Bill to hand over some sort of windfall?"

"That, too," Helen said, her smile smug.

Maddie studied her two friends intently. They were up to something. She'd bet her first alimony check on it. "Tell me," she commanded.

"We'll talk about it when we get to my place," Helen said.

Maddie turned to Dana Sue. "Do you know what's going on?"

"I have some idea," Dana Sue said, barely containing a grin.

"So, the two of you have been plotting something," Maddie concluded, not sure how she felt about that. She loved these two women like sisters, but every time they got some crazy idea, one of them invariably landed in trouble. It had been that way since they were six. She was pretty sure that was why Helen had become a lawyer, because she'd known the three of them were eventually going to need a good one.

"Give me a hint," she pleaded. "I want to decide if I should take off now."

"Not even a tiny hint," Helen said. "You need to be in a more receptive frame of mind."

"There's not enough Diet Coke in the world to accomplish that," Maddie responded.

Helen grinned. "Thus the margaritas."

"I made some killer guacamole," Dana Sue added. "And I got a big ole bag of those tortilla chips you like, too, though all that salt will eventually kill you."

Maddie looked from one to the other and sighed. "With you two scheming behind my back, something tells me I'm doomed anyway."

The tart margarita was strong enough to make Maddie's mouth pucker. They were on the brick patio behind Helen's custom-built home in Serenity's one fancy subdivision, each of them settled onto a comfy chaise longue. The South Carolina humidity was thick even though it was only March, but the faint breeze stirring the towering pine trees was enough to keep it from being too oppressive.

Maddie was tempted to dive straight into Helen's turquoise pool, but instead she leaned her head back and closed her eyes. For the first time in months, she felt her worries slipping away. Beyond her anger, she wasn't trying to hide anything from her kids—not her sorrow, not her fears, but she did struggle to keep them in check. With Helen and Dana Sue, she could just be herself, one very hurt, soon-to-be-divorced woman filled with uncertainty.

"You think she's ready to hear our idea?" Dana Sue murmured beside her.

"Not yet," Helen responded. "She needs to finish that drink."

"I can hear you," Maddie said. "I'm not asleep or unconscious yet."

"Then we'd better wait," Dana Sue said cheerfully. "More guacamole?"

"No, though you outdid yourself," Maddie told her. "That stuff made my eyes water."

Dana Sue looked taken aback. "Too hot? I thought maybe you were just having yourself another little crying jag."

"I am not prone to crying jags," Maddie retorted.

"You think we didn't notice you were crying when we got to the gym?" Helen inquired.

"I was hoping you'd think it was sweat."

"I'm sure that's what everyone else thought, but

we knew better," Dana Sue said. "I have to say, I was disappointed you'd shed a single tear over that man."

"So was I," Maddie said.

Dana Sue gave her a hard look, then turned to Helen. "We may as well tell her. I don't think she's going to mellow out any more than she has already."

"Okay," Helen conceded. "Here's the deal. What have all three of us been complaining about for the past twenty years?"

"Men," Maddie suggested dryly.

"Besides that," Helen said impatiently.

"South Carolina's humidity?"

Helen sighed. "Would you try to be serious for one minute? The gym. We've been complaining about that awful gym all our adult lives."

Maddie regarded her with bafflement. "And it hasn't done a lick of good, has it? The last time we pitched a fit about the place, Dexter hired Junior Stevens to mop it out...once. The place smelled of Lysol for a week and that was it."

"Precisely. Which is why Dana Sue and I came up with this idea," Helen said, then paused for effect. "We want to open a brand-new fitness club, one that's clean and welcoming and caters to women."

"We want it to be a place where women can get fit and be pampered and drink a smoothie with their friends after a workout," Dana Sue added. "Maybe even get a facial or a massage."

"And you want to do this in Serenity, with its population of five thousand seven hundred and fourteen people?" Maddie asked, not even trying to hide her skepticism.

"Fifteen," Dana Sue corrected. "Daisy Mitchell had

a baby girl yesterday. And believe me, if you've seen Daisy lately, you know she'll be the perfect candidate for one of our postpregnancy classes."

Maddie studied Helen more intently. "You're serious, aren't you?"

"As serious as a heart attack," she confirmed. "What do you think?"

"I suppose it could work," Maddie said thoughtfully. "Goodness knows, that gym is disgusting. It's no wonder half the women in Serenity refuse to exercise. Of course, the other half can't get out of their recliners because of all the fried chicken they've consumed."

"Which is why we'll offer cooking classes, too," Dana Sue said eagerly.

"Let me guess. New Southern Cuisine," Maddie said.

"Southern cooking isn't all about lima beans swimming in butter or green beans cooked with fatback," Dana Sue said. "Haven't I taught you anything?"

"Me, yes, absolutely," Maddie assured her. "But the general population of Serenity still craves their mashed potatoes and fried chicken."

"So do I," Dana Sue said. "But ovenbaked's not half-bad if you do it right."

"We're losing focus," Helen cut in. "There's a building available over on Palmetto Lane that would be just right for what we have in mind. I think we should take a look at it in the morning. Dana Sue and I fell in love with it right away, Maddie, but we want your opinion."

"Why? It's not as if I have anything to compare it to. Besides, I don't even know what your vision is, not entirely anyway."

"You know how to make a place cozy and inviting, don't you?" Helen said. "After all, you took that mausoleum that was the Townsend family home and made it real welcoming."

"Right," Dana Sue said. "And you have all sorts of business savvy from helping Bill get his practice established."

"I put some systems into place for him nearly twenty years ago," Maddie said, downplaying her contribution to setting up the office. "I'm hardly an expert. If you're going to do this, you should hire a consultant, devise a business plan, do cost projections. You can't do something like this on a whim just because you don't like the way Dexter's gym smells."

"Actually, we can," Helen insisted. "I have enough money saved for a down payment on the building, plus capital expenses for equipment and an operating budget for the first year. Let's face it, I can use the tax write-off, though I predict this won't be a losing proposition for long."

"And I'm going to invest some cash, but mostly my time and my expertise in cooking and nutrition to design a little café and offer classes," Dana Sue added.

They both looked at Maddie expectantly.

"What?" she demanded. "I don't have any expertise and I certainly don't have any money to throw at something this speculative."

Helen grinned. "You have a bit more than you think, thanks to your fabulous attorney, but we don't really want your money. We want you to be in charge."

Maddie regarded them incredulously. "Me? I hate to exercise. I only do it because I know I have to." She gestured at the cellulite firmly clinging to her thighs. "And we can see how much good that's doing."

"Then you're perfect for this job, because you'll work really, really hard to make this a place women just like you will want to join," Helen said.

Maddie shook her head. "Forget it. It doesn't feel right."

"Why not?" Dana demanded. "You need work. We need a manager. It's a perfect match."

"It feels like some scheme you devised to keep me from starving to death," Maddie said.

"I already told you that you won't be starving," Helen said. "And you get to keep the house, which is long since paid for. Bill was very reasonable once I laid out a few facts for him."

Maddie studied her friend's face. Not many people tried explaining anything to Bill, since he was convinced he knew it all. A medical degree did that to some men. And what the degree didn't accomplish, adoring nurses like Noreen did.

"Such as?" Maddie asked.

"How the news of his impending fatherhood with his unmarried nurse might impact his practice here in the conservative, family-oriented town of Serenity," Helen said without the slightest hint of remorse. "People might not want to take their darling little kiddies to a pediatrician who has demonstrated a complete lack of scruples."

"You blackmailed him?" Maddie wasn't sure whether she was shocked or awed.

Helen shrugged. "I prefer to think of it as educating him on the value of the right PR spin. So far people in town haven't taken sides, but that could change in a heartbeat."

"I'm surprised his attorney let you get away with that," Maddie said.

"That's because you don't know everything your brilliant attorney knew walking into that room," Helen said.

"Such as?" Maddie asked again.

"Bill's nurse had a little thing going with *his* attorney once upon a time. Tom Patterson had his own reasons for wanting to see Bill screwed to the wall."

"Isn't that unethical?" Maddie asked. "Shouldn't he have refused to take Bill's case or something?"

"He did, but Bill insisted. Tom disclosed his connection to Noreen, but Bill continued to insist. He thought Tom's thing with Noreen would make him more understanding of his eagerness to get on with life with her. Which just proves that when it comes to human nature your soon-to-be ex really doesn't have a clue."

"And you took advantage of all those shenanigans to get Maddie the money she deserves," Dana Sue said admiringly.

"I did," Helen confirmed with satisfaction. "If we'd had to go in front of a judge, it might have gone differently, but Bill was especially anxious for a settlement so he could be a proper daddy to his new baby *before* the ink is dry on the birth certificate. As you reminded him on your way out the door, Maddie, he's the one in a hurry."

Helen regarded Maddie intently. "It's not a fortune, mind you, but you don't have to worry about money for the time being."

"I still think I ought to look for a real job," Maddie said. "However much the settlement is, it won't last forever, and I'm not likely to have a lot of earning power, not right at first, anyway."

"Which is why you should take us up on our offer," Dana Sue said. "This health club could be a gold mine and you'd be a full partner. That's what you'd get in return for your day-in, day-out running of it all—sweat equity."

"I don't see what's in it for the two of you," Maddie said. "Helen, you're in Charleston all the time. There are some fine gyms over there, if you don't want to go to Dexter's. And Dana Sue, you could offer cooking classes at the restaurant. You don't need a spa to do it."

"We're trying to be community minded," Dana Sue said. "This town needs someone to invest in it."

"I'm not buying it," Maddie said. "This is about me. You both feel sorry for me."

"We most certainly do not," Helen said. "You're going to be just fine."

"Then there's something else, something you're not telling me," Maddie persisted. "You didn't just wake up one day and decide you wanted to open a health club, not even for some kind of tax shelter."

Helen hesitated, then confessed. "Okay, here's the whole truth. I need a place to go to work off the stress of my job. My doctor's been on my case about my blood pressure. I flatly refuse to start taking a bunch of pills at my age, so he said he'd give me three months to see if a better diet and exercise would help. I'm trying to cut back on my cases in Charleston for a while, so I need a spa right here in Serenity."

Maddie stared at her friend in alarm. If Helen was cutting back on work, then the doctor must have made quite a case for the risks to her health. "If your blood pressure is that high, why didn't you say something? Not that I'm surprised given the way you obsess over your job."

"I didn't say anything because you've had enough on your plate," Helen said. "Besides, I intend to take care of it."

"By opening your own gym," Maddie concluded. "Won't getting a new business off the ground just add to the stress?"

"Not if *you're* running it," Helen said. "Besides, I think all of us doing this together will be fun."

Maddie wasn't entirely convinced about the fun factor, but she turned to Dana Sue. "And you? What's your excuse for wanting to open a new business? Isn't the restaurant enough?"

"It's making plenty of money, sure," Dana Sue said. "But I'm around food all the time. I've gained a few pounds. You know my family history. Just about everybody had diabetes, so I need to get my weight under control. I'm not likely to stop eating, so I need to work out."

"See, we both have our own reasons for wanting to make this happen," Helen said. "Come on, Maddie. At least look at the building tomorrow. You don't have to decide tonight or even tomorrow. There's time for you to mull it over in that cautious brain of yours."

"I am *not* cautious," Maddie protested, offended. Once she'd been the biggest risk-taker among them. All it had taken was the promise of fun and a dare. Had she really lost that? Judging from the expressions on her friends' faces, she had.

"Oh, please, you weigh the pros and cons and calorie

content before you order lunch," Dana Sue said. "But we love you just the same."

"Which is why we won't do this without you," Helen said. "Even if it *does* put our health at risk."

Maddie looked from one to the other. "No pressure there," she said dryly.

"Not a bit," Helen said. "I have a career. And the doctor says there are all sorts of pills for controlling blood pressure these days."

"And I have a business," Dana Sue added. "As for my weight, I suppose we can just continue walking together a couple of times a week." She sighed dramatically.

"Despite what y'all have said, I'm not entirely convinced it isn't charity," Maddie repeated. "The timing is awfully suspicious."

"It would only be charity if we didn't expect you to work your butt off to make a success of it," Helen said. "So, are you in or out?"

Maddie gave it some thought. "I'll look at the building," she finally conceded. "But that's all I'm promising."

Helen swung her gaze to Dana Sue. "If we'd waited till she had that second margarita, she would have said yes," Helen claimed, feigning disappointment.

Maddie laughed. "But if I'd had two, you couldn't have held me to anything I said."

"She has a point," Dana Sue agreed. "Let's be grateful we got a maybe."

"Have I told you two how glad I am that you're my friends?" Maddie said, feeling her eyes well up with tears yet again.

"Uh-oh, here she goes again," Dana Sue said, getting to her feet. "I need to get to work before we all start crying."

"I never cry," Helen declared.

Dana Sue groaned. "Don't even start. Maddie will be forced to challenge you, and before you know it, all of Serenity will be flooded and you'll both look like complete wrecks when we meet in the morning. Maddie, do you want me to drop you off at home?"

She shook her head. "I'll walk. It'll give me time to think."

"And to sober up before her mama sees her," Helen taunted.

"That, too," Maddie agreed.

Mostly, though, she wanted time to absorb the fact that on one of the worst days of her life she'd been surrounded by friends who'd given her a glimmer of hope that her future wasn't going to be quite as bleak as she'd imagined.

Don't miss the Sweet Magnolias,
coming soon to Netflix.
Available now from MIRA Books!

New York Times bestselling author

SHERRYL WOODS

draws you into the emotional journey of a marriage worth saving

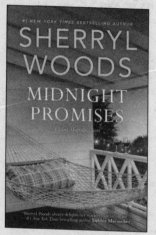

When Elliott Cruz first courted struggling single mom Karen Ames, it was a romance worthy of any Sweet Magnolia fantasy. The sexy personal trainer made it his mission to restore Karen's strength— physical and emotional—and to charm her children.

Now, a few years into the marriage, colliding dreams threaten to tear them apart. Elliott's desire to finance the business opportunity of a lifetime with their hard-earned "baby money" stirs Karen's deep-rooted financial insecurities. It's the discovery that their brother-in-law is cheating on Elliott's sister—and thinks it's justified—that puts their irreconcilable differences into perspective. Will their own loving fidelity be a bond so strong they can triumph against all odds?

Available now, wherever books are sold!

#1 *New York Times* Bestselling Author

SHERRYL WOODS

Chesapeake Shores has always represented home and family for the O'Briens, but in *Lilac Lane*, the community extends its healing powers to a woman recovering from overwhelming grief.

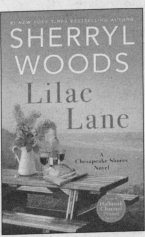

Single mom Kiera Malone, overwhelmed by the loss of her fiancé, is persuaded to visit her father, Dillon O'Malley, and her daughter, Moira O'Brien, in Chesapeake Shores. With the promise of family ties and a job at O'Brien's, her son-in-law's Irish pub, she takes what seems like the biggest risk of her life.

As it turns out, though, crossing the ocean is nothing compared to moving into a charming cottage on Lilac Lane, right next door to Bryan Laramie, the moody chef at O'Brien's.

As these two deal with their wounded pasts and discover common interests, they might just find the perfect recipe for love.

Available now wherever books are sold.

Returning home has never been so bittersweet in this acclaimed novel from #1 *New York Times* bestselling author

SHERRYL WOODS

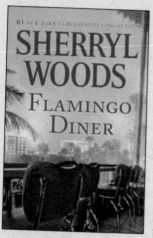

Flamingo Diner has always been a friendly place where everyone knows your name. Unfortunately, in the small town of Winter Cove, Florida, it is also the place where everyone knows everything about you. As a teenager, Emma Killian didn't recognize what a remarkable business her family had created, and so she moved away.

Now her father's tragic death has brought her home to face a mountain of secrets, debts and questions about why and how her beloved father died. As Emma grapples with her out-of-control family, the responsibility of keeping Flamingo Diner afloat and a pair of well-meaning senior-citizen sleuths, she finds support from an unlikely source.

Onetime bad boy Matt Atkins is now the Winter Cove police chief. Matt has always had a penchant for trouble and an eye for Emma. Now it seems he's the only one who can help Emma discover the answers to her questions...and give her a whole new reason to stay home.

Turn your love of reading into rewards you'll love with
Harlequin My Rewards

**Join for FREE today at
www.HarlequinMyRewards.com**

Earn **FREE BOOKS** of your choice.

Experience **EXCLUSIVE OFFERS** and contests.

Enjoy **BOOK RECOMMENDATIONS**
selected just for you.

PLUS! Sign up now
and get **500** points
right away!

Earn
FREE
REWARDS
HarlequinMyRewards.com
Join
Today!

MYR16R

SHERRYL WOODS

60988	A SMALL TOWN LOVE STORY	___$21.99	U.S.	___$26.99	CAN.
36975	FLAMINGO DINER	___$7.99	U.S.	___$9.99	CAN.
33135	A CHESAPEAKE SHORES CHRISTMAS	___$7.99	U.S.	___$9.99	CAN.
33034	ROUGH SEAS	___$7.99	U.S.	___$9.99	CAN.
33028	TROPICAL BLUES	___$7.99	U.S.	___$9.99	CAN.
33008	HARBOR LIGHTS	___$7.99	U.S.	___$9.99	CAN.
33006	FLOWERS ON MAIN	___$7.99	U.S.	___$9.99	CAN.
33004	THE INN AT EAGLE POINT	___$7.99	U.S.	___$9.99	CAN.
32979	MOONLIGHT COVE	___$7.99	U.S.	___$9.99	CAN.
32947	DRIFTWOOD COTTAGE	___$7.99	U.S.	___$9.99	CAN.
31986	ASK ANYONE	___$7.99	U.S.	___$9.99	CAN.
31982	ABOUT THAT MAN	___$7.99	U.S.	___$9.99	CAN.
31876	PRICELESS	___$7.99	U.S.	___$9.99	CAN.
31788	THE CALAMITY JANES: LAUREN	___$7.99	U.S.	___$8.99	CAN.
31778	THE CALAMITY JANES: GINA & EMMA	___$7.99	U.S.	___$8.99	CAN.
31732	DOGWOOD HILL	___$8.99	U.S.	___$9.99	CAN.
31679	THE DEVANEY BROTHERS: DANIEL	___$7.99	U.S.	___$9.99	CAN.
31668	A SEASIDE CHRISTMAS	___$7.99	U.S.	___$8.99	CAN.
31607	THE DEVANEY BROTHERS: RYAN AND SEAN	___$7.99	U.S.	___$8.99	CAN.
31581	SEAVIEW INN	___$7.99	U.S.	___$8.99	CAN.
31466	AFTER TEX	___$7.99	U.S.	___$9.99	CAN.
31391	AN O'BRIEN FAMILY CHRISTMAS	___$7.99	U.S.	___$9.99	CAN.
31339	WAKING UP IN CHARLESTON	___$7.99	U.S.	___$9.99	CAN.
31309	THE SUMMER GARDEN	___$7.99	U.S.	___$9.99	CAN.

(limited quantities available)

TOTAL AMOUNT	$ _____
POSTAGE & HANDLING	$ _____
($1.00 for 1 book, 50¢ for each additional)	
APPLICABLE TAXES*	$ _____
TOTAL PAYABLE	$ _____

(check or money order—please do not send cash)

To order, complete this form and send it, along with a check or money order for the total above, payable to MIRA Books, to: **In the U.S.:** 3010 Walden Avenue, P.O. Box 9077, Buffalo, NY 14269-9077; **In Canada:** P.O. Box 636, Fort Erie, Ontario, L2A 5X3.

Name: _____

Address: _____ City: _____

State/Prov.: _____ Zip/Postal Code: _____

Account Number (if applicable): _____
075 CSAS

mira

Harlequin.com

*New York residents remit applicable sales taxes.
*Canadian residents remit applicable GST and provincial taxes.

MSHW0519BL